On the tempest-tossed seas of peril and enchantment, their love was the most powerful magic of all

"YOU'RE EVEN MORE LOVELY THAN I'D GUESSED."

Startled, Eden's eyes flew open to find Devlin kneeling beside the tub, his gaze avidly perusing her sleek body, which was fully exposed beneath the crystal-clear water.

"Get out of here!" she squeaked, absolutely mortified. "You're not supposed to be home yet. You're supposed to be out with your crew, getting drunk and raising Cain and such."

He laughed softly. "But I'm so enjoying the view. Furthermore, there are certain parts of Kane—*Devlin* Kane—which are definitely being raised at this moment. Would you care to have me show you, sweetling?"

"Try it and I'll scream the shingles off the roof!"

He continued to grin at her, his hand stealing out to lift the hair from the shoulder nearest him. Baring her flesh, he planted a hot kiss at the arch of her neck, sending gooseflesh skittering from Eden's scalp to her toes. "The risk might be worth it, love."

Other Avon Books by
Catherine Hart

TEMPEST
TEMPTATION

CATHERINE HART

HART

SPLENDOR

AVON BOOKS ◆ NEW YORK

SPLENDOR is an original publication of Avon Books. This work has
never before appeared in book form. This work is a novel. Any sim-
ilarity to actual persons or events is purely coincidental.

AVON BOOKS
A division of
The Hearst Corporation
1350 Avenue of the Americas
New York, New York 10019

I dedicate this book to my two lovely daughters-in-law. Remember, girls—never go to sleep with angry words lying between you and your husband. Always wring an apology out of him first!

Love you,
Mom

Chapter 1

1718,
Somewhere in the Caribbean

All the demons of the deep were loose and on a midnight rampage. Stealthily, they struck from the smothering darkness with scarcely a whisper of forewarning before the first magnificent crash of thunder rent the false calm, resounding over the water like a death knell. The sea gave a mighty heave, sending the frigate reeling upon waters suddenly turbulent with gigantic swells. Sails, flapping gently mere seconds before, now nearly exploded with the intense gusts battering them.

The startled crew of the *Gai Mer,* most shaken abruptly from slumber, scurried to their posts, desperate to reef the canvas against the raw fury of this unexpected storm. Shoving his young helmsman aside, the ship's captain hurriedly took charge of the wheel himself, instinctively knowing his advanced experience would be needed if they were to survive this show of power which nature had visited upon them so capriciously.

Over the roar of the gale, Captain Kane shouted orders to his men. The wind whipped his words from his

1

mouth; thunder drowned them in its trembling wake. Jagged spears of lightning split the heavens, slicing through the roiling clouds to release a blinding deluge upon them. Within seconds, the decks were as slick as ice, the rain pelting like a thousand prickly nettles to pierce their flesh.

Drenched sails languished momentarily beneath their own sodden weight, flailing and twisting like a washerwoman's wet laundry, snapping like mad dogs as they strained against the lines and the insistent pull of the wind. Several billowed free once more, cracking loudly, sending sailors sprawling as the frigate lurched in frantic response. Clews groaned, grommets popped, separating canvas from line and line from spars. Shrouds tangled like clumps of twine caught in the hand of a mischievous giant.

On the bridge, Devlin Kane fought the wheel, the muscles of his brawny arms bulging as he strained to keep the frigate's nose angled into the ever-building waves. His booted feet were braced wide for purchase on the slippery deck; his soaked breeches and shirt were plastered the length of his tall, broad-shouldered frame. Eyes as black as ebony squinted against the pouring rain, peering into the night, scanning the deck below him and the skies above. With neither hat to secure it nor thong to bind it, his tawny hair whipped about his head like the shaggy mane of a lion, as wild and free as the man who sported it.

Lightning flashed, and the hoop of gold in Devlin's left ear winked an answering glimmer, as did the strong white teeth now bared in a primal grin. Sleek, sun-darkened flesh drew taut and wet over the slim, straight blade of his nose, the curve of bold cheekbones, the stubborn square jaw with a cleft carved deeply into the center of his chin.

The prow of the ship dipped perilously low into the dark heart of a steep trough of water. Trembling walls

of water rode high all around, threatening to bury the
Gai Mer at any moment. A froth of salt water sprayed
over the bow in a shimmer of lightning-lit lace, dashing
over the decks like the spread of a lady's shawl. Miraculously, the ship rose, balancing precariously on the
wobbly crest of the next wave in a nimble dance of defiance.

With a toss of his head, Devlin let loose a deep, rumbling laugh. "That's the way, m' lady!" he chuckled,
encouraging the frigate as if she were a living thing.
"The dragon's shaking his tail for all he's worth this
night, but 'twill do him little good. Nay! Old Neptune
may aim his trident at us all he wishes, yet we'll dodge
his every thrust! We'll best him at his own game, or
I'm not Devlin 'The Devil' Kane, captain of the heart-
iest crew of pirates ever to sail these seas!"

As if to disclaim Devlin's boast, the waves grew ever
higher, the gale stronger, tossing the ship about as if it
were no more than a splinter upon the ocean. The
planks and masts creaked against every blast of wind
and surf that pummeled the frigate relentlessly. Waves
surged over the sides, claiming three hapless victims
within their foamy grasp before the angered storm gods
were mollified.

By the end of it, Devlin was ready to nod his head
in deference to the mighty power of the sea, that most
haughty and demanding of all mistresses. She'd almost
won this bout, and it was a profound relief to find himself still standing when the storm at last began to wear
itself out. The rain had lessened to a drizzle, the thunder weakened to a few final grumbles, when Devlin finally pried his stiff fingers loose of the wheel and
turned the ship over to his helmsman once more.

Still flexing feeling into his hands, he strode a few
feet to the mizzenmast. On the near side of the mast, a
large peg had been driven into it, with a small slanted
roof fixed a little space above. Shoving aside the scrap

of tarp that had provided added shelter during the storm, Devlin reached out to untie the large, slightly damp, and disgruntled hawk tethered there. Zeus, as the bird was called, was Devlin's trained falcon and the *Gai Mer*'s resident talisman. As he smoothed a calming hand along the sleek plumage, Devlin crooned, "Quite a ride for you, eh, my friend? Aye, 'twas a rough one this time for us all."

With a rustle of wings, the agitated hawk landed atop Devlin's shoulder, his curved beak snapping irritably at a wet strand of Devlin's hair. On a bark of laughter, Devlin swatted at him. "Behave yourself, bird, or I'll be feasting on falcon stew when next I break my fast, and my pillow will be the fatter for your feathers."

The last of his words were nearly drowned out as a tremendous clap of thunder shook the ship, surprising in its intensity now that the storm was all but over. It was followed immediately by the most brilliant blue light, so bright that Devlin reflexively shielded his eyes from it. Unlike the usual lightning, it did not merely flash and diminish as fast as it came. Rather, the glow seemed to brighten. Wondering at this oddity, he cast his gaze upward, and paused to stare in mute wonder, as did every other man on deck, the lot of them struck dumb by the sight.

Though Devlin had been sailing for eleven years, never had he witnessed anything like this. He'd heard of it, to be sure, from other seamen, but he wasn't certain he'd ever believed their tales. Yet here it was before his stunned gaze. The proof of their words. Saint Elmo's fire—skipping along the mizzenmast in a blazing ball of dazzling blue flames!

Everything he'd ever heard about it came rushing to mind. Some said it wasn't true lightning at all, but a phenomenon unto itself. Most agreed it came either at the beginning or at the end of a storm, heralding good or bad weather to follow, which would explain its appearance now, after the worst gale Devlin had ever encountered. The more superstitious sailors believed the strange light to be the souls of drowned seamen seeking solace and a final resting place aboard ship. Others claimed it was a portent of good luck, but only if it remained above the rigging on the mast. If it traveled downward, below the rigging, it was a sign of sure misfortune, most especially if it landed upon the ship's rudder. That most awful event was thought to be what created ghost ships, dooming poor lost souls to wander the seas evermore, sailing eternally through misty realms, caught betwixt heaven and hell forever.

Just thinking about it sent a shiver down Devlin's backbone. Before he had further time to consider the matter, the freakish blue orb began to descend the mast. One and all, the crew stood transfixed, agape with fright. Standing where he was at base of the mast, just below the fireball, Devlin knew he should move back, but his feet seemed rooted to the deck. His feet and legs refused his brain's frantic commands to retreat.

The sphere of light moved slowly, creeping eerily downward until it reached the lower edge of the rigging. There it hovered, shimmering, as if deciding which direction to take. Then, in the blink of an eye, it hurtled toward the deck, where it seemed to explode upon impact in a blinding blaze of sparks.

Caught in its path, Devlin felt a sizzling shock slam through his body. If Thor had thrown his mighty hammer from the heavens and hit Devlin in the chest with it, it could not have stunned him more. His eyes glazed over, his vision blurring. Within his chest, he felt his heart cease its beating. His brain screamed out a warning. *Breathe! Breathe!* Yet he could not seem to make his body obey, could not draw breath into his burning lungs. His limbs began to quake, as if in a fit of palsy, and there was nothing he could do to stop it. Then, even as every ounce of his flesh and bones quivered, a queer numbness enveloped him, sucking him swiftly into a sparkling, spiraling void.

All about him, Devlin's crew watched in fascinated terror as the blue ball of Saint Elmo's fire engulfed their captain. Before their stricken eyes, he began to shake violently, every hair upon his head standing straight on end! And Zeus, upon his shoulder, stiffened and puffed out into a wad of fluff that more resembled a huge dandelion puff than a falcon. Except for the bird's eyes, which bulged out of its head as if on the ends of miniature pokers.

Then, to their further amazement and terror, the pair began to glow. Caught up in the searing blue sphere, both began to shimmer with an eerie iridescence of their own, as if the power of the strange lightning had entered their bodies and now shone from within. White, blue, green. Silver and gold. Bold, lustrous color radiated from them, so luminous it became almost too bright to bear watching.

Gradually, the light began to waver and fade, bit by bit. But lo and behold, to their immense horror, so did their captain and his bird! Those who still watched could not believe their eyes. One minute the captain stood glimmering like a saint come to life—and the next, he had faded away to nothing! Completely and absolutely gone! Not even a pile of ashes to mark the deck upon which he'd trod! Swallowed up in thin air!

Charles Town

Eden Winters gave an inward sigh, clasped her hands in her lap, and gritted her teeth behind what she hoped was a placid smile. Seated directly across from her in the small parlor was the primary cause of her current headache and many of her most pressing problems—one Dudley Finster. By occupation, he was the son and heir of Charles Town's only moneylender, and an accomplished and cunning accountant in his own right. Just now, Dudley Finster was Eden's nemesis, her arch-enemy, and a man most determined to court her into marriage with him.

"Come now, my dear," Dudley was saying, with a stretch of his thin, pale lips that seemed to Eden more of an evil grimace than a smile. "Such reluctance may be your idea of seemly conduct, proper spinster that you are, but it is entirely unnecessary. A simple agreement on your part, followed by a short period of engagement, would be quite sufficient."

"Sir, I do not want to marry you. I have no wish to marry anyone at this time. As you know, I have a company to run and an invalid mother in need of my care. Those endeavors take up most of my waking hours. I do not wish to add the burden of a husband." Eden paused a moment to let him digest her words, then added for further emphasis, "If, indeed, I wished to marry, there are others whom I might also consider as suitors for my hand."

Finster frowned slightly. "Ah, yes, but how many of them would willingly take your mother to their bosoms, Miss Winters?" he asked snidely. "A veritable millstone about their necks. I, on the other hand, am resigned to it, if that be the only means of attaining you as my bride."

Attaining my property is more the truth of the matter, Eden thought grimly. Though the shipping warehouse was currently in her widowed mother's name, Eden managed it, and it would one day pass on to her, as the only child, and thus to Eden's husband and children, should she have them. It was no small holding, being advantageously located on the wharf, large and easily accessible to the many ships that plied their trade in Charles Town Harbor. The only problem was that, under Eden's inexpert guidance, the business was fast losing money. It had been declining steadily since her

father had fallen ill and died three years before—a fact
of which Dudley Finster was well aware, since his
lending house held the note on Winters Warehouse, a
note long past due.

He pressed that point now. "I regret having to say
this, but how many of your prospective suitors would
also be able to assume your debts, even should they be
willing to do so? Whereas, if you were to wed me, the
note would be dissolved immediately upon our marriage, as well as any other outstanding debts you might
have accrued."

His bald statement hung between them like an omen
of doom. In addition to the problems Finster had
bluntly listed, at two and twenty years Eden was ad-
vancing past marriageable age. Not that she wasn't
comely enough to attract a husband, if a man held a
penchant for skinny brown-haired scarecrows. For it
was Eden's plight to be cursed with her father's height,
and bones that refused to pad themselves with abundant
flesh, as was both preferable and fashionable. Her
curves were slight, lending her more the appearance of
a lad than a robust woman. Though she possessed a
slim waist and adequately formed breasts, she also had
a terrible habit of slouching in an attempt to disguise
her height, which successfully hid her best feminine at-
tributes.

Even in her youth, she'd been awkward and gangly
in comparison with other girls. Too late to bloom while
the harvest was prime. And too educated by far for any
man who might care to look beyond her physical shortcomings. It was little wonder than that Eden had pre-
ferred to hide herself away in books while prettier,
rounder maids were giggling and batting their lashes.
With her heart yearning for impossible things that came
so readily to other women, Eden studied. Through her
books she traveled the world, and dreamed of someday
finding a man who would love her as she was, for the

person she was inside herself, for her mind and her wit, and all the pent-up love she had to offer.

As time passed, she'd determined not to settle for anything less, even if it meant remaining a spinster until the end of her earthly days—which it seemed she very well might, if all the world had to offer her for a husband was the likes of Dudley Finster! Or some widower such as Walter Bromley, with eight mewling children and wanting only a warm body in his bed in order to create even more little mouths to feed. Or that aged, toothless lecher Uriah Kempler, who was too old and bent to stand a chance of enticing anyone better. Besides, deep in her heart of hearts, she still waited and hoped for that one man who would make her heart trip over itself and sing wildly with joy.

Meanwhile, here she sat, with the bill collector intent on not only pounding down her door, but also demanding marriage in lieu of debtors' prison. Not just for herself, but for her poor disabled mother! The greedy mongoose!

Why, to her mind, he even looked like a cross between a ferret and a mean little mouse. Surely, *he* was no catch himself on the marriage mart, for he was short and thin, with bony narrow shoulders that seemed barely capable of supporting his clothes. He had close-set hazel eyes, teeth too prominent for his mouth, and sparse brown hair pulled back into a stringy queue. By no stretch of the imagination did Dudley Finster measure up to Eden's idea of Prince Charming, and she'd risk losing her last farthing—nay, she'd beg in the streets for bread—rather than sell herself into his bed, a thought so revolting that it made her shudder in disgust.

"Well, I will leave you to contemplate my offer once again," Finster told her, setting his teacup aside and rising from his seat. "But not for long, Miss Winters. I am a patient man, up to a point—and that point is fast approaching. I will have you, by fair means or foul, the choice of which is entirely in your hands. Do not tarry too long with your decision, my dear. You have one month. At the end of that time I will expect either your acceptance of my proposal of marriage, or your debt paid in full."

He graced her with a thin-lipped smile. "Of course, garnering both would be a superb delight, but since I doubt you will find yourself capable of gaining that amount of coin in such short order, I shall forge ahead with plans for a forthcoming wedding."

He sketched a brief bow toward her. "Good day to you, and please convey my best wishes to your mother for her improved health."

As Finster let himself out the door, as if the Winters's home already belonged to him, Eden collapsed into her chair, a heavy sigh escaping her trembling lips. What had she ever done to deserve being hounded by that mealymouthed vermin? How grandly he'd stated his terms; how graciously he'd extended the brief reprieve! Month? This being the fifth day of the fifth month of the Year of our Lord, 1718, by the first quarter of June, she would either be a reluctant bride-to-be or . . .

Or what, for heaven's sake? Out on her ear, with her mother beside her? With no coin in her purse or any legitimate means of gaining more? Of course, they would probably be able to keep the house for a while, though the warehouse would be forfeit. Perhaps they could take in boarders. Or find someone else who was willing to buy up her note from Finster, or go into the business with her for part ownership. But who? No one Eden knew at present was interested, at least no one with money.

Neither was she aware of anyone in need of lodging, though she could post a notice at the dock prior to the next passenger ship's arrival and hope that someone of good character would apply. It simply would not do to let just anyone take up residence in one's home, of course, so she would have to demand references of some sort, if that became her only recourse.

Mama would not be at all pleased to be brought to such dire straits. But there was only so much a person could do, after all, and at this point Eden imagined only an act of Providence would save the business for them, with perhaps an added miracle to send "Finny" Finster looking elsewhere for a wife.

Maybe she did need a husband after all, Eden concluded with a wry shake of her head. A big, strong, rich, handsome man with enough muscle and sufficient wits to meet all her many needs and solve her problems for her. She chuckled softly. "Aye, Eden, my girl. No doubt he'll come strolling into your life any day now. The answer to all your hopes and prayers. Now, that's not asking for much, is it? Godly intervention, a miracle or two, and all your secret fantasies fulfilled in the space of a month! Ho! What a grand dreamer you are becoming! Such a dotty old maid!"

Chapter 2

Once the shock of Devlin's disappearance began to pass, or to truly set in perhaps, the pirate crew of the *Gai Mer* went crazed. They began running around, screaming and tearing at their hair, scrambling in all directions at once with no place to go, some of them crawling about the decks whining pitifully, cravenly cowering beneath the doubtful shelter of their own arms. A few tried to recall the forgotten practice of prayer, long-dulled from disuse. Four of the men leapt overboard, preferring a quick drowning to whatever else the Fates might have in store for them.

It was to this bedlam that Devlin awoke.

At first, he was aware of nothing more than his own misery, for he felt as if he'd run full tilt into a stone wall. It seemed as though a ton of rock rested upon his chest. While his limbs were oddly weak, there was a strange tingling throughout his body, similar to the sensation of having one's foot fall asleep. His ears were ringing, his vision was blurred, and his head ached abominably. His thinking was very sluggish, and he had only a vague recollection of being enveloped by that eerie blue light, and little of what had happened afterward. Indeed, he had no memory of how he came to be

12

lying on his back on the deck, or how long he'd been unconscious, though it could not have been but a few minutes, for the first pale hues of daybreak were only now streaking the eastern sky.

As his mind began to clear, Devlin became aware of a terrible commotion, an awful din that made his head throb all the worse. By sheer willpower, he rolled to his side, caught hold of the wheel, and pulled himself into a sitting position. He almost wished he hadn't—for the painful effort of moving was certainly not worth the confusion it brought as he witnessed his crew running about like so many chickens with their heads lopped off.

"What in Hades is happening?" he murmured aloud. Forgetting himself, he shook his head, to his instant regret. "Aah! Damn but that hurts!"

Cautiously he levered himself upright, gaining his feet, only to wobble dizzily until the world righted itself again. Despite the pain, he braced himself and shouted down to his men on the deck below him. Twice, thrice, to no avail. The clamor they were making with their wailing was such that they might not have heard a cannon blast in their midst. With no help for it, Devlin stumbled the few steps to the ship's bell, and, clamping his teeth against the resulting agony to his poor head, he gave several hearty yanks to the clapper.

A startled, wary silence fell immediately, as all eyes turned upward toward the imperious signal. Now that he had their full attention, Devlin ordered brusquely, "Listen sharp, you dunderheads! Belay that racket and get back to your stations! We've a ship to sail!"

Rather than obey his commands, the crew stood as one, staring in stupification. "Move, I say!" he roared, his deep, distinctive voice ringing the length of the ship. "Or I'll have strips off all your hides before the day is half-begun!"

Still they gaped openmouthed. Several trembled visibly. One gave a hoarse shout, and, with a running leap, launched himself overboard. Another threw himself down and began to weep like a babe. Beside him, the young cabin boy fainted without a sound. Finally, one brave soul offered tentatively, "Be that you, Cap'n Kane?"

Wondering what had bedeviled his men, Devlin gave a snort of disgust. With his fists riding atop his hips, and his black eyes snapping, he retorted, "O' course 'tis me, you befuddled bilge rat! Who else? Were you expectin' your mother at the helm, mayhap?"

The answer was not what Devlin anticipated. Rather than see his crew turn back to the business of sailing the frigate, they began to murmur excitedly amongst themselves, their mutterings growing louder and more discordant as he watched. Scraps of comments drifted up to him, carried on the early-morning breeze.

"Saints preserve us! 'Tis the Cap'n's ghost!"

"It can't be! We seen 'im disappear! He's gone, I say!"

"Aye, but I know the Cap'n's voice when I hears it! 'Taint another like it thet I've ever heard!"

"Then why are we hearin' 'im an' not seein' 'im?"

"An' what made the bell ring?"

"If it comes t' that, what made the cap'n melt into air like he done?"

"What in bloomin' blazes are you fools blathering about?" Devlin bellowed at last. "Hell's bells and little fishes! Have the lot of you gone daft? What's all this nonsense about disappearings and ghosts? Why, I'm standin' here as big as life, with a head that's about to split wide with all your yammering, and . . ."

"Nay, Devlin—or whoever ye be—ye're not standin' there as big as life. I'd stake my own skin on that." Nate Hancock, the *Gai Mer*'s quartermaster and Devlin's best friend for the past nine years, stepped forward from the rest of the cowering, befuddled group. Like those around him, he gazed upward, toward the point from which the voice was coming, and claimed, "I swear by all the saints, Devlin, I can hear ye, but I'll be double-damned if I kin see ye."

Several others nodded in fearful agreement.

This brought Devlin up short. Certainly he'd never thought to hear anything this crazy. Why, it was ridiculous! Impossible! Suddenly he grinned. Ah! The rotten passel of sea dogs was tweaking his nose a bit, thinking to trick him into believing all this rot. It was a jest they'd brewed up among them, that was all! And a right good one, at that. "All right, lads. You've had your laugh for the day. Now, go fish Harl out of the brine a'fore he drowns, and let's be on our way."

"Ye think we're teasin' with ye, Devlin?" Nate asked incredulously. "Ye think this is a prank? God in heaven, man, I wish it were! Take a look at yerself, and tell me what ye see."

Thoroughly perplexed, and more than a little worried now about the state of his crewmen's minds, Devlin frowned and cast a quick look at his own body. "I see limbs and cutlass and boots and breeches, same as always, Nate. There's nothing the least bit different, and I think this joke has gone too far."

"Touch yerself and tell me what ye feel," Nate persisted.

"Damn it all, Nate—"

"Just do it."

Devlin felt like an absolute fool, but nothing else was going to appease his friend, so he touched his hands to his chest. "Fine. I'm here," he announced tersely. "Aching from my hair to my toes, but all in one piece, as near as I can determine. Does that satisfy you?"

"Actually, no. Do something that'll prove ye truly are standin' up there talking to us. Move something. Pick something up—something we can see."

"Blarst it all, Nate! This has gone far enough. I feel

like a buffoon, set up to play to your warped sense of humor."

Still grumbling, Devlin looked about him. Upon spying Zeus, lying motionless on the deck, he sighed. "Drat! The stupid bird is dead! And just when I had him well-trained!" He walked over and lifted the hawk by his talons, hanging him high overhead. "Now!" he yelled triumphantly. "Tell me you don't see that, you scurvy varmints!"

"See what, Cap'n?" came the reply.

"What are ye doin' that we should be seein'?"

"Blimey! This is sendin' shivers down me spine fit to stand me hair on end!"

"Ye don't have no hair, Jonesie. But I thinks I sees a crop o' gooseflesh sproutin' on yer skull about now."

Nervous laughter broke out, but it did little to ease the strain of the moment.

"Devlin . . ."

"Nay! Don't you dare say it, Nate! Here I stand, holding a dead falcon like a bloomin' flag, and you blind loonies are bound to claim otherwise."

Before Nate or anyone else could answer, the hawk gave a queer little quiver and a pitiful squawk. "I'll be hanged! He's not dead after all," Devlin exclaimed with relief. This was the first good sign since the storm had taken them all by surprise. He gave the bird a sharp shake, and Zeus emitted a loud, angry screech and twisted about to snap at Devlin's hand, demanding release.

"Did ye hear thet?" one sailor cried. "Now, we've not only a captain we can't see, but 'is bird too! I'm tellin' ye, we've all gone round the maypole, mates! We've sailed too close to the Devil's lair this time, an' gotten ourselves caught up in it, like those on the *Flyin' Dutchman* did!"

"The ship's doomed! And us with it!" another chimed in.

"Haunted! Great gallopin' ghosts! What're we to do now?"

The panic was growing again, fueled by mutual fright, but before it could gain full momentum, the ship's bell rang out again with a tremendous clang, almost flying from its mounting. "Nate! Get up here!" Devlin raged.

When his quartermaster hesitated, obviously uneasy about complying, a belaying pin came soaring through the air, missing the man's head by a hairsbreadth. "That's an order, Mr. Hancock!"

With the air of a martyr about to meet his end, Nate slowly climbed to the upper deck. Silent now, afraid to breathe let alone speak aloud, the crew watched apprehensively, waiting for the worst to happen, as their quartermaster walked gingerly toward the bell. Four steps from it, he bumped into something large and solid, an object that heaved a stream of furious, hot oaths into his face.

"By heaven and hell, Nate, if you dare tell me I'm not standin' here cursing you, I'll throw you to the sharks!" Devlin warned darkly.

"Cap'n, I know yer standin' there. I can hear ye and feel ye. Lord, I can even smell ye!" Nate drew in a shaky breath and added hastily, almost cringing with his next words, "But, dang it, I still can't see ye! I'd be a liar if I said differently. Do yer worst to me, but it won't change anything, Dev. Ye've turned into a ghost. A specter."

"Nay!" Devlin denied vehemently. "I'm no phantom, I say! Nor am I a wraith of any sort! I am a man of flesh and blood, the same as ever before!"

Sadly, Nate shook his head. "Deny it if ye must, but 'tis true. When that bolt of Saint Elmo's fire caught ye up in its flames, something queer happened. And now ye're no longer visible to any but yerself. Not even so much as a mist in the air."

Fear clutched at Devlin's belly, cramping it, as he read the truth in Nate's awe-filled eyes. Below them, the faces of the crew echoed Nate's sentiment, most of them still grappling with the notion, but swiftly coming to accept it as fact, though none could begin to comprehend how or why such a calamitous thing had come to pass—or what any of them might expect next.

With a hoarse shout, Devlin shoved his friend aside and raced down the steps. Dashing to the rail, he leaned overboard, trying to catch a glimpse of his reflection in the sea. Far below, the choppy, storm-stirred water offered no aid. Frustrated beyond bounds, he pushed away from the rail, roughly shouldering his way through a throng of anxious, skittish pirates—men now newly alarmed as they hastily attempted to give way to a force they could not see, not knowing which way to go to get out of his path.

His footsteps fell like thunder on the bare planking as he stomped to a nearby barrel and ripped the cover from it with a furious flick of his wrist. The lid went sailing, thudding to the deck. It was still spinning on its rim as Devlin bent over the barrel and gave an awful, agonized gasp.

Dear God, it was true! It was right before his disbelieving eyes to be seen—rather, *not* seen! Oh, merciful heaven, what was happening? How? Why?

Tentatively, Devlin raised trembling fingers to his face. Flesh met flesh without doubt, yet in the calm pool directly below him, no vision mimicked his movements. There came only a faint ripple to disturb the surface of the water, a consequence of the anguished moan Devlin could not contain as, overwhelmed, he hung his head in despair.

A few hours and several tankards of rum later, Devlin sat slumped in the captain's chair in his cabin. Across the desk from him, Nate did likewise. Both were soused to the gills, morosely pondering Devlin's fate as a ghost. "How? Why?" Devlin parroted for the thousandth time.

"Dunno, Dev," Nate commiserated drunkenly. "Mayhap the penalty for the wayward, thievin' life ye've been livin' these past years?"

"If that be so, what of the rest of you?" Devlin retorted in frustration. "I'm not the only pirate on the seas. I may be the best of the lot, but I'm far from the worst. And I sure as hell never set out to be one in the first place. If not for Captain Swift and his band of cutthroats, I'd be a common, law-abiding carpenter now, probably in business with my uncle, with a wife and six little whelps tagging about my coattails. Which, upon reflection, would not be so bad, most especially in comparison to my current, lamentable circumstance.

"But hearth and home were not to be my fate, were they? Nay, not with Swift roaming the seas back then. 'Twas he who attacked the ship carryin' me to the colonies. 'Twas he who dragged me, kicking and screaming, into this brigands' business."

"Aye," Nate agreed solemnly. "Still, 'twas better than gettin' yer gullet slit."

"Better a phantom pirate at the age of seven and twenty than fish bait at sixteen?" Devlin gave a woeful shake of his shaggy blond head. "I don't know, Nate. If I'd guessed it would come to this, perhaps I'd have chosen a swift death eleven years past, when Swift first landed me in his grubby clutches." He lifted his tankard and drained it, then thumped it atop the desk and reached for the small keg of rum nearby, intent upon pouring himself another drink.

Nate swore softly. "Damn, Dev! Do ye have the foggiest notion how dis—discomf—disturbin' it is to see mugs and kegs raise themselves into thin air? T' sit here and talk to ye, and hear ye, and watch things float about as they're doin'? Sweet Jesus! 'Tis like bein' caught up in a walkin' nightmare!"

"Then I wish to God we'd both awaken, because I'm trapped square in the center of it with you. And as long as we're wishin' for the impossible, I'd like to wake up back in England and find myself a beardless youth again, with Mother baking hot tarts and Father teaching me how to plane cabinet doors to fit properly."

"Ye can't bring the dead back to life, Dev. They're gone, both of 'em victims of the cholera the very month ye sailed for the colonies. Ye told me yerself, 'tis the reason they sent ye on ahead to live with yer uncle, so ye wouldn't catch the plague."

"Aye, and much good it did, too. My only consolation is that neither of them lived to see their only, beloved son turn sea robber, or to witness this day's calamity." He raised his eyes toward his friend. "You don't suppose they have any way of knowing about this, do you, Nate?" he questioned hesitantly.

"Why ask me?" Nate grumbled. "I ain't no expert on the habits of the dead. If anybody ought to know if they're spinning in their graves, you should, since ye're halfway there yerself. In body, if not in spirit."

"Another crass remark like that, and I'm liable to forget we're friends, or that you're too drunk on your ear to think before lettin' your mouth overload your arse. Then I'll show you just how much life is left in this body of mine, and you won't even see the punch coming! But I'll damned well guarantee you'll feel it!" Devlin growled.

"Sorry," Nate mumbled, only slightly repentant, "but this whole business has me spooked."

The two were silent for several minutes, each contemplating the situation. Finally Nate said, "Mayhap we're not considering the benefits behind all this, Dev."

With a shake of his head, Devlin frowned in confusion. "Benefits? Nate, old mate, your brains are in your cup, awash with rum. What is there to be gained by being invisible?"

For the first time that day, Nate grinned. "Well, I can name several things, now I've had time to think on it a bit. For one, ye never have to worry about gettin' caught by the Spanish, or the French, or the King's navy. How are they supposed to hang ye if they can't see ye?" he pointed out. "Why, ye might also catch a few of our fellow pirates off their guard, perhaps even discover where Blackbeard has hidden all his treasure. 'Twould be an easy trick for ye to eavesdrop on the hairy buzzard, without his being any the wiser."

He'd caught Devlin's interest now, and with every word Nate uttered, the prospects of the future began to brighten. "Aye, and if we can convince the crew to go along with our plans, there's no reason why I shouldn't continue to captain the ship, is there? After all, I've proven to be a fair and ambitious leader these past five years, ever since you and I organized the mutiny and took the *Gai Mer* for ourselves."

Nate nodded, remembering that time with fondness. "And stranded Swift and his bloody cohorts on that deserted island. That was a touch of genius, if I do say so meself."

"Seeing it was your idea, of course," Devlin conceded with a gruff laugh. "I've often wondered what became of that bunch. Odd that we've never heard or seen a thing of them since."

"More'n likely, they all starved."

Devlin gave an unconcerned shrug of his broad shoulders, though Nate could not see him do so. The quartermaster did, however, hear the enormous yawn that followed. Grinning, he taunted, "Tired, Dev? This is becomin' quite a revelation. I always thought ghosts didn't require sleep. For that matter, I wasn't aware that they could get sloshed on rum, or feel the need to relieve themselves. I'd assumed they were above the more mundane urges of nature." After a brief pause, he asked, "Pray tell me, what are you going to do when next you crave a woman in your bed, if that still be possible?"

A startled expression crossed Devlin's face, a look that would have made his friend laugh had he seen it. "Leave it to you to point out my shortcomings, just as I was beginning to believe this would all work out in the end," Devlin complained irritably.

"Oh, well, I suppose, for a portion of yer booty, I could be persuaded to lure a wench to yer bed for ye," Nate offered, "as long as ye remembered to keep the lamp doused. We wouldn't want the poor girl to run screamin' into the night thinkin' she'd bedded the Devil, or claimin' to be the next Virgin Mary."

Devlin snorted. "Ha! You wouldn't recognize a virgin if you tripped over her, Mr. Hancock. And any doxy you brought to my bed would likely be diseased to her eyebrows. I'll choose my own bed partners, thank you."

"How?"

That was a question, among a multitude of others, which Devlin would ponder long into the night and for many a day to follow.

Chapter 3

A fortnight had passed since Dudley Finster had issued his demands; half of Eden's alloted time now gone, while still she dithered over her reply. What was she to do? Passing a weary hand over her brow, she glared at the open account book on the desk before her, its columns of figures mocking her, and commanded herself to keep her mind on the task at hand. Perhaps by dealing with one concern at a time, thinking no further than the hour and day upon her, she could find some way out of this tangle. Or would that be tantamount to hiding her head in a basket until the inevitable snared her anyway, as it surely would?

Just now, her most pressing problem was attempting to make some sense of the monthly warehouse accounts, a chore she thoroughly detested. As adept as she was at reading and writing, and as much as she enjoyed both, her talents had never stretched to mathematics. Therefore, she had to rely heavily upon her manager's ability in that area, though she had doubts as to whether John Tilton was any more skillful at it. Also, she found herself in the position of having to continually bow to his advice about the operation of the warehouse, and hope that he was both capable and honest in his dealings with her. It was not the most comfortable circumstance in which to find oneself, but there seemed little help for it, unless she wanted to turn her books over to Dudley Finster or his father each month for an additional fee, which she could not afford to do.

She was still struggling to make heads or tails of the accounts when the bell above the office door chimed, announcing the arrival of three men. As she glanced up from her work, Eden's first reaction was one of dismay. By their clothing, it was obvious that they were seamen. It was also obvious to her, since she'd lived in Charles Town all her life and encountered a number of their sort, that they were pirates. The big, handsome fellow in the center wore a red sash about his waist and a gold hoop in his left earlobe, while the man on his left sported an eyepatch, and the one on his right a gold tooth. All were heavily armed, bearing pistols and cutlasses.

For all their fierce appearance, Eden read no immediate threat in their faces—that being no guarantee of safety, of course. Even as fingers of fear rippled through her, despair battled with fright. She needed more trouble like she needed an extra eye in the center of her forehead. And this motley band undoubtedly meant trouble.

In the past, Charles Town residents and businessmen had readily dealt with pirates, glad not only for the increased trade, but also for merchandise the brigands brought into port, goods not always available through ordinary means. In more recent days, however, tariffs and restrictions on imported items had been eased, and the town was thriving without the stolen booty. Indeed, most citizens now considered the pirates more of a nuisance than a benefit, more hindrance than help to legitimate commerce. Not only did they attack lawful trading vessels which were bound into and out of the Carolinas, but when in town they caused quite a disturbance—stealing, whoring, and drinking till all hours, destroying property and generally terrorizing innocent folk.

In the last months, the attitude of the community had undergone an about-face. The citizens were determined to rid themselves of this riffraff. Though not yet a crime, doing business with pirates was severely frowned upon. On the other hand, refusing to do so often brought swift retribution from the angry sea robbers.

Which put Eden in a pickle.

With much trepidation, she swallowed the lump in her throat, dredged up a polite smile, and asked weakly, "How may I help you, sirs?"

The fellow with the gold tooth answered. "We've just put into port, and are lookin' for a place to store our cargo, ma'am. Is the owner about? We'd like to discuss arrangements for transferrin' it to yer warehouse."

Thinking she might have found a way out of her predicament, Eden countered, "Have you dealt with us in the past? We're taking no new customers at the moment."

The man frowned and tossed a quick glance at the pirate in the center, who grunted softly, leaving the first man to reply. "Aye. We've put goods here b'fore, I guess."

"Don't you know?" Eden questioned.

"If the cap'n says we did, then we did," Gold Tooth told her gruffly. "He ain't a liar."

"I didn't mean to imply that he was," Eden said, nervously licking her suddenly dry lips. "Merely that I need a name in order to check our records."

"Oh. Well, I suppose it'd be listed under . . . uh . . ." He hesitated, seemingly unsure how to reply until Red Sash growled the answer into his ear. "It'd be under Kane, ma'am. Captain Devlin Kane, of the *Gai Mer.*"

"And when might you have stored goods here last?"

she persisted. "To facilitate locating the entry in the registry."

"Uh . . ." After again consulting with Red Sash, Gold Tooth blurted. "Three years past."

There was nothing for it but to play along and make a show of finding the old records. Eden was half out of her chair when the bell tinkled once more. Ridiculously grateful for the timely interruption, she turned her gaze to the new arrival, only to find herself faced with the equally unwelcome sight of Dudley Finster.

The accountant looked from her to the pirates and back again, his thin nostrils pinching together as if he'd suddenly smelled something foul. "Might I speak with you, Miss Winters?" he requested archly.

Feeling as if she were caught between the Devil and the deep, Eden nodded. "Sirs, if you will excuse me for just a moment, I will attend to this gentleman and be back straightaway. Or perhaps you would care to talk with our manager in my stead? He is, I must admit, more capable of advising you than I."

Before their designated speaker could reply, Red Sash nudged him and gave a sharp shake of his head. "Nay, ma'am. We'll wait fer ye," Gold Tooth told her.

Within the crowded confines of the tiny warehouse office, there was little chance of conducting a private conversation. So, edging past her potential customers, Eden motioned Dudley to precede her outside. Aware that she was leaving her cash box behind, in an unlocked drawer of her desk, she intentionally left the door ajar, hoping this would deter the pirates from stealing her pitifully small funds.

Once outside, she faced Finster with a stern countenance. "What brings you here in the middle of my workday, Mr. Finster?"

"Why, I've come to receive your answer to my request for your hand, of course."

"My time is not yet up," she reminded him sharply.

"I've two weeks before the limit you have set for me. A fortnight more in which to repay the debt Papa unwittingly bequeathed to me."

He favored her with a tight smile. "Why delay, my dear? Have you any other recourse than to accept my offer of marriage and thus cancel the loan?"

Both knew she didn't unless some rich, heretofore unknown relative appeared suddenly out of the blue.

"Consider how pleased I would be if you were to accede now, rather than make it seem as if I have forced you into becoming my bride," Finster continued. "Our life together would begin on a much more favorable note, and I would be more inclined to be a kind and generous spouse."

"You will have my answer in two weeks, Mr. Finster," she insisted, standing her ground. "I care not if it displeases you. And it remains to be seen whether or not I become your wife. Forfeiting the business would not immediately put me or my mother in the poorhouse, or send me flying into your waiting arms for rescue."

"Though matters are likely to end in the same way, after all is said and done, don't you imagine?" He gave an exaggerated sigh of resignation. "Ah, well, have it your way, if you must. For now. Go attend to those two cutthroats awaiting you, but I might warn you to steer clear of doing business with them. Not only would the town assemblymen disapprove, but you might find yourself courting bodily harm—and as badly as I want you, I would balk at taking soiled goods to wife."

Meanwhile, inside the office, Devlin and his men unrepentantly eavesdropped on the conversation between the proprietress of the warehouse and her would-be suitor.

"Would ye listen to that struttin' fop?" Nate commented. "Actin' fer all the world like some sort of king,

browbeatin' that poor woman into marryin' him when
'tis plain she wouldn't have him on a platter."

"Not that she has much choice as I see it," Arnie put
in. "She looks a mite long in the tooth and too tall by
far to be pickin' and choosin'."

Nate nodded. "Aye. An' skinny as a pike, too. Do ye
suppose she's so bad off that she's been starvin' herself
to save up the money to repay her loan?"

"What's the matter with you two simpletons?" Devlin asked with a frown. "Have your eyes gone as dull
as your brains? The lady may be tall, but not overmuch,
particularly to my tastes. And while she could use a bit
more weight on her bones, neither is she gaunt. Fact is,
I rather fancy the way she looks, with that creamy skin
and those lush lips. Why, I'll wager when she lets her
hair down, it ripples all the way to her waist, soft and
brown and scented. And those big eyes. Now, I ask
you, have you ever seen eyes that color before, like
sun-dappled seas?"

"Oh, ho!" Nate crowed. With uncanny aim, given the
fact that he could not see his target, he slammed an elbow into Devlin's ribs. "Methinks our leader is smitten,
Arnie. And with a spinster lady in dire need of rescuin'.
Think ye that we might work something out here for
him? Do ye reckon she'd consider beddin' a man she
can't behold, rather than mate with that fuss-fidget
who's hot on her heels? I wonder how much that debt
of hers amounts to, anyway? Why, if we all throwed in
a sum, maybe we could offer her enough to meet it and
buy her favors for our dear, nearly departed captain."

"Belay the ill-fitting humor, Mr. Hancock," Devlin
snapped. "Spinster she might be, and well in need of
aid, but 'tis clear she's a lady. So, hold a civil tongue
in your head, if you please."

Nate executed a smart salute and stifled a chuckle.
"Aye, aye, sir!"

At this juncture Eden reentered the room. "Now,

sirs," she said, still trying to collect her scattered wits after the encounter with Finster, "perhaps we can conclude our business without further interruption. Where were we?"

"Ye were about to check yer records, ma'am," Nate offered politely, though his eyes still held a twinkle of humor.

"So I was, though I doubt that will be necessary. You see, I have just recalled how filled the warehouse is at this time. I sincerely doubt we have space for any more goods."

A quick conference was held between the three, whereupon Nate declared, "Beggin' yer pardon, but we saw ourselves through the place afore we come to the office, and there appears to be plenty of room for our cargo."

Eden's face colored at being caught in such a bald-faced lie. "I see," she murmured, chewing her lower lip. "Well then . . ." she hedged.

Again, the center pirate whispered something to his spokesman. It proved more than Eden could tolerate after the morning she'd been through. To her own amazement, as well as that of the men before her, she blurted, "Why is it that your Captain Kane—I assume that's who the fellow in the red sash is—cannot speak for himself? I know he's not mute, for I can hear him muttering to you. Has he some aversion to dealing with a woman?"

All three pirates gaped at her in varying degrees of amazement. "Ye can see him?" Nate asked incredulously, while Devlin continued to stare at her with an expression betwixt hope and disbelief.

"Of course I can," she said. "I'm neither nearsighted nor wall-eyed."

"She can see me!" Devlin exclaimed softly. Then more excitedly, "Blow me down! The wench can detect me! I'm revived! Returned to my normal self once more!"

"Nay, yer not!" Nate corrected quickly, before Devlin's hopes could rise too far, only to be dashed on rocky shoals. "Ye're still a spirit, Dev. Neither Arnie nor I can behold ye. Ain't that so, Arnie?"

Arnie's head bobbed up and down as he struggled to sort out the confusion of having two persons on hand who could not view the captain, and one who could. "I don't know what's goin' on, but I sure can't spot ye, Cap'n. Not so much as a hair on yer head."

"Oh, come now," Eden declared warily, the nape of her neck starting to tingle. "What manner of prank is this? What do you hope to gain by such farce? You'll find no foolish audience with me, sirs!"

" 'Tis no joke we're playing," Devlin assured her solemnly, anxiously. "My men cannot see me. Truth be told, in the last couple of weeks, out of a hundred people, not one has viewed me—until you. Tell me honestly now. Look upon me and describe my person."

Why she complied was beyond her, but her eyes and tongue seemed to have acquired a will of their own, and she found herself studying him and replying, "You are tall, wide of shoulder, and broad of chest. You are wearing boots, dark breeches, and a white shirt, with a scarlet sash about your middle and a gold earring in your left lobe. No hat. Your hair is shaggy, in need of barbering but not unbecoming, blond with lighter streaks in it. Your eyes are dark-brown—no, black. Never have I seen eyes as black as yours. Your chin is cleft, in a strong jaw . . ."

"Enough," Devlin broke in, surprised to find himself somewhat embarrassed by her assessment of him. Still and all, she'd related his features correctly enough that he could not doubt that she saw him quite well.

"So you do see me," he murmured half to himself, a wide smile curving his lips. "By God! You surely do!"

he announced joyously, wonder still pulsing through him. "How this can be, when no one else is capable of doing so, eludes me, but I've never been so grateful for anything in my score and seven years! Oh, lady! If you only knew what a trial I've been through these past days, living the life of a ghost, when I know beyond doubt that I am still an earth-bound man."

The tingle at her nape had spread down her spine, raising chill bumps. It was only now that she recalled Finster commenting on the two pirates in her office. Two, he'd said. Not three, as stood before her, plain as the nose on her face. "Please," she begged. "Tell me you jest. Tell me this is not—"

" 'Tis so," Nate answered. "Sad, but true. Ye ken, several days ago, we had us a hellacious storm." At the shove Devlin gave to his shoulder, Nate said, "Beggin' yer pardon, ma'am, but 'twas. Then we had this bolt of Saint Elmo's fire strike the mast, and it come down and encircled the captain here. And afore ye could spit, he'd disappeared—him an' the bird with him."

"Saint Elmo's fire?" she repeated stupidly. "And a bird?"

"Aye. 'Tis a lightnin' of sorts, I suppose, though not really. An' the cap'n has a trained falcon he keeps aboard ship with 'im," Arnie put in helpfully.

"Oh." Eden nodded, completely befuddled. Certain now that she was caught up in a bad dream, the result of something she'd eaten which had not agreed with her, she longed only to put it to a quick resolution. With that single goal in mind, she rose and started for the door. "Sirs, I must ask you to excuse me, please. I simply cannot sit here and participate in this nightmare any longer. I am going to walk outdoors, where I pray that this will end at last and I will awaken snug in my own bed, and this entire, disastrous day will never have been."

Devlin could not let her go, could not allow the only

person who could see him to walk away. As she sidled past him, he caught her arm. When he did so, another miraculous thing happened. With no more warning than an odd, warm tremor tripping through him, Devlin became visible to his two crewmen. They cried out in shock upon his sudden appearance before their startled gazes.

"Dev!"

"Cap'n! Ye're back!"

"Just look at ye, Devlin! Why, I never knew how much I missed that ugly puss of yers till just this minute!"

"What?" Devlin gasped in delight. "You can see me, too? Both of you?"

"Aye! Ain't it glorious?"

Without thinking, Devlin released Eden's arm. Immediately, he began to fade from sight. Strangely, this time he could actually feel himself doing so. And the dismal looks on Arnie's and Nate's faces told him it was so.

"Devlin! Do somethin'!" Nate implored anxiously. "Ye're vanishin' on us!"

At their initial shouts, Eden had turned back and stared. At the moment when the pirates claimed to glimpse their captain, she realized that she, too, could see the man more vividly, as if what she'd viewed before had been slightly shadowed, not quite as clear as he should have been, though she'd not realized it then. Now, not having the slightest notion what motivated her to do so, she reached out and touched his shoulder. Just that small contact, and Devlin Kane reappeared to one and all.

"'Tis her!" Nate announced in jubilant wonder. "Not only does she see ye when none else can, but when she touches ye, ye become visible. 'Tis the queerest damned thing I ever seen, other than you fadin' away to start with!"

Devlin had to agree. He also knew without a doubt

that he was going to keep this woman no more than an arm's length away from him, if he had to lash her to his wrist to keep her there—for the rest of his life, or however long it took to regain his normal state permanently. Still, the thought of being chained to an unwilling captive for an undetermined length of time, with her ranting and raving the whole while, left something to be improved upon. Far better if he could convince her to go with him of her own volition. And he had just the thing to persuade her, thanks to her unwanted suitor.

Never one to waste time or opportunity, Devlin said, "Miss Winters—that is your name, is it not?"

She nodded dumbly, still shaken, not at all sure her mind hadn't come unhinged. Is this what trying to balance accounts could do to a woman's brain? No wonder men kept warning their ladies away from too much figuring! Was there a cure for what ailed her? Should she consult a physician? Or dare she admit the problem to anyone, lest they lock her away in an asylum, declaring her hopelessly afflicted?

"Miss Winters," she heard the captain saying, "you're not attending my words." Mutely she stared up at him as he clasped warm fingers about her chin and tilted her face toward his. "Now, pay attention, please."

Again she gave a stiff nod, her chin bobbing within his large palm. "I . . . I'm listening."

"I want you to come with me."

"Where?" she croaked.

"Back to my ship. Wherever I go."

"Why?"

"Good God, woman! Need I explain, after all that has happened? You are the one person who can see me, who can make it possible for others to do so. Who can give my life some semblance of normalcy, as long as you are within the distance of a touch. I need you with me."

"Nay."

"Aye. You must."

"I won't," she maintained, turning suddenly stubborn and, to her vast relief, feeling stronger and more herself by the minute.

"I wouldn't hurt you, or allow any harm to come to you," he assured her.

"You don't understand. I have a business to run, and an invalid mother at home. Even if I wished to go with you, which I do not, I could not leave her alone and helpless."

Devlin considered his options, which were few. "Then I'll simply have to stay with you."

"That's impossible. I couldn't allow it. Why, just to do business with you would be risking ostracism by my fellow townspeople. To have you walking about with me, visible or otherwise, would be unthinkable."

"But you *will* do business with me, Miss Winters," he assured her gravely. "And I with you. I shall strike a bargain with you. In return for your companionship, I'll pay off your loan to that puny pup who is sniffing after your skirts. Your warehouse will be yours, free and clear of any debts; and for as long as I stay, it will continue to be so. For your part, you will accompany me wherever I need to go and be seen.

"If that is not agreeable to you, I could very well abduct you now, put a gag between your teeth, and a-sailing we will go. Together." Only Devlin and his mates knew that this threat was a bluff, that unless there was no other recourse, Devlin would never risk his beloved ship by allowing a woman aboard and bringing disaster down upon them all. Miss Winters did not know this, however, and Devlin was not about to enlighten her.

"Or, if you'd prefer," he continued, "I could haunt your home and your business until you relent. I've yet to attempt a haunting, but it shouldn't be too difficult.

And I do so love a challenge." He ended his speech with a rakish grin.

"That's blackmail!" she accused hotly.

"Did you expect less?" he taunted. "I am, after all, a pirate of some repute, and need to maintain my good standing with my fellow buccaneers."

Eden wanted to scream. What a preposterous predicament! She was caught like a juicy bone between two hungry dogs! On the one hand, a priggish moneylender proposing lifelong misery. On the other, a mad pirate promising havoc and hauntings! Not a lot of choice there! Still, of the two, perhaps Devlin Kane presented the better bargain. She'd have the warehouse back, with no mortgage hanging over her head. And there was always the chance he'd soon regain his body and be out of her life much faster than Finster would. After witnessing today's spectacles, surely even that was possible, and it might be worth the risk after all. Besides, if she had to have a man around, why not a handsome almost-ghost instead of a bony accountant?

"I'd want more," she demanded haughtily, thinking to lessen her disadvantage.

"Oh?" Kane raised an arrogant brow.

"Aye. If I were to have you constantly underfoot, I'd need your pledge to discover the reason my business is failing. If the fault lies with me, I want you to teach me how to correct the problem, or hire someone who can. In that way, once you are gone, I can get my life back in order and not have to constantly worry about supporting myself and my mother. And if the fault lies elsewhere, you must help me find a means of resolving the problem once and for all."

"Done."

"What?"

"Are you hard of hearing? I said, I agree. We have a bargain, Miss Winters."

Chapter 4

Struck a deal with the Devil! That's what she'd done, Eden thought in wondrous panic, mere minutes after the fact. What in heaven or hell had possessed her to agree to such an asinine bargain? Or had she? She rather suspected she'd been neatly outmaneuvered, caught in a tangle of her own words and confusion, only to find herself bound to a pact with a man—nay, a pirate specter—she knew nothing about. How did she know she could trust him? That he wouldn't attack her in her bed, or slit her throat in broad daylight? Why, next to him, Finster might seem a piddling bully!

Already, Kane was setting into motion aspects of their agreement to which she'd given little thought, hadn't truly suspected would be part of the plan. Why, the man actually intended to move into her house! With his invisible falcon!

"Absolutely not!" she announced, aghast. "Captain Kane, I can only imagine the type of women you consort with, but I assure you, I am no lightskirt!"

He perused her person most thoroughly, raking his glowing black eyes over her with disturbing familiarity. His intent gaze assessed her stylish lilac day dress, trimmed in contrasting violet lace. The front of the hooped skirt was split and drawn aside, draped over bolsters at the hips and back to reveal the frilled petticoat beneath. At her small waist, the gown was close-fitted, giving way to a snug square-cut bodice, the low décolletage modestly filled with a pleated tucker that rose to band her swanlike neck. She wore no jewelry, save a single brooch at her throat, and no artifice upon her face, though many ladies of the day wore powders and paint, as well as beauty patches, to enhance their features.

"Nay, mistress," he agreed with a brash grin. "You be no tart. Though you do have possibilities. I fail to see how you have remained unwed all these years. Are the men of Charles Town blind to your charms? Or do you hold them at bay with a shrewish tongue?"

Eden blinked up at him owlishly, momentarily dumbstruck. Even while she knew she should be offended, she was also unwittingly flattered. That this handsome, brawny man should think her attractive was beyond belief! Why, it was practically laughable! For years she'd been well aware of her own gawkish looks, feeling much like an overgrown beanstalk stuck amid a garden of pretty primroses.

Oh, she was neat enough in her appearance, and tried to dress fashionably, if not in a manner that would openly invite critical attention. And she'd long since given up hope of attempting an elaborate coiffure, for it invariably emphasized her height, even should she manage to tame her flyaway tresses into something other than a frizzy puff of curls. She'd had to settle for more sedate styles—usually a thick bun, or a fat braid twisted into a coronet or knotted at her nape, or occasionally gathered into a decorative snood, which was the only way she could control the unwieldy mass and wear it more loosely at the same time.

Consequently, she remained eternally conscious of

the limitations which set her apart from others. Now, here was this outlandish pirate tossing glib praise about and likely expecting her to swoon at his feet in abject appreciation! No doubt his objective from the start, the reason behind his pretty lies, had been to worm his way into her home!

"You are no gentleman!" she declared indignantly.

He merely nodded, his smile growing ever more bold.

"You may quit your misplaced flattery, for 'twill gain you naught! You'll not step so much as one boot across my threshold!"

"Come now, my haughty duchess. Think but a moment. Who would know if I did, for who would behold my presence?" he argued. "Also, how do you intend to prevent my doing so? Will you go to the constable and have him arrest me? The man would believe you'd gone simple, would he not, when he came to investigate your claim and found no sign of me in your house?"

"What of my mother?" she countered weakly, his logic fast defeating her. "Surely she would sense that a stranger was abiding in her home. Even should she not see you, would she not hear you? And ponder this, sir pirate. While Jane Winters has not the use of her legs, her mind is as sharp as her ears. Neither is she entirely bedridden. Many a day, with the aid of a servant to help her down the stairs, Mother spends her hours in the parlor, where she entertains friends who come to visit. And what of those friends, and our housemaid?"

Devlin gave an eloquent shrug. "If I take care to be quiet, no great problems should arise. At least nothing that cannot readily be explained. Timbers creak; floorboards squeak. 'Tis natural to expect a few odd noises now and again."

"True," she conceded, with a condemning glare. "However, when the furniture takes on a voice and deigns to speak, I'll be at a loss to account for such a queer happenstance. So, if you insist on moving in, kindly keep your lips buttoned within anyone's hearing. Or they'll fast be proclaiming me a witch. I'll be of little use to you, or any other, once I've been burned at the stake."

"O woman of little faith!" he mocked, sketching a low bow. "Don't you know that I would gallantly rescue you from any harm which might befall you, my beauty?"

She sniffed. "And likely gain me even more trouble in the process. Why must you plague me so?" she lamented.

"Better to ask why the sun must rise or the rain fall," he answered. "Or why I have become a vapor to all but you."

It was decided that the cargo from the *Gai Mer* would be off-loaded the following day, to be stored in Winters Warehouse after all. Immediately thereafter, Nate and Arnie left to relate this news to the crew and see to making things ready aboard ship.

Before departing for home, Eden, with Devlin at her side, went in search of her manager, to inform him of the impending transaction. To her dismay, John Tilton was unaware of Devlin's presence the whole while, dashing her hopes that his invisibility was some elaborate hoax. Apparently, her prayers were not to be so easily answered.

The nightmare continued.

As was customarily proper, Devlin took charge of the reins after assisting Eden into her buggy, neither of them remembering at that moment that no one else could see him. Off they rode, side by side, Eden doing her best to keep even the hem of her skirt from touching him. A slight defiance, at best, but enough to make him aware of her pique.

They'd traversed several blocks when Eden suddenly

became aware that she was garnering strange looks along the route, and it was several seconds before she could fathom the reason. When it came clear to her at last, she uttered a strangled gasp and grabbed for the reins.

Diverted from his own mental fog, Devlin held tight. "What's the matter with you, wench?" he growled. "Cease this fit before you spook the horses!"

Still she battled to strip the thongs from his grasp. "No! Don't you see how people are staring?" Her anxious wail was but a hiss, her lips barely moving in her stiff white face. "Sweet heaven, Captain Kane, leave loose! Turn the team over to me! And do hush! God forbid anyone should hear you! 'Tis bad enough they've witnessed me driving blithely down the street with no one in control of the horses and the reins flapping in mid-air!"

"Oh." Nonplussed, he did as she suggested, berating himself for his oversight. Damn! After a lifetime of being visible, was he supposed to become suddenly accustomed to having it otherwise? Weren't a few lapses to be expected, even excused?

Still and all, he allowed he owed Miss Winters an apology, which he tendered in a rumbling whisper. "I beg your pardon, Miss Winters. I was caught up in my own musings, and caution went by the wayside."

"You buffoon!" she fumed through her teeth. "Your forgetfulness has made a spectacle of me! Already! I can scarcely wait to see what might further develop from our unfortunate alliance."

Though unused to allowing such mutinous behavior to go unpunished, much less to expect it from a female, Devlin wisely let her comments pass. He reasoned that perhaps it was better to let her temper flare a bit now, if it were to cool by the time they reached her home. It would not do to have her too upset upon greeting her mother, and whoever else might be there.

He remained silent until they drew up before a two-leveled sand-colored house built entirely of stone and tabby. It had a mellow, welcoming air of permanence to it, as though it could weather a hurricane and still remain standing for years to come. Vines twined around several sturdy pillars, while the foundation of the surrounding veranda was colorfully edged with blossoming shrubs and flower beds. He had no doubt that Eden's father must have been well-to-do, to have built such a dignified home, for the windows sported real glass panes, and while the place was not a mansion, it was fair-sized and of good construction.

Reminded of a question he'd not posed, he said, "You've spoken of your mother, that she is an invalid with only you and a servant to care for her. Whatever became of your father?"

Sadness furthered darkened her shaded features beneath her bonnet. "He died almost three years past, following a lengthy illness the doctor could neither name nor cure. It was a terrible time for us all, but especially for my mother. On the very day they placed my father in his grave, she lost the use of her legs, and she has not taken a single step since."

Eden gazed past him toward the house, her beautiful eyes dull with sorrow. "The doctor claims it is more a sickness in her mind and soul than a physical condition," she continued on a heartfelt sigh, "but that does not alter the fact that she cannot walk. I doubt she ever will, after all this time. That's why I am so determined to keep the business and the house for her, to see that she is kept comfortable and in want of nothing—thought all she ever wanted was my father, and he is the one thing I can never return to her."

They drove to the rear, to a small carriage house. There Devlin helped Eden unharness and stable the two horses before following her up to the main residence. On the veranda she paused. "For my mother's sake, if not for mine, I implore you to try to remember not to speak or make any undue sounds. Please."

"I'll be as quiet as a mouse," he promised.

She rolled her eyes. "That does little to alleviate my worries, Captain Kane, since everyone knows that mice can be quite noisy."

Suddenly spying the mud he'd tracked onto the porch, she remonstrated stiffly, "And would you kindly scrape the filth from your boots before entering the house, lest you leave ghostly footprints all across my mother's clean floors?"

The door had no sooner opened than Eden's mother called out from the parlor. "Eden, dear? Is that you?"

"Yes, Mama. I'll be right in."

Upon hearing Eden's given name for the first time, Devlin's brow rose in mild amusement. He caught her arm to halt her for a moment, little flickers of heat licking through him as he immediately began to become visible.

"Don't do that!" she warned softly, lest her mother hear her. Pulling loose of him, and noting the odd look on his face, she asked, "What is it?"

"My name is Devlin Kane, but they call me 'The Devil,' " he told her, watching for her reaction. She simply blinked at him and waited for whatever else he would say. "Some have associated my surname with that of Cain, who slew his brother Abel, though mine is spelled K-A-N-E. Don't you think it ironic that the one woman who could prove to be my salvation is called Eden? Is that not a fine joke for the Fates to play upon us, Miss Eden Winters?"

She could not deny that it was, indeed, strange. Neither could she keep her wayward tongue from commenting, "More illogical than a pirate well acquainted with the Bible? You are an extraordinary enigma, Captain."

She stepped into the front hall. "Now, 'tis imperative

to have no more touching. I fear Mama would not take it well to have a ghost in her home. Particularly one who appears and fades at every whipstitch."

Together they entered the parlor to find Eden's mother sitting propped in a chair before the window. On a glance, Devlin compared mother and daughter. Mrs. Winters was clearly slight in stature. She was also more plump than Eden, whether by nature or enforced inactivity, Devlin could not assess. The older woman's pale face bore the markings of time and mourning, though her lackluster brown hair was only slightly streaked with gray and she was clearly not past forty. As she looked up from her embroidery, Devlin's breath caught. It was from her mother that Eden had inherited her magnificent turquoise eyes, but never before had Devlin witnessed such deep sorrow as that displayed in Jane Winters's.

A slight frown creased Jane's forehead as she welcomed her daughter. "My, your step seems heavy this afternoon, dear," she said. She shook her head, gave Eden a loving smile which did little to lessen the sadness in her eyes, and jested, "Are you perhaps feeling weighed down with those nasty accounts you are forced to balance? I know how you dread that chore."

Eden bent to receive her mother's kiss. "They are a trial for me," she admitted. "And I must battle them yet again on the morrow, for I fear they won the fight today. But enough of that dreariness. How was your day, Mama? Did you have a nice visit with Reverend Johnston and his wife?"

"No more or less than usual. Henrietta is still after me to let her paint my portrait, though heaven knows why she would want to commit this wrinkled old face to canvas. I much prefer those she did of your father and me before James's illness. And 'tisn't as if she needs the practice, after all, with everyone in Charles Town pleading for portraits of their own."

Eden nodded in agreement as she loosened the ties of her bonnet. "Yes, she does have a remarkable skill with color and brush." Paying little attention, she tossed the hat toward a nearby chair. It landed on Devlin's knee.

"My stars!" her mother exclaimed, noting the way the hat seemed to hover half a foot above the cushion. "What on earth . . ."

Quickly, Devlin shoved the hat from his knee, causing it to tumble to the floor. Jane stared, then swiftly recovered and offered the explanation herself. "I'll wager that dratted Dora has left half the windows in the house open, as well as the kitchen door. I've tried to tell her what an awesome draft it creates, but she refuses to heed my words, particularly on baking day. Says she cannot work well when the house is so stifling hot."

Eden heaved a tremendous sigh of relief and met Devlin's taunting black gaze. He lifted a broad shoulder in a mute gesture, as if to say it wasn't his doing this time, but hers.

A while later, it was Eden's turn to smirk. As she and her mother dined on tender roasted capon, potatoes, and new peas fresh from the garden, Devlin was forced to sit quietly and watch. The aroma alone was enough to set his mouth watering and his stomach begging for respite. By the time they had finished their meal, he could have eaten the crockery. And as Dora, their stout indentured servant, cleared the table, he could barely withhold a pathetic moan. The gloating gleam in Eden's turquoise eyes did nothing to ease his torment.

He was regarding the remaining dishes with longing when Dora rounded the corner of the table nearest him. It came as some surprise when she lifted the back of his chair and attempted to push it into its proper place, almost toppling him from his seat in the process. No small woman, Dora gave the chair another hefty shove, frowning when it scarcely budged. As she bent to examine the legs, which appeared to be stuck fast, Devlin hastily made his escape.

By this time, Eden could not contain her glee. Though she covered her mouth with both hands, a cascade of giggles bubbled forth, earning her a perplexed look from her mother.

"Eden, what has gotten into you this evening?" Jane inquired. "Why, I declare, you're as skittish as a spring colt. Not at all your usual self. Now this fit of giggles over nothing. Are you sure you are feeling well?"

"I'm fine, Mama," Eden assured her, though she was anything but. "I'm just tired, and a bit giddy with it."

It was not until Dora and Jane retired for the evening that Devlin finally got the opportunity to appease his hunger. As he raided the pantry, Eden stood watching, grimacing he tore into the food as if it were the last morsel he was likely to consume. She'd seen animals eat with better manners!

"Damn me, but I'm starving!" he declared, his head half-buried as he searched the shelves. " 'Twas mean torture, you getting to eat while I sat and watched, salivating over every spoonful that went into your mouths."

"You should have considered that before you invited yourself into my home," she replied, not at all sympathetic. "Perhaps you should rethink your plans. I'm sure this is not the last of the pitfalls you will encounter."

"We," he corrected around a mouthful of food. "As in you and I, my sweet. I am not about to quit our agreement so easily. And if you want that pesky moneylender off your scent, neither will you. 'Twould serve you well to remember that 'tis my gold that will ransom you from his greedy clutches."

Once Devlin's appetite was satisfied and the kitchen tidied once more, Eden showed him upstairs to a spare bedroom, all the while wondering at the amount of food he'd consumed and how she would explain its disappearance to Dora. Though neat, the room was small and sparsely decorated. The bed was shorter than he might have liked, but topped with a plump feather mattress and pillow, crisp white sheets, and a colorful quilt.

"We've quarters above the carriage house, but Dora occupies those rooms. If not for that, you would be staying there," Eden informed him curtly.

"Nay, Eden. I would not. 'Tis here I will lay my head." An arrogant grin, one Eden was fast coming to know, curved his lips. "Here, or in your bed."

"When asses speak the King's English!" she retorted, too shocked to properly watch her tongue.

He chuckled, accepting defeat graciously. "Ah, well, you can't blame a man for trying. If you have a change of heart, come seek me out, my beauty."

For answer, she tartly reminded him to make up his bed in the morning, lest Dora become suspicious, and made good her exit, scurrying to her own room and bolting the door behind her.

Much later, as she lay abed unable to sleep, listening to the clock in the downstairs hall tolling the midnight hour, Eden was reminded of the old French folktale her father used to tell her. It had to do with a girl named Cinderella. Feeling somewhat silly, she nevertheless crossed her fingers and squeezed her eyes tightly closed, on the hope that she, too, would miraculously resume her simpler, saner existence by the time the clock had struck its last.

It was not to be. As the final chime died away, beyond the thin wall separating her bedroom from Devlin's, she heard his bedstead creak.

Cursed fool pirate!

Infernal half-ghost!

Handsome, flattering rogue!

He was fast coming to replace Finster as the bane of her existence.

Chapter 5

"*E*den. Eden!"

She awoke with a start, her heart pounding as she tried to rouse herself from a sound sleep. On a quick look around, she realized it was still night, with not even a hint of light creeping in around the window sash. What had wakened her? Even as the question flitted through her groggy brain, she heard an odd grumbling sound, followed by a loud snuffle.

She was still trying to decipher its source, bafflement furrowing her brow, when Jane called out from the bedroom across the hall. Sleep fled, alarm lending strength to her limbs as Eden tumbled hastily from her bed. Her mother never called for her in the night unless she was sick! Dashing across the room, she yanked at the door, nearly pulling her arm from its socket before she recalled locking it earlier in the evening. Cursing, she fumbled with the bolt, finally dislodging it, and ran to her mother's aid.

"Mama? What is it?" she asked breathlessly. "Are you ill? Should I send Dora for the doctor?

"No, no. Now, shhh!" By the light of the bedside candle, Eden saw the tremor in her mother's hands as she waved her to silence. "I'm fine. Just a bit shaken.

I don't mean to alarm you, dear, but . . . Am I imagining things, or do I hear a man snoring in this house?"

Eden's eyes flew wide, her mouth even wider. Saints above! That was what that strange sound was! It was Devlin Kane snoring fit to lift the rafters! How was she supposed to explain this away?

"Uh . . . uh . . . Oh, Mama! That's impossible!" she stammered, willing Devlin to silence. Evidently, he was not to be shushed quite that easily, for another grunt resounded almost immediately.

"Then pray tell me what it is that I am hearing?" Jane implored, fright aglow in her eyes. "Eden, I fear we have a midnight visitor, though why he would have fallen asleep in our home is beyond me. While I hate to put this problem upon your shoulders, there is no help for it. You must sneak past this intruder and run for help. Oh, but do be careful! There's no telling what he might do if you should waken him! But first, get me your papa's gun from the wardrobe."

"Mama! No!" Eden thought quickly, fabricating the first thing to come to mind. She laughed nervously, trying to display a calm she did not feel. "Oh, Mama! We're such silly geese! Do you know what we're hearing? Nothing more than a stray hog rooting in the yard! Why, I'm almost sure of it! Listen! There it is again! Nothing but a big old pig scaring us half witless!"

To herself, Eden was fuming, thinking it certainly was a big swine making all that racket!

"Are you certain?" Jane queried, cocking her head. "It sounds so close. As if it's right down the hall."

"I'm certain, but if it will set your mind at ease, I'll go check. Now, you just lie down and go back to sleep."

Accepting the explanation, Jane settled against her pillows with a wan, weary smile. "I feel so foolish! Still, promise you won't go outdoors in the dark. Just look from the windows and throw a slipper at it. But do stay indoors. Swine can be temperamental when they take a mind to."

So can riled spinsters, Eden thought angrily. Oh, was Captain Kane in for a rude awakening! And her slipper would be more useful in his big mouth than aside his head!

Retrieving the candle her mother had lit, Eden noted thankfully that Jane was already nearly asleep. Quietly she crept from the room, pulling the door shut behind her. Then, bereft of robe or slippers, wearing nothing but her thin lawn night shift, she charged across the hall, mad as a bull. Not bothering to knock, she threw the door to the guest room wide, and marched toward the bed where Devlin lay blissfully snoring. Barely taking the time to set the candle on the bedside table, she promptly administered a resounding wallop to Devlin's shoulder with the flat of her hand, hitting him so hard that her fingers stung.

One second, she was looking down upon him, the dawning of a satisfied smirk on her lips. The next she found herself hurtling through the air, to end flat on her back on the mattress, his big body atop hers. More than merely startled, Eden's wide-eyed, fear-filled gaze caught the wicked gleam of a knife blade, held in a hand that rested threateningly against her throat. Eyes as black as sin glittered down into hers for countless heartbeats as Eden gasped for air, a single frightened squeak emerging in place of a scream. Dear God! At this fateful moment of impending death, she found she couldn't even close her eyes!

He cursed. Softly. Succinctly. Still holding her pinned with his bulk, he glared down at her and exclaimed, "Damn it, woman! Don't ever creep up on me that way again! Are you trying to get yourself killed?" He tossed the knife aside, relieving the pressure on her neck only slightly.

"N-no!" she squawked, quivers tripping along her backbone. "I only meant to wake you."

"A kiss would have served you better, though it would no doubt have landed you just where you lie now," he growled. His gaze darted to her lips, noting the lower one caught between her teeth to still its trembling. "Have you changed your mind and decided to try my bed after all, my curious cat? Is that what this visit is all about?"

"Absolutely not!" she declared, ire overcoming her lingering fear. Wriggling one arm free, she pushed ineffectually at his, which still lay across her chest and throat. "Get off of me and let me up this instant!"

He stared down at her with a mischievous grin and drawled, "I think not. Not until you have told me why you are here, and why you felt it necessary to slap me awake, when a word or two would have done the trick."

"You were snoring the draperies from their rods, you infernal idiot!" she hissed, remembering to keep her voice low. "You woke my mother, and I had the Devil's own time trying to explain all the noise you were making with your snorts and groans."

"And what did you tell her?"

Eden glared up at him, her eyes narrowed into turquoise slits. "I convinced her 'twas swine loose in the yard—when in truth, 'twas a grunting pig in the house."

"Has anyone ever told you that you have a very sassy, very tempting mouth?" he countered softly.

Eden was calm enough now to become aware of several things she had dismissed in all the excitement. Of their own accord, her eyes drifted downward from his, encountering the mat of blond hair covering his chest. "You . . . you aren't wearing a nightshirt," she stammered, flames licking at her cheeks. And he was lying over her, covering her completely, the heat of his big, hard body seeping through her night shift.

"Sweetling," he answered with undisguised amusement, "I do not own a nightshirt. Nor do I imagine one would do me much good now, except perhaps to startle your maid if she should chance into my room and see a bundle of cloth moving about the bed of its own."

" 'Tis highly improper," she declared stiffly. So was wondering what that swath of chest hair would feel like beneath her fingers; and reveling in the sight of his magnificent torso; and drinking in the warm male scent of him.

He chuckled. "I suppose wearing nightclothes about your hips is more proper than wearing none at all?" he taunted.

Not until now did she realize that, in her tumble, her night shift had risen to drastic heights and now rode about her thighs. Even more alarming, she was feeling not only the heat of him, but also the hair on his legs rubbing intimately against hers. Her eyes widened, her mind spinning with wayward thoughts no virgin spinster should entertain.

"Oh, dear!" she whispered. "Dear me!" Her gaze locked with his, and she silently vowed that she would die before allowing her roving eyes to travel further than they already had. She did not want to see what the lower half of him looked like—truly she didn't, despite an errant curiosity that seemed to have sprung up from heaven knew where. It was bad enough to imagine it, and to feel every intriguing inch of him imprinted upon the length of her.

To her utter mortification, the devil seemed to read her mind. "Go ahead, Eden. Look at me. Touch me."

"Captain Kane!"

He shook his head in mocking reproach. "Ah, Eden, how you do tempt me, spread beneath me, all warm and inviting. Most especially since I've not been with a woman for some time before my unfortunate disappearance. But I prefer my lovers aquiver with passion, not quaking with shame and pretending righteous scorn. I

will let you go, unscathed for now, for the price of
hearing you speak my name. 'Tis Devlin. Say it, Eden.
Softly. Let me hear my name tremble from your rose-
sweet lips."

She stared up at him warily, not at all sure she could
trust him to keep his word, though what she would do
if he did not was unthinkable. Screaming would only
awaken her mother, who could not come to her aid and
would only be more frightened than ever. To fight him
could only anger him and earn her more harm than he
might now intend. Besides, pitting her puny muscles
against his was akin to trying to hold back the tide with
a teaspoon. There was no way she would win in a battle
of strength.

"You'll release me, if I but say your name?" she
asked doubtfully, her eyes searching his.

"Aye."

On a quick prayer, she blurted, "Devlin."

Again he shook his head. "Nay, Eden. I said softly.
Sweetly."

Tears pricked behind her lids. A trembling sigh escaped her lips, and with it his name, like the gentlest
sea breeze. "Devlin."

Unable to help himself, Devlin lowered his lips toward hers, their mouths hovering a whisper apart.
"Eden," he breathed. Then, ever so tenderly, not wanting to frighten her or ruin the fragile beauty of the moment, he kissed her. Just a touching of the lips. A light
brush of flesh against flesh. A fleeting caress, no more
than the stroke of a butterfly's wings.

So surprisingly tender, so exquisite was it, that it
brought fresh tears springing to Eden's eyes. Never
would she have expected such gentleness from this
man. This pirate. For a few precious, stolen seconds,
she forgot to be afraid and let herself revel in the giddy
joy spiraling through her with this, her very first romantic kiss.

It was over all too soon. Reality came crashing down upon her the minute his mouth left hers. Bright flags of color stained her cheeks as he gazed down at her, his eyes dark and fathomless. Before she had time to react, to question whether to push him away or pull him back for more, Devlin levered himself from her, whisking the sheet over his lower body as he went.

"Go, Eden. Escape while you may," he told her gruffly. "Before my desires overcome my sense and I break my pledge."

Stumbling from the bed, still half-dazed, she croaked out. "You already have, Captain Kane. You vowed to let me go upon saying your name, yet demanded a kiss as well."

As she turned on her heel, he caught hold of the braid hanging halfway down her back, halting her flight. "Nay, my saucy kitten. The kiss was but a reward for uttering my name in such dulcet tones. 'Twas anything but a demand, and not taken by force. If you are at all honest with yourself, you will know I speak truly."

When she would have left, he held her fast. "Once 'tis given, I stand by my word, Eden. I lie not. And I tell you this just as surely. This kiss was but a hint of what is to follow between us."

Not daring to turn and look at him, she stood stiffly, held prisoner by the hand still clasping her plait. "Is that a threat, Captain Kane?"

"Nay. 'Tis a promise, my beauty. Fair warning, if you will."

"And what if I decide otherwise? What if I do not want what you offer? Will you then revert to force, and take what you desire, regardless of my wishes?"

He had the temerity to laugh, low and huskily. "I do not foresee that necessity. Though I have little practice in the art of wooing virginal maids, I'm willing to wager I can win you over without undue force."

She gasped, insulted and outraged. "Do I appear so pathetic that you believe a few kisses will have me panting after you, weak to your will? Think again, pirate. Hell will be knee-deep in snow before I yield to you."

"Such will happen sooner than you think, made all the quicker every time you address me as other than Devlin. Unless, of course, you employ a more honeyed term for me, such as 'sweetheart' or 'darling.' That I would not object to at all. But for every time you call me Captain Kane, there will be a penalty." He released her hair and she fled to the door.

"You are a conceited beast!" she hissed back at him defiantly.

His soft chuckle chased after her. "Your barbs will have to be sharper than that to wound my thick hide. At least you remembered not to call me Captain Kane."

To say she was reluctant to face him the next morning was to understate the matter in the extreme. Not that Eden feared him all that much. He'd said he would not harm her, and for some reason she believed him. She was more mortified by her tumble into his bed than truly frightened of him, though if she had a lick of sense she should be scared witless. The man was a pirate, for heaven's sake! A huge, strong, handsome pirate! And she'd gone as giddy as a goose at his mere kiss! Which only proved how dotty spinsterhood was rendering her these days!

She was still berating herself for her lack of self-control as she entered the kitchen. Dora stood at the stove, turning a steaming batch of hash in a skillet—and at her elbow stood Devlin Kane, blithely leaning against the sideboard and pilfering bits of potato from the frying pan!

"What do you think you're doing?" Eden exclaimed

aloud, forgetting herself in her amazement at his recklessly bold behavior.

Dora spun about, almost upending the skillet in her
haste. She gasped, clutching her chest. "Miss Eden!
You scared the bloomin' daylights out o' me!"

While Dora's back was turned, Devlin stole another
tidbit, grinned at Eden, and popped the morsel into his
mouth.

"I . . . I'm sorry, Dora," Eden stammered, still staring
at her smug houseguest, who was now calmly licking
his fingers clean. "I didn't mean to startle you."

"Well, you almost caused my old heart to stop, let
me tell you. And for what? You can see as plain as anything that I'm fixin' the mornin' meal, same as I've
done every day for the last five years." With only two
of the seven years of her agreed term to go, Dora had
long since ceased to be timid in the Winters household,
considering herself more a friend of the family than an
indentured servant.

With a put-upon huff, Dora turned back to her work,
shaking her head. "There must be somethin' in the air,
is all I can figure," she muttered half to herself. "First
I can't find the potatoes left over from last evening's
dinner—and I know good and well I put them in the
pantry—and now you're askin' fool questions, like
you've gone moonstruck. And your mama ramblin' on
about pigs in the yard and wantin' to sleep in, when
she's always pesterin' me to get her dressed and downstairs before breakfast."

Devlin swaggered over and gave Eden a swift peck
on the cheek. "Tell her to pile your plate high this
morning, my beauty," he whispered, his black eyes
gleaming with mischief. "We'll be sharing a trencher,
and I wouldn't want you to starve."

"What was that?" Dora questioned, not bothering to
turn around.

"Oh, uh, I just asked if you could give me an extra

helping," Eden fumbled, glaring at Devlin and swatting at the big hand that came up to play at her nape. "I'm feeling more hungry than usual."

At this, Dora did turn, a smile on her apple-round face. " 'Tis about time you stopped eatin' like a bird, Miss Eden. I swear, you worry every bit of nourishment off your bones."

To Dora's astonishment, Eden ate three times her normal fare that morning. In addition to the hash, she devoured half a dozen eggs and nearly twice that number of jam-smothered muffins. "My goodness, girl! Those long legs o' yours must've gone hollow in the night!" she marveled, ignoring Eden's embarrassed blush, made even more rosy by the ribald gaze Devlin cast toward her lower limbs. "You keep puttin' meals like that under your belt, and I'll need to make more trips to the market. Not that I'm complainin', mind you."

Eden waited just long enough to greet her mother who was still in bed, then hastily made for the door before Devlin could devise any further tomfoolery. "I'll be at the warehouse, Mama, should you have need of me."

"I do wish you could bring the accounts home and work on them here," Jane stated. "Not that I'd be much help, but at least I would have your company."

Devlin tapped Eden's shoulder, nodding that the suggestion had merit. "I'll consider it," Eden said, in answer to both.

"Oh, and dear," Jane called after her, "what should I say to Mr. Finster, should he come looking for you again?"

"I doubt that he will," Eden said with a frown. "At least not today. He stopped by the warehouse yesterday, and I spoke with him there."

"But if he should?" Jane persisted, knowing that the man was pursuing her daughter, and the reason behind his many visits. To her mind, the man was the worst sort of vermin, made more so because after seeing him Eden was always more troubled than before.

"For all I care, tell him to take a long stroll off the deep end of a very short dock, preferably with a large stone tied about his neck!" Eden grumbled. This surprised a gruff guffaw from Devlin, who could not contain his laughter.

Jane's brow wrinkled in concern. "Eden, are you coming down with a cough?"

"No, just a bit of something caught in my throat, Mama," Eden fabricated.

She quickly ushered Devlin out the door and railed at him all the way to the stables. "Drat you and your infernal noises! Because of you, I've told more lies in one day than I've uttered in my whole lifetime!"

"And just how long is that, my sweet spinster?" he prodded with a wry grin, blatantly unrepentant.

"That, sir, is none of your concern."

"Don't be so prickly, Eden. You can't be that old."

"If you must know, I'm two and twenty."

"Ah, a fledgling yet, not even dry behind your ears! Why, I've five years on you, and I certainly don't consider myself ready to retire to my rocking chair."

"You are a man. There is a difference, you know," she said with a sniff.

"So glad you noticed, sweetling. What else caught your interest last night?"

She stopped short, her eyes raking over him like angry blue-green fire. "Captain Kane, you are loud, brash, ill-bred, and totally irritating. There is not a compelling thing about you," she fibbed. *Except your fine body, and your devil-black eyes, and a wealth of chest hair my fingers still itch to touch,* she added silently, despising her own weakness toward him.

One golden brow cocked upward in amusement. "Is

there not? Then why is your face as red as a setting sun? You're a poor liar, Eden."

Quickly, before she could discern his intent, he pulled her into his arms and kissed her soundly, his mouth commanding hers to respond. When her lips remained closed to him, his tongue swept over them, painting them with moist heat. His strong white teeth nipped gently at the lush curves, until her gasp gained him entry.

Shock held her still; his breath stole her own, making her head spin alarmingly; and the touch of his tongue to hers sent flames sparking through her, making her stomach tighten and her limbs quake. When at last he released her, she stumbled against the buggy, stunned and shaken.

Noting with satisfaction the sheen of her passion-dewed lips and the glaze of desire lingering in her eyes, he drawled, "That, Eden, is the penalty I spoke of last evening. The cost of calling me Captain Kane. Now, should you wish more of the same, pray continue addressing me as such. 'Twill be my pleasure to administer the punishment. And yours to receive it."

Furious, humiliated beyond bearing, Eden acted before considering the consequences. Spying the buggy whip so near at hand, she yanked it from its mooring and swung it at him with all her might.

In the blink of an eye, he tore it from her grasp, the thong never grazing his flesh. His sin-black eyes promised retribution as his long fingers bent the limber rod nearly in half. For several dreadful seconds, he continued to flex the whip, his searing gaze trapping hers as Eden slowly backed away and he followed step for step. "I should beat your sweet butt until you plead for mercy, you bloodthirsty little wench. Until you learn a few well-deserved lessons in the manners you claim I lack."

"No!" she squawked, her eyes huge and her throat

dry. Her arms came up across her face, anticipating a blow at any moment. "Please! I'm sorry!"

"Sorry you attempted to strike me? Or sorry I now hold your weapon?" he taunted, daring her to lie to him.

"Sorry I lost my temper," she hedged.

Her answer so deftly sidestepped the trap he'd set for her that Devlin was hard-put not to laugh. With effort, and with high regard for her agility of mind in the face of imminent danger, he left his features stern. "Get into that buggy!" he roared. "Now!"

In a mad flurry of skirts, she scrambled into the seat. There she cowered until he'd hitched the horses and joined her. Without another word, he handed her the reins.

They were some distance from the house when Eden dared to remind him, "You swore not to hurt me."

His gaze caught on her lower lip, which now protruded in an alluring pout. "I haven't," he answered simply.

"You wanted to."

"But I didn't."

"Didn't do it? Or didn't want to?"

He laughed aloud, his shaggy blond head thrown back in his delight at being snared in the same net he'd thrown at her. "Let us just say I should have. You would have deserved it."

"A matter of opinion, Cap—Devlin," she stated stubbornly.

"Ah, Eden," he told her on a deep-throated chuckle, "you are priceless! A feisty feline, all teeth and claws when your back is up. Certainly no dainty, simpering maiden to faint at a man's feet. Yet a lady from the top of your head to the tips of your toes, for all that. You make me wonder why I came to your aid so swiftly, when Finster wouldn't have lasted a month against your stinging wit. You'd have driven him mad in no time."

"I would have tried," she answered simply, a smile playing at her lips.

The way Devlin had phrased some of his comments, she wasn't entirely sure if he'd meant to compliment her or not. But his tone had indicated admiration. His smile warmed her deep inside, though it baffled her that the dubious praise of an arrogant pirate should affect her so. Still, she sat a little taller in the seat, her posture straighter than usual, her turquoise eyes aglow with unleashed humor—and with renewed pride in her own worth.

Chapter 6

While Eden worked on the account books in the warehouse office, Devlin decided to put his invisibility to good use and have a look around the place. It was turning out to be very advantageous to be able to listen in on private conversations without being seen. Or to snoop through the goods stored there with no one being in the least suspicious.

By the time he'd been there an hour, it was plain to him that Winters Warehouse was not being operated with much efficiency. Merchandise was stored haphazardly, with little or no regard for items which might be spoiled or crushed, and no obvious measures taken to safeguard against theft. Under different circumstances, Devlin would have been thrilled to learn this. The warehouse and its treasures were ripe pickings for even a novice brigand. Robbing it would be as easy as pie. But the shoe was on the other foot this time, and Devlin had pledged to help Eden, not steal from her. Besides which, his own accumulation of plunder would now be housed on these premises, and he did not want to see it walk off in the middle of the night, his gains in someone else's pocket. Pilfered or not, it was still his plunder, and he meant to keep it that way.

Other things, too, were readily obvious. The warehouse should have been doing twice the business it appeared to be. Devlin counted at least a dozen workmen standing about doing nothing more strenuous than trading tales with one another and drinking ale. They made no attempt to look busy when John Tilton walked by, merely gave the man a friendly wave and went back to their conversation. It was only when a customer appeared that they wandered off in different directions, to reconvene a few minutes later in another location.

Another ship was berthed at the dock, scheduled to unload before the *Gai Mer,* and Devlin wandered down to observe the proceedings more closely. Tilton was there, involved in a heated argument with the ship's captain.

"See here, man!" the captain argued. "The sum you are demanding is far and above what we were told 'twould be."

Tilton's narrow gaze never shifted as he spat a stream of tobacco, then spoke around the wad in his cheek. "That was the cost of storing your merchandise. There's an added fee for docking and unloading. It'll also cost you extra if my men do the work, but you're free to have your crew transfer the cargo, if you prefer. Or you can forget the whole deal and go to one of the other warehouses. Take it or leave it."

"It'll be another week or more if I contract with another warehouse, and well you know it!" the captain retorted. "Some of the goods could rot by then."

"Ain't my problem, Cap'n," Tilton told him dryly.

With much grumbling, the captain counted out the coin. "You're a thief, Tilton. No better than a common highwayman."

Tilton accepted the payment with a smirk and would have walked off, but the other man caught him by the sleeve. "I'll have a receipt, if you please. Now. In writing. You can write, can't you?"

"Lucky for you." Tilton grinned, pulling a wrinkled pad of paper from his pocket. "Got to be able to keep some sort of record for the boss lady, though she ain't much for figures, poor thing."

Moving closer, Devlin caught a glimpse of the figure Tilton scribbled on the paper. It matched the amount the captain had paid him. He also noted that the money had gone directly into Tilton's pocket, not set aside in a separate pouch for the business.

It was time for a talk with Eden.

" 'Twould be child's play to fleece you blind," he said, after telling her all he'd observed. "And your man Tilton is doing a fine job of it from within, not accounting for anyone outside the business. 'Tis no wonder the warehouse is losing money these days. When, precisely, did it begin to flounder?"

"When Papa got sick and had to turn management of it over to Tilton," Eden admitted weakly, suddenly feeling ill herself. "Are you saying it has been Tilton's doing all the while, and I was simply too stupid to see it?"

Devlin shook his head. "Not stupid, Eden. Grief-stricken at the start, most likely. Untrained and unprepared to deal with the normal running of the warehouse, let alone the problems that began to occur as soon as your father was no longer in charge. Then, of course, Tilton was here to advise you, ready to guide you in the wrong direction."

"Like a sheep led to slaughter." Eden sighed. "Oh, how could I have been so naive? What am I to do now?"

Leaning against her desk, Devlin took a puff of his cigar, letting the smoke roll toward the ceiling as he contemplated the most likely solution. "Do you trust me, Eden? Would you be willing to do as I suggest?" he asked, peering at her through the blue haze.

She, too, took a moment before answering. "I suppose that would depend on what you might ask of me, though I imagine it could not turn out any worse than having Tilton drive the business into bankruptcy."

"What if I told you to replace most of your workmen with men from my own crew?"

She stared at him with wide eyes. "Wouldn't that be tantamount to turning a pack of wolves loose in a hen yard?"

He laughed. "Ordinarily, I would agree with you. But not when they would be under my command. I've given my word to help you, Eden, and that agreement extends to my crew as well. They'll not steal from you. They would, however, provide much-needed protection against unscrupulous scoundrels."

"And what of Tilton? Shall I dismiss him as well?"

Devlin's smile turned wicked. "Not just yet. It's my thinking that once you let the others go, those following his orders and sharing in his mischief, he will go running to whomever is truly to blame for your misfortune."

Eden was stunned. "You don't believe Tilton is the head of this scheme?"

"No. The man is crafty, but not cunning enough to have done this on his own. Unless I miss my guess, someone else is directing him, someone with much more to gain."

"Who?"

"That, duchess, is precisely what we are going to determine."

At that moment, Tilton came walking into Eden's office, an air of satisfaction about him. Now, however, Eden suspected his good humor was caused by more than merely being pleased with himself for holding the reins of her company firmly in his control. His bearing smacked of male supremacy, and above that, she thought he was probably snickering up his sleeve at her.

His swagger came to an abrupt halt just inside the

door, a shocked look on his face as he gazed from her to the smoking cigar.

It was a moment before Eden could discern the reason for the man's perplexity, and when she did, she almost laughed aloud. While she could easily see Devlin's fingers wrapped around the fat roll of tobacco, Tilton could not. To him, it appeared the cigar was balanced on the edge of her desk, and he undoubtedly assumed she had been the one puffing away at it.

He proved her conjecture upon speaking. "Uh, Miss Winters. I . . . ah . . . that is, I had no idea you enjoyed a good cigar now and again."

Eden reached out and slipped the cigar from Devlin's hold, careful not to touch him while taking it between her own slim fingers. "There are a great number of things you do not know about me, Mr. Tilton," she informed him tartly. "Did you have some business to discuss with me?"

"Oh, yes," he said, recalling his purpose. He handed over a scrap of paper, along with a handful of coins. "This needs to be logged into the account book you're working on, so I thought it best to run it straight over to the office myself."

"I see. And what is this in reference to, please?"

" 'Tis the payment from Captain Stuber this mornin'. His crew is almost finished unloading their vessel, and that corsair ship is next up at the dock. If you'll forgive my saying so, I wish you had consulted me first, before dealing with those pirates. 'Tain't good practice to trade with that sort these days, Miss Winters."

"I'm well aware of that, Mr. Tilton. The responsibility will rest on my head if anything goes awry, so ease your mind on that score."

Though he still appeared uncomfortable with the situation, he gave a brusque nod.

Meanwhile, Devlin slid a peek at the receipt Eden set conveniently aside for him. It came as no great surprise to see that the figure listed thereon was but a fraction of the actual amount received. As were the funds for Eden's cash box. When she glanced his way, he pointed to the money and shook his head, silently telling her it was not the sum he'd witnessed being exchanged on the dock.

"Why is it that Captain Stuber's men are unloading their own ship? Is that not what we pay our men to do?" Eden asked suddenly, catching Tilton off guard.

The man drew himself up haughtily, as if offended that she should question him on a matter under his jurisdiction. "Yes, 'm," he said stiffly, "but the captain insisted. Mayhap he thought his cargo more delicate than our hands could manage."

One brow raised over a turquoise eye. "Perhaps he was right, Mr. Tilton. It has come to my attention that a few of our workers have become sluggards on the job. By the end of the day, I will have formed a list of the names of the persons I want you to dismiss. I will also see to hiring their replacements personally."

If Tilton was taken aback at her previous conduct, he was now almost speechless. His face froze, his mouth half-open, then took on a ruddy complexion with his rising anger. "Now wait just a minute, missy," he objected loudly. "I've managed this business since your father turned it over to my keeping, and I'll keep on running it the way I see fit. It's one thing for you to come in here and make a show of trying to do the books, but quite another when you go poking your nose into areas best left to me. The men, and the work they do, are under my direction."

As Tilton's voice rose, so did Devlin. Forsaking his slouched position, he straightened, his arms no longer crossed over his broad chest. His hand hovered at the hilt of his cutlass in an expectant stance, ready to take action the instant Tilton should threaten Eden in any way. A glower darkened his features, his black eyes smoldering.

Eden pretended to ignore Devlin's unspoken defense, though she couldn't help but be grateful for it. Portraying a nonchalance she did not feel, she flicked the ashes from the end of the cigar and calmly studied the glowing tip. "Feel free to add your name to my list if you wish, Mr. Tilton," she told him coolly. "Though I would hate to lose you at this juncture."

Her gaze swept up to clash with his, her demeanor almost regal as she added, "However, let us not lose sight of who owns this business, sir. While I have appreciated your efforts on behalf of my mother and myself, we are still paying your wages. And as your employer, I feel it only proper to involve myself in some of the management, and that now includes the hiring and firing of those who work for me."

"What about Mr. Finster? Does he agree with this?" Tilton blurted out.

"Explain yourself, please, Mr. Tilton," Eden requested, her eyes narrowing slightly. "What say would Mr. Finster possibly have in my decisions?"

"None, as yet, I reckon," Tilton admitted with a slight grimace, as if regretting his risky outburst. "But 'tis common knowledge he's courting you, and only a matter of time before you marry. I assumed you would consult him about any major changes concerning the warehouse."

"You assumed wrongly. Furthermore, I do not appreciate having my private affairs bandied about to one and all." She paused, contemplated the cigar she held, and promptly brought it to her lips.

Devlin held his breath, torn between laughter and concern, as Eden gave a dainty pull upon it. To his surprise, she had enough wits about her not to attempt to swallow the mouthful of smoke. Rather, she puffed it out again, straight into Tilton's stupefied face.

"Now, are you staying with us, Mr. Tilton?" she asked imperiously, her voice slightly huskier than before. "Or shall I look for your replacement as well?"

"With respect for your father's wishes, I'll keep on," he grated out, almost choking on his own words, if not the smoke she'd blown in his face.

"Fine. Then our conversation is concluded for now," she said, dismissing him with a nod toward the door. "Please remember to stop by the office at the end of the day for that list of former workers."

Tilton had hardly closed the door behind him when Devlin let loose a roar of laughter. "Oh, lady!" he crowed. "That was a fancy piece of work! And you are a wondrously shrewd vixen! Why, if you were a lad, you'd have the makings of a fine pirate!"

"If I were a man, I wouldn't be in the straits I find myself now," she reminded him sourly. Then her recently revived humor asserted itself, and she giggled. "Did you see the look on his face when he first spied the cigar? Lands, but I'm glad your hand was resting on the desk at the time, and the cigar not suspended in air!"

"Aye, but now he'll be telling tales about Spinster Winters and her outlandish habits and her high-handed affectations."

At this, Eden sobered. "I suppose he shall, but there's no help for it now. I'll simply have to hope few people believe him. After all, I have lived all my life in Charles Town, and folks know how circumspect I am."

"All prudish and proper and prickly?" Devlin offered, but he chuckled. "They don't know you very well, do they, Eden? All these people who have watched you grow to womanhood. Have they never seen your sharp wit or your impish humor? Have they no suspicion of the fires that lurk just behind your priggish appearance? The surge of emotion lying but a scratch beneath your calm surface?"

"Hah! You are endowing me with traits to fit your own schemes. I am merely a shrewish old maid with a needle tongue and more willfulness than wits."

"Nay, minx." He leaned across the littered desk and trapped her chin in his warm, calloused fingers. His black eyes blazed into hers, all the brighter now that they were touching. "You are a siren just awakening, scarcely aware of her own powers, making the smallest of ripples upon the water as yet. Devil take me, but I want to be the man to tap your capabilities to their fullest, to burn in the heat of your consuming flames, to plumb the heights and depths of your fathomless passions. I want to stir your desires and shake loose the real woman hiding inside."

As if to fit action to words, he plucked the pins from her hair, releasing the looped braid at her nape. Despite her protestations and futile attempts to stop him, he used his long fingers to swiftly unplait it. Then he caught the flowing mass into both fists at either side of her head, letting it cascade across her shoulders to pool onto the desk.

"Magnificent!" he marveled softly. "Just as I knew it would be." His gaze widened as if he'd just discovered the most precious treasure. "And just look what I have found! Unless my eyes deceive me, there is a hint of red amidst these tendrils of mud-brown. Like a flickering flame, tucked carefully away and nearly extinguished within the confines of your pins. Was that by intent, sweetling? Are you embarrassed to have your true colors shine forth? Hiding your light under a bushel, so to speak?"

She tried to pull her hair from his hands, but he held fast. "There you go again, spouting Biblical verse," she sniped, thinking to turn the tables on him.

But Devlin was onto something now, and not about to be steered in another direction. "Why do you wear your hair in such a severe fashion, Eden, when it is so glorious this way?"

"Glorious?" she sneered. "Oh, Captain! You have such a glib tongue, when you know full well that all I sport is a frizzy puff of curls atop my head. And yes, I do try to hide the red, just as I try to tame my unmanageable mop into a more presentable style."

"More presentable to whom?" he badgered. "To yourself, or to that town full of idiots who couldn't distinguish a pearl from a pea?"

"Both," she admitted on a resigned sigh. "Don't you see? As much as I might wish to wear my hair differently, I can't. Not unless I want to solicit more notice to my stature. The prettier coiffures invariably make me seem even taller and thinner than I already am. And the redder hues only draw even more attention toward me."

"Which you would move heaven and earth to avoid," he guessed. At her nod, he shook his head in mockery at her. "Eden, Eden. What are we to do with you, my shy beauty? What will it take, I wonder, to convince you of your own worth?"

"I have my fair share of pride," she assured him wryly.

"Aye. I'm sure you do. But where is your vanity, woman? Where did you come by the mistaken notion that standing taller than most is uncomely? Or possessing a trim body unlovely? Who put such asinine ideas into your head? Those same nincompoops who need a footstool to see over an anthill and can't view their own feet for their fat?"

Laughter bubbled up from some glad spot inside her, spewing forth in a joyous peal of trilling tones, like bells on Christmas morn. Tears of mirth welled in her turquoise eyes, turning them to sparkling jewels. "Oh, Devlin! I truly can't decide if you are going to be my saving grace or my downfall. In a few short hours you have managed to reawaken my sadly languishing sense of merriment, spark my usually serene temper, and raise my flagging esteem. You are either awfully good for me, or terribly, terribly bad."

"I hope to be both, my adorable spitfire-in-spinster's-disguise," he said with a wolfish smile. "Have I told you how enchanting you are when you laugh? Almost as bewitching as when you are angry."

Her attempt at a scowl was ruined by a silly grin, accompanied by tinkling laughter. "You are an incorrigible jackanape, Devlin Kane! A master flatterer, and a dyed-in-the-wool rogue!"

Chapter 7

When Eden professed an interest in seeing Devlin's ship, she received her first indication of how superstitious sailors actually were. Of course, she'd heard such accounts, but she'd never imagined they'd be more cautious than the average person. Upon considering this, she thought it probably had a great deal to do with the fact that they spent so much of their lives aboard a relatively small vessel in the middle of very large, deep, and unpredictable seas. Anything that would bring them better luck and ward off ill fortune was welcomed, and anything contrary to this was avoided like the plague.

Still, she wondered why certain things were designated as evil omens, and how others were selected as denoting good. "Why do you consider a woman aboard ship bad luck?" she questioned, irritated at how maligned her gender was, and how often. Men were constantly denigrating women, excluding them from all manner of activities they deemed exclusively male.

"They just are," Devlin countered. "Always have been, and always will be."

"Then pray do tell me why it is that women regularly

72

sail across the ocean from Europe to the Americas on passenger vessels, with little mishap."

"Pure chance, in most circumstances. Those captains and their crews must cringe in fearful anticipation during the entire crossing. Or pray themselves blue in the face."

Eden gave a wry nod. "Of course. That would explain why a pirate ship would be exempt, since they are not particularly prone to prayer, are they? Though a few among you seem inordinately familiar with the Bible."

"Cease mocking me, wench. Sarcasm does not become you. Nor will it encourage me to change my mind. I've not the time, nor the inclination at present, to dredge up the necessary charms and incantations 'twould take to counter the risk of your boarding; and until I do, you'll not step so much as a single dainty toe aboard the *Gai Mer.*"

"Then your initial threat to abduct me was naught but bluster?" she guessed, arching a brow at him.

"Aye," he admitted with a broad grin. "But we've struck our bargain, and I'll not let you back out of it now."

"Oh, pooh!"

"Pull in that bottom lip of yours before someone treads upon it," he advised. "Though you are very fetching when you pout. Is it another kiss you are inviting, my sweet?"

She wrinkled her nose at him. "Just go unload your stolen wealth," she told him, giving him a light tap on his shoulder.

Immediately, heat streaked up his arm, and he felt himself begin to shimmer, then promptly fade again. "Take care with touching me in public, Eden," he warned. "There are others close enough now to notice, and we can't have me flickering about like a candle flame in a playful breeze. Either I must remain visible or unseen, but not come and gone again within the

same breath. Beyond that, I imagine it appears somewhat strange to have you standing here talking to yourself."

"You're right, of course. I forgot."

"Just don't forget too often, my lady, or we'll both
find ourselves on rocky shoals. Now, you be a good girl
and wait ashore for me, and when I return I'll bring you
a gift."

"I despise it when someone patronizes me," she informed him with a sniff. "Why don't you just give me
a pat on the head while you are about it, much like you
would a trained puppy?"

Devlin laughed. "I dare not, pretty pet, lest I pop into
view again."

By mid-afternoon the *Gai Mer* had been unloaded
and the cargo stored to Devlin's satisfaction. Several of
his crewmen were now in Eden's employ, replacing
those workers Devlin had advised her to dismiss. Not
only would they work during the day, but three men
would stand watch throughout the night, guarding
against theft or any other malicious intent. Eden assessed her new employees with a shudder, and silently
hoped that their rough appearance, and the number of
weapons each sported, would not keep her customers
away as well—and that Devlin could keep his men
under control, as he'd promised.

She could only wonder what sort of treasures Devlin
and his fellow pirates had gained, that they would feel
the need to watch over them so closely. Surely they
weren't taking such measures merely for her benefit.
Still, she hesitated to ask, not certain she really wanted
to know what goods they stored, or the value of their
merchandise, let alone the details of how they had ob-
tained their pilfered wealth. In this situation it was, perhaps, better not to know. Some of those trunks and

barrels might contain skulls and bones, or some such
gruesome remains.

With the immediate business concluded, Devlin was
in high spirits. He made a final trip aboard ship to collect a few personal items from his cabin, things he
wanted transferred to his room at Eden's house. His razor and shaving mug. Extra weapons and clothes. A
store of his favorite cigars and his best brandy. And his
bird Zeus.

Unfortunately, it did little good to gather the fresh
clothing, for the only clothes that allowed him to remain invisible were those in which he had vanished.
When Devlin had first attempted to wear different attire, Nate had laughed himself weak-kneed at the
strange sight of a suit of clothes walking about by itself, especially when Devlin had donned his corsair's
hat with the huge, waving plume. All Nate could see
was a pair of breeches, a shirt, and that ridiculous hat—
all riding in midair, with no discernible body or head
supporting them!

"Egad, Dev!" Nate had cackled. "Ye look like some
washerwoman's laundry, hung out to dry!"

Since then, Devlin had been forced to make do by
washing out his shirt and trousers periodically. For the
time it took his clothes to dry, he simply walked about
naked, and because no one else could see him, they
were none the wiser.

Now, however, there was Eden to take into account.
He couldn't imagine the look on her face, should she
catch him bending over a washtub, his bare arse stick-
ing up behind! So far, she'd been remarkably tolerant
of this nonsense of invisible pirates, more than most
people would have been. But a nude man lounging in
her parlor, while his unseen apparel dried on her wash
line, was a horse of a different color, indeed! He sincerely doubted she'd find much humor in the situation,
especially since he found so little in it himself. It was

becoming a blasted pain, this business of having only one set of clothes!

Before departing the ship, Devlin wanted to leave a few instructions with Nate, since his quartermaster would now be moving the frigate further out into the harbor. His quiet approach went unnoted until he said, "Nate, don't forget to—"

"Aiyee!" Nate turned toward the voice, a scowl pulling his dark brows together. "Damn it, Dev! Would ye kindly stop scarin' the spit out o' me like that? Drat it all anyway! I'm thinkin' we need to hang a bell about yer neck, so we have some inklin' o' where in tarnation ye be!"

Devlin laughed and thumped his friend on the back, nearly sending Nate sprawling. "No bells, Nate. You'll just have to get accustomed to having ghosties bellowing at you when you least expect it. Now, I wanted to remind you to replenish our stores while the frigate is still tied up to the dock. Not that I think we'll have any problems which might make it necessary to sneak off in the dark of night, mind you. But I'll rest easier knowing we're prepared. For the time being, however, it looks as if we'll be in port for a while. And I'm thinking 'tis a good thing our men have something other than bawds and beer to keep them occupied."

"Aye." Nate nodded. "They're not used to bein' ashore for too long at a stretch. T'wouldn't do to have 'em entirely at loose ends. Their work at the warehouse might help to keep 'em from gettin' overly bored, and keep 'em out o' too much trouble with the law."

"If nothing else, 'twill give them a taste of honest labor for a change," Devlin added with a sly grin. "Who knows, Nate? They might decide they like earning their wages by reputable means."

Nate shook his head. "And you, my friend?" he questioned. "Would you give up the merry life you've led to settle down to hearth and home? With the Spinster Winters, mayhap?"

" 'Tis a pleasant change of pace for now," Devlin admitted, "but I've been too long unfettered to stay anchored permanently, I fear. No doubt, I'll soon become restless myself, missing the sea and the raids and the challenges of pirating."

Nate grinned. "Not to mention the rewards. Jewels and gold and your pick of comely wenches in a dozen different ports."

"That, too, I suspect," Devlin said with a laugh. "Lady that she is, Eden's standing her distance."

"No ripe peach ready to drop into your waiting palm, eh?" Nate ribbed. " 'Tis a pity, that. 'Specially seein' as she's the only female who can behold yer handsome face these days. Seems to me ye've met yer match at last, Dev. Ye'll have to do some tall talkin' to get yerself invited into that woman's bed."

"I'm working on it. I'll win her over yet, and sooner than she thinks."

"Aye. That's the sort o' luck ye have," Nate agreed wryly.

"Where was my infamous good fortune a few weeks back?" Devlin asked sourly. "Of all the ships, all the storms the world over, all the men the Fates might have chosen—why was I the one standing in that particular spot, at that precise moment, with that specific bolt of lightning sent down upon my head?"

"No use cryin' over spilt milk," Nate advised. "What's done is done. We've just got to hope there's a way out o' this for ye. Since Miss Winters can see ye, there might be others who can."

"At least when she touches me I can become normal for a time. And if that is possible, mayhap 'twill also be possible to find a way to regain my body permanently someday. In the meanwhile, here I am, stuck betwixt and between. Neither ghost nor flesh."

"At least ye're a friendly phantom," Nate offered. "All is not lost. Tell ye what. Why don't ye join me an' some o' the lads down at the Cock 'n Bull later? We'll drown our sorrows in a mug or two."

That sounded like a grand idea to Devlin. Much better than sitting in Eden's parlor all evening, hearing her and her mother trade feminine gossip, and going quietly insane listening to their knitting needles clack together like chattering teeth. More than that, the thought of actually eating his fill of a hot meal made his mouth water. And a cigar afterward. And a brimming tankard of ale.

"You order me a big slab of braised beef with all the trimmings, and I'll be there," he told his friend.

"Play yer cards right, an' I'll even see what I can do about orderin' ye up a buxom wanton or two, fit to put that dry-bones spinster to shame."

"We'll see," Devlin answered with a wide grin. "Though I seem to be gaining an appetite for longer, leaner morsels of a sudden."

It was a mystery, one neither Devlin nor Eden could comprehend.

After his talk with Nate, Devlin went back to the warehouse office to collect Eden and the account books. By tucking his small bundle of personal belongings beneath his shirt, he discovered he could render them invisible as well, a trick well worth remembering. Zeus he needn't worry about, since the falcon was already vaporous.

Just how much so he was not aware until he entered Eden's office and asked proudly, "Well, minx, how do you like my pet?"

Eden looked up from her books and blinked owlishly at him. "What pet?"

"Those accounts are befuddling your brain, woman. I am speaking of the big bird on my shoulder, as if you did not know. My falcon. He'll be coming home with us this afternoon."

Eden frowned up at him. "Captain, what sort of buffoonery are you up to now? There is no hawk on your shoulder."

Though he could feel Zeus's weight there, and the sharp talons that did not quite pierce his flesh, Devlin cast his head about to look. Sure enough, Zeus was there, plucking at his plumage.

"Come now, Eden. Do not jest, sweetling. If you can see me, surely you can see Zeus as well."

"Devlin, I'm telling you I cannot," she returned with an exasperated sigh. "Why would I claim otherwise?"

Devlin sank onto the corner of her desk, astonished at this latest development. "How can this be?" he mused aloud. "How can you see me and not him? Why?"

Cautiously, Eden reached out her hand, only to have Devlin catch hold of her wrist and hold it shy of her goal. "Nay, Eden. Zeus is particular about who touches him, and I would hate to see you come away minus one of your lovely fingers."

She gazed at him askance, not at all sure whether or not to believe him "Well then, prove to me that he is there."

After considering her request, Devlin gave a sharp tug at the tether which bound the bird to his wrist. Zeus emitted a disgruntled squawk.

Eden jumped half out of her chair. "My stars!" Then her eyes narrowed suspiciously. "Was that really your bird, or did you make that horrid noise?"

"Still don't believe me, eh? All right, my doubting Thomasina. I shall hold his beak closed so that he doesn't nip at you. Then you may safely reach up and touch him."

Devlin's strong fingers clamped over the hawk's beak, while to Eden it looked as if they were hovering around nothing. At Devlin's nod, she once more reached out. This time, her hand connected with smooth feathers.

"Great Gertrude's garters!" she exclaimed. Her eyes were as round as serving platters as she continued to stroke the falcon's back and wings, discerning its size and shape. "It really is true! You actually are bearing a bird!"

Despite Devlin's lingering confusion that Eden could see him but not Zeus, her awe and her odd exclamation urged a chuckle from him. "Great Gertrude's garters?" he mocked laughingly. "Damn me, if I'm not going to have to teach you to swear more fluently, Eden! If you are going to curse, you really should learn to do it properly, my dear. With style."

"Save your energies, Devlin. I am not going to learn how to curse merely because it might amuse you. Nor am I about to abide having that fowl in my house."

"Where I go, Zeus goes also," Devlin stated firmly.

"Then you can both reside aboard your ship—or anywhere else you care to live."

"I thought we'd settled the matter of where I would lay my head."

"*Your* head, pirate. Not your bird's. I don't understand how you can even entertain the idea. It's preposterous!"

"Why? He's well trained. I intend to set up a perch for him in my room and keep him tethered when I must. 'Tis not as if he'll be free to fly all over the house, toppling lamps and whatnot. And I will see to his care and feeding myself. He won't be any bother."

"That is precisely what you claimed of yourself," she reminded him sharply. "Does the bird snore also, or does he merely emit piercing shrieks whenever the mood strikes him? Say, in the middle of the night when he hears a mouse squeak? How, pray tell, would I explain that to my mother, in addition to all the other odd and sundry noises around the house of late? And what is Dora likely to think of Zeus's perch? Am I supposed to tell her it is some sort of newfangled contraption upon which to hang one's coat, perhaps? Or a misshapen hat rack?"

"Zeus does not snore, and I will do my utmost to keep him quiet," Devlin promised with a grin. "As to Dora, you may tell her that you will see to the guest bedroom when it requires cleaning, and we can easily avoid that problem."

"Oh, good!" Eden quipped. "Now, along with my other duties and worries, I also get to clean up after you. How marvelous!"

"You are being a fishwife, Eden. A harridan. A vixen."

"I am very annoyed with you, Devlin Kane, and not shy of showing it," she corrected smartly. "If that makes me a shrew, so be it. Find some other woman to annoy with your problems, if you so dislike my tone and my tongue."

He glared down at her, his stance wide and his arms akimbo. "There is none other, as well you know. However, before you act so hastily, and snip off your own nose to spite your face, recall who has the money you so desperately need. Finster will soon return to demand payment on the note—and your reluctant hand in unholy wedlock. 'Twould be unwise of you to kill the goose that lays the golden egg in your nest, duchess. Or, in this case, the gander, if you will."

"So! Ganders lay eggs now!" she replied archly, resentment plain on her face and in her voice. "Will miracles never cease?" She pointed a slim finger at his shoulder. "No wonder you and that hawk get along so well. You are birds of a feather! Both sleek-plumed predators!"

He nodded, his smile becoming harder, one more fitting her description of him. "Let's not forget to add that we can both be very dangerous, given proper provocation, Miss Winters. Keep needling me, keep pushing and prodding, and you shall discover firsthand just how dangerous and unpredictable I can be."

"You are a devil, Captain Kane."

"Remember it well, Eden. And I'll collect your forfeit at a more appropriate time, when I am not so encumbered with Zeus's great weight. Meanwhile, you can torture yourself with wondering where and when I'll require it."

Her look grew more wary. "Forfeit?" she echoed.

"Aye." In his sun-darkened face, his teeth gleamed white. The gold hoop in his ear seemed to wink wickedly at her, and she could have sworn his hot black gaze was aglow with reflections of fire and brimstone. "You called me Captain Kane again."

Devlin patted his stomach and smiled in contentment. Ah, but he was feeling good! His meal had been hot and filling, the company of his men just what he'd needed. They'd taken a table at the rear of the tavern, stationing their captain in the corner; with ten men gathered around him, he'd been well-shielded from prying eyes as he ate and drank his fill. Not even the serving girl had noticed anything awry, as Devlin's food vanished as if by magic, his tankard and cigars lifting to invisible lips. The hour was late, and he should have been thinking of returning to Eden's house, to his room and his bed, but he was feeling very mellow, and loath to leave his fellows just yet.

The serving girl was back, leaning across the table to replenish their mugs, and, out of long habit, Devlin's hand reached beneath her skirt, his fingers clamping about one plump bare cheek. With a shriek of surprised laughter, the lass spun about, her own hand ready to slap playfully at the man who had grabbed her buttock. When she beheld not the grinning Devlin, but an empty chair, she stopped short, wagging her head in confusion. Then, believing the man on the opposite side of her had done the deed, she promptly clobbered him heartily aside the head.

Poor Nate was not at all prepared for the whack that almost sent his face into his greasy plate. With a roar, he rounded on the woman. "What'd ye do that fer?" he bellowed.

"That was fer grabbing me bum, ye old sea buzzard! It ain't there fer yer pleasure, ye know, leastwise not fer free!"

"Ye're daft! I'm not far enough into me cups to pay out good coin fer the likes o' you!"

Fortunately, there were enough men laughing at the exchange to cover Devlin's own delighted hoot.

"I'll pay ye back fer that, Dev," Nate promised when the woman had gone.

Not long afterward, Devlin was contemplating the possibilities of getting a certain raven-haired doxy into one of the upstairs rooms, when he chanced to overhear a small part of the heated conversation at the next table. Glancing over, he saw a half dozen men grumbling loudly and growing more rowdy by the minute. All appeared to have been drinking heavily, and he was sure each and every one were men Eden had dismissed from the warehouse earlier that day.

With a nudge at his friend's elbow, Devlin caught Nate's attention. Pointing his knife toward the group, he said, "I think I'll wander over and listen in on their talk a bit closer. Unless I miss my guess, those lads are brewing a bit of trouble amongst themselves."

Nate, too, recognized several of the men in question. "Wouldn't surprise me none, and 'tis always better to be alerted."

Devlin's suspicions proved true. In short order, he determined that the men were intent on avenging their lost positions. In fact, they were plotting revenge. Not against Tilton, or Devlin's crewmen who had replaced them; they had no intention of damaging the property at the warehouse, though that might come later. For this evening, their dark schemes revolved around their former employer. From what he could gather, they meant to storm her home en masse, laying ruin to anything they could get their grubby hands on, including the priggish Miss Winters and her lame mother.

Devlin was incensed. With fire in his eyes, he returned to his own table. "Mates, we've a bit of work ahead of us," he informed his crew. "The sort we're meant for."

Quickly he laid out his plan. The maid and her dubious charms now forgotten, he and his men left the tavern well ahead of the would-be mischief-makers.

An hour passed, and more. On the street where Eden's house stood, all was quiet, the residents fast asleep in their beds. The loudest noise was that of crickets chirping softly, courting one another in the grass.

Then, from the distance, a trio of lanterns glowed, swaying in the dark. Drunken voices rent the stillness of the night, rising as they drew nearer. Light gleamed dully over a variety of crude weapons. Axes. Shovels. Prying bars. Hardly a musket or broadsword among the lot.

On they came, their angry grumblings building like the collective hum of a swarm of riled bees. As one, they marched forward, knocking the front gate from its hinges as they crashed through it onto the Winters's front yard.

It was then that Devlin and his men burst from the concealment of the thick bushes and quickly surrounded the unsuspecting marauders. Shouts rang out. Steel clanged against steel.

In the center of the ensuing fray, Devlin dodged the arc of a swinging axe, a diabolical grin splitting his face as he met a challenge not actually meant for him. His opponent never saw the sword that flashed upward, slicing into his arm and rendering him nearly helpless to defend himself further. Almost immediately, a second befuddled man fell victim to this unseen force, knocked senseless with his own pry bar.

Within seconds, the battle was finished. As lights began to glow in neighboring windows, the six attackers lay stunned on the ground outside Eden's home, defeated before they'd begun.

"Well, Cap'n, what do ye say we do with this motley bunch?" one of the pirates asked.

"I say we string 'em up by their privates," another suggested.

Devlin gave a gruff laugh. "Nay, lads. We've laid waste to their plans, busted a few heads, and treated them to a well-deserved lesson. 'Tis merriment enough for the moment, unless they decide not to take heed of our warning. In which case, we can resume teaching them their manners another time. For now, round them up and we'll cart them down to the wharf. No sense leaving rubbish to clutter the lawn."

A few whispered instructions in Nate's ear brought an answering chuckle. "Aye, Dev. Me an' the boys'll see 'tis done good an' proper."

Neighbors were gaping curiously from their window ledges and peering from behind their curtains as Eden threw open her front door. She'd hastily donned her wrapper, which drooped from one shoulder, and her face was a mask of amazement. She watched in dumbfounded dismay as Devlin's crew gathered their fallen prey together and herded them down the street. Two of the victims, either too inebriated or too stunned to walk on their own, were summarily bundled across the backs of two burly brigands.

They were gone before she regained wits enough to speak, leaving only Devlin standing proudly before her, his hands on his hips and a triumphant grin on his face.

Eden promptly slammed the door in his face.

Chapter 8

*T*he door rebounded immediately, sending Eden stumbling onto her bottom. From her position on the hall floor, she met Devlin glare for glare. "What was that fracas about?" she demanded angrily. "That disgusting display at my front steps? I've a certain standing to uphold in this town, and you are not helping my cause one whit!"

"That, my dear Miss Winters," he answered with a superior sneer as he loomed over her, "was me and my men defending you from a drunken mob of the same men you fired earlier today. Their intent was anything but honorable, I assure you. Had it not been for us, you would be screaming your fool head off for help at this very moment, and lucky to come away with your virtue intact, let alone a roof over your head or your precious dignity preserved."

"So you say!" she said with a huff, not yet ready to concede.

"Aye!"

"And how did you gain this information, to come rushing to my aid so smartly?"

"I overheard them making their plans in the tavern."

"Oh," she sneered back, "is that why your shirt is

smeared with food and drink? Why you reek of whiskey and smoke and cheap women?"

"I do not reek of anything, unless 'tis the sulphur spewing from your lips, you ungrateful hellion!"

"You . . . you . . . vile vermin!"

"Eden! Eden? What's going on down there?" Jane called frantically from her upstairs bedroom. "Who are you screaming at? Is someone here?"

"Oooh, *spit!*" Eden clenched her hands into fists, screwed her face up, and gave a small, ineffectual shriek. "Bless your britches! Now see what you've done?" she snarled. "You've woken Mama."

"Me?" Devlin exclaimed incredulously. "Duchess, I'm not the one who's been ranting and raving at the top of her lungs for the past five minutes. The only thing mild about you at the moment are your pitiful curses. If anyone woke her, 'twas you."

"That's right," Eden fumed, picking herself up off the floor and straightening her nightclothes with several vicious jerks. "Blame it all on me, but none of this would have happened if you hadn't advised me to dismiss those men. So stuff that in your smelly old cigar and smoke it, Captain Kane!"

With that, she flounced up the stairs to calm her mother's continuing cries.

Not about to let Eden have the final word, Devlin was hot on her heels. "Come back here, you nasty little witch!" he hissed.

Thinking that once she reached Jane's room, she would be safe from any reprisals Devlin might have in mind, Eden burst through her mother's door. "Mama, you must calm yourself," she began, rushing to the bedside. "You'll make yourself ill, going on like th—aah!" Without warning she found herself spun about, her arm caught in Devlin's huge hand.

The next scream came from Jane, who was staring and pointing and gurgling excitedly, too panicked for coherent speech. At the same instant, Eden and Devlin realized her dismay—and its cause. The moment he'd touched her, Devlin had abruptly materialized before Jane's startled eyes. Caught off guard, Devlin then dropped Eden's arm, whereupon he promptly vanished again.

It was too much for the distraught widow. To Eden's utter astonishment, Jane suddenly leapt from her bed. Out into the hall she ran, as fast as her wobbly legs could carry her, shrieking hysterically and pulling wildly at her hair.

"Mama! Mama! Wait! I can explain!" The guilty pair dashed after her.

Jane had reached the top of the stairs, where her shaking limbs carried her no further. Still intent on escape, she was scuttling down the steps on her backside, her night shift flapping behind her like broken wings.

Devlin caught up with her at last. Seeing no help for it, he scooped the woman into his strong embrace. Jane gave one last anguished cry and fainted in his arms. Above them, at the head of the steps, Eden watched anxiously, scarcely able to deal with the shock of it all. The many upsets of the day, topped by seeing her mother walk—nay, run—after all this time!

"Oh, dear God!" she exclaimed, her arms outstretched and her eyes glittering with tears. "Is . . . is she hurt? Is she dead?"

"Nay, Eden, merely unconscious. Which is probably best for us all just now. 'Twill gain us time to decide what to tell her and how to go about it once she wakes."

"Shouldn't we try to revive her?" Eden questioned shakily, trailing behind as Devlin swiftly carried Jane back to her room and placed her gently upon the bed. She caught hold of her mother's wrist, almost gasping in relief upon finding the rhythmic pulse.

" 'Twould be better to let her come about on her

own, rather than jolt her back to reality quite so abruptly, don't you agree?" he proposed. "However, I do have some brandy in my room that might ease her frustrations once she regains her senses. I'll fetch it."

Devlin had no sooner left than he was back. "We've another problem, Eden," he informed her solemnly. "Your housekeeper is downstairs, no doubt wondering about all the commotion in the street. Then again, your mother was yelling fit to wake the dead."

"Oh, dear! What shall I do?"

"I suggest you go down and calm her before she takes it into her head to come upstairs," he said dryly.

"But what if Mother wakes while I'm gone? I can't leave her like this!"

"I will stay and watch over her until you return," he told her, firmly urging her toward the door. "Now go get rid of Dora!"

It was several minutes before Eden could convince Dora that all was fine, that the furor in the street had amounted to no more than a brief, drunken conflict.

"I was sure I heard your mama scream," Dora insisted.

"The noise and the fighting upset her," Eden informed her. "She's settled comfortably now, fast asleep in her bed." All true to some extent, though not nearly the whole of the tale.

At last Dora wandered back to her own quarters, grumbling about drunkards and brawlers requiring only a sharp rap aside their heads with a stout rolling pin to set them to rights. Eden charged upstairs again, just in time to witness her mother's first feeble stirrings.

"She's coming around," Devlin whispered. "And she'll be wanting an explanation."

Eden spared a moment to wring her hands. "Oh, dear! What a tangle this is turning out to be!"

She knelt and took her mother's hand in hers, tenderly stroking it. "Mama? Mama, can you hear me, darling?"

Jane groaned out her daughter's name. Slowly, as if fearful of what was to be found, her lids fluttered open. "Eden? I had the strangest dream!"

If she'd thought that would be the end of it, Eden might have been tempted to allow her mother to go on thinking it had all been a nightmare. But there was far more to take into consideration now that Jane had regained the use of her legs. Also, Eden was sure more incidents were bound to crop up, with Devlin residing beneath their roof, more now than ever before, if Jane was going to be up and about in her home.

"Mama, I want you to listen to me very carefully, dear. And I don't want you to become too distraught over what I tell you. Just lie calmly and sip a bit of this, and hear what I have to say."

She propped the pillow at her mother's back and placed the brandy glass into her hands, wrapping Jane's trembling fingers securely around the bowl. " 'Twas not a dream, Mama." At her mother's frantic, questioning look, Eden shook her head. "'Twas all real." Fresh tears misted Eden's eyes as she reached out and caressed the older woman's cheek. "Oh, Mama! You walked! Truly, you did!"

"And the man?" Jane's voice trembled over the query. "What of that ghostly vision?"

"He's real, too. Though not quite a ghost as we think of one." Eden cast a glance toward Devlin, who stood listening to her faltering explanation, his head cocked slightly in wry expectation. His sand-colored brows were raised over his dark, glittering eyes, and there was a derisive twist to his mobile mouth.

"He's . . . he has form, and it's not as if he can walk through walls and such."

Here Eden halted, her features reflecting her confusion. "You can't do that, can you, Devlin?" she asked him speculatively.

"Nay. Neither, however, can I view myself in a mirror, which makes shaving something of a hazard," he replied, his tone denoting more frustration than amusement.

At the sound of his deep voice, Jane gave an involuntary yelp. Her hands fluttered to her chest, the brandy glass somehow landing upright in her lap. "Oh!"

"Mama, it's all right. Honestly," Eden hastened to say. "I know this is very confusing, and I'm not explaining it well at all, but he's not here to harm you. Please believe that. If anything, Devlin is aiding us."

"H-h-how?" Jane stammered, peering into the shadows with wide, frightened eyes.

"He's providing the funds with which to pay off our debt to Mr. Finster. And he's trying to discover why the warehouse is losing money, and a means to correct the problem."

"A guardian angel?" Jane asked softly, incredulously.

Eden almost laughed. "No, I wouldn't put it quite that way. More of a helpful hindrance. The lesser of two evils, if you will," she supplied with ripe sarcasm. Devlin scowled at her. "You see, for some unknown reason, I appear to be the only person who can view him. Others can readily feel him and hear him, but only I can actually see him."

"But I saw him," Jane interjected. "I'm certain of it."

"Yes, but only because he and I were touching at the time." Eden sighed, wondering how to explain this strange phenomenon. "That is another aspect of this oddity. Bizarre as it is, no one else can make him visible but me. Only when we touch can others see him. In exchange for my services in this area, he is helping us."

"This is all too fantastic!" Jane exclaimed with a

shake of her head. "A ghost who isn't a ghost? An angel who isn't an angel? A man not really a man?"

"Now that is where I draw the line, madam," Devlin put in on a grunt of exasperation. "I will not have doubts cast upon my manhood."

Jane blinked in surprise. Then, to their vast amazement, she began to chuckle. "I stand corrected." In an aside to her daughter, she said, "He's a man all right. As vain about his masculinity as any of them. Now, let me hear how all this came about. Start at the beginning, please, and do try not to muddle your story too dreadfully in the telling of it."

By the end of their tale, with Devlin adding his own comments to Eden's, Jane had a fair idea of what had occurred, though she didn't really comprehend the why's and wherefore's of the events any more than they did. "Am I to understand that you, sir, are using my daughter to be seen? To assume form when needed?"

At his affirmative reply, she continued. "Is it your hope that in the process, you will somehow stumble upon a means of regaining your usual appearance?"

"Aye."

"And you are currently residing in my home? With few people aware of that fact?"

"True, madam. And I would prefer that my presence remain unknown."

Jane cleared her throat delicately, directing a stern gaze toward him—or where she thought him to be. "As would I, young man. We do have Eden's reputation to consider. What of Dora?"

"She suspects nothing as yet," Eden assured her. "I hope to keep it from her. You know how excitable she is over the least thing."

"You're right, of course. Luckily, Dora does not sleep within these walls, to hear loud grumblings in the middle of the night," Jane quipped tartly, pinning her daughter with a quelling look. "Swine, eh? Just how long did you expect to get away with such an outrageous lie?"

Eden cringed. "I'm sorry. It seemed the only thing to do at the time."

Jane's attention returned to Devlin. "You are a sea captain, then?"

He debated the wisdom of his answer for only a moment. "I'm a pirate, ma'am."

She merely stared toward him, apparently not at all shocked at his confession. "I see." After a slight hesitation, she asked, "Are you very good at it?"

This surprised a chuckle out of him. "Aye. The best," he replied, laughter adding warmth to his rumbling tones.

Jane drew herself up straighter on her pillow. "You may stay," she informed him imperiously. "For now. But if I should learn that you are in any way besmirching my daughter's honor, or scheming to steal from us, or intent on other harmful misdeeds toward my family, out you go. Am I making myself quite clear, Captain Kane?"

"Indeed, madam. Explicitly."

"Fine." Jane tipped the brandy glass to her lips, helping herself to a hefty swallow. Then she directed a commanding wave toward the hall. "As much as I have enjoyed our talk, I would prefer that both of you retire to your respective rooms now, and let me get some sleep before the sun rises. You seem to be making a habit of disturbing my rest, and if I am to continue my miraculous recovery, I am going to need all the stamina I can muster."

They were closing the door after them when she called out, "Captain Kane?"

"Aye."

"While I would not ordinarily be grateful at being frightened into hysteria, in these circumstances I find I must tender my appreciation. I might never have tried to walk again, but for the shock you gave me this night, and I am thankful to have been torn from my self-imposed lethargy, even by so dramatic a means. 'Tis a pity it did not occur sooner."

"You are most welcome, madam."

"And Captain? Molest my daughter, and I will personally shoot off your ears. Your screams will tell me how truly I have aimed."

Two seconds later, Devlin seemed to have forgotten Jane's warning. In the hall, he turned to Eden, graced her with his most sensual smile, and suggested, "Your bed or mine, sweets?"

Eden smiled back. "Both. You in yours, and I in mine, pirate. Separately, with a wall between us. That, or I shall return to Mother's room and load Papa's gun for her, and your ears will pay the price."

Upon entering the house the next morning, Dora was astounded to discover her mistress dressed, downstairs, and walking about cautiously on her own. "Blessed saints! 'Tis a bloomin' miracle! How? When?" she blathered excitedly.

Lifting her hands palm-upward in an attitude of uncertainty, Jane shrugged. "I can't begin to explain it, Dora. It simply happened," she said. "But isn't it grand?"

Eden gaped, wondering how her mother could embroider the truth so smoothly. To hear her now, one would believe she was accustomed to fabricating lies at a moment's notice. It was a stunning revelation, to learn this about one's own mother!

Devlin's smirk only added fat to the fire.

The morning meal passed in much the same manner as the one before, with Devlin sharing Eden's larger portions. Jane hid a smile upon seeing the food disappear from her daughter's plate so mysteriously. "Ah, so that is how you manage it without rousing Dora's suspicions," she commented, the servant in question safely out of sight and hearing. "I was curious. But how did you explain to her that you have suddenly developed a taste for coffee, Eden, when she knows you prefer tea?"

Eden grimaced. "I told her 'tis what I drink at the warehouse, and that I've grown fond of it. With my expanding appetite, I request both drinks with my meal. In that way, Devlin can have one and I the other. Of course, by now the entire town is probably aware that I am eating enough for four normal people." She aimed a snarl at Devlin, who answered with a wicked grin.

The meal resumed in silence, or what would have been silence if not for Devlin's chomping and slurping. Jane frowned, but held her tongue, even as she witnessed her linen tablecloth acquiring more fresh stains by the moment. Eden suffered the aggravation for as long as she could, then blurted, "For pity's sake, Devlin! Must you make such atrocious noise when you eat? Can't you chew with your mouth closed? I swear, the table is gathering more food than your stomach! 'Tis little wonder your clothing looks and smells so bad! Verily, it amazes me that you have remained undetected all this while, for surely every dog in town must be acting strangely, yapping and trailing about in your wake, disturbed by your scent, yet unable to locate its source."

Devlin stared at her, completely flummoxed.

"In your own sweet, roundabout way are you trying to tell our guest that he stinks, Eden?" Jane choked out past a giggle.

With a sigh, Eden cast her gaze overhead, as if seeking celestial intercession. "Yes. If you want it put bluntly, he reeks to high heaven!"

"I do not!" Devlin blustered.

"You do, Devlin. Both you and your clothing could use a good scrubbing."

"I hate to say it, Captain, but she's right," Jane concurred. "A good dousing is overdue."

Devlin glowered.

In an uncharacteristic gesture, Eden poked her tongue out at him. "Told you so!" she caroled.

"Eden! Behave yourself! Why, you have never acted so outrageously in your life!" Jane wavered between laughter and embarrassment. On the one hand, she had taught her daughter better manners; on the other she'd also been painfully aware that Eden had always been more withdrawn and less gleeful than other girls her age, even as a child. It was a joy to see her exhibiting a more playful attitude for a change, no matter the reason.

Eden excused herself by saying, "Devlin brings out the worst in me, Mama," and continued to eat her porridge.

"That is another thing I've been meaning to ask about," Jane commented, her narrowed gaze traveling from her daughter to the chair in which Devlin sat. How she wished she could see his expression now! "Why is it that you address the captain so informally, and on such short acquaintance?"

Eden nearly swallowed her spoon, her teeth clacking against it before she pulled it from her mouth. Her startled eyes sought him, but Devlin's bland demeanor told her she could expect no help from that quarter. Never had she seen anyone so devilish suddenly look so angelic!

"Trouble with your spoon, Miss Propriety?" he asked too sweetly.

"Remove your elbows from the table, and stop slouching like some spineless creature," she retorted.

"Eden? I believe I asked you a question, dear, and I would like an answer, please," Jane reminded her.

"Uh . . . uh, he requested that I address him so, Mama. Quite adamantly, in fact."

"Is that so?" Jane turned the question to Devlin.

He hesitated for so long that Eden was certain he

was not going to confirm her statement. Finally, he answered. "Aye. As I have told your daughter, it delights me to hear my given name when she speaks it. Her voice makes it sound different to me somehow, almost musical. Because of this, I have entreated her to refer to me in the more familiar manner."

Jane sent him a skeptical look. "Entreated, or demanded, sir?"

"Whichever applied at the moment," he replied, not at all ruffled by her tone.

Jane stood her ground and met him square about. "You, Captain, are so full of yourself that 'tis a wonder you don't burst your seams. 'Twill be my pleasure to see you get toppled from your high horse now and again—whether by my hand or Eden's."

Chapter 9

*T*hey were just rising from the table when
there came a pounding at the side door. Fearing it was
Finster come to pester her again, Eden was relieved to
find young Willie Moffet, the lad who took their milk
cow to pasture every morning and back again each evening. This morn, however, he was running late collecting the animals.

As she opened the door to him, she asked, "Is it
payment time already, Willie?" It seemed she'd just issued his due for the chore.

"No, ma'am, er, Miss Eden," he answered excitedly,
fairly dancing into the house. "I jest had to stop and see
if ye'd heard the news yet."

"What news?"

"Why, 'tis all over town!" he declared, his eyes sparkling with delight at being the first one to relate this
juicy bit of gossip. "They found six fellows tied up
down at the wharf this mornin', all bound and gagged
and laid out in a row like hogs at the market! And ye'll
never guess what else! They was naked, each an' every
one!"

"William Moffet!" Jane reprimanded him sharply,
coming forward to give a tug on his ear. "Watch your

98

tongue, young man, or I'll be advising your mother to take lye soap to your mouth!"

The boy grinned up at her, then gaped. "Miz Winters! Ye're walkin'!"

"So I am," Jane agreed simply. "Now, please go on with your story. What were these men doing tied up as they were? Do you know who they were?"

"Oh, yes, 'm! Know'd all o' them! Know 'em even better now!" He giggled. Jane wagged a warning finger at him, and Willie sobered somewhat, though not by much. "There was Mr. Smythe, and Mr. Browning, and Danny Everett's pa."

As he went on to list three others, Eden recognized them all as the men she'd dismissed from employment the day before, the same men who'd been involved in the confrontation on her lawn last midnight. She turned to look at Devlin and found him leaning casually against the window frame, listening with obvious amusement.

Willie was not yet done recounting the delicious details. "They was a-layin' there tied up tighter'n Christmas geese, each with some sort o' tool or somethin' laying next to 'im, and they all had big printed signs hung round their necks, tellin' why they was there."

"Could you read what the signs said, Willie?" Eden wanted to know.

"No, but Ned Travis could, an' he told me. They said something like 'I took up this weapon agin' defenseless women. Now you use the same agin' me.' An' folks was doin' it, too, they was!" he added gleefully. "Old Ed Browning got a good wallop with 'is own shovel, an' the Widow Gooding took the end o' Mr. Everett's axe handle to his noggin! Oh, but was that a sight to see!"

"I can imagine it was," Eden replied, struggling to hold back a chuckle. Beside her, Jane was coughing delicately into her handkerchief, her eyes sparkling with merriment.

"Well, we must thank you for relating the latest news, Willie," Eden went on. "But the cows await you, and I think you'd best run along about your usual business now, or 'twill be time to bring them back before they ever reach the pasture."

"Yes 'm. Oh, an' Miz Winters, I sure am glad to see ya on yer feet agin'. Wait'll I tell Ma!" He dashed off, happier than a dog with two tails at having yet another morsel of gossip to add to the first.

"That lad is worse than an old woman!" Jane declared, laughing and shaking her head. "He's turning out just like his mother, and I vow her tongue is hinged at both ends!"

She turned to find Eden doubled over at the waist, clutching her stomach with both arms and emitting strange squeaking sounds. "Eden? Are you all right?"

"Ooh! Ooh!"

"She's fine, or she will be as soon as she quits cackling fit to lay eggs!" Devlin announced on a snicker of his own.

It was several minutes before Eden could recover enough to speak. Wiping tears of mirth from her cheeks, she heaved a tremendous sigh. "Heavens! I can't recall when anything has struck me so silly!"

"Nor can I," Jane concurred wryly. "Am I correct in assuming those were the same men who created all that fuss outdoors last evening?"

"The very same."

"Then I'm glad to see that they've all been taught their lessons, and quite appropriately. Captain Kane, did you apply those measures, by some chance?"

"Indirectly. My men did the actual work of it."

"But it was your devious brain that derived the scheme," Jane surmised.

"Aye."

A slow smile crept across her face. "Sir, you have earned my profound admiration. I can only add that I am sincerely grateful that you are aligned with us and not against us."

Among the three of them, it was decided that Eden and Devlin should go to Dudley Finster's office to tender repayment of the loan. At Jane's suggestion, they would take an impartial witness with them, to verify that the debt was paid in full, and the canceled note and receipt collected on the spot.

"Since we and the Finsters all attend his church, perhaps Reverend Johnston would be a good choice," Eden offered.

"Excellent," her mother agreed. "There is not a more respected or honest man in Charles Town."

"Mama, now that you are walking again, shouldn't you be the one to do this?" Eden asked.

"No. Finster has been dealing with you for some time now, and you deserve the reward of seeing the look on his face when you hand over the money. Also, it would not be a bad idea if Devlin were to be seen escorting you, boldly visible to one and all."

"Oh?" Eden and Devlin spoke simultaneously.

"My, yes! Can you imagine Finster's bafflement, should he suddenly find another man courting his chosen bride?" Jane asked, a sly smile curving her lips. "Why trounce him with one blow, when you have two at hand? The loan paid and a rival for your affections, all at once."

"Oh, Mama! You are so wicked!" Eden marveled.

"Aye," Devlin agreed. "And might I return your compliment by saying I'm heartily glad you are not my adversary, madam?"

"You may. And do keep that thought foremost in your mind, Captain."

* * *

Before they could put their plan into action, Eden thought it best that Devlin launder his clothes and himself. "If you are to play the part of my suitor, you will present a well-kept image," she announced firmly. "I refuse to be seen about town with an unkempt beau. 'Tis enough that people will soon discover you are a pirate."

"I wouldn't be quite so high and mighty if I were you, Miss Priss," Devlin advised. "This *pirate* is still holding the purse strings."

She answered with a pert wrinkle of her nose. "Release them long enough to wield a bar of soap for a change."

He agreed, not to please her or to let her have the upper hand, but because he truly needed the scrubbing. Jane did her part by creating an extensive list of errands for Dora, which would keep her conveniently away from the house for an hour or more. Devlin dragged a big tin washtub into the kitchen, and the two women set about filling it with hot water.

" 'Tis not as if I never bathe, you know," he informed them grouchily. "Truth be told, I'm cleaner than most. You wouldn't smell like roses either, were you forced to wear the same clothing day in and day out. Which presents another point. Since I'm to be fully visible today, I could very well do so in an altogether different suit of clothes, and save all this fuss. 'Twould be a treat to vary my wardrobe from time to time."

"As long as Eden doesn't let loose of you and have you disappear, with only your clothing left behind," Jane pointed out.

"That's fine with me," Eden put in, "but you can't apply clean clothing on a filthy body. Besides, your invisible apparel still needs washing, for those times when you need to remain undetected. Unless you intend to stroll about in your bare skin," she added. "However, the way your luck has been running, I wouldn't risk it.

You would undoubtedly encounter some other poor soul who could discern you, and embarrass the daylights out of both of you."

"Unlike someone else I could name, I am not ashamed of my body," Devlin retorted.

Eden gave an indignant sniff. "I don't doubt that you are as vain as a peacock, but that's not to say the rest of us need to see you strut your feathers." She tossed a bed sheet at him. "Use that to cover yourself once you have washed your clothing." The tub now filled, she started from the room.

"What's this?" he called after her with a gruff laugh. "Aren't you going to stay and scrub my back for me, sweetling?"

"You are a crude lout!"

"And you are a chicken-heart!"

The tub was too small for his large frame, requiring much twisting and turning, until Devlin thought surely he was tying himself into knots, but at last he was as clean as a whistle. He then set about laundering his clothes. Once he'd finished, he carted them outdoors, draped them over a drying line stretched between two small trees, and dumped out the tub of dirty water—completely unconcerned that he did so without a stitch covering him. After all, who was to see him but Eden? And she was cowering in the parlor with her mother.

Except that Eden was not hiding in the parlor. Upon hearing the kitchen door slam, she'd gone to investigate. Finding Devlin and the tub missing, she failed to notice the bed sheet tossed into the corner. Whereupon, she erroneously concluded that he'd ventured outdoors draped in the huge white sheet which anyone might chance to see floating across the yard. Rushing to the window, she peered out, inwardly cringing.

It was not what she'd expected to see. Oh, no, not at all! There he stood, in all his glory, the sun shining down upon him like a blessing—and the sight literally stole her breath away. Where before, trapped beneath him on his bed, she had carefully avoided looking below his chest, she now found she could not tear her eyes from him.

He was magnificent! Until now, the only nude male forms Eden had viewed were those in books, pictures of stiff, lifeless statues, many with hairless bodies and their private parts shadowed or covered. There was nothing in the least lifeless about Devlin Kane! His whole being practically shouted of bold vitality. Tall, perfectly proportioned, beautiful enough to put Michelangelo's *David* to shame!

Below the waist, his powerful body was pale, his long limbs darkened with only a sprinkling of tawny body hair. Above, his skin was sun-kissed to a rich, warm bronze, his broad chest carpeted with a wide vee of shimmering gold, which trailed a thinner line over his taut stomach. As he moved, a symphony of muscles played in perfect accord with one another, stretching along his calves, his thighs, his buttocks, rippling across his sleek back and sinewed arms.

As Eden watched him, unable to make herself turn away, a feverish heat sizzled through her, turning her first hot, then cold, then hot again. Her flesh tingled and burned. Her breasts seemed to swell, as if seeking release from the confines of her bodice, their suddenly sensitive tips protruding against the soft fabric of her chemise. Her knees felt like pudding, her mouth as dry as cotton, and her heart determined to gallop away with itself.

He shifted his stance, turning more fully toward her, his leg no longer hiding his manhood, and Eden nearly choked. There *it* was, cradled in a nest of thick, amber curls. Even as she watched, it lost its flaccid state, growing in size and strength before her stunned eyes.

"Oh, my stars!" she whispered, her hand flying to her heaving chest.

Her gaze flickered upward, gooseflesh forewarning her, and she found herself staring straight into Devlin's blazing black eyes. Never had she seen a look so brash, so challenging, so blatantly sensual! His eyes were like glowing polished ebony; his nostrils flared slightly, as if to catch her scent; the flesh was drawn taut over his strong cheekbones; his teeth gleamed in a smile as brazen and beckoning as sin itself. Even at this distance, it jolted through her with lightning force.

With a muted cry, she stumbled backward and ran from the kitchen.

Eden was hiding in her room, wondering how she was ever going to look him in the eye again, when her mother called up the steps to her. "Eden? Darling, could you come to the kitchen, please? Devlin is in need of your help."

Devlin was in need of a good thrashing!

"Eden?"

She sighed. She was going to have to face him sooner or later, so it might as well be now, with her mother there between them. "Coming, Mama."

She stopped just shy of the kitchen entrance. There she took a deep breath, straightened her shoulders, and tried to arrange her features into placid lines. But the moment she entered the kitchen to find Devlin grinning at her like a cat stalking a mouse, her composure slipped. However, it did help somewhat that around that arrogant grin, he had shaving soap lathered all over his cheeks. And the sheet was now anchored firmly around his trim waist, at least covering the lower half of him.

"You were supposed to wear the cloth over your entire body, Captain, not just the lower portion," she snapped.

"And go about looking as if I were on my way to a Roman feast? Not on threat of death, duchess! You'll simply have to ignore my hairy chest, if it disturbs you." His look said that he was fully aware of how much he disturbed her—and where—and in precisely what manner.

"What do you want?" she asked irritably.

"A leading question, if ever I've heard one," he answered glibly.

"Your pirate is having a bit of trouble handling his razor," Jane explained. "He keeps cutting himself, and unless you want to be escorted by a man with half a face, it might be best to lend a hand. I'd offer to do it, but I fear I'd be as lacking at it as he, for neither of us can see more than a smear of shaving soap. Whereas you, dear, see the whole of him."

"More than you know," Devlin said on a soft chuckle, low enough that only Eden caught his words. He winked at her.

She glared at him. "He's not my pirate, Mama. And what makes either of you think I'd do a better job than he can? I've never attempted to shave a man before." She gave him a simpering look, though her eyes continued to shoot daggers at him. "Why, I might end up slitting his throat—entirely by accident, you understand. And what a pity that would be!"

Devlin stared at her with narrowed eyes, as if gauging the extent of her malice. "I think not," he decided, relaxing once more. "I'm willing to wager you will be extremely careful with my person. At least until Finster has his gold."

She shrugged, feigning disinterest. " 'Tis your neck."

In short order, Devlin was half-reclined on a kitchen chair, a towel draped around his neck, and Eden bent over him with the shaving brush. When he attempted to bring up a hand mirror to watch what she was doing, she shoved it aside. "I'm novice enough at this, without you making it more difficult." Before he could argue the point, she slapped a glob of soap onto his face, landing the brush squarely in his open mouth.

Sputtering and spitting, he reared up. "You witch! You did that on purpose!" he accused, swiping at his tongue and teeth with the towel.

"Oh, don't be such a baby! Besides, if anyone's mouth needed washing out, 'tis yours!"

By this time, Jane was openly chuckling at their antics. "Now, children," she admonished. "Let's get on with this, shall we? Dora will be home soon."

It was a trial for the wary pair. In order to keep her balance, Eden found she had to lean into him. Feigning assistance, he helped to steady her with a hand at her waist, his wandering fingers caressing her there. The contact sent a hot quiver through both of them, and Eden's fingers were visibly trembling as she raised the razor to his face. "Easy now, lass," he told her, his dark eyes burning into hers. "I like my nose the length 'tis."

"So do I, actually," she admitted tightly, taking a short, quick breath.

All in all, it went fairly well after that. He sat as still as the statue with which she'd mentally compared him earlier, and she managed to control her trembling enough to execute the deed with moderate success. She nicked him only twice. Once near his right ear, and once while trying to negotiate around the deep crevice in his chin.

Both heaved audible sighs of relief when it was finished. At which Jane commented laughingly, "To hear the two of you, one would think you'd just gained reprieve from the gallows!"

"An apt comparison," Devlin allowed, paler than usual. "Mayhap I'll consider growing a beard, until such a time as I regain normalcy."

"Oh, pooh!" Eden grinned cheekily at him, feeling perky now that she'd gotten a bit of revenge on him. "And just when I was beginning to get good at it!"

* * *

When Devlin returned from his room a short time later, Eden was surprised, and impressed, by his improved appearance. He was attired in a snowy-white shirt, with wide sleeves and ruffled cuffs, over which he wore a black brocade waistcoat, beautifully embroidered at the edges with rich red trim. Encircling his waist was the scarlet sash, his cutlass tucked into it; at his throat lay a white satin cravat, perfectly tied. His knee breeches were also black, and fitted him so faithfully that they were just short of indecent. Indeed, they left no doubt that he was definitely a man—and well-endowed into the bargain!

He'd foregone shoes in favor of his jackboots, which were now shined to a high gloss; and in his hand he carried a cavalier-style hat, complete with waving scarlet plume. Other than the fact that he sported no outer coat over his waistcoat, Eden could find little fault with his appearance.

"Well, milady," he queried, turning about for her perusal, "will I do?"

"Quite nicely, indeed," she answered by way of a compliment. "Is the lack of a coat an oversight, or merely a personal preference?"

"Preference, sweetling. An overcoat is cumbersome, and often in the way when one is trying to draw one's sword."

"I would think 'tis also much too warm in the summer," Jane added. "My late husband shed his as often as he dared." She sighed sadly in remembrance. "I loved him so dearly, and letting go of him has been most difficult for me, but 'tis best now to put my terrible grieving aside and hold only to the warm memories. I think I am ready to do that at long last."

"I'm glad, Mama. I want to see you happy again." Eden rose and kissed her, then turned and took Devlin's arm, thus affording her mother her first full look at him, inside of all his finery.

"Ah, that is much better!" Jane said on a watery laugh. "You can't know how peculiar it is to see a set of clothes wandering about with no body within them! 'Tis enough to send shivers up one's spine! Just see that you keep a firm hold on him, Eden, for all our sakes!"

Eden started for the door, only to be drawn to an abrupt halt as Devlin refused to budge. "What is it now?"

From inside his waistcoat he withdrew two finely carved tortoiseshell hair combs. He handed them to her. "The gift I promised you yesterday," he explained.

Then he reached out and swiftly pulled the bonnet from her head. Next, the pins from her hair, where she had it bundled into a tidy knot at her nape. Her tresses fell in a shimmering brown mass across her shoulders. "Oh, Devlin! Now see what you've done!" she wailed. "It shall take me a good quarter hour to repair it!"

"Nay," he corrected. "'Twill take but a minute or two to draw up the sides with the combs, and let the rest fall free." When she would have argued, he shook his head sternly. "If I am to appear the suitor you wish me to, then you ought be the sort of lady I would fancy courting. Fair is fair, Eden."

"But 'twill look horrid!" she lamented.

"Nay. 'Twill be most lovely. Trust me."

With a pleading look toward her mother, Eden sought support. "Mama, tell him."

Jane smiled, her face more alive with tenderness than Eden could recall since her father's death. "Wear it down, Eden," she said softly. "He's right, my dear. When you were small, I used to love arranging it that way for you."

Off Eden flounced, to return once more with the bonnet atop her head, though her hair was now streaming out behind it. She was three steps inside the room when Devlin again snatched the hat from her. "If you require some means to keep the sun from darkening your fair skin, pray employ a parasol until we can purchase more fashionable headgear for you." He eyed the hat with distaste. "This god-awful thing looks as if a ragman's wife would turn her nose up at it. For that matter, I prefer to see your hair in all its abundant splendor, not just a swatch of it hanging down your back like a horse's tail."

"I don't give a whit what you prefer, Captain!" she railed at him, her eyes smoldering. She made to grab the hat back from him, but he held it out of reach. Much to her dismay, he then ripped it in half and tossed the remains over his shoulder with blatant disregard, while Jane sat staring at them in gleeful anticipation.

"You should care, Eden," Devlin insisted, "as my sense of style seems far superior to yours."

"You wouldn't know fashion if it perched on your nose, you oaf!"

"I know when it's perched on your head! Or not, as in this instance."

"Eden, please!" Jane implored. "All this shouting is ridiculous. And for what? If he can go without a coat, then surely you can go without a bonnet for once. And it does make your hair look ever so much better this way. After all, 'tis not as if you were bald!"

Shooting a glare at both of them, Eden snatched up a parasol and swept from the room, and might have kept on going if Devlin had not caught her arm and slowed her to a more dignified pace. With haughty aplomb and a devilish twinkle in his black eyes, he bowed and offered his arm toward her. "If you please, duchess," he said with a broad grin. "I am ever at your service."

She grabbed at his arm, grumbling irritably. "You're ever a thorn in my backside, Devlin Kane! That's what you are, you wretch!"

Chapter 10

To Eden's disgust, it took Devlin all of ten minutes to charm Reverend Johnston, a usually perceptive man. Apparently the minister had a blind spot when it came to devious sea rogues.

"Have you never considered giving up your lawless ways?" Johnston asked as the three of them piled into the carriage, on their way to Finster's office.

"Well, I did have what you might term a spiritual encounter recently that made me look at myself in a new manner," Devlin admitted, tongue-in-cheek.

"Was it at all enlightening, young man?"

"Fairly blinding, sir," Devlin granted, ignoring the sharp poke Eden administered to his rib cage.

"Good. Good. And will you be staying in Charles Town, perhaps seeking a new means of earning a living?"

"For a time, though I must point out that pirating is not something one can quit at the drop of a hat." At the reverend's questioning look, Devlin went on to explain. "You see, sir, I have my crew to consider, some thirty men who have no other employable skills. 'Twould take a while to see them set up in other work. To be perfectly frank, many might not easily convert to lawful society. Buccaneering is a daring, exciting profession, and once in the blood it is not readily quelled."

Johnston nodded. "I can understand your dilemma. But do work on it, won't you? Piracy is a dangerous career, and not long-lived if our government has much to say about it. In short order, our sea-lanes will be cleared of brigands, so they claim, and I would hate to see such a man as yourself laid to waste in the process."

Seated between the two men, Eden gave a violent quiver at the thought of Devlin killed or hanged. Aware of this, the good minister was immediately contrite. "Oh, dear! I fear I have served you quite a fright with my thoughtless words. Still, 'tis something both of you need to contemplate. You must keep it uppermost in your mind, Miss Winters, if you are tempted to entertain Captain Kane as a suitor. And you, Captain, must not trifle with her tender emotions unless you can see your way clear to spending a lifetime with her."

His sermon delivered, Johnston settled back for the ride, leaving the younger couple to ponder his wisdom.

Though at Jane's suggestion Devlin was merely *posing* as Eden's suitor at the moment, he suddenly felt uncomfortable. Had the minister somehow divined his intentions to entice Eden into his bed? Was he warning him against it? Reminding him just how detestable such an action would be? Tweaking his conscience?

Devlin shook off that thought. His conscience was conveniently at bay, right where he wanted it, and there it would stay until he'd bedded the lovely spinster. He'd made up his mind to have her, and nothing would deter him. Certainly not a mere preacher spouting morals.

Furthermore, when it did happen, which it most surely would, Eden would be more than willing. She would be as eager for him as he was for her, equally responsible and therefore unable to lay the whole blame upon his head. Besides, it wasn't as if she wouldn't be gaining her own sweet pleasure from it as well. He would see that she did, would make damned sure it was the most marvelous, memorable experience she'd ever known.

For her part, Eden was stunned at just how much Reverend Johnston's comments had affected her. Lands! She'd known Devlin but three short days, and already she was devastated at the thought of harm coming to him. Still, the thought of him as an actual suitor was preposterous! While he seemed serious in his intention to lure her into his bed, the idea of him seriously courting her was laughable. The man was a rover. An itinerant charmer! Here today, gone tomorrow. In more ways than one!

Sweet heavens, the man was the closest thing to a ghost she was ever apt to meet! Not precisely choice pickings as a husband, by any stretch of the imagination. A life together? Not likely! Magnificent as he was, beguiling as he might be, he was an impossible fantasy, and best left at that.

If only he'd cease tempting her so!

When Eden entered his office, Finster came half out of his desk chair, his thin lips stretching into a parody of a smile. "My dear Miss Winters, I could scarcely believe my ears when Mr. James told me you were here to see me. To what do I owe the pleasure?"

It was only then that he noticed the two men alongside her, and his smile faded in confusion. "And you, sirs? Might I inquire why you are here as well?"

Eden plunked her fat purse onto Dudley's desk, the coins inside clinking noisily. Gesturing toward it, she said, "I have come to pay off Papa's loan, Mr. Finster, as agreed. Captain Kane and Reverend Johnston are here to bear witness to that fact, and to remind me to collect the canceled note and a proper receipt."

Jane had been right. The look of surprise and dismay

that crossed Finster's mouselike features was priceless! Why, the man appeared about to swoon, as if the brush of a feather could have sent him fluttering to the floor in a faint! His face turned ashen, his tiny eyes bulged, and his mouth worked soundlessly as his stunned brain struggled to comprehend her blunt announcement.

Finally he blustered, "We-well, fine!" He gestured toward the chairs set opposite his. "Please, be seated. I'll just run this out to Mr. James and have him tally up the total."

As Finster's scrawny fingers reached for the money bag, Devlin's came down hard atop it. "I think not, Mr. Finster," he drawled. "Miss Winters would much prefer that you count it here, so there is no mistaking the amount."

"And who are you, sir? Her appointed keeper?" Finster dared.

"Mr. Finster!" Rev. Johnston protested, before either Devlin or Eden could speak. "Kindly recall that you are in the presence of a lady, sir! Captain Kane is merely watching out for Miss Winters's best interests, as am I."

Properly chastised, Finster resumed his seat, while Devlin took up a defensive stance behind Eden's chair, his hand resting lightly upon her shoulder to maintain the contact necessary to keep him visible.

As Dudley spilled the coins from the cloth and began to count them, Reverend Johnston did his best to ease the tension in the room. "Have you heard the news, Mr. Finster? Miss Winters's mother has regained the use of her legs. My wife is visiting with her as we speak, and I shall be going over to tender my own congratulations upon leaving here."

Dudley frowned, his concentration broken. "Yes. I had heard, though I've not yet had the opportunity to extend my best wishes." He shot a hard glance at Eden from across his desk. "How did this miraculous event come about?"

"It's really Mother's tale to tell," Eden replied, neatly sidestepping his question. "Suffice it to say that Captain Kane had something to do with it, and that we are all extremely grateful to him." She turned limpid eyes toward Devlin, much enjoying her rare chance at flirtation.

"Oh? And is he also the person responsible for your abrupt turn of fortune?" Finster insinuated nastily, waving a hand over the pile of gold before him.

"Whyever would you think such a thing?" Eden asked in an offended tone. "I informed you weeks ago that I would pay the debt, long before Captain Kane ever set foot in Charles Town."

Finster made a production of separating the coins into several neat stacks. "Forgive me if I made an incorrect assumption. Still, it does seem peculiar that you should suddenly come by the necessary funds, when everyone is well aware that your warehouse is failing. Also, does it not strike you queer that there are thirty coins in this lot? An odd coincidence, I'm sure, but quite Biblical, wouldn't you say, Reverend?"

"As you say, a coincidence, Mr. Finster, and surely lacking the same interpretation as those thirty pieces of silver paid out to Judas," Johnston answered with a severe frown. "Might I also take this opportunity to remind you that 'tis not at all Christian to make rash judgments of your neighbors, lest ye too be judged."

"Amen," Devlin intoned softly, hiding a smirk.

Eden was still trying to deal with the fact that Devlin had placed thirty coins into her purse, though these were gold rather than silver. A shiver ran up her spine. Had he intentionally presented her with this traditional sign of betrayal? But who was she betraying? She'd simply made a bargain with him, a fair agreement. If she were betraying anyone at all, placing anyone's soul in jeopardy, it was hers alone. Still, it was an eerie thought.

Devlin's voice brought her out of her dark musings. "Your concern about Miss Winters's business is misplaced, Mr. Finster," he was saying. "And not entirely correct. The warehouse is simply mismanaged, a situation the lady is currently taking steps to rectify."

"Ah, yes! I have heard that she has replaced a number of long-standing workers with new ones. Would these be members of your own crew by some chance, Captain?" Finster inquired with a snide look.

"News does travel fast in a small town, doesn't it?" Eden remarked frostily. "And just how did you come by this information so quickly?"

"I . . . uh . . ." Finster made a pretense of being caught up in his accounting. "Why, I ran into Mr. Tilton last evening. He was concerned with the drastic measures you have suddenly employed."

Eden's brows rose. "So much so that he felt it necessary to tattle all my private dealings to you?"

Finster's color rose. "Well, I imagine he felt compelled to inform me, since I am courting you, my dear."

"Ah, but are you in fact doing any such thing?" Eden countered quickly, a mocking smile on her lips. "Name me one instance to prove your point, Mr. Finster. Have you once been invited to my home for Sunday supper? Have you at any time brought me flowers, or sweets, or quoted poetry to me? Have we been seen promenading the lane, or perched on the porch swing together? Nay, I say. Therefore, I fail to see why anyone would assume that you are courting me, or that I might be at all inclined to allow it of you."

"I . . . I've sat beside you in church a number of times," Finster stammered. "Even the good reverend can attest to that."

Eden gave a humorless laugh. "So has my mother, yet I'm not being courted by her! And Mr. Langford sat down beside me last week, and the Widow Ames the previous Wednesday evening. Am I being courted by them as well?"

Reverend Johnston cleared his throat noisily in a bid for attention. "Another lesson to be learned, I think, Mr. Finster. That of not counting one's chickens before they hatch. And speaking of counting, could you get on about the business at hand? I told Henrietta I would be along shortly, and time is passing."

In quick order, the money was counted and found to be the correct amount. Though he had to be reminded, Finster did write up a receipt and produce the loan documents, which he marked as paid in full.

On their way out of his office, one hand placed securely within the crook of Devlin's elbow, Eden hesitated. Over her shoulder she said, "A final suggestion, for future reference, Mr. Finster. A woman likes to feel precious to a man who courts her. That includes doting attention and small gifts to win her heart. Even if the lady in question appears to be a lonely spinster whom most people consider long past such fanciful dreams."

She touched slender fingers to the comb in her hair and turned a loving gaze up to meet Devlin's laughing black eyes. "Is that not so, Captain?"

"Aye. But I do hope you weren't alluding to yourself when you mentioned spinsters, sweetling." His fingers came up to cover hers on the comb, lingering to stroke her silken curls. "I prefer to think you were merely biding your time, awaiting my arrival before offering your heart."

By the time they reached the street, Eden was nearly choking with mirth, and bursting with a dozen other emotions, not the least of which was a trembling desire conjured up by Devlin's slight touch. She stood watching, saying not a word, as Devlin politely offered their carriage to Reverend Johnston.

"We've a bit of additional business to conduct yet,"

he told the minister, "but we know how anxious you are to be off. If you would, please tell Mrs. Winters that we'll be along shortly."

"But your carriage, Captain," the man objected.

"We'll hire a conveyance."

Thus it was that Eden found herself alone with Devlin. "What other business have we?" she inquired hesitantly. "Are we bound for the warehouse now?"

"Nay, wench." He grinned down at her, his earring winking at her. "We're not." With that he sketched a bow and proposed merrily, "Would you care to stroll the lane with me, Miss Winters?"

She laughed back at him, the joyous sound rippling from her throat and attracting a few curious stares. "I would indeed, sir."

Down the street they wandered, arm in arm, her parasol bobbing gaily over her head, a playful breeze tugging at her bright hair.

"What a milksop that Finster is!" Devlin said, shaking his head. "I can't countenance your letting him court you. I am a much better catch."

"The man did not court me, as I told all of you just minutes ago." She sighed. "I am ever so glad Reverend Johnston was along with us today. Now he will tell Henrietta, and she will make certain everyone knows Finster is not my suitor."

"Greedy little squirrel, isn't he?" Devlin added.

"The man is a repulsive toad. I shall remain unwed till my dying day, and be thankful for it, if that is the best I am offered."

"Why settle for codfish, when you can have oysters, duchess?" Devlin suggested with a wag of his brow. "I stand ready to serve you, and serve you well indeed—any time you decide to grace my bed."

She declined his offer with a shake of her head and a dry smile. "I'm not that hungry, thank you. And I detest oysters."

"Tastes can change," he countered smoothly. He gallantly steered her around a ladder which was propped against the front of a leather shop. "Eden, I think Finster may be behind all of your financial problems," he said, turning their talk back to the accountant. "Something about him strikes me wrong, and I don't think Tilton went running to him merely on the assumption that you and Finny were engaged. There is more to it, I'm sure."

"Like the two of them being in league with each other from the outset? And Finster courting me more to get his grubby hands on the business than for any love of me?" she asked wryly.

He slanted her a solemn look. "Aye. I'm sorry if that hurts your feelings, but—"

"Oh, don't gnash your teeth over it, Devlin. 'Tis not as if I didn't wonder about it many times myself. Not the part about Tilton and Finster being aligned, of course," she clarified. "The reason behind Finster's attentions. I'm just glad it's over and done with."

"It may not be yet."

"Meaning?"

"Meaning that I do not believe Finster will give up hope of owning the warehouse that easily. I expect we'll be hearing more from him."

"Gad!" she cursed. "You don't think he'll still attempt to court me, do you?"

Devlin shrugged. "Perhaps. Or maybe he'll look for other ways to ruin your business, hoping you will then be forced to turn to him for another loan. Failing that, he might resort to nastier measures."

"Such as?"

"Threats. Physical harm. Destroying your property or your credibility, or both."

"Oh, I can't believe he'd go that far," she argued. "He's a mean little weasel, but surely he would not risk darkening his own reputation merely to get back at me, or to gain my business."

"No, he'd undoubtedly hire someone else, like Tilton, to do his dirty work for him and catch none of the blame himself," Devlin hastened to point out. "Also, if he's smart, he'll try to shift the fault onto some other likely party, someone he deems a threat to him and his plans."

"Someone like you," she guessed. "Oh, Devlin, I'm beginning to think you have gotten the worst of our bargain."

Her concern was touching, but he couldn't let her burden herself unnecessarily. "No need to fret, fair lady. I've butted heads with far worse than Finster in my day, and am more than capable of taking care of myself— and you. However, 'twould be to our benefit to see that Finster continues to underestimate us. If he considers me a brutish dolt, let him keep on thinking so."

Eden nodded. "And if he considers me a silly old maid, with her head in the clouds and not a lick of sense, then all the better for us. Am I catching your meaning correctly, Devlin?"

He grinned down at her. "For someone who can't add two plus two, you are a very smart lady, Eden Winters."

She chuckled. "From you, I will accept that as a compliment, but the credit really goes to my mother."

"Partly," he agreed. "You do take after her."

Their wandering had taken them down by the docks after all. "Perhaps we ought to look in at the warehouse and see how Nate and the lads are bearing up under Tilton's supervision," Devlin mused.

Before they could act on his suggestion, a voice called out his name. "Kane! Over here!"

Turning, they scanned the crowds and finally spotted a man waving to them from outside a nearby eatery. He was a handsome young fellow, though dressed rather garishly in a brightly patterned calico shirt, with several large rings flashing on his fingers.

"Who is that?" Eden whispered, instinctively sidling closer to Devlin.

"That, my dear, is the one and only 'Calico Jack' Rackham," Devlin informed her with droll humor. "Just our luck to encounter him. Not that he's such a bad sort, as pirates go. 'Tis just that he no doubt wishes to bore me with exaggerated tales of his latest escapades. He's a fair brigand, but a notorious braggart."

By now Jack had caught up with them and was urging Devlin along with a hearty clap on the shoulder— dragging Eden with them, as she dared not let loose of Devlin's arm. "Come join me in a mug or two, Kane. I'd heard the *Gai Mer* was in port, but no one could tell me where you'd gone off to." Jack glanced to Devlin's other side, winking lewdly at Eden. "Now I see why you've been makin' yourself so scarce."

As it turned out, Calico Jack was not alone. Awaiting them at the outdoor table was a pretty young lass with whom Eden was previously acquainted. Whether Anne Bonny or Eden was more surprised to see the other was anyone's guess. "Eden Winters! Why, of all the people I'd least expect to see traversing the docks!"

"Oh, you two already know each other?" Jack put in. "Good." Then, as Devlin politely held Eden's chair for her, Jack proceeded to ignore the women altogether, content to bend Devlin's ear.

"Hello, Anne," Eden greeted her. "How have you been? I've not seen you at church for a while."

"And not likely to any time soon, either," Anne replied tartly. "Bunch o' goodies who wouldn't help a body in need if their lives depended on it! I'm shocked no end that you're willing to be seen talking to me."

"Oh, surely not!" Eden protested, though there was more truth than fiction to Anne's claim. The girl had always been wild, and when she had recently defied her rich father's wishes and married a common sailor, he had promptly cut Anne off without a farthing to her name. Whereupon, it was rumored, her sailor had slipped away to sea, leaving poor Anne behind to handle the consequences of her rash actions alone.

Apparently, Anne was not spending her days mourning the loss of her bridegroom, nor trying overmuch to get back into her father's good graces. If the bright color in her cheeks and the determined glint in her eyes was any indication, the girl was smitten with Calico Jack, and bound to see her affections returned.

"What are you doing roaming the dockside? You haven't taken up the trade, have you?" Anne asked with a toothy grin.

Eden almost sputtered, doubly so when she felt Devlin's hand tighten over her knee, sending a sensual tingle through her. She slid a glance in his direction, to find him smiling broadly at her. The infernal idiot! Trying not to draw too much attention to herself, she brushed at his hand as she would an insect. He simply shook his head at her, from which she determined that he was taking full advantage of the fact that they had to maintain contact, and had chosen this means to do it.

To Anne Bonny, Eden replied as calmly as she could, "I doubt I would make a credible doxy. As to my reason for being here, Captain Kane and I were on our way to my warehouse."

"Oh." The young woman gave a negligent shrug. "I'd forgotten you owned that property." In the blink of an eye, she changed course and asked, "Is it true that you are going to marry that smug little wart of a moneylender?"

Eden could scarcely believe her ears! However, Anne had never been noted for diplomacy. "If you are referring to Dudley Finster, no. I am not going to marry him, no matter what the man might be saying to the contrary."

"Good. You'd do much better with this one." Anne motioned toward Devlin. "He's a damned sight better-looking, for one thing, and I'd wager he's a hell of a lot more virile."

Eden didn't need to look to know that Devlin wore a gloating smirk. She could feel it echoing between them like a living thing. Neither did she require a looking glass to know her face had turned as red as a boiled lobster.

"Now me," Anne continued, blithely unaware of Eden's discomfort, "I'm getting set to weigh anchor with Jackie here. We're gonna sail the seas together and see the world."

Eden didn't know what to say. "Anne, are you serious?" At the woman's nod, she hesitantly offered counsel, unsolicited though it was. "Hadn't you better think this through more carefully, dear? What will your father say?"

"My *father* wouldn't spit on me if my hair was on fire, and that's the bare truth of it. You know it as well as I do. The entire town knows how he's thrown me out to starve. At least Jackie pays me some mind. He's my passage out of this stinking hole, and I'd be a fool to let him go." Anne slid closer and winked conspiratorially. "Besides, he's a handsome jackal, ain't he? And a regular devil betwixt the sheets, if you take my meaning."

At long last, Devlin took pity on Eden and made their excuses. With her face aflame, she bid Anne farewell.

"You too, honey," Anne called out loudly. "And you stick with that dashing rogue of yours. He'll have you out of those stiff old stays before you know what hit you. And I'm willin' to bet you won't regret it, either."

"I already do." Eden groaned, pulling her parasol down to cover her face and nearly tripping.

"But, *honey*," Devlin mimicked on a husky laugh, "how could you? After all, I'm such a dashing, virile rogue!"

She glared at him from beneath three inches of pink parasol fringe and snarled, "If you don't want to be an empty suit of clothes standing in the middle of the street, you'll shut your miserable mouth this instant!"

Chapter 11

The next few days were only slightly more peaceful than the previous three. Though Jane now knew of Devlin's presence in her home, it was still something of a trial to keep that startling fact from Dora, or anyone else who might chance to visit. And with the news of Jane's miraculous recovery, well-wishers were arriving in droves.

To add to the confusion, there was Zeus to take into account. While Devlin swore the big bird was trained to obedience, Eden was not so easily convinced, most especially when she considered who had educated the falcon. She was simply waiting to see which of the two of them—Devlin or Zeus—would create the most havoc.

In order to escape the deluge of visitors in the house, and gain a bit more privacy, Devlin and Eden spent a good deal of time at the warehouse. There, they concentrated their efforts on finding discrepancies in the accounts which they might use as legal proof against Tilton and Finster. The work was tedious, with no results, which was vastly disappointing to Eden. She would have liked, if only for her own satisfaction, to have been able to prove that Tilton had been stealing from the warehouse for the past three years, and that

Finster had somehow benefited from her failing business. For she doubted she'd ever see the return of one stolen pence.

After three days of fruitless searching through past accounts, Eden threw up her hands in despair. "I give up! If I keep at this much longer, I swear I'll go blind! Or mad! Or both! If I were any good at figuring, I might see some sense in it, but—"

"Sweetling, if you were any good at figuring, you wouldn't be in this mess to begin with," Devlin put in bluntly.

Eden graced him with a sour smile. "Why, how gallantly phrased, Captain. And might I remind you that you seem to be faring just as badly? I thought pirates were supposed to be able to tally their stolen booty with the utmost ease and precision. What's wrong, Devlin? Did you run out of toes and fingers upon which to count?"

He tweaked the end of her nose. "Fear not, my beauty. I've not lost my talent with numbers. The problem is that I do most of my own tabulating in my head, where no one can tamper with the figures. I'm not accustomed to dealing with ledgers, where sums can be manipulated to appear correct when they are not. Since you can find no inconsistencies, 'tis my guess that Tilton, most likely with Finster tutoring him, has only registered the figures he wanted you to see. In doing so, the accounts appear to balance perfectly with the receipts and expenses."

"So what do we do now?"

"I suppose the next move would be to fire Tilton before he can cause any more harm. He doesn't seem to be leading us toward a solution, as I'd hoped he would once he was aware that you might catch onto his game."

"Did you honestly think he was going to confess all,

Devlin?" Eden asked with an arched brow. "Merely on the suspicion that I could stumble across the truth?"

He shrugged. "He might have. For that matter, he still could, given the proper incentive."

"Such as?" she prompted.

"A few imaginative threats might do the trick, and have him squealing for mercy and naming Finster as his accomplice. Or a chance meeting in a dark alleyway with a few of my more bloodthirsty mates. They wouldn't necessarily need to hurt him too badly. A couple of broken bones might make him willing to talk."

Eden gave a delicate shudder. "Why don't we simply dismiss him first, and see what happens then? As much as I dislike the man and what he has done, I can't see how roughing him up will regain my losses. I'll simply have to content myself with preventing further failure of the business."

"Are you sure, Eden?" Devlin questioned. "The man might have hidden the money somewhere, in which case you could see some of it returned to you. For all we know, he might be banking it."

Eden snorted. "Where? The only banking institution in Charles Town belongs to Dudley Finster and his father, and if that is where Tilton has put it, you can rest assured 'twill never be found by either of us. You could probably drag Tilton into Finster's office by his ear, written confession in hand, and Dudley would deny all knowledge of wrong doing, or of any such account, if one exists."

"All right, we'll do it your way for now, since you are bent on being squeamish. Dismiss Tilton, and we'll watch to see what their next move will be. But I can't help thinking you're wasting a fine opportunity to throttle the bastard. And asking for more trouble in the bargain."

"Perhaps," she agreed. "But as you pointed out at the start, 'tisn't merely Tilton we want to net. If Finster is the mastermind, I want him squarely caught. I don't want him to catch wind of this and cover his tracks before we can collect the proof we need against him."

Devlin grinned. "Again you surprise me, duchess. You may not have a head for figures, but you've a fine mind for battle tactics." He gave an exaggerated sigh. "Ah, wench, what a pair we would make, if only you were a man! Then I could take you sailing with me, and we'd really put your brain to good use."

"A shame, to be sure, Captain. Were I a man, there are a great many things I could do that I cannot do now. I could travel the world at will, and most likely run this company more efficiently without everyone trying to cheat me out of it. Moreover," she added with a wry smile, "I wouldn't have Dudley Finster attempting to court me, or you sniffing at my skirts, would I? Indeed, life would be so much simpler, had I been born a man."

Black eyes glittered into hers as he conceded the verbal contest to her. *"Touché!* You have shed light on my erroneous thinking. Upon further reflection, I can see that 'tis much better that you are a lass. For both of us."

With that, he bent and placed his arms on either side of the chair in which she sat, effectively trapping her there. Then, ever so slowly, as if to tantalize her with anticipation of his touch, he leaned forward until their lips were a mere whisper apart. "Have you been wondering when I would repay you for calling me other than Devlin? I haven't forgotten, little one. Oh, no! Never think that I have. I've simply been biding my time, letting you dwell upon that moment when I would collect my due, savoring the thought of it in my mind. Have you been doing so as well, my sweet? Dreaming of it, perhaps, while you lie in your virginal bed with just one thin wall separating us? I've heard your restless stirrings in the night, you know."

He didn't give her time to deny it, but brought his lips over hers in a warm caress, a sliding of flesh upon

flesh, until her mouth trembled in invitation beneath
his. His teeth nibbled at her lips, his tongue laving
them, tasting her, sucking at them until her lips parted
beneath his. Then his tongue intruded to parry with hers
in a heated duel that sent the blood spinning to her
brain.

Eden's breath caught in her chest, crowding her
thumping heart. Her limbs went hot and weak, her body
tingling to life as it seemed to only when Devlin
touched her. She felt a strange need to be closer to him,
a yearning so strong that it overcame her natural inhi-
bitions. Almost of their own accord, her arms rose to
twine about his neck, her fingers sifting through the
tawny hair at his nape, drawing him nearer, until the
male scent of him filled her head. Through the haze
that clouded her thinking, she registered his touch as his
hand closed over her ribs, searing her skin through the
fabric of her dress. Her surprised gasp served only to
seal his lips more tightly to hers, his tongue delving
deeper into the sweet, hot recesses of her mouth, his
mouth sipping at hers like a bee for nectar.

Slowly, inexorably, his fingers worked their way upward, until they rested against the outer slope of her
right breast. In promise or threat, Eden wasn't sure
which. Nor did she care. It was she who completed the
touch, twisting until her breast fit to the curve of his
palm, nestling within his long, strong fingers like a
fragile flower turning its head toward the sunlight.

Devlin groaned, a low growl deep in his throat. The
weight of her full, firm breast in his hand was an almost unbearable pleasure, even through all the cloth
that separated their flesh from actual contact. How long
had it been since he'd touched a woman this way?
Weeks? Months? It was nearly more than he could
stand, and it took all his willpower not to rip her
clothes from her back and toss her to the floor, then and

there, so hotly was his blood thrumming, demanding release for his tormented body.

Though he knew he was tempting fate, still he could not make himself release her just yet, not when she was offering herself to him so sweetly, so openly. His thumb strayed further, barely skimming across the peak of her breast. The hidden nipple budded immediately, cresting within his palm like a wave.

Now it was she who moaned with burgeoning passion, pressing her breast forward, rubbing against his yearning flesh like a feline wanting to be stroked. Catching the nub between finger and thumb, he tugged gently at it, imagining his lips replacing his fingers, his tongue sleek against her silken breast, envisioning its texture and color, the contrast against his darker flesh.

A breathless whimper escaped her lips, a quiver rippling through her, and Devlin silently swore he had never before felt so powerful, so masterful—so proud. She squirmed slightly, as if in need, yet not truly knowing what it was she sought, and Devlin was lost to reason. It mattered not that they were in her office at the warehouse, that the door was unlocked, or that anyone could walk in on them at any moment. He had to have her. Here. Now. Before his next breath. Before he had time to think about what he was doing—before she had time to realize what they were doing.

Eden was caught up in a cloud, a delightful mist of the most marvelous sensations she'd ever experienced, or had ever hoped to experience in this lifetime. Pure, raw feelings were tumbling through her, buffeting her like ocean waves, relentlessly pushing her toward an unknown shore.

Suddenly, without warning, the bell over the office door clanged, announcing an intruder and bringing both of them to their senses. Abruptly, as if they'd been doused with a bucket of icy water, they sprang apart—Eden's face now aglow not with passion but with guilt and embarrassment. Instantly, Devlin sought to reestablish contact, reaching out to grab her arm as he felt himself begin to fade from view.

Thankfully, the interior of the small room was dimly lit. Tilton appeared to notice nothing more amiss than his spinster employer in very intimate contact with the pirate captain. The foreman's gaze traveled from one to the other, his eyes narrowing as he stared hard at Eden's flushed features and moist, kiss-swollen lips. Eden could almost hear the man planning to run to Finster at the first opportunity, spreading tales of her most recent misbehavior.

Tilton's apology and the knowing smirk that curled his lips were at odds as he said, "Beggin' your pardon, Miss Winters. If I'd have known I was about to walk in on such a cozy scene, I would have knocked first."

Perhaps the knowledge that she was going to dismiss him gave Eden's reply an added dose of venom. Her ire was at its peak, her hackles up, and Tilton's impertinence was all she needed to push her patience past its limits. Extending her hand toward him, palm up, she demanded frostily, "Turn in your warehouse keys, Mr. Tilton. All of them. As of this minute, you have a quarter hour to collect anything which might belong to you and get off this property. I never want to see you here again. Your services are no longer required."

For several stunned seconds, the man stared in dumb disbelief. Then he frowned, his eyes squinting at her in warning. "Now just hold on there, missy. Mayhap you'd better consider what you're doing. You can't dismiss me just like that." He leaned forward, snapping his fingers before her nose. "I've given more time and effort to running this company than you can begin to know. Why, I've worked myself ragged trying to save this place for you and your ma. And this is the thanks I get?"

"That and whatever pay you have coming to you,"

Eden said, refusing to be intimidated by such a worthless worm. Glaring back at him, she longed to tell him all she truly knew, and what more she suspected. Such as how he'd been lining his pockets at her expense, and deliberately trying to ruin her business. Somehow, she held her tongue, knowing now was not the time to spill the beans from that particular pot. "I'll also have all the monies you have collected this morning on behalf of the warehouse, Mr. Tilton. And the receipts for the logbook, if you please." Consulting her pendant watch, which hung suspended at her waistband from her father's gold watch chain, she told him, "By my calculations, you now have twelve minutes. If you have not left the premises by that time, I will have you forcibly removed."

"At the point of my sword," Devlin put in for good measure, noting the malevolent gleam in Tilton's eyes, and the way the man leaned toward Eden as if he wanted to launch himself at her.

Under Devlin's Satan-black gaze, Tilton backed down, though not without a final word of warning. "This won't be the end of it, Miss High-and-Mighty Winters." Digging into his pockets, he threw a crumpled wad of hand-written receipts and money onto her desktop. Next, the company keys came clanking, tossed with such force that they skittered off the edge of the desk onto the floor, dragging coins and papers with them. "You haven't heard the last of me, not by a long shot! You'll regret this day for years to come. And you'll regret putting in with this passel o' pirates. Mark my words, girl. There'll come a day when you'll beg to have me back here running this place for you, but my help won't come so cheap then."

He stormed out of the office before Eden could think to tally his final pay, leaving her limp from their heated exchange and his lingering threats. While she was more than justified in firing Tilton, she still wasn't accustomed to standing toe-to-toe and nose-to-nose with a man in verbal altercation, despite the practice she'd had of late with Finster and Devlin. It left her distinctly shaken, even as she felt a glimmer of pride expanding within her chest.

"Now then." Devlin chuckled, recalling her attention to him. "Doesn't that warm the cockles of your heart, seeing old Tilton dash off with his tail tucked betwixt his legs?"

She frowned up at him. "Devlin, he didn't seem particularly cowed to me," she hastened to point out. "In fact, he seemed extremely angry and vengeful. And he practically promised to make future trouble for me."

Devlin gave an unconcerned shrug. "Don't fret your pretty head, duchess. If 'tis trouble he wants, I'll be glad to see he gets it. Meanwhile, we'll bide our time."

"And do what until then?"

The devilishly wicked look he gave her, with those gleaming dark eyes and that seductive smile, should have singed the laces on her chemise. "Where is your imagination, wench?" he teased. "By the stars, I swear I must have found my way to Charles Town simply to save you from withering away from sheer boredom. To rescue you from yourself, and the likes of Finster, who would have shriveled your soul and wrung you dry of all life. Sweetling, when are you going to realize that there is more to living than simply existing from day to day, always doing what others expect of you, never veering from the path of righteousness? Let down your hair a bit, love. Shake loose of those stiff stays, and taste the world as it was meant to be tasted. Glory in it while you may."

"And go to hell in a hand basket?" she countered, giving him look for look, trying to resist the temptation in his twinkling eyes, the promise of passion lurking beyond his teasing words. "Should I sell my soul to the Devil for a few minutes' pleasure?"

"Not your soul, Eden. Your heart, your lovely body, the sweet essence of yourself. Freely given, never sold. And to no other devil but me."

"And what would you give me in return, Devlin? Other than a broken heart, a body no longer pure, and my reputation in tatters?"

He could not promise her what he knew she longed to hear, and he refused to lie to her, yet there were some things he could pledge in good faith. "I would teach you desire, and ecstasy, as can only be shared between a man and a woman. I would offer you freedom from the confines of the tiny cage into which society has locked you. I would give you passion beyond your wildest imaginings, and a treasure trove of memories to last all your days."

A sad, regretful smile etched her lips. "I rather think you would bring me great sorrow, Devlin, should I ever take a bite of this tempting apple you offer me."

"Mayhap," he conceded quietly, nodding, "but I could also bring you great joy, Eden. 'Tis for you to decide if the prize be worth the risk."

Devlin was not used to taking no for an answer. Thus, he set out to change Eden's mind, through fair means or outright trickery, whichever worked faster or better. He began by deluging her with gifts. He bought her a new parasol, which she adored at first sight. Still, he practically had to beg her to keep it, for she insisted that ladies never accepted articles of clothing from gentlemen.

"Ah, but there you have it," he informed her with a victorious smile. "I am no gentleman, so you needn't worry. Moreover, I fail to see how a parasol can be considered clothing, since you but carry the thing, you do not wear it."

He used the same argument when he presented her with a beautiful silk fan, intricately gilded with pure gold. "Oh, but Devlin," she moaned, unable to tear her hungering eyes from the magnificent gift, "'tis far too expensive."

Fearing that she would further object if she knew it had cost him nothing, that it was part of his booty from one of his raids, he offered instead, "Eden, take a lesson from the Trojans, and learn not to look a gift horse in the mouth, will you?"

"Ah, but in this case, perhaps I should question your motives," she said. "What do you expect in return for such an extravagant gesture?"

"What would you give me? Your sweet body lying naked next to mine? Passionate kisses in the dark?"

When she started to hand the fan back to him with a frown, he relented. "I'll settle for a smile to replace the glower you are about to bestow upon me. Nothing more, at least for the moment."

She reconsidered, obviously reluctant to part with her fine treasure. "A smile, then. And something more."

His hopes rose, only to be quickly dashed again as she added with an impish grin, "I shall teach you proper manners. For a start, you may begin by removing your feet from the sofa table. If you must prop them upon something, please use the hassock."

She continued to instruct him in gentlemanly behavior, and he continued to bring her gifts. Brightly colored hair ribbons and a garland of flowers for her hair. "Though your glorious mane needs little enhancement," he told her, flattering her yet again. He was continually complimenting her hair, her eyes, even her nose, which Eden knew was not among her best features. Still, his pretty praise did turn her head, though not enough to make her leap into his arms and immediately forfeit her maidenhood.

His most unique gift was a large copper bathing tub,

ornately scrolled, with a raised headrest. Even Jane was taken aback, considering it too intimate a gesture.

Devlin promptly brushed the women's objections aside. "I know not how long I'll be required to stay here, and that old tin washtub you possess is far too cramped for my tastes. If you wish me to remain clean and presentable, then please allow me to do so in comfort. Of course, 'tis for your use also, and will remain yours when I am gone."

But once Eden had accepted his gift, and tendered her thanks, he could not keep from teasing. "I shall envision you in the tub, you know, all sleek and bare and wet, the water softly caressing every sweet curve of your body," he whispered privately, his flashing dark eyes traversing the clothed length of her. "Think of me when you bathe in it, pet. Imagine my hands replacing the water, stroking your dewy, flushed flesh."

"I will not!" she claimed, though she feared she would now do just that.

He gave her a wink and that outrageously roguish grin. "Then think of me when I use it. Picture me hot and naked and longing for your touch. Better yet, imagine the two of us enjoying it together, both immersed in warm water, our limbs tangled and our skin slippery with soap, my body sliding sensuously against yours."

Eden's cheeks burned, and she could not meet his gaze. "Please cease such ridiculous prattle, Devlin. You tempt only yourself with such talk."

"Do I?" he countered with a knowing smirk. "I sincerely hope not, duchess."

Chapter 12

*H*aving never kept company with a gentleman, and having gained a reputation as a circumspect unwed female, Eden had never before encountered any public censure, as she did now whenever she was seen out and about upon Devlin's arm. Not that she was snubbed outright by most of her acquaintances, but they stood their distance, both curious and watchful of her and Devlin, as if reserving judgment upon them. Such behavior reflected the current attitude toward pirates in general these days, more than any particular prejudice toward Devlin himself. Still, it was disconcerting to Eden to be met with speculative looks rather than pleasant greetings, and concerned frowns in place of friendly, open smiles.

Also, the townsfolk seemed confused that Eden should suddenly adopt a change of feathers, when they were so accustomed to her as an unassuming, somewhat dowdy spinster. Indeed, Eden had changed almost overnight from a quiet little mouse into a confident young lady. Though she'd always been pleasant and polite, now it was not uncommon to see a smile on her face, or to hear her laugh like a carefree child. Her walk seemed to have a more lively spring to it, her posture straight and proud alongside Captain Kane's superior height. While she dressed no differently than before, she was styling her hair more attractively, frequently abandoning the stiff bun in favor of letting her tresses flow long and loose down her back. There was a new twinkle in her blue-green eyes, and an added bloom to her cheeks. From a plain little mudhen there had emerged a comely woman no one had ever imagined existed. In large part, the change was due to Devlin's continued praise and attention.

The residents and businessmen of Charles Town received yet another shock when Eden, in company with Devlin, began visiting places she would never have entered before. On one such occasion, she walked right into a local brewery without so much as the bat of an eyelash, and waited as the pirate captain placed an order for five kegs of ale. On another, she actually sauntered through a dockside tavern, as if she did so every day, and took a seat at one of the tables. There she remained, as pretty as you please, until Devlin had concluded his conversation with another sea captain. It became customary that wherever Devlin Kane was to be seen, Eden was found at his side, be it at the sailmaker's, the smith shop, the shipyards, or any of the more common merchant establishments.

Only Devlin and Eden knew the real reason for her constant attendance upon him in such unusual quarters—or how embarrassing it was for her at times. However, it was the only way she could uphold her end of their bargain and allow Devlin, with full competence and visibility, to go about his normal business and to market his pirated merchandise. Many a time, when she would have balked, she needed only to remind herself how willingly he had set himself to the task of rescuing her warehouse.

Besides, as the days wore on, she was intrigued to be gaining a startling insight into a rougher, darker side of

life to which she would never have been privy otherwise. Truth be told, she was both fascinated and re-
pelled by much she learned at Devlin's side.

Even should she have been allowed in such places,
without Devlin's presence she would never have dared
to go. With him, however, she felt utterly safe. His tall
frame and broad shoulders, not to mention the fire that
seemed to spark from his black eyes, were enough to
intimidate anyone who would have approached her with
ill intent. As ridiculous as it was, she actually felt cher-
ished by this brawny pirate, precious and protected—a
feeling she hadn't experienced since her father's
death—and it was marvelous.

Still and all, when the two of them realized that the
average citizenry did not wholly approve of her association with him, it became apparent that something more
must be done. "Papa worked long and hard to build his
company, and I have vowed to maintain his high stan-
dards now that he is gone," Eden said. "We cannot allow respect for the family or the firm to diminish. I'll
not tarnish Papa's memory, or my own reputation."

It was Devlin who came up with a solution. "'Tis because I am a pirate, you say?" he mused, as they discussed the problem over dinner one evening. "Then
methinks I must improve my image to these people, lest
your reputation suffer for it, Eden. Why not tell them
that I am your new business partner? Surely, if they
think me engaged in a legitimate venture, they will
view me more kindly, and you in turn. And who is to
claim otherwise, now that you have dismissed Tilton?"

Eden looked dismayed. "Yet another lie, Devlin?
Heaven knows, I shall soon become so adept at deceit,
I'll be hard-put to tell the truth, or to decipher the dif-
ference betwixt the two."

"Need it be a lie, daughter?" Jane put in calmly. "If
'twould bother your conscience so, why not make it
fact? I'd not object, so long as Devlin pledges not to

sell his interest to anyone else without our prior approval, or to do anything that would be a detriment to the company. Would that be satisfactory to both of you?"

"Aye." Devlin nodded. "You but set the amount, and I'll meet it."

Still Eden frowned, foreseeing pitfalls in her mother's suggestion. "And what happens when Devlin's business in Charles Town is at an end, Mama? What if he should regain his normal sense of being soon and decide to go on about his brigandry? Do we then lay claim to a partnership with a criminal? I vow business would take a turn for the worse then, for sure, more so than with Tilton and Finster executing our downfall."

Devlin arched a golden brow in Eden's direction. "Criminal, am I? And what, pray tell, is Finster, if not painted with a blacker brush? At least I go about my piracy openly, for all to see."

"How so, when it is impossible for others to discern you?" she argued, not backing down. "And you must admit that I have plausible cause for concern. Pray, what is to happen to your portion of the business when you leave?"

"You could always hold it for me, and set aside my part of the earnings until next I make port in Charles Town. Or, if it would make you more comfortable to regain full ownership at that time, you can buy my share back again before I sail."

"What if, God forbid, we have even worse financial reversals in the meanwhile, are forced to spend those monies you would pay us now, and cannot remit it to you when the proper time comes?" she persisted stubbornly.

Devlin heaved an exasperated sigh and rolled his expressive black eyes. Then his gaze centered on her face, his white teeth flashing in a roguish grin. "Don't get your shift a-twist in knots over it, Eden," he counseled with a dry chuckle. " 'Twill only make you more contrary than you already are. At any rate, you are forgetting that I promised to look after the warehouse for you until I sail again. Trust me to see that you do not go to the poorhouse in a tumbrel, will you, please?"

Thus it was that Devlin became part owner in the warehouse, and was henceforth introduced as Eden's business partner, though in actuality he was more Jane's partner than Eden's, at least legally. Even Eden was amazed at what an immediate reversal the general populace executed, tradesmen and townsfolk alike extending polite smiles and a fair dose of congeniality toward their newest fellow merchantman.

A few even invited him into their homes, now that he was reputably employed, and Eden was quick to note that those who asked him to dine invariably had homely daughters or unwed nieces abiding beneath their roofs. She couldn't decide whether to laugh or be offended, for it was as if they were saying, *"Come look my daughter over, sir. If you can cast your sights on Eden Winters, then surely you will be more pleased with our offering."*

It salved her wounded vanity that Devlin had to refuse their invitations, unless they also included her, for he was incapable of doing so without her, unless he wanted to attend as a phantom. Also, to his credit, Devlin appeared not to have any desire for female companionship other than hers, giving everyone the distinct impression that he was content with the woman he had and could not be tempted from her side. False impression or not, it bolstered Eden's feminine pride no end, especially since all of Charles Town had previously considered her a dowdy. And if he were at all sincere, it also spoke well of Devlin's loyalty.

When she mentioned this to him in passing, trying not to put much weight behind her words for fear of hearing him declare that the only reason he was true to her was that it was impossible to have a relationship with anyone else, he laughed. "What sort of fickle fellow do you take me for, lass? Aye, I'll not deny dallying where my nose has led in the past, but I am loath to veer from your scent, it seems. There is something about you which lures me, wench, that challenges me to see you yield."

"And should I do so, you would then be off to greener pastures, I suppose. So fast you'd leave naught behind but a trail of dust!" Her pert nose rose by several inches.

To her surprise, and his own, he shook his head. "Mayhap, but I think not so quickly. Nay, methinks 'twould take longer than that to have my fill of you, my beauty, for you are a rare treasure. A pearl which promises to glow ever brighter with the polishing."

"Pretty phrases, but rendered next to nothing since they are uttered with the sole purpose of seducing me, a feat you'll not accomplish, pirate," she countered haughtily, determined not to let his smooth tongue entice her to grief. Yet, even as she once more denied him, her heart ached painfully within her breast, yearning for something she could never have—his undying love.

"I suppose it means nothing that I care for you more than I have any other woman?" It amazed Devlin to find he truly meant the words, that he really did care what she felt for him, what she thought of him.

"It matters, Devlin. It matters a great deal. But not enough to sully myself for pleasures which could be gone with the next tide. I will not sacrifice my pride merely to grant you another notch on your bedpost."

"I never kiss and tell, milady. Nor do I keep a tally of my lovers on my bedpost."

"No doubt your mattress would be resting upon the floor if you did, the bedpost having been whittled away to nothing!" Her beautiful eyes glared up at him.

"However, notches or not, I will not be added to your list of lovers."

"Keep telling yourself that, Eden, if you must. But you are fooling no one except yourself," he told her with a taunting smile. "You will succumb, and revel in your surrender."

Eden was luxuriating in the new brass tub, up to her neck in hot water and enjoying every blessed moment of it. As tall as she was, the old washtub had been a bit short for her, and it was delightful to be able to stretch out full-length, even though this tub took half again as many bucketsful of heated water to fill it. She was warm, drowsy, and content, not at all concerned about being interrupted in her bath, since her mother was in bed, and Devlin was out carousing with his mates and would not return until late.

Or so she assumed, until a deep voice sounded softly near her ear. "God, Eden! You're even more lovely than I'd guessed."

Startled, Eden's eyes flew open to find Devlin kneeling beside the tub, his gaze avidly perusing her sleek body, which was fully exposed beneath the crystal-clear water. Her first reaction was to sit upright, which only served to bring her breasts bobbing above the waterline, water cascading from them in gleaming sheets. Realizing her mistake, she immediately hunched down again, drawing her legs up toward her torso, attempting to shield her most intimate parts with them, while she covered her breasts with folded arms.

"Get out of here!" she squeaked, absolutely mortified.

"But I'm so enjoying the view," he retorted, unrepentant. He dangled the wash cloth before her, just out of her reach. "Shall I scrub your back for you? Mayhap lather those delicate toes? Those long legs of yours? Those pert pink breasts you are trying so desperately to hide? Shall I pull the pins from your hair and wash your burnished tresses?" He put words to action, and her carelessly upswept hair tumbled down over her shoulders, the ends floating brightly in the water.

"You're supposed to be out drinking with your crew!" she accused in a shaky voice, near tears at being caught in such an awkward position. "You should be getting drunk and raising Cain, and such. You're not supposed to be home yet."

He laughed softly. "But I am home, and just now I am becoming very drunk, indeed. On your beauty. Furthermore, there are certain parts of Kane, Devlin Kane, which are definitely being raised at this moment. Would you care to have me show you, sweetling? Mayhap I could join you in your bath and fulfill at least one of my fantasies—and yours?"

"Try it, and I'll scream the shingles off the roof!" she grated through clenched teeth. "Then you'll see just how true Mama's aim can be!"

He continued to grin at her, his hand stealing out to lift the hair from the shoulder nearest him. Baring her moist flesh, he planted a hot kiss at the arch of her neck, sending gooseflesh skittering from Eden's scalp to her toes. "The risk might be worth it, love."

His lips caressed a burning path to the upper curve of her breast, that portion not covered by her quivering hands, and Eden suddenly forgot how to breathe.

In a strangled voice, she gasped, "Don't!"

His fingers were gently prying hers away, to afford him better access, when Jane called out from the top of the stairs. "Eden, dear? When you've finished with your bath, would you please bring a cup of warm milk up to me? For some reason, I simply cannot get to sleep this evening."

Devlin muttered a curse. Eden stared back at him, nearly spellbound by the desire reflecting in his sin-black eyes. "Answer her!" he hissed.

"Uh . . . yes, Mama!" she stammered loudly. "I'll be right up with it. Straightaway."

He rewarded her, and himself, with a swift, hard kiss to her lips, then stood and raked impatient fingers through his hair. "I'll keep trying, duchess," he promised with a rueful smile. "You won't always have your mother near to preserve your virtue."

Eden was not the only one who showed signs of physical improvement lately. Jane was almost aglow with renewed health. The change was dramatic. Perhaps it was because she could move about normally, but her complexion was far less pallid now, her body more firm with each passing day. Though still peppered with strands of gray, her hair had regained its former luster. There was new life in her face, a gleam of interest in her eyes. She appeared ten years younger.

Here was yet another reason to be grateful for Devlin, for not only had he been responsible for the fright that had forced Jane to her feet once more, but his presence, and all the mystery and secrecy involved in it, seemed to intrigue her greatly. After three long years, Jane seemed to have accepted her husband's passing at last, and was finding a new level of peace within herself. No longer did she simply watch as life went on around her, a shadow of her former self. Now she chose to participate, to involve herself in the scheme of things.

There was plenty of opportunity for that these days. Jane, Eden, Devlin, and Nate often held evening conferences once Dora had retired to her quarters. They discussed problems at the warehouse and possible solutions for them. In the process, Eden and Jane came to know Devlin's quartermaster fairly well.

Though Eden thought the older man as ill-bred as Devlin had been when he'd first come into their house, she abided Nate. For a brigand, he was moderately considerate of ladies and made a halfhearted effort to curb his salty language in their presence, which was more than she had expected.

Jane, on the other hand, did not seem to find Nate in the least offensive. Soon she began taking pains with her dress and hair when she knew Nate was coming. Moreover, she appeared to bask in the man's awkward praise, obviously enjoying his company immensely. His witty remarks, off-color though they frequently were, brought a chuckle to her lips and a sparkle to her eyes.

For this, too, Eden was thankful. After years of mourning, Jane had discovered laughter again. Eden was less thrilled when Nate began appearing at the house more regularly for the specific purpose of visiting Jane—alone. More than once, Eden entered a room unannounced to find them seated unnecessarily close together on the divan, both looking slightly guilty, as if she'd nearly caught them in an embrace.

In turn, Jane was amazed and delighted at the transformation of her only child. Eden was evolving into the attractive, winsome daughter Jane had always hoped to see, bickering with Devlin at every turn, her timidity forgotten as she challenged the handsome pirate captain with outright impudence. She'd sprung from her shell, a bold new creature, so vibrant that Jane could scarcely believe the change in her. And amidst it all, there was never a dull moment, only endless surprises popping up at the oddest times.

To her dying day, Jane would never forget the afternoon Devlin washed his invisible clothing for the second time. For once, they had no company, and Dora had gone to visit a friend, at Jane's suggestion. Eden, Jane, and Devlin were alone in the house. On the excuse that someone might decide to come visiting and catch him in more detectable clothing, which he would then have to hurriedly discard, Devlin again chose to don a bed sheet to conceal his nakedness. Eden suspected he did so more to irritate her than for any other reason, but since he was modestly covered, and her mother was there to keep him on his best behavior, she ignored his taunting smile and kept her comments to herself.

They were all in the sitting room, Jane tatting lace and Eden sorting through the yarn which had made a tangle of her sewing bag. Devlin was lounging in a chair, regaling them with tales of his travels. None of them heard the back door open, and they were totally unaware of approaching footsteps until Dora suddenly appeared in the room.

"I'm back," she announced heartily, as the others looked up in surprise. "I brung a nice chunk o' venison back with me, to roast for dinner. Mary's man just bagged it this mornin', and there was too much for just the two of them, without some goin' to waste."

"How nice of them to share it," Jane answered weakly, deliberately keeping her gaze from the chair where Devlin sat. "But you needn't have rushed home so soon, Dora. 'Tis not so often you get to spend much time with your friend."

Dora shrugged. "Couldn't be helped, not if you want to eat afore midnight. And now I'm glad I did," she added, dividing a stern glare between the two ladies. "Which one o' you has been mucking about in my kitchen and slopped soapy water all over the floor? Why, to mind you, ye'd think I have nothin' better to do than to go around all day pickin' up after you."

As if to prove her point, her eyes lit on the sheet draped over a nearby chair. Two quick strides, and Dora had her hand on it. Another second, during which the other three held their collective breath, and she gave it a stout yank. Only Eden could see the way Devlin's eyes widened as the sheet pulled taut about him, a goodly amount of it trapped between him and the chair. When the cloth did not immediately come loose, Dora frowned, muttering, "Why'd you tuck this old thing into the cushions anyway? And in such a muddled knot?"

"Uh, leave it, Dora," Jane suggested breathlessly. "Captain Kane stopped by, and he had dirt on his britches. We covered the cushion to protect it from soiling." Once again, Eden was amazed at how smoothly her mother could lie when the situation warranted it.

Dora was nothing if not conscientious about her household duties, however, much to everyone's current dismay. "Well, he's gone now, and there's no sense leavin' the room cluttered." She gave the cloth another tug, and there was nothing for it but for Devlin to cooperate in the matter. With one hand on the arm of the chair, he levered himself slightly, enough for his weight to be lifted; with the other he unwound the sheet from about his body. Dora whisked it away, unknowingly exposing his nude body to Eden's view. With a satisfied grunt, Dora shuffled off, still grumbling to herself as she folded the sheet in her ample arms.

After one quick, unwitting glimpse, which was more than sufficient to give Eden a memorable image of Devlin's personal anatomy, she squeezed her eyes tightly shut. "Oh, my stars!" she wailed softly, hellfire licking at her cheeks as she raised shaking hands to cover her face. "My blessed stars! Mother! Do something!"

It was a rare occurrence which struck Jane Winters speechless, but this was one of them. For several long seconds, all she could do was stare at her daughter, then at the empty chair where Devlin still sat, if the dent in the cushion was a true indication. Though Jane could not see him herself, Eden's mortified reaction was clear evidence that she had seen more than a maiden should. For just a moment, knowing from those times when he was visible to her what a fine figure of a man he was, Jane wished she, too, could view what Eden had. Then, with a slight shake, she collected her senses. "Captain, kindly do cover yourself," she commanded softly.

Devlin sat with one hand inadequately covering his privates, and the other cupped about his chin, half-hiding a silly grin. "Would you happen to have a fig leaf convenient?" he quipped, casting about for anything within reach which would do the job and finding nothing available to him. "Or perhaps you could stitch up a lace doily while I wait? That is, if Miss Eden promises not to peek."

Across from him, Eden gave a strangled choke. "You infernal beast!" she hissed. Blindly, she dug into her sewing bag and produced a partially finished shawl. Still without looking, she tossed it in his direction. "There! Now, be gone!"

Not yet fully recovered, Jane would have given a king's ransom to have seen the entire picture. As it was, all she witnessed as a tattered piece of pink-and-white knitting floating from the room, leaving behind a trail of unraveling yarn.

While Jane had become accustomed, as much as anyone could, to the idea of having a pirate ghost inhabiting her house, Zeus was an entirely different matter. No matter how hard she tried, she could not grasp the concept of an invisible falcon roosting in the upstairs guest room. Of course, the big bird often went out with Devlin and Eden, which helped immensely, for Jane could not imagine what Dora might do if the fowl decided to set up a fuss, or how she would ever explain the current state of affairs to the servant. It was work enough trying to hide Devlin's presence from her, to invent ways to get her out of the house when need be, and to excuse the growing list of curiosities which seemed to occur daily.

As it was, Dora was becoming increasingly suspicious and on edge. Something queer was going on in the Winters household, but she couldn't figure out what. For one thing, the house constantly stank of cigar smoke. Eden had suggested that, with all the visitors they'd had of late, it was to be expected. Dora thought otherwise, particularly when she smelled it so strongly upon first entering the house each morning. Jane had hinted that perhaps Dora was imagining it, since she herself failed to notice it.

Then there was the matter of various articles of male clothing found here and there. A glove was one thing, easily dropped by anyone. And Captain Kane had once forgotten his plumed hat. Even the neckcloth left behind was not unreasonable, given the uncommonly warm weather they were having. But a stray man's stocking? A dirty one? Dora simply couldn't accept Jane's lame explanation that it must have been one of her late husband's, accidentally put in her own drawer. The lady claimed it must have gotten tangled within the folds of one of her petticoats and not been discovered until now. Dora doubted that, since she'd found it in the upstairs hallway, in plain sight, still stinking—after three years? Ha!

What really set Dora's hair on end was the morning she caught a glimpse of Eden and Devlin headed toward the carriage house. Granted, the sun was extremely bright that day, and the kitchen window was a bit streaked with cooking grease and in need of washing, but Dora could have sworn Captain Kane had no head upon his shoulders! To her immense fright, it seemed his hat was floating in midair, all of its own! When she'd gone running to Jane, almost hysterical at what she'd witnessed, Mrs. Winters had merely shaken her head, laughed that soft laugh of hers, and said, "Dora, my dear, when are you going to stop being so vain and go see Dr. Myers about a pair of spectacles? I shall pay for them, if you do."

Two days later, Dora was hanging laundry outdoors

to dry. Upon hearing a piercing shriek, she turned, startled, and imagined she saw a mouse fly into the air. With a scream of her own, she dropped the clean dress she'd been holding and ran around the corner of the house as if the Devil were on her heels. She was so frightened that she nearly ran smack into Eden and Captain Kane, who were enjoying a walk in the side flower garden. "Oh, sir! Miss! Did you hear that! Did you see?" she gasped, stumbling over her words.

"Whatever are you so upset about?" Eden asked with a concerned frown. "Honestly, Dora, you are acting so oddly lately that I fear you must be going daft on us!"

"That ungodly noise, didn't you hear it?" Dora cried.

"The only racket we heard was you yelling fit to raise the dead," Devlin told her with a shake of his head. "And we didn't see a thing out of the ordinary. Did we, Eden?"

"Certainly not," she concurred. "What is it you saw, Dora?"

Hesitant now to tell them, lest they have her locked in the madhouse, Dora mumbled halfheartedly, "Well, I could've swore I saw a flyin' mouse, but now I ain't so sure."

Taking pity on the poor befuddled woman, Eden put a comforting arm around Dora's shoulder. "There, there, now. A flying mouse? Surely not. You know, I think you must be working too hard these days, Dora. And the sun has been unbearable hot lately. 'Tis bound to give a person a fit now and again, especially someone who's getting on in years and whose eyes and hearing aren't as sharp as they used to be. Why don't you go to your room and lie down for a bit, dear? And tomorrow, have Mother give you a couple of hours free to see Dr. Myers." With a gentle pat, Eden steered Dora toward her apartment over the carriage house. "Go on now and have a good rest."

Dora was no sooner out of sight than Zeus, with a

heavy rustle of wings, landed upon Devlin's shoulder. Eden cast a dark look at Devlin, and another in the direction of the falcon. "I told you that bird would be trouble," she snapped. "Drat it all! Between you and your invisible friend, poor Dora must think she's losing her mind."

Devlin cocked his head to one side and attempted a boyish smile that was not quite innocent enough to pass muster. "Not a great loss there, I'd wager," he offered. "But I must commend you, Eden. You think fast on your feet, almost as well as your mother. It must be an inherited trait, like your eyes."

Those eyes were blazing at him. "You are a scoundrel of the first order, Captain Kane. You and your nasty bird. I can't for the life of me understand why anyone would care to keep such a vermin-ridden creature for a pet."

"I'll make a bargain with you, duchess. When you agree to take Zeus's place as my prize pet, I'll turn him loose."

"Cows will sooner sing opera, so I suppose we're stuck with both of you for the duration." She sniffed, lifting her nose into the air as if she smelled something rotten.

Even with Zeus complicating matters, Devlin managed to lean down and steal a hard, quick kiss, his tongue delving deeply into Eden's mouth to vanquish hers. "You still haven't learned to mind orders, have you, wench?" Then he grinned and smacked her sharply on the rump through her skirts. "Ah, but I do love chastising you, sweetling, so pray do continue your rebellion a while longer, will you?"

Chapter 13

*F*or a full week following Tilton's dismissal, everything was fairly calm, if one discounted all the general complications of having Devlin and Zeus haunting the house, and Dora acting as jittery as a bug in a hot skillet. With the help of the employees Eden had kept on—those who had been more loyal to her father than to Tilton—and the men Devlin supplied from his own crew, the warehouse was running quite smoothly. In just a few short days, business was already improving, and Eden could not believe the increase in profits now that Tilton no longer had his fingers in the cash pot.

She'd scarcely drawn her first tentative sigh of relief, almost daring to hope her troubles were finally at an end, when she entered the warehouse office one morning to find it in a shambles. So suddenly did she stop, as if turned to stone, that Devlin, who entered just behind her, almost sent her careening onto her face. Together they stood staring in dismay.

Whoever had ransacked the room had done a thorough job of it. Ledgers were strewn about the floor, pages ripped out and shredded. Not a cupboard or drawer had been left untouched, the contents thrown willy-nilly. Even her desk had been desecrated, the beautiful walnut finish now sporting numerous deep scars, as if someone had slashed it time and again with a knife. Likewise, her father's chair was no more than a pile of kindling, the leather seat sliced to ribbons and the stuffing pulled out.

Devlin had never seen Eden cry. He'd seen her sad, worried, angry, happy, even frightened—but he'd not seen her shed so much as a single tear. Now she gave a hoarse little cry, turned her face into his chest as if to shut out the sight of the devastation, and clung to him like a kitten to a tree limb. Enfolded in his arms, her slight body trembled so that he wondered how it stayed intact. With each deep sob, her shoulders heaved, and within minutes her tears had soaked his shirt through.

She wept as if her heart were breaking, and Devlin felt so sorry for her that his own heart ached for her. Never having had much experience or patience with weeping women, he was at a loss as to how best to comfort her. Awkwardly, he brought a hand up to stroke her head, and crooned to her, "Sweetling, don't cry. It can all be set to rights again."

"N-not Papa's chair!" she wailed.

Devlin winced, not knowing what to say. Over the top of her head, he viewed the remains of the chair and had to concur. It was, indeed, beyond repair. Still, he had to say something to make her stop sobbing. "I could try to find someone to rebuild it," he offered lamely.

"No." She sniffled. Her face was flattened against his chest, her words muffled and watery as she added, "It wouldn't be the same."

He sighed, then grimaced slightly as she rubbed her nose back and forth over the front of his shirt. Blast it all, he was going to have to launder his shirt again, and it was about two threads shy of being a rag now. "Tell me what I can do to make you stop crying," he said, ready to promise almost anything.

Her reply surprised him. It was the last thing he expected to hear her say. "Teach me to curse."

On a half-laugh, he asked, "What?"

"Teach me to curse," she repeated past a quivery hiccup. "You once said you would, and I could use a few good curses more than anything else just now, because if I don't get rid of some of this rage building up inside of me, I'll surely burst." She pulled back far enough to turn red-rimmed eyes and a cherry nose up to meet his wondering gaze. "If you were standing in my shoes at this minute, what would be the first words off your tongue?"

"Son of a . . ." The words dwindled off.

She raised a delicate brow in query. "Go on with it. Son of a what?"

He couldn't do it. He just couldn't teach her that particular word. "Bear," he offered. "Son of a bear."

She gave him a disbelieving frown. "Somehow that doesn't sound right. What else?"

"Damnation."

She nodded. "That will do nicely. Let's hear another."

"Hellfire." He hoped she stopped adding to her list soon, because he was already running low on his list of milder curses, and he was loath to teach her the more scalding ones.

Eden was not to be put off that easily. "Yet another, if you please."

"Tarnation?"

"Try again, Devlin. A really good one this time."

"Jackass. Horse's bum. Crupper."

"Too tame," she insisted with a shake of her head.

"Blarst it all, Eden! A lady shouldn't say such things, and I'll be double-damned if I—"

"Just one more, and I promise I'll be satisfied."

"Gadzooks."

"Gadzooks?" she echoed. "What sort of word is that? Did you make it up? I'll bet 'tis not a curse at all."

"Would you really care to wager on it, duchess? After all, I'm the one teaching this lesson."

"Then what does it mean?" she challenged.

" 'Tis an oath sworn by the nails driven into Christ's hands at the Crucifixion."

"Truly? You swear it?"

"By everything that's holy. And as you have pointed out repeatedly, I am well versed in Biblical fact."

She still wasn't sure she believed him, given the teasing twinkle in his eye, but she decided to grant him the benefit of the doubt. Besides, it was a wondrously unusual word, and worthy of being put to good use.

As she turned to view the ruin of her office, she tried it on for size. "Gadzooks! How I would love to catch the person responsible for this deed and hang him by his . . ." Here she paused to wrinkle her brow in concentration. "What is it you would hang him by, Devlin, were you me?"

"His ears, sweetling," he supplied with a long-suffering grin. "Most definitely by his ears."

Dora got her new spectacles from the doctor, which meant that she began seeing things even more clearly than before, things she wasn't supposed to observe. Every so often she would pop into a room and catch an invisible Devlin with a spoon or cup halfway to his mouth. Or worse yet, witness a chicken leg suspended in midair.

At first she simply shook her head and said nothing, lest Jane and Eden think she'd gone daft after all. But when she twice caught Devlin stealing kisses from Eden, only to have him disappear from view a second later, she finally complained, shakily and with pitiful hope clearly written on her face, that the doctor must have given her the wrong prescription for her eye-glasses. Feeling guilty, but still unwilling to confide their secret to their flighty servant, Eden and Jane agreed that the physician probably had made an error. That, or Dora simply had to give herself time to become accustomed to the strength of the new lenses.

Meanwhile, Devlin was still plotting to get Eden into his bed. When all else failed, he decided to play on her sympathy. At breakfast one morning, he began coughing and sneezing and complaining of a sore throat.

Though his forehead felt cool to her touch, Eden suggested with a frown of concern, "Perhaps you should see the doctor, Devlin."

"Nay. I'll not go wagging into his office with you at my side, like a sniveling lad needing his mama along for courage. You are not the only person with a reputation to uphold, sweetling, and I'll not have it bandied about town that I was too much a coward to seek a doctor by myself, which we both know is impossible at this point."

"Shall I get him to come here, then?"

"And stand hovering at my bedside all the while? I think not."

"Well, then, why don't you go upstairs and lie down for a while?" Jane suggested. "More than likely, 'tis just a sniffle. I'll send Eden up in a bit with some broth for you, and mayhap a poultice for your throat."

Which was precisely what Devlin had hoped when he'd devised this scheme.

A short time later, he lay lurking in his sickbed, the sheet pulled up to his chin, and wearing absolutely nothing but hard, hot flesh beneath it. He tried his best to curb the wolfish smile which kept curving his mouth as he awaited Eden's imminent arrival. Soon she would discover that the only ailments he suffered were pangs of acute desire. And the only cure required was her sweet body thrashing beneath his, her moans of longing

matching his, her hands caressing his feverish body—
soothing, or exciting, everything but his brow.

Upon hearing her tread in the hallway outside his
room, Devlin gave a pitiful moan, in the advent that
Eden might already suspect his devious trickery. The
doorknob turned, and Devlin held his breath. Just as the
door swung open, Zeus let loose with a loud squawk.

An even louder, human shriek echoed the hawk's.
Devlin bolted upright in bed and stared in disbelief as
Dora tossed an armful of linens into the air and tore off
down the hall as if demons were fast on her heels,
screaming at the top of her lungs.

He'd scarcely managed to leap from his bed and don
his breeches when Eden entered the room. She took one
hard look at his sheepish face, long enough to accu-
rately determine the state of his health and his obvious
guilt, and launched into a hushed tirade, no less effec-
tive for its lack of volume.

"You snake! You scheming worm! Now see what
you've done? Dora is downstairs, quaking and screeching about ghosts! And if we don't quiet her soon, the
entire town is going to be alerted. Blast your randy
hide!" She tossed the onion plaster into his face and,
while he was still trying to peel his way clear of the
soggy, smelly hank of cloth, she upended the bowl of
broth on his head. "I wish you truly were sick. For a
hoax such as this, you deserve to cock up your toes!"

Fortunately, Jane was able to calm Dora sufficiently.
As it happened, the servant had suffered a knock to the
head the day before, when a large pot had come tumbling off a high kitchen shelf. Jane suggested that Dora's hallucinations were a result of the blow. This the
woman reluctantly conceded as possible, though she
continued to mutter about ghosts and haunted houses
for long afterward, claiming she would never, under
any circumstances, enter that upstairs guest room again.

Thereafter, they could hardly encourage her to venture to the upper level of the house to clean any of the bedrooms unless she was accompanied by Jane or Eden. It took a costly bolt of silk from Devlin's pilfered treasure before mother and daughter forgave him for his part in this inconvenience.

Just when it seemed that Charles Town was ready to put aside all reservations about Devlin, and forget the fact that he was a pirate as well as a partner in the Winters Warehouse, four brigand ships, with upwards of four hundred rowdy cutthroats, sailed into port and promptly began to terrorize the town. The attacking horde of marauders swept through the streets like an angry swarm of riled wasps, armed to the teeth and destroying everything in its path. Within hours, a large section of the town nearest the dock was reduced to a shambles, all shipping trade brought to a jolting halt beneath this unforeseen assault. Throngs of drunken, sword-wielding raiders pillaged at will, ransacking and burning businesses. In their mad frenzy, they ravaged, maimed, or slaughtered anyone or anything not wise enough or fast enough to flee, while the citizens of Charles Town recoiled in abject terror.

Word of this terrifying onslaught spread like wildfire, and within minutes of the attack Devlin and Nate were being apprised of the situation by their mates. "'Tis that devil Blackbeard and his crew," one fellow informed them. "Along with others who've joined up with him for a time. Looks as if they mean to sack the entire town and leave it smolderin' in their wake."

This was not heartening news to Devlin's ears, for Edward Teach, better known as Blackbeard, was a crazed, murdering bastard who through his ruthless antics was continually earning all pirates a much worse reputation than the majority of them deserved. Numerous of the more civilized brigands of the day limited their attacks to merchant vessels, opposing pirates, or galleons filled with New World treasures headed for Europe; they did not generally prey on passenger ships or common townsfolk in their search for wealth, nor menace and maim indiscriminately. Not so the infamous Blackbeard. His very name struck terror in many a heart, for he had well earned his notoriety as one of the most ferocious and bloodthirsty pirates known to mankind.

With a shake of his head, Devlin gave an agitated sigh. "Damn the man! Why did he have to attack Charles Town now, when I was finally gaining some favor with the townsfolk here? He is going to destroy every bit of goodwill Eden and I have managed to garner."

"Aye," Nate concurred, "and with the number of men under his command, there's little we can do to stop him."

"Methinks we need to hie ourselves down to the docks and investigate the matter further," Devlin suggested. "Mayhap there is something Teach wants, something which would appease him enough to make him cease his rampaging and seek his sport elsewhere."

With that in mind, the men stopped by the house long enough to warn Eden and Jane to stay safely ensconced behind locked doors and shuttered windows. "I'm leaving a couple of my men on watch outside as added protection," Devlin told them, "but if anyone tries to break into the house—"

"We'll shoot first and ask questions later," Jane finished for him.

"Ye do that, Janie girl," Nate said with a chuckle, giving her a quick buss on the lips. "We'll collect the bodies later, along with any bounty they might have on their heads. Jest be mighty careful and make certain yer aim is true. This be a scurvy bunch o' bilge rats Blackbeard has gathered about him."

As accustomed as Devlin and Nate were to pirate

raids and the mayhem that usually resulted, they were sickened by the sight that met them when they reached the docks. At least a dozen hapless victims lay injured or dying in the streets, their bodies riddled with wounds. Dead animals, including carcasses from a local butcher shop, littered their path. The stench of rum and blood was everywhere.

Several shops were aflame, the fires untended and raging, threatening bordering establishments. Drunken pirates chased about in all directions, looting and shouting and fighting even among themselves. As Devlin watched, a young lady managed to escape her would-be rapists, while they pummeled one another to see who would ravage her first. From a nearby brothel, panicked screams revealed that even those women willing to sell their favors were not safe this day, and would not be paid for what was being taken so violently.

Amidst this ongoing melee, Teach was still ridiculously easy to spot. Standing a half foot taller than the average man, he towered above the crowd like a huge, bellowing giant. His shaggy black mane and the bushy beard that had earned him his name were braided into a multitude of long, spike-like plaits and decorated with pieces of brightly colored ribbon. Oddly, this unsightly coiffure served to make him appear all the more fierce, like some demented demon from hell. The mere sight of this scowling hulk was enough to send any prudent person running in the opposite direction. And if additional intimidation was required, Blackbeard had been known to twine bits of candle into his beard and light them, making his hair appear to be ablaze, the better to inspire fear in an opponent.

Their weapons in hand, Nate and Devlin waded into the fray, readily insinuating themselves into the confusion. While Nate concentrated on gathering information from lesser pirates, Devlin invisibly sidled closer to Teach, eavesdropping on the man's conversation. He soon learned that Blackbeard and his unholy troops had by now succeeded in plundering several ships in Charles Town Harbor. Not satisfied merely to steal goods, disrupt trade, and create havoc, they had taken a number of the passengers hostage, including several women and children. In exchange for these hostages, Teach was demanding that the town send him a chest of medicine for his sick crewmen. He threatened to sever the heads of his prisoners and deliver them to the governor if his demands were not met.

So that's his game, Devlin thought darkly. *A bout of revelry and ransacking for his men, some booty into the bargain, and medicine as the final reward from terrorized citizens eager to see the last of him.* Devlin also knew that, in accordance with Blackbeard's murderous code, if innocent people were sacrificed in the process, so much the better. Teach would relish every moment of tormenting his helpless prisoners, and gleefully kill them afterward.

The man was an ogre, completely without conscience, and Charles Town was in a panic to be rid of him. Their hackles raised, all their old antagonism toward pirates immediately reborn, the frightened people demanded revenge. They wanted the governor to do something. Now. Before more lives could be forfeit, or more of their hard-earned livelihood destroyed.

But Governor Johnson decided to take the matter under advisement before acting, stating that he did not want to make any rash decisions which might put the town in further peril. In the interim, Blackbeard and his pirates were running amok through the town, parading boldly through the streets and terrorizing one and all. More innocent bystanders were abducted and taken aboard Blackbeard's ship.

During this time Devlin received unwelcome news of his own. Several of his crewmen came hurrying to him with reports of his old enemy, Captain Swift. "He still be alive, Cap'n," one man declared. "Talk is he was in the Tortugas a while back."

Nate, too, had heard this latest supposition. "A number of Blackbeard's men claim to have seen him. 'Twould appear maroonin' the bloody bastard didn't rid us of him for good and all, Dev."

"More's the pity," Devlin mused. "I'd hoped he was dead. And for all we know for sure, he might be, since these latest tales of him are naught but rumor."

"Mayhap, but if they be true, ye know he'll come lookin' fer us, sooner or later," Nate predicted. "'Specially if Teach's men tell him where to find us."

"I hope they do. 'Twould save us the trouble of having to run him to ground," Devlin responded with a contemplative smile.

"Then we're not goin' after him?"

"Nay. Not now, at least. I've promised Eden my help with Tilton and Finster, and we'll not be leaving Charles Town until I've rid her of their menace. With luck, by the time that deed is accomplished, my visibility will have returned to normal as well. Then we'll be after Swift, if he's still alive, and if he hasn't found us first. Either way, the next time we meet, his blood will stain my sword."

Meanwhile, Blackbeard's terrible antics were creating dismay and concern for everyone, Eden included. "Can't you do something, Devlin?" she asked, turning immense, pleading turquoise eyes on him.

He shook his head at her naiveté. "What would you suggest, Eden? I have fewer than forty men. Shall I pit them against four hundred? The odds would not be in our favor."

"But you know him, don't you? You are in the same business, so to speak. Couldn't you talk with him, pirate to pirate? Make him see reason?"

"There is no reasoning with the man. Plainly put, he's insane."

"That being the case, do you think he will honor his word and release the hostages unharmed if he gets the medicine he wants?" she questioned further, sympathetic tears turning her eyes to glistening jewels. "Or will he murder them anyway?"

"I cannot say, Eden. There is no determining what the man might do. He derives diabolical pleasure from terrorizing others, is famous for his unpredictable temper, is quick to the trigger or the sword, thrives on bloodshed, and is absolutely fearless."

An odd look crossed her features, one Devlin could not immediately read. "Is he truly? Fearless, I mean? Is he also as superstitious as the usual sailor, despite the fact that he's holding women aboard his ship even as I speak?"

"What is going through that devious female mind of yours?" Devlin asked, a frown drawing his golden brows together.

She offered him a gamine smile, a look of pure mischief about her. "Well, I was thinking our fierce Blackbeard might be uncommonly afraid of ghosts," she suggested lightly. "Now, if a certain phantom pirate I know were to approach him, mayhap whisper a few dire threats into his ear, he'd be liable to reconsider his demands, would he not?"

Devlin's white teeth flashed in an answering grin as he doffed an imaginary hat at her. "Aye. He just might at that, duchess."

In the wee hours of the following morning, enshrouded by the black mist of predawn, Devlin rowed himself out to Blackbeard's ship. So dark was it that he had little fear of being seen by anyone—rather, of having anyone see the dinghy rowing itself out into the harbor, and he was careful to make as little noise as possible. Blackbeard's crew was so confident of their superiority, so blatantly arrogant, that they had left the boarding ladder hanging over the ship's side. Devlin climbed aboard without ever having to wet the soles of his boots.

He swaggered past several men on the main deck, none of whom took any notice. Not that he'd thought they might. From the lay of the ship, he quickly calculated the most reasonable place to find Blackbeard's quarters. Then, instead of choosing that route, he took the hatchway leading into the bowels of the vessel.

Just as he'd suspected, he found the prisoners, at least a fair number of them, locked in a single barred cell in the hold. A lone sentry guarded them, or would have, if he'd been awake. It was child's play for Devlin to rap the sleeping man over the head with the butt of his flintlock and slip the keys from his belt. It was slightly more difficult to unlock the cell door without waking any of the hostages, but he managed this also. As the door swung open with a loud squeak of rusted hinges, they stirred drowsily. Suddenly, one fellow gave a disbelieving gasp and cried out softly, "Look! The door's open!"

"Saints be! We're saved!" another exclaimed.

Rousing their mates, they started hesitantly toward the open doorway. "Do ye think 'tis a trap, so they can slay us and claim we were trying to escape?" someone hissed.

"I don't care if 'tis," a woman said. "I'd rather die trying to swim to shore than here in this stinking hole."

"What of the others? How can we go without them?"

"We have yet to be gone ourselves," another hastened to point out. "And we'd better be about leaving before someone comes and we lose our best chance to do so."

A second woman piped up in a frightened whisper. "I can't swim! Neither can most of the children."

Devlin wanted to tell them about the dinghy, and about the half dozen men on deck they would have to elude, but he was forced to silence.

As if the fellow had read his mind, a hostage suggested, "If luck is with us, we'll find a rowboat. If not, hold onto someone who can swim. Now hush, for surely they have someone standing guard above." Assuming the role of leader, the man began ushering people from the cell. "Keep the children quiet and try to stay in the shadows."

Devlin followed them on deck, his sword in hand, ready to defend them if need be. Somehow they made it to the ladder and over the side undetected, the adults carrying the children. Once assured that they had found the dinghy and could row themselves safely to shore, he left them, cursing the fact that he had not thought to tow another dinghy behind the first, for now he could not free any other hostages he might happen to find unless they were strong swimmers. He estimated he'd saved fewer than half of those reported to be aboard, but there was no help for it now, unless he could manage to frighten Blackbeard into releasing the rest.

As silent as a wraith, Devlin made his way to Blackbeard's quarters. The door was barred from the inside, but he made quick work of that problem, the blade of his longknife sliding effortlessly through the crack and shifting the latch aside. Without a sound, he crept toward the bed, where Blackbeard lay blissfully unaware, snoring loudly.

Devlin had to hold back a laugh as he perched on the edge of the pirate's bed and croaked out in his best imitation of a wavering, ghostly voice, "Teach! Edward Teach! Awaken, you scurvy arse!"

Blackbeard awoke with a start, reaching immediately for his cutlass. In the inky darkness of the room, Devlin could scarcely view the man's movements, but he managed to see well enough to bring the point of his knife against Blackbeard's throat. In the process, Devlin inadvertently sliced off a thick strand of braided beard. Again, he had to choke back a chuckle as he imagined Blackbeard's ire when he realized that his precious beard had been mutilated. Still holding the burly pirate at bay with his knife, Devlin slid the loose skein of beard beneath his shirt, where it would remain undetected for the time being. Then, with the toe of his boot, he kicked Teach's cutlass beneath the bed, out of reach.

"Who . . . what?" the man stammered in confusion.

"Teach! Listen to me," Devlin told him in the eeriest, wobbliest tone he could manage. "I have come to warn you to leave Charles Town."

"Who . . . who's there? Show yerself, by damn!" Once more, Blackbeard tried to arm himself against his unknown attacker, snaking a hand toward the pistol atop the stand at his bedside, only to feel strong fingers clamp about his wrist, holding his hand shy of the gun. The knife point pricked sharply at his throat, following the bob of his Adam's apple as he swallowed reflexively.

Devlin thought he felt Blackbeard's arm tremble slightly. "Your weapons will do you no good, Blackbeard. Not against the likes of me," he prophesied with an evil hiss.

"Who are ye?" There was a distinct note of panic in Teach's voice now, and Devlin could have crowed with delight.

"I am the Phantom of Fate! Your fate, Edward Teach!"

"Ye're a lying sack o'—"

"Tsk, tsk," Devlin chided mildly, even as he gave the man's wrist a wrench hearty enough that Blackbeard released an involuntary groan. "However, since you seem reluctant to believe me, I will allow you to light a candle. Then we'll see who is the liar, and who is not." The tinderbox seemed to float into Teach's hand.

It took several tries before Blackbeard could accomplish the simple task, so shaken was he by now. But his original fright was paltry compared to that which crossed his hairy features when he had the candle lit and still beheld no one in the room with him. And all the while, he felt those fingers about his wrist!

"Where are ye, ye devil?" he roared, his famously fearsome gaze searching his quarters. He nearly leapt from his skin as Devlin replied with an awful chuckle, "No need to shout. I'm right here."

Incapable of more than a hoarse whisper at this juncture, Blackbeard asked fearfully, "Wha-what do ye want?"

Devlin could not resist the temptation. He tried, for all of a heartbeat, then answered in his most terrifying voice, "I want your soul. You named me the Devil, and quite correctly. I want your soul for my amusement."

"Why?"

Devlin's demonic laugh raised gooseflesh over Blackbeard's skin. "Because 'tis mine, for all the evil you have done, and now I am here to claim it for all eternity."

Amazingly, Teach was still coherent enough to argue the point. "Nay, Devil. I'm yet young, with many a year left to me, and plenty of fight in this body."

"You dare to gainsay me, mortal?" Devlin crooned nastily. "To deny me that which is rightfully mine to take at any time I deem proper?" He let the question lie between them, unanswered, for just a moment before continuing in a considering tone. "Then again, perhaps I could wait a bit. There's no hurry. After all, a year to you is as a blink of the eye to me. However, if I were to grant you a reprieve, I would have something in return for my benevolence."

"What might that be?" Blackbeard asked hesitantly.

"That you set your hostages free, unharmed, and leave Charles Town forthwith. And never set foot or anchor in this place again."

Blackbeard pondered but a moment. "Aye. But I need those medicines."

"Then take them, by all means, but should you harm one hair upon the head of any of your prisoners, I shall prepare the hottest coals of hell for your immediate arrival."

Again Blackbeard looked confused. "What sort of Devil are ye, that ye would want to keep these priggish maggots from harm? I'd think ye'd dance a jig if I cut 'em to ribbons and fed 'em to the fishes."

For just a moment Devlin was at a loss, but his quick mind came to his rescue. "Nay, Teach. There are those among them who will go on to do my will and my work here in Charles Town, and I need no interference from you. Either you abide by my decree, or suffer the consequences. And think not to defy me, pirate, for there is no way you can escape my wrath."

Slowly, cautiously, Devlin eased from the bed as he spoke, hoping his words would hold Blackbeard's attention, even as he lowered the man's hand and gently let loose of it. "Before I go, tell me the whereabouts of Captain Swift."

"I don't know where he is, and I care less. Ye should know better than I."

Realizing his error, Devlin added hastily, "No matter, Teach. I'll find him, just as I did you. You," he repeated softly, a faint echo shadowing his words as he backed soundlessly toward the door. "You."

He let his voice become weaker, fading into nothing by the time he opened the door and sprinted through it. He was out of the passageway and onto the deck before he heard Blackbeard's roar trailing after him. As he leapt to the ship's rail, he caught a glimpse of Teach's huge, naked, apelike body lumbering into the open, pistol in hand.

Devlin spared but a moment of regret for the soaking his boots were about to take, and one last, gloating laugh for Blackbeard. Then, before the pirate could decide where to aim his shot, Devlin launched himself into an arcing dive and plunged below the murky waters of Charles Town Bay.

Chapter 14

"*D*amn me, if I didn't put the fear of the Devil into that old goat!" Devlin crowed. "Why, I could have trod the boards as an actor, so good was I!"

"And so modest, as well." Jane chortled, shaking her head.

"And wet," Eden added, eyeing his large, dripping frame, and the growing puddle beneath his soggy boots.

"Ah, but where is a properly appreciative female when you want one?" he lamented theatrically, throwing his arms wide and rolling his eyes. "A woman ready to fall at the feet of the conquering hero and grant him any boon? Do I get a kiss of gratitude for risking all? Nay, I say. I get a heartless laugh and a scowl for my trouble. Where is the justice?"

"Justice is due to march into this kitchen at any moment and land a broom on someone's head when she sees this floor," Eden told him, reminding all of them that the sun had risen and Dora would soon arrive to prepare the morning meal. "And you, my poor, ill-praised prince in pirate's clothing, are due for some dry apparel, which I hope will smell less of fish than those you are presently wearing."

Devlin grimaced in mock dismay. "What a harridan

you have for a daughter, Jane. I pity the poor man who actually weds her, for she'll flay him alive with her tongue. Thankless wench! Especially when I return so victorious from my mission of mercy—one of the few I have ever ventured upon, I might add—and come bearing such a glorious trophy as this!" Reaching inside his shirt, he drew out a long, sodden black ropelike object and waved it before Eden's nose.

It stank worse than Devlin's bay-soaked clothes, and Eden backed away from it, her nostrils wrinkling in distaste. "Ugh! What, pray tell, is that horrid thing?"

Devlin laughed. "Why, 'tis a good portion of Teach's beard, duchess. And I would soak my boots twice over just to see his face when that vain peacock views himself in the mirror this morn."

Eden's eyes widened. "Oh, my stars! Devlin, is that truly part of his beard?" She peered at it with careful awe, as if to judge for herself.

" 'Tis, indeed," he told her with an imperious nod. "Still plaited and tied up in its scarlet bow."

Now that they'd been informed, both women recognized the limp red cloth dangling from the black strands for the ribbon it once was.

"Captain, you are a delightful rogue!" Jane pronounced gleefully. "Quite ingenious at your craft. You have my unfailing admiration."

He sketched a bow, though she could not see it. "I thank you, ma'am. At least you can value the worth of a man's work, even if your daughter does not."

"Oh, but I do, Devlin," Eden countered. "I beg your pardon if I've seemed ungrateful, when in fact, I am quite proud of you. You, and you alone, saved the lives of those unfortunate hostages, and hopefully more than the number you managed to free last evening. I just wish there were some way of letting everyone know what you have done, that they might also thank you and give credit where 'tis rightfully due."

"I agree," Jane said. "The citizenry should know what Devlin has done, and be properly beholden. The problem is how to manage it without confusing the matter with such triviality as ghosts."

A light dawned in Eden's eyes. "There may still be a way. Devlin, go change your clothes, and let me study the idea a bit more."

"While you're about your thinking, consider what I might wear to the breakfast table, if you will," he suggested with droll humor. "Until my invisible clothing dries, anything I put on will be visible to Dora."

"Oh, dear." Jane frowned and tapped a fingernail at her lip. "This having but one set of clothing which cannot be seen is becoming more trouble by the day. Are you positive you have nothing else to wear? Perhaps a cloak?"

White teeth flashed in a taunting grin, for Eden's eyes alone, as he shook his head. "Nay, madam. Nothing but a smile."

Eden's eyes glittered a scathing warning. "If you dare come to the table that way, you will regret it for the remainder of your days. That I promise you."

"What is it you threaten me with, Miss Propriety?" he teased. "A deluge of maidenly blushes? An outraged shriek or two?"

She offered him a gamine smile that made him wonder what she'd been like as a child, before she'd begun to be scorned by her playmates. "More than that, Devlin," she pledged with such overdone sincerity that he was made immediately leery. "Don't forget that while I may not be as well-traveled as you, I am well-read. By any chance, have you ever heard of a eunuch?"

Devlin's mouth flew wide in surprise that she'd even heard of such a thing, let alone uttered the word. Before he could think how to reply, Jane spoke up. "Oh, yes, Eden dear. I'm certain he has. I'm also certain that, between the two of us, we could render him just as unmanned. Of course, since I can't see him, you would have to wield the scissors, and 'tis bound to be a bit gruesome, but we could manage it somehow."

Devlin cast the pair of them a horrified look, not entirely sure that either was simply jesting. With squishy, mincing steps, he edged past them, bound for his room. "Just bring a plate upstairs to me. I'll eat where Dora can't see me."

"I'm not your serving girl," Eden called after him, sharing a grin with her mother behind his fleeing back. "And get those wet boots off this very instant, before you track up the entire house!"

Half an hour later, wearing a sheepish scowl and a change of clothes, Devlin sat at Eden's side, their shoes touching beneath the dining table. Eden had come upstairs to fetch him, silently and pompously escorted him to the front door, waited as he pretended to knock, then presented him to Dora and her mother as their breakfast guest—thus solving his predicament, if not his embarrassment at having been so successfully cowed by two women. Blast! If any of his men ever got wind of this, he'd never live it down!

Within the space of the meal, Eden also resolved the problem of how to gain Devlin credit for the safe release of Blackbeard's hostages. "We'll simply have to involve ourselves in the exchange," she told him. "To be there when the medicine is handed over to Blackbeard."

"We?" he questioned. "Have I a mouse in my pocket, Eden? If not, there is no *we* to it. I will not have you near that unconscionable madman. And since I cannot 'appear' without you, there you have it. End of plan." He offered a shrug, palms outspread, not at all apologetic at having shot holes in her newest plot. It mattered little to him whether the townspeople ever knew of his part in freeing the hostages. He did not need their acclaim, regardless of what Eden might believe, though he did see her reasoning. The better they thought of him, the better it would be for her, as they were in such constant association with one another.

"Mayhap not the end at all," she said with a sly smile. "If you would be willing to part with the prize you collected last evening, there may still be a way to remind Blackbeard of his demonic visitor's threat and ensure his compliance."

Now she had hit upon his true worry, though he was baffled to find himself so concerned with the lives of a few people he didn't even know. Still, it was not in his nature to stand by and watch as women and children were brutally slain. If there were any way to make certain that Blackbeard spared the remaining hostages, he was willing to try, for he was not positive that his solitary ghost act would entirely do the trick.

A short time later, Devlin found himself accompanying Eden, Jane, and Reverend Johnston into council chambers, where Governor Johnson and several of the most prominent citizens of Charles Town were gathered. Their appearance, obviously considered an ill-timed intrusion, was met by glowers all around.

"Pardon our presumptuousness, sirs," Reverend Johnston began, "but we believe we may be of some assistance to you. May I present Captain Devlin Kane of the *Gai Mer,* with whom some of you may not yet be acquainted?"

"His reputation as a pirate precedes him," one council member stated baldly, glaring first at Devlin, then at the rest of the small party. "To what do we owe the, er, pleasure?" As though the air in the room had suddenly become foul, he brought a scented handkerchief to his nostrils.

"If you'd get the snuff out of your nose long enough to clear your head, John Longstreet, mayhap you'd see that Captain Kane has come with an offer of aid to you and the town," Jane said haughtily.

"How so?" the governor queried. "And by what authority?"

"By the authority of knowing Blackbeard personally, and having spoken with him recently," Devlin said, stepping forward. His abrupt movement caught Eden unaware, and she nearly lost hold of his coat sleeve as she scurried forward with him.

"Did he send you with more demands of us?" the local physician asked. "What more could the man want that he has not already taken by force?"

"Nay, I'm not his man. He does not command me. On the contrary, 'tis I who may be able to direct him, to some extent. If you will allow me, I should first like to ask a question of you gentlemen." His dark gaze included all of the men present at the meeting. When none objected, Devlin went on. "From your communications with Teach, what is your opinion of his intentions? Do you truly believe that he will release his prisoners unharmed, should you turn over the medicines he has requested? Or do you think he will abscond with the chest and commit further atrocities upon those unfortunate victims?"

"Why should we tell you what we think?" one fellow asked belligerently.

Devlin's brow rose in silent rejoinder, as if berating the man for his supreme stupidity. After a lengthy silence, he answered, "Because I know Blackbeard better than any of you possibly could. I know he is mad as a March hare, utterly without conscience, and thrives on spilling blood. There is very little the man fears. However, he does have a few weak points in his armor. I've thwarted him before, and know where best to strike at him."

"Forgive me, but would you be doing this yourself, or would you require help?" the governor inserted dryly, gaining a few weak laughs for his effort. "After all, the man has an army of brigands behind him."

"So did Goliath, but David felled him nonetheless, with naught but a stone."

"So you would meet with him, one man against the other?"

"Nay, I did not say such, did I? The moral of the tale lies not in the might of the warriors, as the good reverend could tell you, but in God's intervention. However, as the Lord seems to have left us to our own devices in this matter, a well-planned strategy may do nearly as well. Therefore, if you are done with pricking me with your puny thorns, mayhap you are now ready to listen to reason."

" 'Twouldn't hurt just to listen, would it?" a merchant suggested. "Heaven knows, we haven't come up with a workable plan betwixt the lot of us."

Privately, Eden thought if brains were gunpowder, this group didn't claim enough collectively to clear the wax from their ears.

"Fine. We'll listen," the governor decided reluctantly. "But do get on with it, if you please, Captain. The noon deadline which Blackbeard has set for us is fast approaching, and that leaves us very little time to execute any plan you might suggest."

" 'Tis time enough for what I have in mind," Devlin told him with a cocky nod. From beneath his coat, he withdrew the hank of beard. "This, gentlemen, is a length of Teach's beard, which I cut from his face with my own blade not long ago. I hold the distinction of being the only man ever to have relieved Blackbeard of such a treasure. 'Tis my hope—nay, my belief—that when he sees this, he will reconsider whatever treachery he has further planned."

"And which brave soul gets the privilege of presenting it to him?" Longstreet asked snidely. "You know what too often happens to the bearer of bad news."

"Are you volunteering, John?" Jane queried jeeringly. She paused for effect, then continued thoughtfully, "Wasn't it you who ran screaming from your cellar just last week, when you chanced upon a den of harmless black snakes?"

Her comment sent sniggers echoing through the room, and high color flooding Longstreet's face. " 'Twas an honest mistake, Widow Winters. The cellar was dark, and the snakes were nestled in dry leaves. The rustling noise they made led me to believe they were rattlesnakes."

Bound to keep the peace, Reverend Johnston inserted, " 'Tis quite understandable, John. But let's do get back to the business at hand, if we may. I believe Captain Kane was about to enlighten us further."

"Contrary to what Mr. Longstreet thinks, none of you need imperil yourselves more. I am only suggesting that this plait from Teach's beard be placed in the chest, atop the medicine. Thus, when he opens the lid, 'twill be the first thing he sees—a blatant reminder of the man who stole it from his person and what I might do to him next, should he think to go back on his bargain with you."

"Is it not extremely vain of you, to imagine he fears you so much that the mere sight of his missing locks would send him running with his tail tucked betwixt his legs?" Governor Johnson asked. "My God, man! There are people's lives at stake here! Women! Children! And you come to us with this outrageous proposal? We have more important tasks at hand than to consider childish pranks such as this!"

Before matters got too far out of hand, Eden interceded. "Mayhap you would do well to consider who knocked the guard unconscious aboard Blackbeard's ship last eve, gentlemen. And who unlocked the cell to free those fortunate souls who escaped Blackbeard's clutches. And who left his own dinghy available for their safe conveyance to shore, and himself swam the entire way back. Need I tell you who this brave man was, who put his own life in peril to release the others?"

"Kane?" the doctor questioned incredulously. "Well, why didn't he say so at the start?"

"And why didn't you show yourself last night, or lay claim to the fact before now?" another asked.

"Some men have no need to flaunt their achievements for their own glorification," Reverend Johnston answered quietly, shaming several of the men. "Good deeds do not go unrewarded, but neither must they be proclaimed from the rooftops."

An imperious knock at the door, followed by a rough demand, brought the meeting to an abrupt halt. All eyes now turned to Devlin. His remained locked with those of the governor. "Have you anything better to propose?" Devlin asked simply.

"Put the hair in the chest," the governor commanded dourly. "And may God be merciful."

Within minutes, the chest of medicine was being carted away by three of Blackbeard's crewmen, on its way to Teach. In the midst of the excitement, Eden and Devlin slipped away unnoticed.

They raced their carriage through the streets, careening around corners in their mad return to the Winters's house. There, Devlin quickly changed back into his wet clothes, wincing as his every step brought a loud squish. "Damn Teach for a fool if he doesn't hear me coming this time," he muttered.

"Mayhap 'twould be better not to chance it, Devlin," Eden said, casting a worried gaze at him.

His laugh was pure deviltry, as was the gleam in his black eyes. "What? And miss seeing the fright on his face when he opens that chest? Never!"

From the warehouse dock, Devlin commandeered a

dinghy and several of his own crewmen to row him out to Blackbeard's ship. "And how did ye get out here last night, if not on yer own?" Nate grumbled, hauling hard on an oar.

"This is faster," Devlin countered cheekily. "Besides, 'twould look a mite queer, a boat rowing itself in broad daylight, now mightn't it?"

"And I suppose after doin' all the labor, we get to sit below and miss all the fun?"

"Now, Nate, old chap, you wouldn't want to throw a Jonah to the plan, would you? There's a good fellow."

"Good fellow, my bloomin' arse!"

Devlin arrived aboard just in time to make his way to Blackbeard's side as the man lifted the lid of the chest. Only those nearest to him heard the pirate's slight gasp upon seeing the plait of hair atop the medicine. Teach's eyes seemed to bulge from his face, his neck and cheeks growing suddenly mottled as if with a raging fever. His shaking fingers rose to his chin, seeking out the very spot from which that braid had been cut.

When he made no comment, a crewman called out loudly, "Well, what's it to be, Cap'n? Do we run 'em through now, like ye said?" He gestured toward the fearful hostages, bound and lined up along the deck.

Beneath the cover of the babble of excited voices, Devlin leaned close. His breath was hot against Teach's ear as he whispered in an eerie voice, "Don't do it, pirate. I warned you what would happen. Last night. Remember?"

Teach crouched there as if frozen. Slowly, as if fearing what he might see—or worse, what he would not— he turned his head toward the voice. "I was sure 'twas a dream," he murmured at last. "Naught but a dream."

Devlin changed sides, leaning to speak into Teach's other ear with an evil hiss, causing the man to swivel about so abruptly that Devlin barely pulled his nose back in time to avoid a nasty bump. "Nay, Teach.

'Twas I. The Devil come to haunt you. Defy me now, and you won't live to draw another breath." As if to prove the truth of his words, Devlin plied the blade of his knife along Teach's bushy chin, deftly severing more strands of hair. They drifted to the deck where they lay like black omens.

"Cap'n?" his second in command questioned. "What's yer orders?"

"What's it to be, Blackbeard?" Devlin taunted softly, boldly, swearing to himself and sweating profusely as he played his final card in this fatal game of trickery. "Their death brings yours as well."

After what seemed an eternity, Blackbeard shouted, "Release the prisoners! Strip 'em of their finery and set 'em adrift in a smallboat—the one with the leak in it. And be quick about it. We sail b'fore the tide changes."

"But, Cap'n, we've a handful of men still ashore, and the tide be changin' any minute."

"Then they'd best be gettin' their lazy carcasses back aboard ship, if they have to sprout wings to do it, b'cause I say we're weighin' anchor, with or without 'em. I've done with this stink-hole they call Charles Town. And if I never set eyes on it again, 'twill be too soon."

One crewman dared to risk Blackbeard's ire for one last question. "Should we give the prisoners oars when we set 'em loose?"

Blackbeard answered with a mighty roar that threatened to set the masts quivering. "Nay, ye daft bilge scum! When I say adrift, I mean adrift! Let their fine townspeople come to their rescue—or let the Devil take 'em! Though why he wants the likes o' them I fail to see."

Chapter 15

*F*ollowing Blackbeard's departure, Charles Town was divided in its opinion of Devlin. While most of the residents were extremely grateful to him for aiding in the rescue of the hostages, there were still a number who were so set against pirates of any sort that they would not be easily won over. It was to this group of citizens that Dudley Finster played his tune of discontent, targeting Devlin as a perfidious villain who might turn on them at any moment.

"I vow, if that man were to wander into the swamp and be swallowed whole in a bog of quicksand, 'twould be the happiest day of my life," Eden claimed irritably. "He is like a pesky mosquito. The moment you think he's gone to bother someone else, he appears again to buzz about your ears!"

As if her complaints of him had conjured him up, she answered a knock on the door to find Dudley on her step, a small spray of flowers in one hand and a box of sweets in the other.

Squelching the urge to slam the door in his face, she gave him a weak smile—the best she could summon—and said, "Mr. Finster, what a surprise. I suppose you've come to wish my mother well, now that she is recovering so nicely?"

For a moment she held some small hope that this might be his mission. Until he said, "While I do, indeed, wish her well, that is not the purpose of my visit. I have come courting, Miss Winters, in the proper manner you prescribed not long ago."

Eden stifled a groan. Blast the man! Did he have to take her words so literally, when anyone else would have recognized them as a means of declining his attentions? Knowing she couldn't just leave him standing on the doorstep, as much as she might wish to do so, Eden relented enough to invite him inside, prompted solely by propriety even as every bone in her body urged her to get rid of him.

When Eden led him into the sitting room, Jane surreptitiously rolled her eyes in silent commiseration. "What brings you our way, Mr. Finster?" she asked. "We haven't seen you in some time." *And hoped it would be even longer,* she added to herself, shooting a quick look toward the chair where Devlin reclined in invisible silence.

"He's come courting, Mama," Eden explained flatly, her tone clearly lacking enthusiasm.

"Oh? Well, this certainly is unexpected," Jane remarked. "I really hadn't counted on having suitors just yet, though there is one fellow I've had my eye on of late." Though she was being deliberately obtuse, her dry humor caught all of them off guard. While Eden stared in mute stupefaction, from the corner chair arose a hoarse cough, covered only by Finster's blustering attempt to correct her misconception.

"Madam, uh, with all due respect, you have misconstrued my intentions. 'Tis Miss Eden I have come calling upon." He twisted his hat nervously in his hands, aware that he had yet to be invited to sit down.

"Really? But why? She already has a suitor."

By now Devlin was beginning to enjoy the way Jane was slowly and thoroughly raking poor Finster over the coals. A wide grin split his face, and he sent Eden a broad wink.

"If you are referring to Captain Kane," Finster went on, "surely you wish better than that brigand for your daughter, ma'am. He is a pirate, after all."

Devlin's smile melted into a scowl as he mentally drew and quartered the mealymouthed limp-wrist who was defaming him.

"So he is," Jane concurred, as if it bothered her not at all. "He is also our business partner, and doing a fine job of it, too."

"He'll rob you blind. Mark my words."

Jane shrugged and arched a delicate brow at him. "I don't suppose he'd be the first to try such a thing, would he?" Finally relenting a bit, she waved him toward a seat. "Do sit down, Mr. Finster. Not that you are quite as tall as most men, but I do hate to crick my neck so, simply to carry on a conversation."

Spying Eden's sewing at one end of the divan, Finster promptly availed himself of the cushion next to hers. Whereupon Eden chose the only remaining single chair in the room, merely to spite him.

Devlin's grin returned, full-blown. With a devilish twinkle turning his eyes to polished ebony, he pushed himself from his chair and eased himself onto the arm of the divan, at Finster's elbow. Though she said nothing, Eden's brows rose questioningly, which Finster mistook as directed toward him. Immediately, he recalled his mission and thrust the bouquet toward her. "I suppose you should put these in water before they wilt," he suggested with a weasel-like smile.

Before Eden could reach for them, the flowers seemed to fly from Finster's hands and scatter about the floor. To the man's amazement, the blossoms appeared to crumble before his startled gaze, as if crunched beneath an unseen foot.

Jane caught her lip between her teeth, her eyes watering with the effort not to laugh. After taking a moment to compose herself, she exclaimed, "Why, I don't believe I've ever seen flowers die so quickly. Have you, Eden?"

"Never, Mama," Eden croaked. The sight of Devlin looking all too pleased with himself proved too much, and she promptly burst out laughing.

"You'll have to excuse my daughter, Mr. Finster. She often has this compulsion to laugh at the oddest times," Jane told Eden's would-be beau.

Perplexed, and more than a little perturbed, Finster calmed himself with visible effort. "Well, no real harm done, I suppose. And there are still the sweets for her pleasure." With a flourish, he tore the top from the small box, revealing a dozen chocolate-covered cream candies, a truly rare and costly treat just recently invented. "I had them imported all the way from Switzerland," he boasted.

This time he held the candy package firmly in hand. To no avail. Even as he presented them for her perusal, the chocolate treats appeared to pop open like cracked eggshells. One by one, until each was smashed, the gooey centers oozing their filling.

"Well, I'd say they suffered a little through the lengthy transport," Jane commented wryly, as Eden turned away, her shoulders shaking suspiciously. Even with her back to him, Eden knew Devlin was merrily licking chocolate and sugar filling from his fingers.

At length, Eden managed to control her laughter long enough to show a thoroughly bewildered Finster to the door. "I really don't care for chocolate anyway," she fibbed, wanting to discourage him from bringing more, though she was extraordinarily fond of it. "It gives me indigestion," she blurted with a timely belch.

"Then I shall endeavor to bring you something which you might like better, when next I come," Finster replied smartly.

"Oh, please don't bother yourself. You see, Mr. Finster, as flattered as I am, I am well content with the beau I have."

"A lady can have more than one suitor at a time," he was fast to point out.

Drat the man! Couldn't he simply take no for an answer and go his way? Did she have to batter him over the head with her refusal? "No, thank you. That isn't acceptable to me."

Pulling himself up to his full height, which was still slight, he responded stubbornly, "I shan't stop trying."

"I sincerely wish you would," she answered bluntly, all traces of humor gone now.

"That man will leave you high and dry," he predicted. "You'll awaken one day and curse yourself for a fool. You'd do much better to put away your giddy, girlish dreams and accept my attentions while they are still being so cordially tendered."

She offered him a false smile, her eyes snapping. "How graciously and romantically stated," she replied mockingly. "Finster, has it ever occurred to you that I would rather slit my own throat with a dull knife than marry you?" With that, she did what she should have done at the first; she slammed the door in his face.

As it happened, Jane had told Finster the truth, and the fellow she had her sights set on was none other than Nate Hancock. Even as Eden had seen their romance developing bit by bit, she still could not fathom the appeal Nate held for her mother. In fact, he was the last person on earth Eden would ever have suspected her mother to show a romantic inclination toward. While likable for the most part, Devlin's quartermaster was rough-spoken, uneducated, and uncouth in more ways than one. Though he and Devlin were the best of friends, Nate was a good ten years older, which still made him three years younger than Jane.

While he was not bad-looking, Eden considered him far from handsome in his baggy sailor's clothes, his face lined and weathered from the sea and the sun. It also seemed to her that the man had little to offer her mother, aside from an adoring smile and an immediate, obvious attraction, which Jane promptly reciprocated. From the first moment they set sight upon each other, stars danced in both their eyes.

Eden was at a loss to understand it, or Jane to explain. Finally, after several failed attempts, Jane gave a helpless shrug and said, "I just don't know, Eden. Maybe it's that gold tooth of his. All I know is, when he smiles at me, it's like the sun just popped out from behind the clouds, and the world is brand-new again. The grass is greener, the flowers more fragrant, the air sweeter than it's been for a very long time. When I'm with him, I feel younger, so carefree that I find myself believing in rainbows and promises again."

"False promises and stolen rainbows, Mama. The man is a pirate!"

"So was your grandfather, my own dear papa," Jane told her daughter with a stern look. "Or have you conveniently forgotten?"

"Nay. Nor have I forgotten that Grandfather's lawless rovings nearly cost him his life upon the gallows, and broke Grandmother's heart, driving her to an early grave."

"She'd have had no other, Eden. Mother loved him dearly, as he loved her."

"Then why didn't he give up pirating? For her sake, and for yours, when you were born?"

"'Tis not for us to judge the way others decide to spend their lives. He did as he saw best, and eventually mended his ways."

"Too little, too late," Eden said sadly. "Too late to spare you and Grandmother all that grief, or to save her poor heart. And now you want to make the same mistake with Nate?"

Jane shook her head in pity at Eden's lack of understanding, unable to find the means to convince her daughter of the right of things. "The human heart has a will of its own, dear, as you will someday learn for yourself. I loved your grandfather, just as he was. I loved your father, and our respectable life together. I wouldn't have changed either of them. Nor would I change Nate, or the love we now share."

It was as simple, and as complex, as that. At least for Jane. For Eden it was another matter. She found herself struggling with profound feelings—wanting to be glad for her mother's newfound joy, and at the same time fighting resentment and jealousy that another man had taken her father's place in Jane's life.

Her turmoil was evident to one and all, though she did her best to be pleasant to Nate, for her mother's sake. With all her worrying and lack of sleep, Eden soon became short-tempered and snappish, until finally Devlin could stand no more. Following her into her room one evening, he bolted the door behind them and promptly took her to task.

"You are a snob, Eden. A nasty little narrow-minded shrew. What is it about Nate that grates against you so? Isn't he rich enough? Landed enough? Literate enough to suit you? Well, I have a bit of news for you, sweetling. 'Tis not you he has to please, but your mother, and he's doing that right well. Are you so mean, so contrary, that you can't allow your own mother her happiness, and rejoice in it?"

"Should I be thrilled that she has found love again with a man who will only leave her more desolate than he found her?" Eden countered angrily. "At least when my father died, she had the comfort of knowing he didn't want to go, that he had no choice. What will she do when the *Gai Mer* sails, Devlin? How will she console herself then?"

"That is something Nate and Jane must decide between themselves, Eden. 'Tis not for you to interfere."

"And who will be left to pick up the pieces when you and Nate are gone, if not me?" she asked. "Do you think I look forward to seeing the light dim in her eyes again, to having to coax every morsel of food down her throat, to seeing her wither away a little more each day?" She was shouting now, sobbing out her frustration and fear of what was to come.

Devlin could stand against her temper, but not her tears. Tenderly he gathered her into his arms, disregarding her struggle not to be held. "Eden, have you spoken with your mother about this?"

"She doesn't seem to care what tomorrow brings, not when today holds such joy. I've tried to warn her, but she won't hear me. Oh, Devlin, how can I shield her when she doesn't want to be protected?"

"Mayhap you could try accepting it instead of fighting the idea so hard," he suggested. "You might trust your mother's judgment a little more. She's not a stupid woman. Nor does she strike me as being rash or irresponsible."

"No, she's not." Eden sniffled. "She's very bright and loving. 'Tis just that she is so devoted, once she gives her affections. She doesn't do so lightly."

"And you think Nate does? That he's just amusing himself at her expense?" Devlin held her apart from him enough to turn her face up to his. "Eden, as long as I've known Nate, I've never known him to take such a tumble for any woman. Have you seen the way he looks at her? The way his gaze follows her every movement? The man is arse over applecart in love, plain as day. He's as likely to be hurt as she is, mayhap more so."

Eden wiped away her tears, her eyes imploring him for the truth. "You really think so?"

"I know it. And here is another thought for you to mull upon. 'Tis not fair to go on comparing Nate to your father. To do so can only cause more hurt and ill will for everyone concerned. Jane loved her husband, and she grieved mightily for him. For her to love Nate takes nothing away from the love she and your father shared, so put your jealousy to rest, Eden. Do not bind your mother to the past. Set her free to enjoy what she feels for Nate, without having to account to you or to feel guilt where none is justified."

Eden heaved a huge sigh, as if the weight of the world had been lifted from her slender shoulder. "I'll try, Devlin. I truly will try. 'Tis not that I don't like Nate. 'Tis just that I've never seen my mother act this way before, not even with Papa. And it hurts. I feel as though she's betrayed him somehow, and me as well. In my mind I know she hasn't, but my heart doesn't understand that yet."

"Give it time, minx," he advised.

She answered with a tentative smile, so at odds with the tears still staining her cheeks that Devlin's heart turned over. Dear God, what was it about these Winters women that scrambled a man's brains so? That made him yearn for things better left untouched? Was he, too, in jeopardy of losing his heart? To this woebegone waif with sea-sparkled eyes and spiked lashes? This sassy kitten with all the spirit of a tigress?

"Ah, Eden," he murmured, "have you any notion how lovely you are? How tempting?" Gently, he traced her damp cheekbones with the pads of his thumbs. Then, as if no longer able to deny himself, he bent and kissed her tearstained face, slowly, as if savoring the taste of her. His tongue flicked out to lick the salt from her cheeks, the delicate curve of her jaw—working his way lingeringly, inevitably, toward her lips.

"You taste of spindrift," he told her huskily. "Salt spray on the sea breeze. I can never get enough of it. Or of you, it seems."

Then his lips found hers, and words were lost to both of them. His tongue was much too busy communing with hers in a more intimate language. His teeth nibbled, his mouth suckled, his breath stole hers from her body, replacing it with his own. His long fingers tangled in her hair. Pins tumbled to the floor, unheeded.

Somehow her own fingers became enmeshed in the laces of his shirt, loosening them. Then her hands were seeking new territory beneath the cloth, spreading over his broad, hair-sprinkled chest. Never had she felt anything so sensuous as that warm, downy nest of fur. It sprang up between her stroking fingers and tickled her palms like shaggy velvet. It was wondrously soft over a bed of taut, sun-baked flesh.

As her fingernails lightly skimmed his flat male nipples, he drew in a sharp breath, his muscled chest pressing against her hands. To her surprise, his nipples peaked, as hers had once done at his touch. His every thundering heartbeat echoed into the center of her palms, his racing pulse speeding hers. His heat, his desire, seemed to transfer themselves to her at every point where their bodies touched.

The kiss deepened, tongues stroking, mouths devouring, as they clung to each other in a passionate embrace. Once again Eden experienced that sizzling jolt as Devlin's hand found her breast, molding his strong fingers around it, cupping, kneading. Through her dress, his thumb repeatedly grazed the crest, and a sweet ache coursed through her, building with every slight caress.

By the time Devlin had found and loosened the small clasps at the back of her dress, Eden was nearly senseless with yearning. He pushed the top of her gown down, over her shoulders, letting it fall about her waist. Only when the cooler air of her bedroom met her flushed skin did she think to object. But by then it was too late, and she was caught up in the mad spell Devlin seemed to be casting over her. In any case, he gave her neither time nor breath to demur, for no sooner had he bared her breasts to his view than his mouth left hers to claim this newfound prize.

The shock of his hot, moist mouth enclosing her bare breast so shocked her that Eden's knees buckled beneath her. Only Devlin's arms about her waist, anchoring her to him, kept her from falling to the floor. Her gasp became a strangled moan as he suckled her, sending streaks of fire from her breast to her abdomen. A strange, liquid heat pooled in that secret place between her legs. With tiny nibbles of his teeth, and the insistent flicking of his tongue, he laved her breasts. First one, and then its twin, while Eden melted and burned in the throes of a desire such as she had never envisioned.

As she lay arched over his arm, her fingers digging into his shoulders for purchase, her head spinning dizzily, Devlin's free hand found its way beneath her petticoats. With the first, unexpected contact of his hard fingers on the sensitive flesh at the back of her knee, Eden nearly leapt free of him, but he held her fast.

"Easy, sweetling," he murmured, his lips vibrating against her breast. "There's nothing to fear. Only pleasure. Such glorious pleasure."

All the while, he continued to stroke her leg and tongue her breast, while she quivered in his arms. Then his fingers found her inner thigh, and for Eden it was as if he'd branded her flesh with his. Her heart was pounding so violently, she thought surely it would explode. Her breath came in short, harsh pants.

"Devlin!" she rasped. "Oh! Stop, or I'll surely swoon!"

"Don't do that, pet," he answered on a hushed chuckle, "or you'll miss the best part."

Whatever she expected next, it was not his hand

covering her mound, his fingers sifting through the thick brown nest that guarded her most private parts, then separating the velvet folds in tender, seeking discovery.

"God, love!" he exclaimed softly. "You feel like hot, wet satin. I could burst just touching you."

Eden felt as if she already had. All of her thoughts, her senses, seemed to scatter, only to promptly converge on Devlin and where he was caressing her so intimately. His mouth claimed her breast once more, and the combined sensations made her cry out in wonder and alarm. He stroked, he pressed, and everywhere he touched, her body pulsated with tingling flames.

The tip of one finger probed at the portal to her most special feminine place, seeking entrance into her body. At the very moment it pushed into her, his mouth gave a sharp pull on her breast, and Eden's world shattered. Her eyes flew wide in awe, as rainbows seemed to dance over her head. Her body stiffened and quivered like a hunter's bow from which the arrow had just been released. Then, at the height of this magical, mystical phenomenon, Eden gave a queer little shriek and went limp in Devlin's arms.

It took a moment for Devlin to realize what had happened, and when he did, he wasn't sure whether to be offended or merely surprised. The wench had actually fainted!

With his own body still throbbing to the point of bursting, he gave a rueful laugh. Well, she'd certainly left him in a fine fix, hadn't she? That he probably deserved it was beside the point. However, he now had two choices left to him, neither of which held much appeal. He could either take her while she lay unconscious and unknowing beneath him, little better than a warm corpse, or he could put her to bed, in virginal solitude, and take himself off to the bay for a cool swim.

Deciding to be a gentleman for once in his life, he carried her to the bed, quickly stripped her down to her chemise, and tossed the bed sheet over her. "Another time, duchess," he promised with a wry chuckle and a shake of his head. "You won't always elude me so easily. Nay, I'll have my satisfaction yet, so rest well and gather your defenses, love, for surely you are going to need them."

Chapter 16

*E*den's prickly attitude did not take an immediate change for the better, at least not until her embarrassment over the intimate activities she and Devlin had engaged in had begun to abate. Even then, there were moments when her wayward mind would suddenly wander back, and she would mentally relive those stolen kisses, those heated caresses—and her body would burn anew with forbidden desire, her face flaming with telltale color.

Perversely, this always seemed to occur when Devlin was present to witness her discomfort, and he never failed to give her a shrewd smile or a knowing wink. The hateful wretch! Under his watchful eye, she began to feel like a mouse being stalked by a huge cat. A big, beautiful golden cat, with velvet paws and an agile tongue and a lean muscled body. Gadzooks! What spell had the man cast upon her? She could scarcely dare to look in his direction, lest she begin to pant like a bitch in heat!

Hers was not the only strange reaction occurring these days, however. Of course, no one seemed to notice it at first, but one afternoon shortly after Blackbeard's departure, Jane suddenly became aware that

Devlin's image was prone to linger for a few minutes after he and Eden had ceased touching each other. Always before, the instant they had broken contact, he had disappeared immediately.

Devlin was ecstatic with this new development. "Mayhap 'tis a sign that I'll soon be restored completely," he suggested. "Ah, to be normal again! 'Twould be bliss!"

"That may take some time yet," Eden warned, wondering why the idea of Devlin's recovery did not thrill her as much as it should. After all, consorting with a ghost was not the most convenient arrangement, and once he had his full self back, she would not need to be constantly tied to his coattails. They could both get back to their normal lives then.

And Devlin would leave. He would have no more need of her. Off he would sail, with hardly a thought of her.

Therein lay the cause of Eden's downheartedness. Not only had she become accustomed to having the arrogant beast practically shackled to her, but in these past weeks, she had truly come to love him. Ironically, Eden's words of warning to her mother had now come home to roost at her own doorstep. Nor was this a simple case of desire, though there was that also. She honestly loved him, with her whole being. When he left, as he surely would, her heart would be shattered, her entire life destroyed. Of this she was certain, and she could not look forward to it without being filled with dread.

On the other hand, the longer he stayed, the more he was around her, the better chance she had of convincing him to remain in Charles Town. Already he had insinuated himself into the fabric of their lives, and she knew he must care for her in some way. Obviously, he admired her mother, and Jane returned the affection. Besides, there was more to his life now than piracy; he was part owner of the warehouse and seemed to enjoy overseeing the work there.

If only the day would come when he would give up his hopes of returning to the sea, to that carefree outlaw life he'd had before. If only he loved her enough to stay. Not only for her sake, but for her mother's, because when Devlin sailed away, Nate would go too—and there would be two brokenhearted women left behind to weep and live on memories for the remainder of their lives.

Eden shook her head, berating herself for such fantasies. And what good would it do her if Devlin were to set down roots in Charles Town if he remained a phantom? Even were he to stay, to declare his love for her, what kind of life could they actually have together? How could they marry? How could they function as normal families did, if she had always to be at hand in order for him to be visible to others? How would they ever have children—if it were possible even to conceive a child from a man who was half-spirit? And, if it were, how would they explain Devlin's invisibility to their children, and manage to keep the fact hidden from everyone else all the while?

No, even as Devlin's condition was the only thing that truly kept him here now, it also stood between them—an impossible obstacle. Either way, she was bound to lose him eventually. She could only hope that the day would not come too quickly.

Eden soon had more to worry about than the consequences of Devlin's invisibility, or the duration of his stay. In spite of the additional security which had been posted in and around the warehouse since her office had been ransacked, yet another midnight incident occurred. This time it was a theft of goods in the warehouse itself, specifically of Devlin's cargo. Fortunately, very little was taken, since the guards discovered the theft soon after it began.

"There were five of 'em," Nate reported, having gathered the information from the guards. "Our fellows didn't get a good-enough look at any of 'em to be able to identify 'em, though. The minute they knew they'd been discovered, they run like rabbits, scatterin' goods all over the place as they went. One thing was mighty peculiar, if ye ask me. As dark as it was, all of those thievin' arses seemed to know their way around the inside of the warehouse like it was the back o' their hands. And that's probably the only reason they managed to get away like they done."

Devlin nodded. "Most likely, they were former employees. Tilton and his men." Devlin was searching the area himself, trying to find any evidence the men might have left behind. "Have you noticed that none of the doors show signs of being forced open, and that none of the windows are broken?" he asked with a thoughtful frown. "That leads me to believe that someone, probably Tilton, still has the keys to the locks."

"But, Devlin, you saw the man hand them over to me in the office the day I dismissed him," Eden commented.

"Aye. But who's to say he didn't have a second set made for himself, or for Finster, at any time during his employ? Since he was the manager of the place, no one would have questioned it if he'd professed to need them."

"Well, isn't this just a fine kettle of fish!" she exclaimed in disgust, her small fists atop her hips. "If the man can come and go as he pleases, so conveniently and quietly, what's to keep him from picking the entire warehouse as clean as a bone some night?"

Devlin grinned down at her, thinking she looked for all the world like a spirited, feather-ruffled hen. "For one thing, we're going to hire a locksmith and replace all the locks. If they have to force their way in next time, chances are the guards will hear the racket and be able to catch them sooner. And once we have one of them, we'll quickly have the others, for I doubt any of them are being paid well enough to take the blame alone. He'll squeal louder than a stuck hog."

Meanwhile, someone else was back to squealing his own tune. Dudley Finster was out to malign Devlin in any way he could, which mostly consisted of telling anyone who would listen what untrustworthy curs all pirates, and Devlin in particular, were. Not that everyone was listening to the mouthy little accountant. By now, most of them were well aware that jealousy was likely prompting his pique. Still, it was a sore point with Devlin and his crew, and to Eden and her mother.

Finster's latest verbal ammunition had to do with the recent theft at the warehouse. It was particularly galling that Finster, who was probably masterminding the scheme from behind the scenes, was now pointing his finger at Devlin. He was loudly heralding "that unscrupulous jackal" as the culprit, claiming Devlin was trying to disguise his true purpose behind a thin cloak of respectability.

"Well, if that ain't the pot callin' the kettle black!" Nate declared. "Someone ought to stick a rotten apple in that nasty shoat's mouth and roast him over a pit! Ye just say the word, Dev, an' me and the mates'll take care o' this problem for ye."

Devlin shook his head. "Not just yet, Nate. I'm thinking I'd like to have myself a bit of fun with this fellow first. The kind of pranks a ghost does best, if you take my meaning. If I could set the fear of the Devil into Blackbeard, why, I imagine I'll hardly work up a sweat spiking Finster's puny guns."

Jane nodded her agreement. "I ask only that you keep the bloodshed to a minimum, if you please, and not drag our good name into the mess while you're about it."

"Mama!" Eden was aghast. "What a thing to say!"

"Now, daughter, don't be such a faint-heart. Can you honestly stand there and tell me, after all that man has put you through, that you don't want to see him get a bit of his own dirt shoveled back into his face?"

"No, but I would hope the matter could be resolved in a more peaceful fashion than by breaking bones and shedding blood. Thief he might be, but he hasn't physically harmed anyone."

"Not yet," Devlin put in. "And I promise to conduct this mission of revenge in the most politic way possible. Does that satisfy your sense of propriety, duchess?"

She turned her nose up at him. "I won't know that until I see the result, will I?"

Devlin's first opportunity to put his plot against Finster into effect came the following afternoon. He'd just returned from his ship and was sauntering down the street in search of Eden and her mother. The two women had gone shopping for sewing materials and feminine furbelows, and since his own business hadn't required that he be seen, they'd gone their separate ways. With his personal errands accomplished, Devlin now thought he'd pop in on them and lend a hand with their purchases.

He'd just peered through the window of a small tea shop and spotted them at one of the tables when who should appear at his shoulder but Dudley Finster. Unseen as he was, Devlin watched as Finster mimicked his own actions. However, upon seeing the Winters women inside, Dudley did not immediately enter the shop. Rather, with a tight-lipped smirk, he continued down the street, where he entered a dusty establishment which dealt in books.

Curious, Devlin followed, entering the store so close behind him that the bell over the door chimed but once. He watched silently as Finster selected a book of poetry. "Is this a proper book of verse for a lady?" he questioned the proprietor.

"Indeed, and quite pleased she should be to receive it, too. I've only these two copies of it, and the other is already promised to Reverend Johnston for his dear wife."

"I'll take it." Finster counted out the proper amount and left the store, looking pleased.

Devlin didn't need to be a prophet to know that he'd bought the book for Eden, and most likely intended to give it to her immediately. As soon as the proprietor's back was turned, Devlin snatched up the remaining volume and stuffed it beneath his shirt. His fingers were on the door handle when he stopped short. Damn! Why had his conscience begun to plague him so relentlessly of late, when it had been so conveniently quiet for the past decade or more? Hurriedly, he dug into his pocket for the price of the book, tossed the coins behind him, and ran from the store.

Devlin dashed into the tea shop, fast on Finster's heels. He arrived at the table just in time to see Finster extend the book to Eden. Pushing up close to her, with his back to Finster, Devlin whipped his own volume from his shirt and dropped it into Eden's lap.

For all the confusion of the moment, Eden kept her head. As did Jane, who had seen the second book emerge from thin air. She watched with avid anticipation as Eden glanced first at the book, then up at Devlin, and then to the book Finster was yet holding out to her, an impish light dawning in her eyes.

"Why, Mr. Finster, I do believe you've purchased the exact volume of poetry I already own," she cooed, retrieving the book from her skirts and holding it aloft for his perusal. "Amazing, isn't it, that two people as different as you and I should select the same reading material?"

Devlin's smile grew as Finster's face fell. "But . . .

uh, how . . ." the man blustered. "The clerk at the book-store swore that he had only two copies left, this and one reserved for Henrietta Johnston."

Eden gave him a simpering smile. "Then I do hope you enjoy the author's work, since it appears to be at such a premium, sir. If not, perhaps you can return it and have your money refunded to you."

"And I hope Henrietta gets her copy before it disappears entirely," Jane interposed wryly, spearing a stern look toward Devlin, or where she supposed he was standing.

Not content to be so easily defeated, Finster dredged up a thin smile. "Again, I seem to have chosen my gift unwisely. Will you let me make up for it by buying the two of you another cup of tea?" Without awaiting their consent, he promptly seated himself at Eden's side and motioned for the serving girl.

While Finster was thus diverted, Eden cast a quick look at Devlin, who wagged his brows at her, grinned, and nodded. In turn, Eden gave a slight signal to her mother. "That would be most kind of you, Mr. Finster," she answered belatedly.

When the fresh pot of tea was delivered, Eden poured each of them a cup of the steaming brew. Then she and Jane sat back and waited.

As Finster tried to chip a bit of sugar from the sugar cone, cone and spoon went sailing through the air. As luck would have it, the weighty cone bounced off of a neighboring patron's bald head, nearly knocking the poor man senseless. The fellow's portly wife was the recipient of the flying spoon, which landed in her cup and splattered tea from her hat to her mighty bosom.

The couple's yowls were heard throughout the shop, and every head turned to witness the lady rising from her seat, a-drip with tea and as enraged as a bull. With narrowed eyes, and a threatening scowl, she glanced about for the culprit, while Finster did his best to appear innocent and insignificant.

The formidable woman was not to be denied, and Eden was perfectly willing to oblige her in her search. In a voice that carried to the four walls, Eden wailed, "Oh, Mr. Finster! How perfectly clumsy of you! Just see what you have done!"

Those terrible, fiery eyes leveled themselves on Finster, and he literally shrank down in his seat. With a bellow that would put a charging elephant to shame, the woman grabbed up her parasol and lunged toward him.

Finster ducked the first swing, but the second whacked him squarely upon the head. The third sent his chair toppling out from under him; the fourth caught him aside the ribs. The next few minutes were complete havoc as Finster scuttled crablike toward the entrance under a continual rain of blows, fellow patrons hooting with laughter and hastily making way. Dudley was last seen limping down the street toward the doctor's office, one arm shielding his head and the other wrapped around his ribs.

Eden was among the many people in the tea shop who wiped tears of mirth from their faces. "Land's sake, but that was a sight to see!"

Devlin, who in the midst of the fracas had slipped behind a screen with Eden, grabbed hold of her arm, and become visible without notice, righted Finster's empty chair and joined the ladies. "I had no idea 'twould turn out so well," he told them, still chuckling. "I swear, that old harridan swings her parasol like a battle-ax! I wonder if I could persuade her to join my crew."

"I'd like to know where she bought such a stout sunshade," Jane piped in.

"I was under the distinct impression you would sooner be boiled in oil than allow a woman aboard your ship," Eden said, wrinkling her nose at him.

"True," he agreed. "Damned inconvenient at times, but true."

Eden shook her head mockingly. "I despair of you, Devlin. Verily, I do. Your silly, superstitious nature will be the end of you. I've seen you step into the street to avoid walking under a ladder, knock on wooden objects to ensure good fortune, and thrown salt over your shoulder if you accidentally spill it. Why, I declare you would have turned purple if that lady had opened her parasol indoors."

Devlin's chin came up defensively. "Laugh if you will, Eden, but an ounce of prevention is worth a pound of cure, and these notions are not of my invention. They had to arise from some truth, otherwise there would not be so many people who believe in them. So put that in your bum roll and sit on it, milady."

"I'm not wearing a bolster at present," she countered saucily.

He grinned and arched a sardonic brow at her. "I noticed."

"How crude of you to observe such a thing."

"No more indelicate than you pointing out the fact."

Jane sighed. "Drink your tea, children, and Mama will take both of you home and put you to bed for a nice long nap, so that I may have some peace at last."

Devlin's eyes brightened. "And will the nice mama put us to bed together, by chance?" he asked with a boyish grin.

Jane answered with a lemon-tart smile. "Only bound and gagged in individual parcels."

Quite inadvertently, mother and daughter were soon treated to another prime example of a sailor's superstitious nature. Nate had come to dinner, and the four of them were just finishing their meal when Willie Moffet brought the cows home from pasture. He was later than usual, and Dora had already retired to her quarters, so

Eden volunteered to feed and bed the animals, while Jane conversed with the men.

When Devlin gallantly offered to help her, Eden politely declined. Not only was the pirate captain inept at handling livestock, but she had a keen suspicion he only wanted to corner her in the haymow for another session of touch and tickle. And Eden had had quite enough of that. From now on, she intended to avoid all temptation.

She'd finished with the milking and had just stored the fresh pails in the well-house to cool when she felt something small and furry brush against her leg. She gave a lively start of fright before hearing the tiny meow. Looking down, she found a small black kitten, its golden eyes peering up at her in the most pathetic manner.

"Oh, just look at you!" she murmured, bending to scoop the little mite into her arms. "If you aren't the cutest thing since Christmas!" As if in full agreement, and to further entice her, the cat rubbed its head under her chin and began to purr contentedly.

Eden laughed. "You win, puss. You can't have the fresh milk, but there's a lick or two left in the pitcher in the kitchen, and I'm sure no one will begrudge the little you will drink. I'll bet there are even a few scraps from the table you could have. How does that sound?" The kitten somehow managed to purr and meow in the same breath.

When Eden entered the dining room with the cat, to show the sweet little thing to her mother, she watched in awe as both burly pirates blanched as white as starched linen and went twice as stiff!

"Get . . . get that creature out of here!" Devlin croaked, his voice as raspy as sand, his eyes resembling two huge burn holes in a sheet. Nate nodded mutely, his head bobbing so vigorously that, had it been attached to the handle of the churn, they would have had butter in seconds.

"Oh, come now!" Eden scoffed. " 'Tis but a tiny, harmless kitten. One would think I'd just come through the door with a full-grown lion!"

" 'Tis black!" Devlin declared, pointing an accusing finger at the animal. "Pure black! An omen of misfortune, should it cross your path! I'll not have it near me, I say!"

Had he not pointed that finger so directly, all might not have gone so awry. As it was, Zeus, who was perched invisibly on the back of Devlin's chair, took this as a command to attack. With an ear-piercing shriek, and mad churning of wings, the bird launched himself at the cat. So heartily did he do so that the thong binding him to the rung of the chair uncoiled itself before Devlin could think to prevent it.

Even as the falcon squawked his warning, the kitten reacted in fright. Its needle-sharp claws bit into Eden's arm, the fur on its back standing straight up like porcupine quills. It leapt from Eden's arms, leaving behind eight long red welts for her efforts to hold it.

Eden's yelp of pain, and her cry of alarm, were scarcely audible for the cat's frantic yowling, Zeus's horrid screeching, and the shouts of the other three humans.

"Get the bird!"

"Catch the cat!"

"The hell with the blarsted cat! Grab hold of Zeus's leash!"

"Watch out!"

"Oh, no! My best lamp! Eden, quick! Fetch the broom!"

In the process of trying to douse the fire from the toppled oil lamp, Jane tossed an entire pitcher of water into the crotch of Nate's britches. "Sorry," she apologized lamely. "Eden! Bring more water! Quickly!"

Devlin, who was the only person present who could see the dratted hawk, was dashing around like a madman, whistling at the top of his lungs—all the while keeping one eye on the cat and trying mightily to stay out of its path.

Frightened witless, the kitten was scurrying hither and thither in an effort to elude Zeus. Under tables, around chairs, up the draperies it went, the bird in hot pursuit.

Nate, who also had no ambitions toward catching the kitten, applied himself to putting out the fire and trying to rescue further breakables from flapping arms and wings.

Jane manned the broom, chasing after both demented creatures as best she could, while Eden scampered over and around furniture, trying to snag the fleet-footed kitten. At one point she almost had hold of him, until she caught her head in the rungs of a chair and nearly strangled herself. She could have cheerfully throttled both animals and urged her mother to put the broom to better use—on the men!

At long last, when Eden was sure she had not one more breath in her body, or one more ounce of strength to go on, Devlin caught hold of Zeus's thong and reeled him in. Using the leash, he bound the hawk's lethal feet and employed a table napkin as a hood to finish the job of restraining the frantic bird.

Seconds later, Eden captured the kitten, which she promptly deposited outside the back door. The instant the cat's paws hit the grass, it was off like a shot. Eden doubted they'd ever see hide or hair of it again—not if the poor thing had an ounce of brains!

She walked back into the dining room and stared about in disbelief. "Merciful heavens!" she exclaimed. "It looks as if a hurricane struck!"

Chairs were overturned, the draperies drooped on their rods and were scarred with snags, and the linen cloth was half off the table, the dishes balanced precariously on the edge. Goblets were toppled, the chandelier was askew, and Jane's prized Persian rug had a wet scorch in it.

"I don't even want to look." Jane groaned from her resting spot against the wall, her eyes closed in weary defeat. "When I do, I'm going to be sick."

Eden noted that both men were now conspicuously absent. "Where did those two worthless ninnies disappear to?"

Jane gave a tired chuckle. "They ran for their lives, as all brave men are wise to do when faced with a woman's fury. Devlin went upstairs to calm his beloved bird, which I am considering poisoning. And Nate bussed me on the cheek and fled to the ship, assuming that would be far enough from my reach for safety. Little does he know how long I can hold a grudge, the silly fool!"

"And they call Finster a milksop!" Eden declared, sinking down beside her mother. "Heaven help us both, Mama! We've fallen in love with a pair of very contrary rogues!"

Chapter 17

With Jane miffed over the desecration of her dining room, and Eden keeping her distance and acting wary of him these days, the highlight of Devlin's life was his continued campaign against Finster. He delighted in devising new ways to publicly discredit the accountant, just as Finster had tried to do to him. The difference lay in Devlin's more devious methods.

He took to following the moneylender around town, shadowing his activities. He listened in on private transactions and conceived of ways to scotch the most advantageous deals Finster had in the offing. This he did cheerfully, with the knowledge that if he ruined the man financially it was no less than Dudley had meant for Eden.

As he had done in the tea shop, Devlin continued to plague Finster with perplexing accidents. The fellow would be walking down the street with a favored client and suddenly lose control of his limbs, his arms and legs thrashing about unaccountably in every direction as Devlin nudged his elbows or tripped him up. After several such incidents, people began to shy away from him, as if he had contracted some strange disease they were loath to catch.

But Devlin's crowning achievement, the one he most enjoyed, occurred right in the man's own lending house, with his father looking on in horror. The previous day, a ship had landed in the harbor bearing several important officials from London, who had arrived to inspect various business establishments in Charles Town. They were presently touring the offices of the accounting firm, having been ushered inside with much formality.

Naturally, since there was a lord or two among them, they had gathered a large contingent of curious followers, and the main receiving room was full to overflowing. The elder Finster had designated his son to present a bouquet of flowers to Lady Chamberlain, who had accompanied her husband on the voyage. Puffed with pride, his hands filled with flowers and all eyes upon him, Finster announced pretentiously, "Lady Chamberlain, it is with great honor that I offer you this small token of our esteem."

At precisely this point Devlin chose to strike. Conveniently unseen, he held out the invisible blade of his sword and swiftly sliced the buttons from Finster's trousers! The accountant's britches dropped to his ankles with the speed of a falling stone, while his shirt stayed crumpled at his waist. Since he wore no drawers beneath, his intimate anatomy was completely displayed to one and all, but most especially to Lady Chamberlain!

A collective gasp ran through the crowd, even as the baroness cried out in shock and swooned into her husband's arms. Finster, as stunned as the rest, abandoned the flowers and hastened to retrieve his trousers.

The irate baron sputtered, finally got hold of his wits, and declared pompously, "I'll have satisfaction, by God! At dawn on the morrow, you shall meet me with your sword and your second!"

"But my lord! I know not how to wield a sword!"

"Then it shall be a duel of pistols."

"But your lordship, he has no second!" a voice tittered from the rear of the room.

Finster's father stepped forward, his face blistered with shame for his son, but ready to defend him nonetheless. "My lord, please! 'Twas an unfortunate accident which we much regret. Is there no other way to rectify this unfortunate incident? I beg your mercy. He's my only son."

"Then I pity you, sir, for you got a raw bargain," the baron assured him. "You would be well rid of him."

"Of late, I would agree. But not through his death. I implore you to spare him."

Devlin would have liked to have argued the point and urged the nobleman to insist on the duel, but as he was presently invisible, he could not. This same hindrance, as well as his own moral code, was what had thus far deterred Devlin from personally engaging Finster in mortal combat, since it wouldn't be sporting to do so as a spirit, with the man unable to see him. It was one thing to go up against a rowdy band of misfits such as had planned to attack the Winters's home, or to tangle with cutthroat buccaneers who themselves had no scruples. But Devlin did not deem it fair to remain invisible when facing an opponent less skilled than himself, particularly one generally thought to be a gentleman. Thus, by his own honor, he was forced to limit his revenge against Finster to milder confrontations.

The baroness was quickly reviving from her faint, and it was she who next claimed her husband's ear. "Harold!" she whimpered. "Did I hear mention of a duel? You promised me, upon your sacred oath, that you would not indulge in such perilous endeavors again. I care not what becomes of this horrid man, except that I never set eyes on him again. Let us return posthaste to England, where we are accorded the respect so lacking in this filthy backwoods colony."

Blast and damn the woman! Devlin could have spit nails! Just when he'd finally cornered the little weasel good and proper, it looked as if Finster was going to escape without the least consequence, not even so much as a slap on the hand!

But perhaps not entirely. As the disgusted crowd began to disperse, several comments were offered up.

"'Twill be a cold day when I do business here again."

"Mr. Finster, you'll not see a pence more from me as long as your son is working here."

"Far as I'm concerned, ye can get yer meat from another butcher, sirs."

"That goes for me as well. I don't do business with perverts."

"That lad's gone as queer as a three-legged goose!"

Devlin's retelling of the tale set Eden, Jane, and Nate rollicking. "I'll wager his father will choose the business over his son, and send him packing off somewhere until the dust settles," Jane predicted. "That old man is so tight with his money, he probably takes it to bed with him each night."

"Well, the sooner Dudley is gone, the better it will suit me," Eden announced.

Nate agreed. "And good riddance to the varmint! I just wish ye'd told me what it was ye were up to today, Dev. I'd have paid to have seen it."

"Well, I'm more than glad Eden and I were absent, thank you. I don't wish to have my daughter viewing such a spectacle. Once was quite enough," Jane put in, obliquely referring to the day Dora had whisked the sheet from Devlin's nude body, exposing him to Eden's eyes.

Eden blushed. Devlin merely laughed and said, "Truth be told, there wasn't much to see today. Mayhap that's why the lady fainted. Mayhap she thought him malformed!"

Jane glowered, but commented sweetly—too sweetly. "Captain Kane, your mouth could do with another soaping from your shaving brush, anytime you'd care to oblige."

"And I wield a wicked razor, too, if you'll recall," Eden added.

Under their dual assault, and much to Nate's amusement, Devlin sought a swift retreat. "Methinks I've decided to grow that beard after all."

Though Devlin had never had much to do with farmyard animals, there was one area which could almost be termed domestic in which he excelled. In the days following the episode with Zeus and the cat, he put his knowledge of carpentry to good use, as a means of getting back into Jane and Eden's good graces. It also served to keep him occupied when he wasn't needed at the warehouse, or when Eden was otherwise engaged.

Within a short time, he had repaired two sagging dresser drawers, replaced the chipped cornice above the corner cupboard, refitted the loose rungs of several chairs, and refinished the top of a drop-leaf table. He also mended Eden's office chair, the one that had been all but destroyed when her office was ransacked. It would never be quite the same, but at least he'd managed to save it from the kindling pile.

Jane was thrilled, and very grateful, for these needed repairs. Eden was moved to tears, and properly astounded. "Devlin! I had no idea you were so talented. Where did you learn such a wonderful skill?"

A shadow crossed Devlin's face. "From my father," he admitted. "He was a carpenter by trade, and he taught me."

"How marvelous to have such skill run in the family. Where are your parents now?"

"In England," he answered brusquely. "In their graves."

"Oh, Devlin! How thoughtless of me to ask such a thing." Though grieved that her curiosity had obviously brought him pain, she could not help questioning him further. "Has it been long?"

Squatting back on his heels beside the window frame he was bracing, Devlin let the wedge of wood he was holding drop unheeded to the floor, his mind turning backward in time. Just when Eden had decided he was not going to answer her, he spoke in a voice made husky with emotion.

" 'Twas eleven years ago. We were planning to move to the colonies, where my father was going to join his brother in the carpentry shop he had begun here. Before we'd completed our packing, and the sale of our house and shop there, London was hit with the cholera. It swept through the city like wildfire. Fearing for my health, Mother and Father decided to send me on ahead of them to the Americas. I didn't want to leave them behind, but they insisted. You see, by then the port officials were reluctant to allow ships out of port, fearing the transport of the disease. My parents promised to follow as soon as possible."

"And you left? All by yourself?" Eden queried in soft commiseration. "Did you have no siblings, no other relatives to come with you?"

"There were just the three of us, though I'm sure Mother wanted more children. I was sixteen, well able to fend for myself, and big for my age even then."

"How long was it before you learned of their deaths? I assume they died of the cholera, did they not?"

"Aye, and it took me six interminable years to know of it."

Eden was aghast. "Six years!" she exclaimed. "My word, Devlin! Why so long?"

He gave a chilling, mirthless laugh. "Fate, my sweet.

A black-hearted pirate by the name of Swift took it into his head to attack the ship transporting me to the colonies. The only thing that kept me from a watery grave was my youth, my size, and my carpentry skills, which the *Gai Mer* was badly in need of. Even that would not have saved me had I not agreed, under duress and much persuasion, to sign the Articles of the Brethren, thus effectively, and upon my solemn oath, joining the order of pirates."

"If the *Gai Mer* is yours, what became of Swift?" Eden wanted to know.

"First of all, the *Gai Mer* jointly belongs to Nate and me, since we organized the mutiny against Swift some six years after my capture. As for Swift, who made so many years of my life a living hell, I may be granted yet another opportunity for revenge against him, since rumor now has it that he is still alive. In days past, I'd joyously imagined his bones, and those of his loyal followers, adorning the beaches of the uninhabited island upon which we marooned them."

Eden grimaced delicately. "What occurred after that?"

"I, Nate, and the part of the crew who had decided to align with us headed back to England. There, finally, I learned of the death of my parents, and for the first time set flowers upon their graves. My sole consolation was that they never knew that their beloved only son had become involved in such a nefarious life."

Tears swam in Eden's eyes. "Then why did you not give it up and join your uncle, as was originally planned?"

Devlin returned her look with a smile of self-derision. "By then, my dove, I had become accustomed to a much richer life than the carpentry business could provide. Piracy can be very seductive, as can the sea itself. I thrived upon it, and upon commanding my own vessel."

"Did you ever visit your uncle? Does he know what became of you?"

Devlin shook his head. "I suppose he may have heard, but I've never gone to see him. He's not the sort to condone brigandry, and I felt 'twould only embarrass him, were I to show up at his door. He has his family to consider, and I wouldn't want to shame them."

"And what of you, Devlin? Do you not long for the companionship of your own kin? Do you never wish for a home and family of your own? To quit your lawless wandering and settle down to one place?"

He caught her gaze with his, holding it and reading the yearning she tried to hide from him. "Eden." He sighed. "My sweet Eden, if anyone could tempt me 'twould be you. But sailing is in my blood, lass. I could not forsake it for long."

She ducked her head to conceal her disappointment. "But must it be piracy? Many a man is content to sail the seas lawfully. Why not you?"

He shrugged. "That could be somewhat difficult, wraith that I am. If this ghostliness proves to be permanent, I would be a most formidable sea robber, don't you see? At any rate, I fear I am too restless to make a good husband."

She dared to look at him. "Do you know what I fear, Devlin?" she said softly. "I fear for your life, if you continue down this path of crime and violence. I fear for your soul." She rose and made her way slowly to the door, as if weighted down with her bleak thoughts.

There she turned to deliver a final, solemn comment. "You say you would not make a good husband? Could it be, great strong rogue that you seem, that you are afraid of committing yourself to one woman, to one place? If so, you are condemning yourself to a lifetime of loneliness. And it may prove to be a very short one, at the rate you are going."

* * *

Eden could have cut out her tongue, for she had inadvertently revealed more of her feelings to Devlin than she'd wanted. Indeed, more than she should have, since Devlin had felt it necessary to warn her away from thoughts of marriage to him.

Lord, but she felt such a fool! Here she was, the dowdy Spinster Winters suddenly thinking herself so irresistible that a man as handsome and footloose as Devlin should fall over himself to gain her hand and her heart? Ha! What a farce! And how humiliating to be so bluntly reminded otherwise! The man had no designs on her heart, no desire for her hand. The randy rogue only wanted beneath her skirts. That was the long and the short of it, and high time she faced up to that fact once and for all!

But, drat it all, he had seemed to care. When he hadn't been trying to sweeten his way into her bed, they'd talked and laughed together. True, they'd yelled and argued equally as often, but they'd also shared private portions of their lives. He'd held her as she wept, and dried her tears with his kisses. Was this the act of a man who did not care?

While Eden was wallowing in mortified confusion, Devlin was busy flaying himself with self-derision. Blarst! He felt as if he'd just tromped on a helpless chick! The pain on Eden's face had torn at his heart. But he could not rescind his words, for they were true. Indeed, he did love roving the seas; he did enjoy the life of a pirate; he would make a poor husband. And there was possibly some unfinished business with Swift, which could soon take him sailing again.

Yet he could not deny that he had led Eden down the garden path a bit in his pursuit of her. Oh, he'd never declared undying love, or anything of that sort. No, he'd been much more subtle, more underhanded. Without committing himself, he had led her to trust him, to believe in him. He'd watched her blossom beneath his praise and attention, and just when she'd felt secure, he'd pulled the rug out from under her feet! All in the name of lust! And damn him if he didn't still want her, even as guilt gnawed at him.

Before leaving Charles Town, he would keep his vow to her. He would rid her of Finster and the problems at the warehouse. He would also keep his pledge to himself. He would make love to Eden, right or wrong, regardless of her mother's threats or any other consequences—and mayhap then he could rid himself of this obsessive desire, this relentless need for her. Perhaps then she would cease to haunt his every thought, waking and sleeping, stop taunting him in his dreams each night. Aye, he had to have her, if just once, before he sailed. Then he had to make certain he never set foot in Charles Town again, because Eden was much too bewitching to resist twice in one lifetime.

The two of them proceeded to tiptoe around one another like a pair of wary alligators. Even as she accompanied him to town, while Devlin continued to sell and trade the merchandise he and his crew had stored at her warehouse, Eden remained uncharacteristically aloof and quiet.

Then Devlin did something curious, something that shocked her out of her morose musings. He ordered Nate to bring the *Gai Mer* ashore, to beach the frigate on the short stretch of sand next to the warehouse wharf. She couldn't help but question this command, or die of inquisitiveness, all the while hoping it somehow meant he'd decided to give up sailing after all.

Her prayers were not to be so easily answered, however. "I've decided we might as well careen the ship, since we have the time and the opportunity," he explained. "Besides, we've been in port so long that the men are beginning to get restless. They need more to keep them occupied, lest I lose them to another captain."

"Careen?" Eden echoed. "What is that?" She stared at the huge vessel, now toppled helplessly on its side on the beach, wishing he would tell her it meant to dismantle the ship for all time.

"To scrape the hull free of barnacles and sea debris," he told her, blithely unaware that he was deflating her hopes once more. "A ship's underside needs a good cleaning every now and again, and 'tis a job that can only be done correctly on dry land, since the timbers usually need to be re-tarred as well. Unfortunately, we've let the *Gai Mer* go longer than she should, and she's showing signs of sluggishness."

At Eden's puzzled look, he went on. "The cleaner the hull, the faster the ship will sail, and in my business, speed is essential."

"Then you are making ready to sail soon," Eden surmised, swallowing a lump in her throat and blinking back sudden tears.

Devlin shrugged, scarcely noting the added brightness of her eyes or the extra huskiness of her voice. "I've no definite plans to do so, Eden. There is still this business with Tilton and Finster to finish, and I'll not go until I've seen it to a satisfactory conclusion. However, I want the frigate ready when I am, and it takes a while to do the chore properly."

"How long?"

"A couple of weeks, give or take a few days."

Eden wanted to scream. Two weeks? A mere fortnight more of having Devlin in her life? Oh, God! How would she ever bear it, knowing he would be gone so soon? No wonder he'd been so intent on selling his cargo and clearing it from the warehouse. Even then, he'd been thinking of leaving, anticipating his departure.

"What of your invisibility, Devlin?" she asked hesitantly. "I thought you intended to remain in Charles Town until you got your body back."

"I may never get it back, and I can't remain here forever. As I said, the crew is already showing signs of restlessness. However, I'll stay as long as I can, and hope for a miracle before I go."

As will I, Eden thought. *A miracle to keep you here. A miracle to make you love me too much to leave me.*

Chapter 18

A week had passed since the incident in the lending house. The offended baroness had taken the first ship back to England, as had the remainder of their visiting party. Gossip was still rampant, and the Finsters' banking business was in a decline as a result. And still, though Eden hoped for his departure with great anticipation, Dudley remained in Charles Town.

"What is keeping him here?" she wondered aloud, knowing she would not draw a full breath of relief until she'd seen the last of him. On the other hand, Dudley's departure would, in all likelihood, precipitate Devlin's, and Eden would rather have the threat of Finster hanging over her head forever than to see Devlin leave.

"Mayhap he's waiting for the talk to die down, thinking folks will soon forget and all will return to normal again," Jane suggested.

Nate nodded. "Given enough time, it just might. Looks to me like the man needs another nudge or two, Dev."

"Aye," Devlin agreed. Then he shook his head and added, "Who would have thought we'd have this much trouble with the likes of Finster? Blimey! Even Blackbeard wasn't this hard to convince!"

"Blackbeard didn't have as much to lose," Eden reminded him. "Dudley's entire future, and everything he's striven for, are now at stake."

"Which makes the man more dangerous than ever," Jane predicted.

Devlin nodded. "Give him another day or two, and if he still hasn't left, I'll see what else I can do to hurry him along."

Later that evening, Eden was undressing for bed. She'd disrobed down to her chemise, and was attempting to unravel a knot in the laces, when Devlin spoke from the darkened corner of her bedroom. "Need help with that, pet? I'm uncommonly handy at aiding ladies out of their undergarments."

Swallowing a startled gasp, and clutching her hands over the lacy, low-cut bodice, Eden retorted breathlessly, "I don't doubt you've had abundant practice, Devlin, though probably more with loose women than with ladies." She peered into the shadows and found him lounging in the chair near the window. "I, however, do not require your help. I have been removing my own clothing for more than twenty years now, and can continue to do so quite nicely, thank you."

"Not as *nicely* as with my assistance."

"I'll manage. Now, kindly remove yourself from my bedroom."

"But I've come bearing gifts, my dove." He rose and sauntered toward her, his hands extended. In one he held a silver-backed brush, in the other an ornate silver-edged comb, a matching set. "I was hoping you'd let down your hair and grant me the pleasure of brushing it for you."

Even as she reached for the beautiful offerings, she commented skeptically, "Since when are you a lady's maid, Devlin Kane?"

"Ah, but sweets, I am a man of many talents, as you

would know, if you would but permit me to demonstrate a few of my better abilities."

Eden turned toward the lamp on her dressing table, comb and brush in hand, the better to examine their intricate design. No sooner was her back turned than Devlin's fingers were delving through her upswept hair in search of the restraining pins. Eden's head snapped up, a ready reprimand on the tip of her tongue, as her eyes sought Devlin's in the mirror.

The retort froze on her lips. Her eyes widened in wonder. She could feel Devlin's breath on the nape of her neck, his warm presence just behind her, though his hands were no longer tangled in her hair. She knew he was there, and if she were to turn toward him again, she was certain she would behold the teasing smile on his face, the sparkle in his dark eyes. Yet, for the life of her, she could not discern his reflection in the mirror before her!

It was too strange! So eerie that gooseflesh peppered her skin. In all these weeks, while everyone else was experiencing this phantom phenomenon, Eden had always been able to see him. Never had she truly experienced him in this ghostly mien, as others had. Until this very moment.

He'd told her he could not view himself in a mirror. She'd believed him. She'd also believed when others could not see him. But she'd never witnessed the oddity for herself, and it came as a jolt now.

Her heart hammering a drumbeat in her breast, Eden whirled to face him. On a sigh of relief, once more her gaze met with sun-kissed flesh, actual cloth, and a substantial man.

"Oh, Devlin!" she breathed gratefully, wilting against the solid breadth of his chest. "'Twas so queer! So frightening, not to be able to see you in the mirror! At last I realize just how immense a shock this must have been for everyone else. For you most especially."

Her words cleared the perplexed frown from his face, and Devlin chuckled, enclosing her firmly in the shelter of his arms. "Scary, isn't it, duchess? Particularly the first instance or two. I've become so accustomed to your ability to see me, the thought never occurred to me that my reflection would be every bit as invisible to you as 'tis to me. Served you somewhat of a fright, eh?"

She nodded. "Upon consideration, however, more's the wonder that it did not happen sooner. Of all the shop windows and shiny objects and mirrors we've passed, not once have I noticed the absence of your image in them."

"Most likely because we were touching then," he supposed. "At those intervals when I am totally visible to all, so is my reflection." He turned her toward the mirror once more, removing his hands from her arms before she caught a glimpse in the glass. For the moment, hers was the only likeness reproduced.

"Watch, now," he instructed, laying a hand to her shoulder. Upon contact between them, his image flickered into view.

Eden giggled. "'Tis like magic!" she murmured, enthralled. "A marvelous illusion! Do it again, Devlin."

Laughing, he complied. "You are easily entertained, Eden. So like a delightful, enchanting child at times. And so like a beguiling temptress at others," he added softly, his deep voice rumbling near her ear.

Their eyes caught and held as desire sparked between them, even through the looking glass. As Eden watched in breathless fascination, his hand slid from her shoulder, his touch ever-present as his fingertips lightly caressed the curve of her neck, the ticklish rim of her ear. Retracing the same path, he pushed the strap of her chemise aside, baring her shoulder and the high slope of her breast.

Her eyes widened, their turquoise tint changing from

light to dark as she anticipated his next move. His own eyes blazed with fiery intent, gleaming like polished jet in the shimmering lamplight.

His tawny head lowered, inch by inch, until his hot, moist mouth closed over the arch of her shoulder, his teeth nipping gently at the sensitive tendon just beneath her skin. Instantly, a wild tingling streaked through her. As if at his personal, unspoken command, the peaks of her breasts hardened. Her belly burned; her knees threatened to buckle beneath her. Closing her eyes, she bit back a weak moan.

"Nay," he directed in a hoarse whisper. "Open your eyes, Eden. Look. See how your body responds to my touch. Feel it. Know it. Want it."

Her lashes fluttered open in helpless obedience, her gaze locking with his. As if spellbound, like a hare entranced by a hawk, she watched him adroitly unlace her chemise, his nimble fingers defying the knots with ease. Just as deftly did he deal with her corset, and suddenly Eden found herself completely bared to his view—and her own.

His arms closed about her from behind, drawing her firmly against the front of him. Beyond the silvered surface of her mirror, she saw his hands rise, the palms cupping to cradle her breasts, his thumbs brushing the aching crests. Though she caught at her lower lip with the edge of her teeth, her answering gasp would not be stifled. Nor could she suppress the immediate quickening of her body to his skillful manipulation, the flames that shot through her, heating her blood and bringing a telltale flush to her flesh.

Even so, his sun-bronzed fingers made a startling contrast as they rested over her pale breasts, as they plucked gently at her rose-hued nipples, sending lightning deep within to pierce her womb. One dark hand wandered lower, resting for a moment on the flat plane of her stomach, making her muscles clench ever tighter, then venturing further to delve into the nest of red-brown curls that sheltered her womanhood. A whimper escaped her, a wispy breath born half from yearning, half from apprehension.

"Look, love," he commanded yet again. "See how my hands adore your body, how they stroke and entice your loveliness." He edged a knee between her own, parting her thighs and causing her to lean more heavily into him, to clutch at his upper arms for support.

With her head cushioned against his broad shoulder, compelled by Devlin and by her own burgeoning longings, Eden watched in passion-glazed awe as his fingers parted her, darting unerringly to the very heart of her desire, that small kernel of flesh that seemed to house the soul of her sensual feelings. At that first, stunning contact there, she lurched in his arms and cried out softly. Reflexively, she closed her eyes, only to have them spring open again as Devlin continued his sweet torment, the fingers of one hand plucking at her nipple in concert to the rhythmic stroking he applied below.

Her legs shook, her stomach trembled, her flesh felt seared to the marrow of her bones. Moist heat pooled inside her, flowing like lava in her loins. Everything tightened in intense anticipation. She ached. She burned. She wanted.

"Tell me," he urged softly, his mirrored eyes burning into hers. "Tell me what you feel."

"Hot!" she mewled. "So hot . . . and wet . . . and tight . . . and . . . empty!"

Devlin slid a finger inside her, and she swallowed a muted cry of mixed relief and need. Instinctively, she moved against him, arching and twisted and reaching for more.

And still she could not tear her eyes from their reflected image, from the sight of his flesh invading hers so intimately, the vision of herself writhing so wantonly in his embrace. His fingers stretched up inside her, plumbing, probing, while the heel of his hand tantalized that outer nubbin of desire. Incredibly, her passion rose further still, until she thought she would go mindless, forever and blissfully crazed with this splendid craving.

Then, suddenly, it was as if a dam burst within her. As if a tightly compressed inner volcano had erupted full-force, thrusting her out of herself and into the bright, blinding glory of a thousand suns.

Only then did she squeeze her eyes shut, her shout of joy smothered against Devlin's muffling hand as he held her quaking body tightly to his, sheltering her against the onslaught, supporting her through the rapturous journey.

"Be mine now," she heard him beseech her.

And she heard herself answer meekly, willingly, "Aye."

Devlin swung her into his arms, cradling her against his thudding heart as he carried her toward the bed. He placed her gently upon it and had just begun to unbutton his shirt when a tremendous pounding arose at the downstairs door.

"Fire!" someone shouted loudly. "Fire at the warehouse! Hurry, Cap'n Kane!"

Eden hastily yanked her night shift over her head and rushed out into the hall. Two steps beyond her door she ran headlong into Nate—the man having just emerged from her mother's bedroom, buttoning his britches on the way!

Though she'd begun to suspect by now, this was the first time Eden was confronted with the indisputable fact that the quartermaster spent his nights in her mother's bed. Heretofore, the older couple had been very circumspect, but the cat was out of the bag now, and Eden was caught speechless.

She and Nate stopped short in mutual shock. She gaped at him in surprise, all the while hoping God would not see fit to restore Devlin to normal visibility at this disastrous moment, and praying that her own guilt was not shining forth like a blazing beacon for all to see.

Evidently, Nate was having much the same problem with his conscience, for he stood as if turned to stone. Devlin's timely intervention was a mixed blessing, as he noted their stupefied looks and said gruffly, "You two can thrash this out between you at a more convenient time. Or have you forgotten we've a warehouse to save?" With a push to get him started, the still-invisible Devlin ushered Nate toward the stairs.

"Oh, mercy! The warehouse!" Eden shrieked, coming out of her stunned state.

She started down the hall, only to have her mother call after her. "Eden! You're in your nightdress! Let Nate and Devlin go on ahead, and you and I will follow as soon as we can."

Eden had never dressed so quickly. Foregoing the usual number of petticoats and bindings, she dove into her wardrobe and came up with an old brown day gown, the dress she usually reserved for housecleaning and gardening. She yanked on the first pair of stockings her fingers touched, and shoved her feet into her shoes, waiting to lace them until she and Jane were in the buggy and on their way. Only then did she realize that she'd left the house with neither shawl nor cap, but propriety be damned! Little did her lack of head-covering matter now, with her warehouse going up in flames. Better a bucket than a bonnet. And if her bare arms offended anyone at this hour of night, they could just go hang!

As their buggy careened through the dark streets, Jane was the first to introduce the touchy subject on both their minds. "Eden, did Devlin come out of your room with you when the alert first sounded?"

Hoping the darkness would cover her guilty blush,

Eden returned the question in kind. "Did Nate exit your room, Mother?"

Jane did not attempt to confuse the issue. "Aye. He did. However, I am a widow, and you are a maiden, and there is a large gulf betwixt the two when it comes to what I may do and what you may not. You *are* still a maid, aren't you?"

"I am," Eden replied stiffly. "However, I fail to see why you should be permitted to break society's rules so readily, yet deny me the same right. If my own mother can bed down with a pirate, then why shouldn't I be allowed to choose a lover of my own? I am of age, an adult, and mature enough to make my own decisions."

"And your own mistakes as well? Are you mature enough to bear the consequences of your actions? What will you do when he leaves, Eden? What if you find yourself with child after he is gone? Have you thought of these things at all? Have you considered how you will be ruining your chances of marriage in the process? All for lust?"

"Not merely lust, Mama. Love. And regardless of whether Devlin stays or goes, my heart is his. I want no other, and I doubt I ever shall. I cannot help it; nor would I change it. And I most assuredly will never apologize for falling in love with him."

"Nor do I feel any need to justify my love for Nate," Jane concurred solemnly. "To you, or anyone else. Please understand that, Eden. Accept it, if you will."

Eden nodded, then added softly, "I hope you can do as much for me, Mama, and love me despite what I might decide, for I want no conflict between us."

"Darling, I shall always love you, no matter what happens. I just want you to choose your path with care and caution. God knows these sea rogues can be a tempting lot, with enough charm to lure the birds from the trees. I don't want to see you heartbroken, or to spend the rest of your days repenting a hasty liaison."

Eden sighed. "Let us both pray for that, Mama, for I greatly fear the two of us will be left behind, alone and weeping, with only each other for comfort."

At first glance, it appeared to Eden that half the town was at the scene, most of the men lending a hand in the water brigades. To her amazement, she spotted Finster midway along the line, passing a bucket to the fellow next to him.

"Why, that snake! Do you see what I see? Do you believe it?"

"Not for a minute," Jane assured her. "Like as not, he tossed a torch shortly before he took up this helpful pose. I just wish one of our guards could have caught him at it."

Though there were several fires spread among the warehouse buildings, the major conflagration was located toward the front, furthest from the river. This was where Devlin and most of his crew concentrated their efforts, while a handful of others managed to contain the smaller flames.

There was very little the two women could do to help other than stay safely out of the way and let the men do their best. From the buggy they watched, and worried, and prayed. They'd been on the scene for perhaps a quarter of an hour, though it seemed much longer, when Eden's gaze caught a movement in the shadows. When she recognized Tilton skulking about between the buildings, she was glad her attention had wandered in his direction.

"Mama! Look! 'Tis Mr. Tilton!" As she spoke, Eden was hopping down from the buggy.

"Eden! Where do you think you're going?" Jane asked frantically.

Eden halted and frowned up at her mother. "After Tilton, of course."

"To do what, dear? The man is undoubtedly up to no

good, and most probably dangerous. You cannot just go running after him by yourself and confront him."

"Who else is there to do it?" Eden countered impatiently, her eyes searching the area where she'd last seen the man. "Our men have all they can do fighting the fire. We can't just let him get away! We've been looking for evidence against him for too long!"

Without waiting for further objections, Eden gathered up her skirts and dashed toward the shadows.

"Wait! Eden, for the love of God!" Jane called out. As quickly as she could, she, too, climbed to the ground, running after her daughter, who had already disappeared from sight.

Tilton was no longer in the darkened pathway between the buildings into which Eden ran. Hardly slowing to allow for the lack of light, she sprinted toward the rear of the structure. There she stopped to catch her breath and listen, but all she heard was her own thudding heartbeat.

Cautiously, she peered around the corner, looking both ways. To the right, some distance away, she saw a furtive movement. As quietly as she could, she edged along the back of the building, hardly daring to blink lest she lose sight of him again.

Ahead of her, the man stopped. After a brief look about him, he bundled something around his arm, raised it, and struck the glass from a small window. Before Eden could call out, or do anything else to stop him, he lit some sort of torch and tossed it quickly into the building. Almost instantly, smoke and flames began to belch from the window.

Without thinking or caring about anything but stopping him, Eden bolted forward. Launching herself at him, she caught him by the arm. "You thieving beast!" she shrieked. "How dare you do this!"

Tilton whirled, and suddenly Eden was caught in a relentless grasp. By the light of the fire he'd just lit,

Tilton glared at her with wild eyes. "You!" he barked.
He let loose a harsh laugh. "Well now, if this isn't a
fortunate turn of events. You're just the person I need
to talk to, missy."

"Let loose of me!" Eden was kicking and struggling,
but Tilton seemed to have ten times her strength.

He shook her hard. "Shut yer trap and listen to me!"
he ordered gruffly. "I left a metal chest here, hidden in
one of the buildings. I came looking for it before, but
you and yer pirate lover took it upon yerselves to move
the merchandise around. I want that trunk, missy. I
want it now."

"I . . . I don't know what you're talking about," Eden
gasped. "Even if I did, God alone knows how many
trunks and boxes there are in this place. It could be
anywhere, probably aflame at this very minute."

"You'd better hope it isn't, lovey," he growled,
bringing his face close to hers. "Now think fast. 'Tis
red with black straps, about two foot long and high.
Full of books."

She blinked up at him. "Books?" she scoffed. "I'll
wager the only books you've ever cared to open were
our account books, and that only to steal from the company. Even then, Dudley Finster probably had to decipher them for you."

His smile was more evil than anything she could
have imagined. "Figured that out, did ye, dearie? Took
ye long enough. And good old Finster thought he'd
have ye wedded and bedded b'fore you knew anything
about it. Well, that's his bad fortune. Me, I just want
my money, and you're gonna tell me what you've done
with it, or I'll break your scrawny neck here and now."

One huge hand moved up to close about her throat.
Hating herself for her own cowardice, Eden begged,
"Please! I don't know where it is!"

Hard fingers threatened to close off her air as Tilton's
thumb pressed hard against her windpipe. "Lying bitch!

You've got half a minute to remember where you hid it, or the next face you see will be your Maker's."

"I don't know where the men put it," she insisted frantically, tears blurring her vision. "They went through all the goods stored in each building, cataloging which cargo belonged to whom. Anything they couldn't account for went into the big room over the office for safekeeping, until we could locate the owners. Mayhap your strongbox is up there."

Even in this light, Eden saw Tilton's face blanch as he realized that the structure housing the office was the one where the worst of the fire now blazed. "Damn and blast ye and yer meddling friends!" he cursed.

He threw her from him, already racing toward the office as Eden's head struck hard against the wooden frame of the warehouse behind which they stood. Without a murmur, she slumped to the ground beside the burning building.

Eden was beyond hearing the shot that rang out mere seconds after she fell. Nor was she aware of her mother kneeling beside her, nearly hysterical as she hastily tossed the smoking pistol aside and tried to determine the extent of Eden's injuries. Unable to awaken her, aware of the peril to them both, Jane caught Eden beneath the arms and, with extraordinary might, dragged her daughter's limp body a safe distance from the fire. There, she collapsed next to Eden and gave way to her tears.

Eden awoke to the sound of her mother's sobbing pleas. With effort, she forced her eyelids open, though the pain lancing through her head demanded otherwise. "Mama?" she croaked out.

Gentle hands stroked the hair from her brow. "Oh, baby! My brave, foolish child!" Jane wailed. "You might have been killed! I tried to warn you."

"He got away, didn't he?" Eden groaned.

"Not without a ball from your father's gun," Jane replied. "I think I hit him in the leg, but I can't be certain."

"You shot him?" Eden asked incredulously, then gasped at the pain the slight exclamation brought.

"That I did, but don't fret about that now. We've got to get you some aid, darling. You mustn't try to move until we see how badly you are injured. Where is the pain, dear?"

"My head. I fell against something."

"Do you hurt anywhere else? Your back? Your limbs?"

"Nay," Eden denied weakly. Then she qualified her statement. "At least, I think not."

"Can you stand, if I assist you? I hate to leave you here alone while I go for help."

Together, they struggled to their feet. Eden's head threatened to explode, and she had to wait several seconds for the colored lights to stop dancing before her eyes, but she managed to stay upright. Slowly, with Jane supporting her all the while, they made their way back toward their buggy.

Eden was slumped against the front wheel, her mother beside her, when Devlin came dashing up, his face blackened with soot. "What happened?" he demanded with a worried scowl.

"Tilton," Jane answered shortly. "I shot at him, but he still managed to get away."

"Nay. I know where he's gone," Eden wheezed. "The room over the office. He went after a red coffer full of books—and money. Our money."

Promise of unholy retribution blazed in Devlin's dark eyes. "I'll kill him for harming you!"

Before Eden could dissuade him, Devlin was gone again. She watched him go, wondering if any man could be so angry and not love the woman he was about to avenge.

She watched Devlin lope toward the burning office.

Just as he reached the bottom of the outer staircase leading to the second story, Tilton emerged from the upper doorway. Unaware of Devlin's approach, he limped down the steps, his coveted tin of treasure wrapped in a scorched blanket and clutched in his arms. Devlin was three steps up—and Tilton three steps down—when the staircase gave a violent shudder. With an ear-splitting creak of rending wood, it tore away from the smoldering building. For several breathless seconds it seemed to stand on its own, tilted precariously in midair—just long enough for Devlin to leap free. Then it collapsed, crumbling down like a house of cards, hurtling Tilton with it. Within moments, the man was crushed beneath the heavy rubble, his torso flattened by a huge beam.

The crash brought several men running, Finster and Nate among them. They were still gaping at the gruesome spectacle when Devlin bent over Tilton's bloody form. The first to recover his wits, Nate approached cautiously, inching his way carefully over splintered wood toward the body.

"He's dead, Nate," Devlin announced softly, giving Nate yet another fright, since Devlin was still invisible.

Nate answered with a hearty "Blimey!" which the others attributed to the bloody sight before them.

Finster made his way forward to stand at Nate's side. " 'Tis Tilton," he proclaimed to one and all. "The poor, gallant man! To lose his life trying to save the warehouse, even after being dismissed so precipitantly. How loyal!"

As the others shook their heads and began to disperse, returning to the task of dousing the fires, only Nate and Finster lagged behind—and the unseen Devlin. Spying the metal coffer, Finster's eyes took on a speculative gleam. "It appears that Tilton saved a small bit of merchandise as he fell. I'll take it and put it safely with the other rescued cargo."

As Dudley reached to retrieve the box from amidst the fallen timbers, Devlin hissed in Nate's ear, "Don't let him have that chest! 'Tis Tilton's stolen wealth Finster is about to pilfer for himself."

Thus spurred, Nate drew his cutlass and waved it menacingly beneath the accountant's nose. "I wouldn't be so hasty to put me hands on Miss Winters's property, were I you, Mr. Finster. Now, be on yer way, and I'll take care of the matter meself."

Anger twisted Finster's face, but prudence had him backing off. "How dare you threaten me, you good-for-nothing ruffian! I'll have the constable after you!"

"Then why don't ye just go fetch the man now," Nate suggested. "He'll be wantin' to view Tilton's remains and arrange to remove them for burial, in any case."

Finster marched off in a huff, spouting dire warnings, and Nate lost no time in uncovering the strongbox and delivering it directly to the safety of Eden's buggy.

As the last of the fires were finally extinguished, Devlin, Nate, and the Winters women wearily assessed the damage. It turned out to be much less than they had at first feared, thanks to the speedy arrival and dedicated aid of so many volunteers.

The office building was the only structure that had been entirely demolished; fortunately, since the previous ransacking, Eden had removed all the important documents and files to the house for safekeeping. Also, as she had informed Tilton, the only merchandise stored there was unclaimed items. Thus, it wasn't likely anyone would now come demanding reimbursement for them.

It also proved prophetic that they had recently redistributed the cargo in an effort to store it in a less haphazard fashion. By doing so, they had inadvertently thwarted Tilton's attempts to destroy the most valuable merchandise. Changing the locks had been a fortuitous move as well. Denied their usual entry, Tilton and his fellow arsonists had resorted to breaking windows and blindly tossing torches within, never knowing they were setting fire to less costly goods than they suspected.

Where expensive tobacco had been stored previously, only a shipment of animal hides had been singed, causing more smoke than flame. As was the green cypress awaiting transport to England, the wood being too freshly cut to burn. Very little of either was lost. In another area, the wooden crates holding crockery had burned, leaving the dishes blackened but still of good use—discounting the few which had cracked in the heat. The load of cast-iron goods had sustained no damage at all; a few barrels of rice had been scorched before the remainder was successfully removed from harm's way.

Luckily, numerous bolts of valuable cloth had been replaced just the previous day by a cargo of popping corn, which had cooked in the heat and spread fluffy kernels throughout one huge room. The mass had also mysteriously acted to smother the very flames which sought to consume it, thus saving the building and the rest of the merchandise within. All in all, they had survived this latest attack with limited damage to goods and the loss of only one life—Tilton's own.

Still, Devlin was so incensed over Eden's injury that he swore, "If the man weren't already dead, I'd kill him with my bare hands! And Finster with him!"

"And what of Finster now?" Jane wanted to know. "Eden told me that Tilton admitted that Dudley was involved in the theft of money from the warehouse, just as we have suspected."

Eden nodded. "Can we have the constable arrest him on just Tilton's confession?"

"I doubt it," Devlin said with a shake of his shaggy blond head. "'Twould be your word for it against

Finster's, without Tilton here to add weight to the accusation."

"What a shame the bastard had to die as soon as he did, then," Nate put in.

"Nay. I've something much more fitting in mind for our mewling accountant," Devlin told them, his black eyes twinkling with devilment. "A penalty more just than a quick and merciful hanging or a few years in prison, with his father's money buying him nearly as much comfort as his own home. But first, before we see the last of him, he must be made to face the error of his ways, to relinquish that which he stole." Devlin's smile was diabolical. "Maties, methinks 'tis time for another haunting."

Chapter 19

Since no one had gotten any sleep during
the night, they decided it was only fair to put the warehouse workers on four-hour shifts, at least for the day.
The night guards would maintain their vigil as usual,
for while Tilton was no longer a threat, Finster had yet
to be dealt with. As soon as they could, Jane and Eden
headed home to a bath and bed. Because Dora would be
up and about, Devlin had to bathe elsewhere before
seeking his own rest—as did Nate.

Not until late afternoon did they all gather in the parlor to examine the coffer Tilton had forfeited his life to
save. With everything that had transpired the night before, they were naturally a bit tense and out of sorts. Of
the four of them, Devlin seemed least affected, though
he, too, was aware of the strained tone in the room.

How could be not be? Eden was gnawing at her lower lip, and refused to look him directly in the eye, as if
newly embarrassed by their latest romantic interlude.
Nate kept nervously clearing his throat and fidgeting
like a guilty schoolboy expecting a rap on his knuckles,
his face set in mutinous lines. Jane was unusually quiet,
and cast several sidelong glances between Eden and the

chair Devlin invisibly occupied, a thoughtful frown creasing her brow.

"What the devil is going on here?" Devlin asked, his frustration rising at the feeling that he was the only one who hadn't been included in some secret pact. The other three exchanged pained looks.

Finally, Eden spoke up in a quiet voice, though she still could not meet Devlin's gaze. "Mama, Nate, forgive me for being such a hateful shrew these past weeks. Your relationship, though it does affect me in some ways, is not for me to rule or judge. I'll make an effort to be more reasonable about it in the future." *If there is a future for the two of you, or for Devlin and me—and I pray there will be,* she thought to herself.

Nate relaxed visibly. "I wouldn't hurt yer mama for the world, Eden," he replied.

Eden nodded, as if trying to believe him.

Jane offered her daughter a weak smile. "Thank you, Eden. Believe me when I say that I fully appreciate your concern, and what it is costing you to trust us in this matter." She slanted a worried glance in Devlin's direction, and back again to Eden. "I will honestly attempt to return the favor, though 'tis uncommonly hard for me to do so."

Devlin was still confused. While he understood the apology from Eden, Jane's response seemed to contain undercurrents he could not fathom. With the looks he'd been sent along the way, it appeared Jane's words held a double message, which only she and her daughter could decipher, and if it had something to do with him as well, he could not determine precisely how or why.

Whatever had passed between the women, it served to lighten the mood, and for that Devlin was as grateful as the rest of them. "Shall we have a look at Tilton's treasure now?" he suggested.

As the others gathered round, he broke open the lock and threw up the lid. Eden and Jane gave twin gasps.

Amid a tumble of scorched books, the centers of which had been hollowed out, lay a fortune in cash and coin.

"My word! Would you look at all that money!" Eden exclaimed, her eyes wide with surprise. "Surely Tilton could not have pilfered that amount from us!"

Jane blinked and agreed. "Surely not. Why, there must be thousands of pounds there! Mayhap he had not yet shared his stolen wealth with Mr. Finster."

Nate snorted in disgust, while Devlin shook his head. "Both of you are so naive 'tis unbelievable. Little wonder the two of them were able to fleece you so easily. Judging by the amounts charged, and those actually received the few times I was on hand to witness Tilton's actions, this amounts to only Tilton's share. Believe me, Finster gained an amount equal to or larger than your former foreman's. Do not forget, ladies, that these men had three long years in which to accumulate their stolen wealth."

Eden knelt and ran both hands through the coins, letting them rain back into the box. "This is incredible! 'Twill more than pay for the office to be rebuilt, for needed repairs, and any other improvements we have been delaying. Not to mention monies to be repaid to customers for damaged goods."

"Aye," Devlin concurred. With a teasing smile, he added, "And a whole wardrobe full of fashionable new bonnets and gowns for the recently prosperous Winters ladies. Before you know what is happening, you'll both be turning suitors away from the door by the droves."

Three frowning faces rounded on him at this latest statement, but only Nate challenged it aloud. "I don't think I care for the notion of anyone else tryin' to take me place in Jane's life, thank ye very much, Devlin Kane. So just tend to yer own affairs, and I'll tend to mine, and we'll see who comes out the better, shall we?"

* * *

At the stroke of midnight, Devlin hoisted himself through Dudley Finster's open bedroom window. A floor below, the mantel clock was still tolling the witching hour as he grabbed the skinny accountant by his bony shoulders and gave him a rough shake. "Finster!" he hissed.

The man came awake with a violent start, clutching both hands to his meager chest. For a moment Devlin thought the fellow was about to go into apoplexy. But that would have been too easy, and too swift an end for him. He deserved to suffer much more.

Savoring what was to come, Devlin lounged against the corner bedpost and waited, silently chuckling to himself as Finster peered into the murky shadows of the room, perhaps sensing Devlin's presence but unable to detect him. Cautiously, the man reached his hand out toward the nightstand, and the new spectacles he'd recently purchased in the hope of remedying his sudden, inexplicable bouts of clumsiness. The fragile eyeglasses rattled noisily in the still room as Dudley's shaking fingers came into contact with them.

Devlin laughed aloud. Dudley cried out. His hand jerked reflexively, causing the spectacles to crash to the floor and shatter into tiny pieces. "My, my! What a bloody awful shame!" Devlin commiserated mockingly. "But don't fret, Finster. Where you're headed, you won't need to see any further than the end of your nose."

"Kane?" Dudley guessed. "What are you doing here? What do you want?"

"Justice, my little man," Devlin told him, his deep voice ringing with barely muted menace. "Why don't I light a candle so you can properly see exactly what you are pitting your puny efforts against?"

Broken glass crunched beneath his boots as Devlin stepped up to the nightstand, from whence he took candlestick and tinderbox. As the wick fired, he turned full view toward the bed, and was immediately rewarded by Dudley's gasp of horror upon witnessing the candlestick floating in midair.

"Not quite what you expected, eh, Finster?" Devlin continued with an evil croon.

"Who . . . what are you?" Dudley wheezed, his thin chest heaving beneath his nightshirt.

"A specter? A phantom? Mayhap your worst nightmare?" Devlin suggested tauntingly. "Ah, but you guessed who I was at the start—you simply underestimated *what* I was, didn't you? A fatal mistake, Finster. As were your schemes against Miss Winters. For which you will now begin to pay, and continue to do so for many long days to come." He crossed to the fireplace mantel, left the candle there, and continued to stride about the room, confusing the accountant even more as Dudley attempted to pinpoint his opponent's ever-changing position.

"Now then," Devlin intoned with deceptive casualness, "I believe we have come to the point in our talk where I inform you what I wish of you. And if you are at all wise, you will do precisely as I request. After all, what choice have you against my superior wit and might? You must admit that I do hold the advantage over you, Finster. I could slay you on the spot, and none would know 'twas I. Even should they suppose it, what could they do to me? 'Tis nigh on impossible to catch a ghost."

"No! Don't kill me!" Dudley whimpered, huddling against the headboard and tugging the covers half over his face. "Let me be, and I swear I'll never go near Eden Winters again!"

"That is a fair start, but not near enough to barter for your life."

"What more?" the accountant squawked. "I'll do anything. Anything at all."

Devlin's chuckle was demonic. "I thought you

might." For endless seconds, during which Finster quaked in fright, Devlin let the man wait. Finally, he said, "Hand over the funds you stole from Winters Warehouse. All of it. Every last pence. And don't try to hold any back for yourself, because I know the sum you took."

"I . . . I can get it to you tomorrow, first thing in the morning," Finster pledged frantically. "As soon as the bank opens."

"Nay, Finster. Now. You and I both know that money is not resting in the bank, where your father might chance upon it." He strode to the bed and yanked the quivering man to his knees, pulling him from the bed. "Get it, man. This minute. Or begin to pray for a merciful death."

Stumbling on watery legs, Dudley made his way toward the hearth. There, he knelt and clawed with fear-numbed hands at the cornerstone, until at last he pulled it loose. From within the gaping crack, he pulled a sack, then another, and finally a third. These he placed in a pile on the floor, then scuttled away from them as if afraid to be near Devlin when he retrieved them.

From nowhere, a hand closed over the back of his nightshirt, administering a sound shake. "I said all of it, Finster. Or don't you care for breathing?"

On a defeated sob, the man again reached into the hole and withdrew two more sacks. "There," he wailed. "You can check yourself if you don't believe me, but that is the sum of it."

"Fine. Now pick them up and let's be on our way."

"Where? Where are you taking me?" Tears streamed down his sunken cheeks. "You're going to slay me after all, aren't you?"

"Nay, weasel. Not as long as you do as I say." When Finster failed to move, Devlin gave his shoulder a rough nudge. "The bags, Finster," he prompted. "And you may choose either the window or the door for leaving, but make so much as the smallest squeak, and your father will purchase your coffin on the morrow."

A short time later, Devlin relieved the quaking accountant of his burdensome booty and delivered him into Nate's care.

"Ye brought him in his nightshirt, Dev?" Nate crowed. "Damn me, if old Cap'n Grumble ain't gonna get a charge out of this! His new pretty boy, all dressed and ready fer his bed! Ho!"

"Captain Grumble?" Finster parroted.

"Aye," Devlin answered with a gruff laugh. "He's going to be your new master for a time—a very long time. You see, Finster, I've sold you to him, and he takes quite a liking to mewling men such as you. Treats them real special, if you catch my meaning. You'll have many a day to reflect upon your sins and repent of them, endless days and nights to plead for mercy—or the death you begged me not to grant to you."

Finster's disappearance came as no great shock to anyone save his own family, and that only because he'd left in the dead of night with no word of farewell. Eden was at once relieved and anxious, for the work careening the *Gai Mer* was nearly done, and Devlin might decide to leave soon. Each day, she watched for signs of his imminent departure, becoming more and more nervous as time went on. Each night, awake in her bed, she listened long into the night, treasuring each sound that came from his side of the abutting wall. Each morning, before opening her eyes, she breathed a fervent prayer that he would not yet be gone when she arose. At moments she almost wished he would go and get it done with, for she felt as if she were walking about on pins and needles, just waiting for the inevitable.

Meanwhile, Devlin and Nate went about business as usual, or what passed for usual these days. Beyond tending to the frigate, they were also overseeing repairs at the warehouse.

This went on for nearly a fortnight, with Eden holding her breath against the day Devlin would announce his intention to weigh anchor with the next tide. Then came news of a different sort, and Eden's heart soared with renewed hope. The King of England was offering amnesty to all pirates who would apply for it. All they were required to do was to sail to New Providence in the Bahamas by the fifth of September and renounce their unlawful ways of life publicly before Governor Woodes Rogers. All who did so by the deadline would be granted pardons for their sins against the Crown, as long as they swore to be peaceable citizens henceforth, and stood by their oath never to return to piracy.

"Oh, Devlin! This is wonderful news!" Eden proclaimed.

"Is it now?" he replied sourly. "Well, I suppose that all depends on which side of the fence you are standing, doesn't it? As for me, I think it stinks!"

Her face fell, her smile wavering. "But, Devlin, think of it. A full pardon for all your past crimes. A chance to start your life fresh, with no marks against you."

The look he gave her was the same an adult gives to an ignorant child, one who simply will not understand. "Sweetling, if I wanted to reform, don't you think I'd have done so before now? With or without the King's benevolent consent? As it happens, I like my life just as it is. Or as it was before I became half a ghost," he qualified. "Piracy suits me, Eden. 'Tis what I do, and what I am good at. I am loath to give it up now, merely because the Crown requests it. Besides, they've been attempting to rid the seas of pirates for centuries, and have had little success at it. What they ask now is nothing new."

"Perhaps," she conceded softly. "But what they offer

in return is, Devlin. Amnesty. No reprisals. A chance to begin again, on the right side of the law."

"Ah, but look at what they expect me and my men to relinquish at the same time. Jewels, treasure, wealth beyond your dreams. And to do what, Eden? To find some menial job ashore and live on remembrances of past adventures for the rest of our days? To dine on regret evermore and become more bitter with each passing year?"

"Nay," she told him stubbornly. "You needn't give up sailing altogether. Simply employ your favorite skills in a more lawful direction. Would that be so terrible?"

He gave a negligent shrug. "Mayhap not, but the earnings would be a pittance compared with our current gains. I might have a mutiny on my hands at the mere suggestion of it to my crew."

Eden stomped a dainty foot at him, both hands bunched into small fists and planted atop her hips, her eyes narrowed into angry turquoise slits. "Horse feathers!" she spat out. "You're just too greedy and too lazy to want to work for your pay. You'd rather steal it from someone else, which makes you hardly better than Finster!"

Fire seemed to spew from his black eyes, and anyone else would have run for his life at the scowl that drew Devlin's brows together. "Why, you tart-tongued harridan! You dare to say such a thing to me, after all I've done for you?"

"I dare more than that, *Captain Kane*," she retorted smartly. "Beyond all else I've mentioned, you are also too much a coward to want to try living a normal existence—for fear you might fail!"

Her verbal darts fell too close to the truth for Devlin's comfort. It wasn't just the wealth and the excitement that lured him on in his pirating ventures. Or the vengeance he still meant to visit upon Swift, when next they met. It was also a deep-rooted fear of not being able to measure up to what his dead parents would have expected of him. It boiled down to that. After all the time that had passed, he was still afraid to disappoint them, and himself—despite the fact that he had recently tested his rusty carpentry skills, and been fairly satisfied with the result. Or that, for several weeks now, he'd been land-bound and was not suffering overmuch from it. He'd even enjoyed certain aspects of working at the warehouse.

But he was not about to admit any of this to Eden, when he was scarcely able to admit it to himself. Rather, he stood glaring down at her, wondering why he would think she looked so fetching, so downright beautiful at this moment, when she seemed set on being her most hateful. Her color was high, her eyes sparkling with defiant fury, her nose tipped at a haughty angle— she was the most glorious sight he'd ever beheld.

His hands shot out to pull her to him, his head lowering close to hers. "Even when you're spitting at me, you're a beguiling little witch! For tuppence, I'd turn you over my knee and spank the meanness out of you!"

"Nay, Devlin." Her arms rose to twine about his neck, her slender fingers threading through his hair. Her lovely eyes implored him even as her lips formed the words he longed to hear. "I beg a kiss instead."

Their lips met and clung, hers soft and pliant beneath his. The taste of them was sweeter than the finest wine, and far more potent. It must have been the same for her, for she sighed softly, and when she did, he sucked her tongue into the hot depths of his mouth, there to tangle with his.

With little urging, her body arched toward him; nearer still, as he spread his legs to draw her tightly into the cradle of his thighs. The points of her breasts brushed teasingly against his chest, even through the layers of their clothing. One large hand cupped her buttock, while the other roamed the contours of her back. Warm fingers teased the ridges of her spine, from neck to bottom, raising gooseflesh in their wake. They sought the curve of her waist, caressing there, then meandered upward to lightly stroke the side of her breast.

On a muted whimper, and with an agitated twist of her torso, Eden wordlessly conveyed her wishes—and Devlin gladly complied. His hand glided smoothly between them, capturing her yearning breast at last—cupping it, fondling it, the crest thrusting into his palm in sweet entreaty. An answering ache flamed in his groin, and he instinctively pulled her closer, grinding her pelvis against his aroused manhood. He swallowed her moan, only to echo it in the same breath.

Somewhere in the house a door slammed. Nate's voice called out Devlin's name. Footsteps resounded in the hall. Only then did Devlin come to his senses and realize that the two of them were standing in the downstairs study, where anyone might chance upon them.

Reluctantly, he set her apart from him, his body objecting to the move. It soothed him little to note that Eden was in similar straits, unable to stand on her own, her arms still reaching out toward him, her lips wet and rosy, her eyes hazy with desire. His hand stroked her mussed hair, a shudder quaking through him. "Oh, my beauty. One of these days, we'll see this to its proper end. That I promise you."

" 'Twould please me better were you to pledge to apply for pardon," she replied, a catch in her voice.

A mocking smile curved his mobile mouth. "Was that what this bit of seduction was all about, then? To lure me into changing my mind? Well, duchess, I assure you, 'twill take more than a mere kiss in the corner to do the trick. At any rate, you are forgetting one imperative fact. In order to apply to the governor, I must be seen. And that I cannot do."

"You could if you took me with you," she argued not yet ready to give up her dreams.

"Nay. You know I cannot take you aboard the *Gai Mer.*"

Eden's mouth pursed into a pout. "What? That dratted superstition again? Surely there is a way around it. You said yourself there are charms and such to counter it."

"Forget it, Eden," he advised gruffly. "I won't chance my ship and the lives of my crew simply to satisfy your whims."

"Not even for something as important as amnesty?"

As he said the words, he knew he was hurting her, yet he could not stem them. " 'Tis only important to you, lass. Not to me."

She flinched as if struck, each syllable rending her heart like the sharp slice of a knife. Then she drew herself up proudly, tears glistening in her eyes. "I shall endeavor to remember that in the future, Captain. But should I forget, I'm sure you will remind me in your usual forthright manner, for it seems the only time you lavish tenderness upon me is when you are attempting to ravish me. Which invariably clouds my better judgment, fool that I am. I shall try to correct that particular fault of mine."

"You do that, sweetling," he challenged with a rakish grin. "And I shall continue to try to charm my way beneath your skirts." He paused and arched a blond brow at her. " 'Twill be interesting to see who wins."

Chapter 20

*I*t seemed Devlin had more supporters of his seeking amnesty than just Eden. No sooner had his argument with her concluded, than Nate began on the very same topic.

"I want that pardon, Devlin, whether ye do or not," his friend told him. "I'm gettin' to an age where I'd best be thinkin' about settlin' down, if I'm ever gonna do it. And Janie's the woman I want to do it with, so I guess the time is ripe."

"Damn it all, Nate, I need you with me! Besides, half the *Gai Mer* belongs to you. We can't just split her in half so that you can sail legitimately, while I continue my raiding."

"Well, ye could always consider applyin' for amnesty, too, ye know, and make things simple. That way, the two o' us could still sail together, like always—only on shorter jaunts, o' course. I will want to spend some time with me bride, ye understand."

"Bride?" Devlin almost choked on the word.

Conversely, Nate appeared to puff up with pride. "Aye. The lady has agreed to marry me, as soon as I return with me pardon. Can ye beat that, Dev? Imagine me wed to a real lady. And the grand thing is, I won't even have to go lookin' fer a way to make me livin'. I'm gonna keep on overseein' the runnin' o' the warehouse."

Devlin gave a gruff laugh. "I'll wager Eden is thrilled to her toes over that!"

"Uh . . . well, she doesn't know yet. Janie's supposed to tell her today," Nate admitted sheepishly. "I don't reckon she'll be real happy over it, but what can she do? It's her ma's warehouse, after all."

"Well, I wish you good luck then. But don't expect me to join you."

"I truly wish ye would, Dev. We both know, with more and more countries plyin' the trade lanes, and puttin' out naval ships to guard the ports, that corsairs are enjoyin' their final days. Ye can list on yer fingers the number of ports we can sail into now without a mob linin' up to lynch us." Nate shook his head. " 'Tis sad, but true. 'Twas good while it lasted, but now is the time to quit, while we still have our hides."

The corner of Devlin's mouth pulled up in a wry grimace. "I never thought I'd see the day when you'd talk this way, Nate. When you'd so readily trade in your sea legs to become a landlubber."

Nate's smile was a bit remorseful. "Aye, but that's the way o' it. And I'm not the only one, ye know. Several o' the crew are thinkin' along the same lines, now that they can do it legal, with a real pardon."

"What? How many?" Devlin asked, aghast at the thought of losing more of his faithful crew.

"I don't know. About half, I reckon. Which brings up another matter. Ye may be the cap'n, but accordin' to the rules, there has to be a vote b'fore ye go tryin' to decide the fate o' the crew."

"I know that, Nate," Devlin concurred. That had always been one of the best parts of being a buccaneer, even before he and Nate had gained control of the *Gai Mer*. Every member of the crew got not only a share of the booty, but also a vote on every major matter of concern to them and the ship. "They'll have their say."

"And what if most want amnesty?" Nate questioned further. "If the vote goes against ye, will ye quit piratin'?"

"Nay," Devlin answered with a frown. "I'll take those who want to sail with me and search the docks for others to fill the crew. That is, if you agree to sell out your half of the frigate."

"And if I want to keep her?" Nate suggested. "What then?"

"Then you can buy out my share, and I'll go looking for another ship," Devlin stated stubbornly. He heaved a heavy sigh, running his fingers through his hair in an agitated gesture. "Blarst it all! Just when I thought things were starting to look up, this has to happen! I not only lose my body, but my best friend deserts me for a rich widow!"

"Now, Dev, don't ye be talkin' about me and Janie like that. What she owns or doesn't is of no real concern to me. I love her, plain and simple."

"I know that, Nate. I'm sorry for the way it sounded. I'm just not real glad you're not going to be sailing with me."

"It saddens me, too, after all these years," Nate admitted. "But, Dev, as to all this happenin' now—do ye think it could be a sign o' some sort? Do ye think someone might be tryin' to tell ye somethin'?"

Devlin gave a disgusted grunt. "Aye. Probably telling me to look at my friend and beware of getting caught in the same trap. Whispering in my ear that 'tis high time I weighed anchor and set out after Swift."

"Mayhap so, but first we have to finish careenin' the ship, and see how many o' the crew want to go to New Providence. And don't forget, if ye're outnumbered, those o' us who want amnesty are gonna vote to take the ship to the Bahamas to get it. 'Tis only fair. And once they give their pledge to the governor, they shouldn't be seen immediately afterward in league with known brigands who don't swear to forego the life. All o' which means they shouldn't be seen with ye, nor those who side with ye, goin' or comin' from New Providence—not if ye don't apply as well. So, if ye don't mind, those lads and me'll be takin' the ship out ourselves, and ye can stay here an' make yerself useful lookin' after the warehouse for me until we get back, if ye would."

Devlin threw up his hands in defeat. "Damn me! Is there anything else?"

"Not that I can think of, off the top o' me head." Nate grinned and slapped in the direction of Devlin's unseen shoulder. "Brace up, Dev. 'Tisn't the end o' the world. And if it gets too rough, ye can always change yer mind and throw in with us."

"Not bloody likely," Devlin grumbled.

Nate shrugged. "Have it yer way, ye stubborn scoundrel. Meanwhile, what say we amble down to the tavern and hoist a few for old times' sake, while I still have some say in me own life? B'fore long, I'll have a wife to monitor me comin's and goin's, and ain't that gonna take some gettin' used to!"

Jane attempted to reason with Devlin. Nate tried. As much as it went against her grain, Eden relented and began hounding him once more. And still Devlin stood fast. Nothing they could say would sway him. Nor did the fact that nearly two-thirds of his crew were deserting him make any difference. He simply announced, grim-faced, that he'd put the word out for new men to take their places. To Eden's mind, the man made a jackass appear agreeable.

Reluctant to give up trying to persuade him, but getting nowhere individually, the three quickly joined forces against him. Together, and secretly, they met to discuss possible strategies. Finally they hit on a workable plan, though all agreed to employ it only as a last resort. If by the time the work on the *Gai Mer* was finished Devlin still had not agreed, they would simply abduct him and take him by force to New Providence. How they were going to get him to utter the requisite vow they had not yet worked out, but Eden swore she'd get him to agree if she had to stand Devlin before the governor with a gun to his ribs.

Meanwhile, also surreptitiously, the trio set about conjuring ways to counter the evil of having Eden aboard ship, for she would have to go along on the voyage. In this, Nate proved particularly knowledgeable, most likely because he, too, had a sailor's superstitious nature.

"Now, here's what we have to do," he told the two women. "First, we have to find a priest."

Eden grimaced. They'd hit their first snag before they'd gotten a good start. "Does it have to be a priest, or would Reverend Johnston do?" she asked hopefully. Though there had to be at least one Catholic in Charles Town, any who laid claim to that faith took care to conceal it, since to the colonists of the region the term Roman Catholic was, although unjustly, equated with the Spanish—and thus aligned with their enemies. Being Catholic was not something to shout aloud about these days, at least not in the Charles Town area.

"Nope," Nate said. "We got to have a priest."

"But we don't have one anywhere around Charles Town," Eden protested. "What do we do now?"

Jane tapped her daughter on the shoulder and gave a sly wink. "You just leave that part to me," she advised them. "I happen to know a few people—who know a few people. And unless I miss my guess, there's a priest lurking in a woodpile somewhere around here."

"Well, you sniff him out real quick, Janie, my love," Nate suggested, " 'cause we're sure gonna need him, along with some o' that holy water o' his and a few hearty blessin's."

He went on to list some of the other items they would need. "Eden, can ye get yer hands on a horseshoe, and maybe a fresh caul or two?"

"A caul?" Eden echoed. "What is it?"

Jane took up the answer. "A caul is the birth sac of a newborn animal, and we might have a time finding one this far into the summer. Most young calves and kids are born in the spring. Still, there must be at least one creature in the area about to give birth. We'll just have to make inquiries."

"I'll take care o' gettin' more codfish stones," Nate went on, "though most o' the crew already have 'em. They put 'em in little sacks and hang 'em around their necks to protect 'em from drownin'. Ye see, 'tis reasoned that if these stones, which come from the ear of the codfish, can keep the fish afloat, 'twill do the same fer any person who wears 'em. There's bound to be a ship dockin' soon from up Plymouth way, carryin' a load o' codfish."

"Then get a couple of stones for me, too," Eden decided, "because I can't swim a stroke!"

Between them, they managed to gather everything they needed. The priest, who until now had been doing an excellent job of keeping his profession a secret from all but his handful of parishioners, had no problem with Nate's request not to wear his black robes. Though Devlin himself and a few of his mates often wore black, it seemed that any ship's visitor or passenger who wore this "color of death," particularly a priest or a widow, brought bad fortune aboard.

On the day chosen to conduct the blessing of the ship, Jane was designated to keep Devlin busy at home, lest he witness the ceremony and begin to ask questions no one wanted to answer. The crew had been sworn to silence, upon Nate's threat to have the priest exclude them from his blessing should they whisper so much as a word about these proceedings to their captain.

"I'll try," Jane promised, "but do be as quick about it as possible. 'Tis hard to keep an eye on a man I cannot see, and he could be off and gone long before I know it."

Her plan was to put Devlin to work repairing an old bed frame in the attic, while she kept Dora occupied in the kitchen. Nate would not be missed, as he usually spent a good portion of his day at the warehouse. Eden's absence would be explained as a shopping expedition.

"Be sure to stop in town and purchase some small item before coming home," Jane reminded her. "We don't want Devlin to become suspicious."

All went well, considering the speed and secrecy in which they had to conduct the service. First, the priest invoked a blessing on several small items: the caul, the cloth amulets containing the codfish stones, three silver coins, a horseshoe, and the wine which would be used to bless the ship. Then he performed purification rites for the frigate itself and the crew. At Nate's suggestion, he invoked a special sanctification on Eden, since she was the primary reason for all of these preventative measures.

"I feel like a fool," Eden complained, as she knelt to submit to the ritual.

"Better that than a Jonah," Nate told her. "Now, shut yer trap and let's get on with it."

She kept her comments to herself after that. Anything that would get her aboard the *Gai Mer* without causing a riot among the crew, and enable them to get Devlin to New Providence for his pardon, was well worth a few minutes of looking silly.

As soon as his part was done, the priest left. Eden stayed and watched in fascination as the caul, holding three precious codfish stones, was tacked to the main-

mast below the horseshoe, which was hung upside
down to catch and hold good luck. It took several stout
men in the bowels of the ship to lift the three masts,
one at a time, just far enough to slip a single silver coin
beneath each. Her own little sack of codfish stones she
tucked into her pocket for safekeeping.

"Now don't ye go forgettin' this when we sail," Nate
admonished as he handed the sack to her, "or all our
good work might go for naught."

It was done. The *Gai Mer* and her crew were as
ready, and as protected against evil, as ever they would
be. The ship was nearly fit to be put back into the water. With luck, they would all be on their way to the Bahamas, Devlin included, within a few short days.

The following evening, in celebration of Jane and
Nate's engagement, the four friends went out to supper
together at a local inn. It was an uncommon treat for
the women, as they rarely dined out except when invited to someone else's house. Eden could count on one
hand the number of times she'd eaten her evening meal
in a public establishment.

In honor of this event, Eden took great pains with her
toilet, arranging her hair several different ways before
she was satisfied with the result, and changing her
gown at least four times. She finally decided upon a
creation of lustrous silk damask in a shade resembling
polished bronze, with stomacher and flounced under-
skirt of lemon satin, and soft kid slippers and gloves to
match. The outfit, fashionable but still sedate, was the
most colorful in her wardrobe, a lack she had yet to
rectify. She tied a yellow ribbon about her throat, and in
lieu of a bonnet, all of which Devlin seemed to dislike
immensely, she wore a lace-trimmed pinner, held in
place with the tortoiseshell combs he had given her.

Then Eden did something which was, for her, outrageously daring. Dampening her handkerchief with her

favorite perfume, she dabbed the scent liberally into her hair, behind her ears, and on the insides of her elbows and wrists. From her mother's dressing table, she borrowed a small pot of rouge. Foregoing face powder, she applied the scarlet coloring sparingly over her lips and cheekbones. A pinch of lamp soot darkened the tips of her lashes, lengthening them and heightening the unusual hue of her eyes. As a crowning touch, she affixed a small golden beauty patch in the shape of a butterfly to her right cheek.

Stepping back to view the result in her looking glass, Eden was not at all sure she didn't look like a harlequin, unused as she was to wearing face paint. However, minutes later when she entered the parlor, the appreciative gleam in Devlin's dark eyes reassured her, as did his immediate praise.

"I've called you 'beauty' before, Eden, but this night you surely earn the title. You are a vision."

"Well, blow me down!" Nate exclaimed. "Would ye look at that! Lass, I tell ye truly, I'd never have believed ye could turn into such a comely gal, when ye seemed such a skinny dowd at first. Now I see that yer ma passed the best o' her looks on to ye, after all. That she did."

The glow of their praise lingered through the better part of supper, which consisted of succulent quail and pheasant roasted to perfection, dressing and gravy, yams and greens, and plum pudding. While they ate, the men entertained the ladies with tall tales of their pirating ventures, exaggerating their skill and triumphs to the extreme, and with several sailor's ditties, duly revised to be more suitable to mixed company. Devlin even composed one of his own, in Eden's honor.

With a teasing gleam in his dark eyes, he singsonged, "There once was a Charles Town spinster, annoyed by a suitor named Finster. A rogue came to the aid of the comely young maid, haunting all those who would pinch her."

Amused, and more than a little pleased with his effort, Eden made him promise to write the verse down before he forgot it. She wanted to keep it as a remembrance of the evening.

The one sour note to the dinner was that their serving girl could not seem to keep her eyes off of Devlin for more than a few seconds at a time. Nor her body, for that matter. The little tart was ever at their table, bending over him and brushing her hips and breasts against him at every opportunity, affording him bountiful glimpses of her breasts, which were fairly leaping from her low-cut bodice.

Of course, who could blame her? Devlin cut an extraordinarily dashing figure. Once more, he had declined to don a coat, understandable considering the summer heat. Indeed, Eden wished she might have done the same with her half dozen petticoats. He wore a snowy-white shirt with abundant ruffles at the cuffs and an equally decorative cravat, expertly tied. Over this, he sported a hip-length waistcoat of dark-blue brocade, lavishly trimmed with gold braid. His breeches were in a matching shade of blue, tucked neatly into the tops of his jackboots. About his waist hung a heavily fringed gold sash, into which he had tucked his sword. The gold hoop in his ear and the tawny color of his hair seemed designed to accent his apparel, or the other way round, perhaps. Certainly, a powdered wig would not have suited him half as well as his own sun-streaked locks.

Still, Eden fumed, the serving girl had no call to flirt with him as openly as she did, no matter how appealing he was. And Devlin, in his turn, need not preen under her attentions quite so much. After all, he was Eden's escort for the evening! Beside which, it wasn't as if Eden had come out in rags, with warts dotting her face. As much effort as she had taken with her own appear-

ance, she deserved his undivided attention, which she
was definitely not getting!

The longer the flirtation went on, the more peevish
Eden became, until finally she could stand it no longer.
Leaning close, she hissed into his ear, "Captain Kane,
must you act a lust-crazed fool over a simple tavern
maid? 'Tis disgusting, the way you are practically
drooling into your plate!"

Her comment seemed to amuse him greatly. On a
laugh, he said, "But, duchess, that is precisely what I
am, much to my own dismay. Since you have not seen
fit to invite me to your bed, how could I be otherwise?
I am but a carnal creature, with natural hungers which
must be appeased from time to time."

She glared back at him. "Nay, sir! You are a lout! A
flaming lecher! Moreover, you are making a disgraceful
spectacle of yourself, and the rest of us in the process."

He simply smiled at her. "Having a fit of pique, are
we, pet? Mayhap venting a bit of jealousy? No need for
it, you know. You are more than welcome to fulfill my
desires at any time you choose."

"Mother, please make this jackanapes cease his lurid
prattle, or I swear I shall take my leave," Eden implored. "In which case, you and Nate will be seated
with a stiff suit of speaking clothes, and left to explain
the matter."

"Please do hush with such unseemly talk, Captain,"
Jane complied, spearing him with a stern glower. "You
have made it plain that you will be departing Charles
Town as soon as you can manage to do so. Under those
circumstances, I find it totally reprehensible, dishonor-
able, and in poor taste for you to remain bent on seducing my daughter."

Devlin, knowing that Jane's accusation held more
than a grain of truth, and feeling the slightest bit guilty
because of it, managed to behave moderately well after
that. Until the walk home. With the evening so balmy,

and the two men at hand to take charge of any problems they might encounter along the way, the foursome had decided to walk the short distance from the inn rather than employ the carriage. They were but a few steps along when a buxom young doxy strolled past, her bodice barely covering her breasts. She reeked of cheap perfume, her black hair streamed down her back like a witch's mane, and her face had been painted with a heavy hand. As she came even with them, she glanced sideways through kohl-laden eyes, spotted Devlin, and winked.

Caught up in each other, Nate and Jane witnessed none of this. As Eden stopped short in dumbfounded shock, the older couple continued walking. Devlin halted as well, and stood staring wistfully after the harlot, his eyes faithfully following the beckoning sway of the woman's hips.

His lips pursed in a soundless whistle. "Now, there's a sight worth its weight in gold!" he sighed dramatically.

"Then you just have your fill of it, you randy hound!" Eden spat out. "For all the good 'twill do you! And I hope your eyes fall right out of their sockets!" She yanked her hand from the curve of his arm and strode angrily after her mother, leaving Devlin to his own devices.

For all of a minute Devlin remained in full view. Then, predictably, he began to fade, leaving only his fine apparel to be seen.

Several yards away, slouched in an alleyway with his precious flask of rum, an old drunk beheld the strange transformation with boggled mind. The befuddled fellow gave a sharp shake of his head, as if to clear his drink-fogged vision. "Blimey! I must've gotten me a powerful batch o' rotgut this time! This keeps up, I'm gonna have to start cuttin' back on the bottle! And what a bloomin' shame that'd be!"

Chapter 21

Almost before Eden could fully comprehend what she was about to do, the day arrived when the repairs to the *Gai Mer* were finished, and the frigate was launched back into the bay. Fresh stores were laid in, and Nate announced he would be sailing on the early-morning tide of the following day. Jane was properly saddened, more than Devlin could know, for not only would she be parted for several long weeks from her betrothed, but also from her only child. The reality was almost more than she could bear.

"Must you go so soon?"

"Now, Janie, the sooner I leave, the sooner I'll be back, love. And the sooner we'll be wed. Surely you can see the sense of that."

"But anything could happen. To you. To me." *To Eden.* This last thought remained unspoken, because Devlin was standing close by, but her fellow conspirators understood it nonetheless.

"Nay," Nate told her. " 'Twill be smooth sailin' all the way, and I'll be back almost afore ye know I've gone." He gave her a wink and added for Devlin's benefit, "B'sides, ye'll have Dev and all yer fine friends to look out for ye. And dependable help at the warehouse, as well."

The remaining crewmen, those who still did not wish to apply for pardon, had agreed, with the promise of a hefty bonus, to stay on in Jane's employ until Nate's return. They were a loyal lot and had given their solemn oath, and Nate was assured that they would not go back on it, even without Devlin present to monitor them.

Jane sniffed tearfully. "Well then, in honor of our last night together, I've some excellent brandy I've been saving for just such a special occasion. Let me fetch it, and we'll all share a toast."

It was all part of their scheme. In the kitchen, Jane would pour their drinks. Into Devlin's, she would add a prescribed amount of sleeping powder. Within a short time, he would fall into a deep sleep, and when next he awakened, he would be aboard the *Gai Mer*, bound and gagged and far out at sea.

But in her haste and nervousness, Jane failed to stir the potion well enough. Devlin took only one sip and spied the undissolved powder at the bottom of his goblet. His brow furrowed, and he turned accusing eyes on all three of them.

"Ho! What's this? Could it be I'm being duped by those I trust most? Is that why, in the past two days, you have all ceased nagging me to go to New Providence?"

"Whatever are you yapping about now?" Eden demanded, praying that her face was not flaming with guilt. "Devlin, you are making absolutely no sense."

He held out his cup to each of them in turn. "Then explain, if you can, what is at the bottom of my drink. Methinks you all planned to drug me—did you not?"

Jane took up the defense. "Devlin Kane, you are being ridiculous! I've never heard such rot in my life! That"—she pointed to his goblet—"is nothing more than sediment from the bottom of the cask. Not that I meant to serve it to you, but in my hurry, I must have become careless in the pouring. An error which I shall rectify straightaway."

In one smooth motion, she snatched the cup from his unseen hand and started again for the kitchen, muttering for all to hear. "I've never been so insulted! Why, to be accused of such a thing, right in my own home! And by someone I considered a friend!"

"Dev, ye should be properly ashamed o' yerself!" Nate claimed, shaking his head. "Aye, ye should."

Devlin wasn't so sure about that. Turning on his heel, he stomped out of the room. Over his shoulder he said, "Tell Jane to forget pouring more brandy for me. I'm not certain the next serving would be any better than the last. Nor am I sure I trust any of you further than I could throw you."

Once he'd gone, Eden slumped into a chair. "Tarnation! What do we do now?" she wailed.

"For a beginning, you can watch your tongue, young lady," her mother admonished, stepping back into the room.

She, too, fell into a seat on the divan, leaving the cushion next to her for Nate. "'Tis all my fault for getting into such a rush about it," she admitted. "But 'tis too late to change that. Rather, we must concentrate on finding another means to outmaneuver him."

"I could try slipping into his room while he sleeps and bashing him senseless," Nate offered.

"How well do you imagine that would work, with that dratted noisy falcon to alert him the instant you opened the door?" Eden said.

"Aye," Nate agreed with a resigned sigh. "I'd forgotten about Zeus."

"Well, we must find some means of lulling the man into lowering his guard," Jane said.

The glimmer of a notion teased the back of Eden's brain, growing brighter with every passing moment. "I think I have an idea which might work. 'Tis a bit precarious, but it does have some merit." On a deep breath, before she lost her courage, she blurted, "I propose that I should seduce him. Only up to a point, you understand."

"What!" Two voices blended in exclamation.

"Well, can either of you suggest anything better?" she challenged. "The man is practically obsessed with bedding me, and after his extended abstinence he is certainly primed for seduction."

"So much so that a ewe will not be safe near him soon," Nate put in succinctly.

Eden grimaced. "How graciously stated. Not that I appreciate the comparison. Still and all, if I were to entice him, I believe he would snap at the bait like a starving shark."

"An apt analogy, daughter, and one to keep foremost in your mind. Properly provoked, he could be every bit as dangerous."

Eden nodded. "True, but is it not also a proper assumption that, once beguiled, his thinking will be muddled, his suspicions at bay? Would it not then be easier to persuade him to share a drink with me, simply to ease my fears of what he imagines will transpire soon afterward? But, in reality, I shall be sipping very little of the wine, while he will be consuming a greater quantity. Before the seduction can be accomplished, he'll be flat on his face, snoring the curtains from their rods."

" 'Tis a gamble, but it could do the trick," Nate concurred. "Certainly, he'll take great care about what he eats and drinks in this house for many a day to come, but once overwhelmed with lust, he's bound to be less cautious." He turned to Jane. "Think ye 'tis worth a try?"

"I don't know," she answered, worrying her lower lip with her teeth. "There's so much at stake, and too much that could go wrong. The slightest slip, and Eden could easily lose her virtue. 'Tis not a thing to take lightly, or to put in jeopardy without just cause."

"Mama, this *is* a just cause," Eden proclaimed. "The man I love is about to throw his future away, and mine with it. I will do anything to prevent that, and if the price is my chastity, then the cost is well worth the paying."

"And what if you forfeit your innocence for naught?" her mother counseled gravely. "Your life could lie in ruin."

"Mama, I thought we'd agreed that the choice would be mine, if and when the time came. Besides, I think we are putting the cart before the horse. If all goes well, I will come away as pure as I begin. However, if the worst should happen, I shall bear the consequences without regret, for I'd rather know one night of passion with Devlin, than a thousand with anyone else. Just as I have changed from the prudish old maid I once was, so have my values and my ideals. I want to know the glory of lying with the man I love, if only once in my life. I'll gladly go to my grave a fallen woman, than die never having taken this chance at a future together with him."

The trap was set once more, awaiting only the moment to spring it. Much to Devlin's confusion, Nate sailed the next morning as intended. What he did not know was that his quartermaster took the *Gai Mer* only a short distance down the coast, with plans to return again that evening under cover of darkness. Meanwhile, though perplexed, Devlin still had not relinquished his suspicions, refusing to eat his meals with the Winters women that day, or to drink anything they offered him. It was going to be tricky to dupe him now; everything depended on Eden's untried powers of seduction and the whims of fate.

All was ready. Devlin had retired to his room for the

night not ten minutes ago. In her own room, attired in her most becoming nightdress, with tampered wine at hand, Eden whispered a quick prayer and put her scheme into action. Very deliberately, she set about creating as much noise as she could, all the while making the sounds appear normal. First she clomped about the room in her shoes, slamming bureau drawers and wardrobe doors. At length, she flopped heavily onto the bed, making it squeak in protest. Then she removed the hard-heeled shoes and dropped them, one at a time, onto the hardwood floor.

All this she was certain Devlin was hearing through the connecting wall. How could he fail to, when he'd told her he'd heard her restless turnings many a night before, when she'd been trying her utmost to be quiet? With that in mind, Eden bounced about on the bed. Then, with a loud sigh, she got up, went to the window, and slammed it shut. A few minutes later, she threw the window open again, smiling at the loud squawk the frame emitted. Only she and her mother knew how laboriously they had worked earlier in the day, soaking the wood with wet towels to make it swell.

She walked to the rocker, which she had intentionally positioned directly opposite the head of Devlin's bed, with only the thin wall separating them. The rocker, too, had been treated to a good dousing, and as Eden put it into motion, it protested with a chorus of groans and creaks. Back and forth, over and over again, she rocked, until she was tempted to put her own hands to her ears for respite. She could only guess, and pray, that the sound was equally irritating on Devlin's side.

She was beginning to give up hope when there came a pounding against the wall near her head. Three sharp raps. Smiling to herself, Eden answered with two taps of her own. She ceased rocking, mentally allotted him three minutes of blessed silence, then rose and went again to her wardrobe. With calculated clumsiness, she rumbled about, finally retrieving a pair of mules from the bottom shelf. These she fitted onto her feet, and the next sound was that of flopping heels clip-clopping repeatedly over bare floorboards, as Eden began to pace. Every now and again she would stop long enough to rattle bottles and jars on the top of her dressing table, or to drop something on the floor, or to clang the side of her silver goblet against the crystal wine decanter on her nightstand.

She continued in this manner for a quarter of an hour, then finally settled herself once again in the rocking chair. Loud creaks sounded in tandem with her clicking heels, and, to add insult to injury, Eden began to softly hum off-key—all the while trying to listen for sounds from Devlin's side of the wall.

Just when she was beginning to think nothing would disturb him sufficiently, she heard his bedstead creak, followed by muted sounds which she could not interpret. Then she heard his bedroom door open and shut. She prayed he did not intend to leave the house. Finally her pleas were granted, and he knocked softly on her door.

She was halfway to answering the summons when she remembered the wine. Backtracking quickly, she gave the decanter a brisk shake to blend the potion well, and poured a generous amount into her goblet. With drink in hand, she went to the door.

Cracking it open just enough to allow him an adequate view of her in the fetching nightdress and her flowing tresses, she peered at him. By the light of her lamp, which now shone on him, she noted that he'd taken the time to yank on his breeches, but nothing else, and the sight of his bare chest threatened to give her an instant attack of the vapors, as if she were not already nervous enough. "Yes?" she questioned weakly.

He frowned back, his shaggy hair handsomely rumpled. For a moment he said nothing, merely staring

down at her. Little did she know that the same lamplight that enabled her to see him so well was also
shining through her white batiste gown, very clearly sil-
houetting her curvaceous bare body. His voice was
husky as he finally replied, "Is something wrong?"

She pretended ignorance. "Why do you ask?"

He countered with an exasperated look. "Why?" he
echoed in disbelief. "Because you are making enough
racket in there to wake the dead!"

On a negligent shrug, she offered, "I'm just restless
for some reason. I can't seem to light in one spot for
more than a minute."

"I've noticed."

She elaborated—very innocently, of course. "I seem
to have a bad case of the fidgets. First I'm too hot, and
there doesn't seem to be enough air in the room. Then
there is too much. Even my skin seems extraordinarily
sensitive this evening."

"Are you running a fever?" he queried, apparently
concerned. "Do you hurt anywhere? Should I fetch
your mother or the doctor?"

She waved a slender hand at him, dismissing the
idea. "I'm not ill. I suppose my nerves are simply on
edge."

"Have you tried drinking some warm milk?"

"Nay, but I did pour myself a dram of wine, in the
hope it would help relax me enough to sleep." She
lifted the goblet for his perusal.

It was filled almost to the rim. "A dram?" he
mocked, his brow rising. "Duchess, that is definitely
more than a dram, and quite sufficient to set you back
on your heels."

She considered this. "I suppose so," she agreed
lightly. "And 'tis my second glass."

At this, the other blond brow rose to meet the first,
his eyes lighting speculatively. "Why don't I come in
and sit with you for a while?" he proposed. "You really

shouldn't be imbibing so freely on your own. You could have an accident, mayhap fall and hit your head. And no one would know you were hurt."

"You wish to join me?" she asked, seeming to weigh his suggestion. Then she shook her head. "I think not, Devlin. But if you want to share my wine, you may."

She offered the chalice to him, but he pushed it gently back. "Nay, sweetling, I do not want your wine. I only meant that I might keep you company while you drink it."

"Aye, no doubt with the intent of taking advantage of me when I've consumed enough to cloud my judgment, you scoundrel!" She glared up at him while with one hand she flipped a length of burnished hair over her shoulder. Then she made to close the door on him. "Go back to bed, Captain Kane."

His sly smile was that of a fox trying to convince a hen that he meant no harm. "Gladly, if that bed be yours."

"When roosters lay eggs," she retorted sweetly, reaching out to give him a little shove, allowing her fingers to caress his bare chest in the same movement. Her eyes went wide and slightly unfocused.

Devlin drew a sharp breath. "Let me in, Eden," he coaxed softly, convincingly.

"Nay." Her hand dropped slowly to her side. She swayed slightly toward him, her lips still parted, before she caught herself and took an unsteady step back. "Go, Devlin. Please. While I still have the strength to resist your charms."

Her words rocked him. In that moment of hesitation, Eden gently closed her door on him. She was shaking, whether more from this mad gamble she was taking or with desire for him, she was not sure. She sensed him still standing in the hall outside her door. Then she heard the quiet tread of his departing footsteps.

Taking a deep breath, hoping she was not overplaying her hand, Eden once more opened her door. He stood in the shadows, ready to enter his own room. There he halted, waiting for her to speak.

Small white teeth gnawed at her lower lip, her indecision evident, and quite endearing. When finally she spoke, her voice was quivering and wistful. "Is it awfully sinful for me to want you so, Devlin?"

Within the space of one heartbeat and the next, he was beside her, his arms gathering her to him as he ushered them both inside her room and closed the door behind them. Then his lips were devouring hers, giving her no chance to demur. His hands were in her hair, at her waist, stroking the length of her back, moving eagerly as if to touch every part of her at once. At last, when her world was spinning recklessly, he allowed her a breath of air.

"God, Eden, have you any idea what you do to me?" he groaned.

"If 'tis anything like what you do to me, 'tis indeed dangerous," she answered on a wobbly sigh.

His mouth lowered toward hers again as he pulled her nearer still, curving her soft body into the hard contours of his. "Wait!" she protested mildly, pushing at his shoulder.

As he drew back slightly, she looked down at the goblet trapped between them, tilted precariously in her trembling hand. "My cup runneth over," she quipped with a giggle.

His gaze followed hers, and he gave a rumbling laugh. "So it seems," he agreed, reaching out to relieve her of the vessel. He glanced about for a place to set it down, but none was near enough to suit. Without another thought but ridding himself of the encumbrance as speedily as possible, Devlin brought the cup to his lips—and as Eden watched in breathless jubilation, he drained the brew in four swift gulps, then carelessly let the empty goblet fall to the floor.

"That," he murmured, his arms banding about her waist to gather her near again, "takes care of that problem. Now, you tempting little witch, we'll take care of another. One that's been tormenting me since the day I met you."

"Me as well," she admitted daringly, rising to her toes to present her lips to his. "Oh, Devlin. Make me yours. Ease this ache I have for you."

Her words, so bold and provocative, were more potent than any ancient aphrodisiac could have been, making his body leap in immediate response. Yet the part of his brain which was still functioning past his lust warned him to go slowly, reminding him that no matter how much she professed to want him, she was yet an innocent, and must be tenderly introduced to the powerful hunger now clawing at him. With effort, he gentled his caresses, his kisses, savoring the feel and the taste of her, relishing every moan of desire that tore from her throat. He spent endless minutes holding her, whispering to her, inviting her inquisitive touch. Only when she was quivering so intensely in his embrace that her legs began to fail her did he sweep her into his arms and carry her to the bed.

As he lowered her to the mattress, her arms clung about his neck, reluctant to release him. Passion-glazed eyes stared into his, large and liquid, like sparkling turquoise pools, and he felt himself drowning in her tremulous gaze. "Oh, sweetling! When you look at me that way, I would grant you almost anything."

It was on the tip of her tongue to request yet again that he apply for amnesty, but she bit the words back, knowing that to do so would immediately cool his ardor. Even as shaken as she was, her desires nearly overwhelming her, some inner voice warned her not to ask it. Rather, she implored huskily, "Hold me. Love me."

Before the wondrous longing once more swept her beyond the point of reasoning, she realized that the sleeping potion did not yet seem to be affecting him. She pondered vaguely whether it would render him unconscious in time to save her virtue—or if she even wanted it to. Then she was once again caught up in the enchantment of his sweet, persistent persuasion, arching into him with wanton delight as he joined her on the bed.

His hands were everywhere, setting her body aflame. Taunting. Teasing. Arousing. And all the while, his mouth was making sumptuous love to hers. She did not know exactly when he had removed her gown and his breeches; had not the time nor the patience to fathom how he had managed the feat when his hands and lips seemed never to leave her. She only knew that his flesh was now searing hers with a heat that threatened to set her ablaze.

Just holding her, rubbing his bare body along hers, burying his face in her sweet, soft flesh, was heaven to Devlin. The pebbled tips of her breasts probed his furred chest, burrowing into the fleecy nest as if to melt themselves into him, and he knew if he died that very instant, he would perish a happy man. Her hair tangled about him, stroking him with its fragrant length, beckoning him to bury his face in its silken strands. Everywhere he touched, her skin was like warm satin. Her body was flawlessly formed, sleek and firm where God had intended it to be, yet incredibly soft and pliant in all the proper places.

She was perfection—and in a few short minutes, she would be his. Completely. The mere thought of it, of possessing her totally, his body claiming hers at last, seemed to make his head spin. Fuzzily, he tried to recall if craving any other woman had ever made him quite so dizzy with desire.

Eden was afloat on a sea of strange and magical sensations of her own, all directly related to Devlin and the fascinating feelings he was awakening within her. Of a sudden, her body seemed to have acquired a thousand places which were now exquisitely attuned to his touch. Her nipples were uncommonly sensitive, supremely ticklish and tingling as his chest hair caressed them teasingly. Wherever it rasped over her bare flesh—her throat, her shoulders, her breasts, her stomach—the shadow of bristles on his usually clean-shaven face seemed to evoke an erotic quickening. Even the coarse hair of his legs as they grazed across her more tender limbs was curiously titillating.

At every point at which their clutching, passion-misted bodies met, soft against hard, rough against smooth, the differences between them formed a marvelous contrast, yet at the same time were wonderfully complementary. Except, perhaps for one. She did not need to see it to know that the hot, hard protrusion pressing against her thigh was his engorged manhood. She'd inadvertently observed it twice before, and felt it through her skirts numerous times. Still, feeling it against her bare leg, with nothing covering either of them, was quite a different matter, and almost as alarming as it was exciting.

Even with his mouth now suckling at her breast, sending a quiver of fiery desire to her loins, fear darted through her. In preparation for what might occur this night, Eden's mother had reluctantly described the mating process, but even with Jane's explanations, Eden could not see how her body would ever accommodate Devlin's organ. Surely, it would rend her asunder! To what, precisely, had she committed or condemned herself?

Oblivious of her fears, Devlin continued to stroke Eden's trembling body. His fingers trailed upward along the silken skin of her inner thighs until they found the sheltering nest of curls at the delta and delved through them in search of that most treasured pearl of passion.

Suddenly Eden was lost in a shower of sensual pleasure. Stars seemed to dance in her head in time to the wild beat of her heart and the throbbing between her legs, where Devlin was so deftly caressing her. His thumb continued to fondle that special place that had her writhing beneath him, while his fingers slid lower, searching, probing. One eased inside to stroke the warm, moist passage hidden there. Then two fingers stretched up inside her, readying her for what was to come.

As he levered himself over her, she was panting, her breath coming in short, harsh gasps. No longer was she afraid. Her mind had no place for fear now, or for anything beyond gratifying this intense longing.

He was murmuring to her, meaningless phrases her brain was too befuddled to interpret, as he positioned her quaking legs about his waist. His shaft pushed into her where his fingers had gone before. He paused briefly, his own breathing labored now as he strove to control his passion, to allow her body sufficient time to accustom itself to him, lest he hurt her more than he must. Then, with his mouth over hers to muffle any cries she might make, he thrust himself full within her tight, wet sheath, piercing the thin obstruction in his path.

For all her previous fears, Eden felt little more than a twinge of discomfort as Devlin shoved past the barrier that proved her virginity. There was a brief burning sensation, an incredible fullness as her inner chamber stretched to accommodate him. Again he had paused, and a moment later it was she who lifted her hips upward in a wordless gesture of need.

He chuckled softly, lifting his mouth from hers to gaze into her flushed face. "Your wish is my command, duchess," he assured her with a roguish grin, even as his hips began the age-old rhythm.

His thrusts were long and deep, once more igniting her passions to delirious heights. Soon she was writhing beneath him, mindlessly matching his every movement with her own. Together they climbed ever onward, upward, toward the blazing heavens, their ecstasy building until Eden thought they would surely be burned alive in the fierce inferno that enveloped them. Then the sun seemed to shatter, spewing forth a fountain of dazzling rays, showering her and Devlin with golden brilliance. On gilded wings of rapture, they soared—and when their radiant flight was done, they glided gently down to earth once more.

When next she was aware of her surroundings, she lay with her head gently pillowed on Devlin's broad shoulder. His hand tenderly stroked her head, brushing the damp curls from her face. "Sleep, my beauty," he whispered drowsily, "and dream sweet visions of glories yet unshared between us. Splendors yet to come."

Past a stifled yawn, he added teasingly, "In the morn, when my head has ceased its peculiar spinning, you and I must inspect your chicken pen, sweetling—for certainly the rooster will now be laying eggs."

Eden was still considering an appropriately clever retort when Devlin began to snore sonorously. At long last, the sleeping draught had taken its toll.

Chapter 22

*D*evlin awoke slowly, groggily, his mouth like cotton and his head throbbing. Before he opened his eyes, he could tell that doing so was going to be painful, for through his closed lids the room seemed brighter than normal. It also seemed to be swaying dizzily, much as it had when he'd fallen asleep the night before.

If it didn't hurt so much, he would have smiled, recalling the night which had passed, and the wonders of making love with Eden at long last. She'd turned out to be quite a delight, practically a wanton in fact, once he'd finally rid her of her silly, virginal qualms. Perhaps he'd stay abed a bit longer this morn and feast again on her delicious charms.

With this thought foremost in his mind, Devlin attempted to move his hand in search of her warm, bare body. It was then that he first discovered that his hands were bound above his head, securely tied—to what? Why? Instantly, at the same time that his eyes popped wide in alert reaction and he found himself in his own quarters aboard the *Gai Mer*, Devlin's befuddled brain recognized several other facts. The bed was rocking, not because he was still dizzy but because the frigate was under sail. And if he'd had his senses about him, he would have realized before now that he could hear the creak of the timbers, the slosh of the waves, the familiar flapping of canvas.

Not only was he now at sea aboard his own ship, but he was trussed up in bed like a Christmas turkey, secured hand and foot! Damn him for being the biggest fool God had ever set breath into! Despite all his suspicions and precautions, he'd still been properly duped, abducted, and bound. By his trusted mate, and the refined little lady who had come to be like a second mother to him, and that spiteful wench who'd had the audacity—the absolute temerity—to seduce him free of his better judgment!

Unless he missed his guess, the ship was on its way to New Providence, and he with it. Devlin's brow furrowed as he contemplated his predicament. Then he gave a gruff laugh. They might all have thought they'd outfoxed him, but they had made a major miscalculation. Nate could haul him all the way to the Bahamas, could even hold a gun to his head, but it would all be for naught. Without Eden along, he still couldn't "appear" before the governor. It would be he who would have the last laugh after all.

And if Nate, or someone, didn't trot his rotten carcass in here soon and untie him, there would be bloody hell to pay! How dare his crew treat their captain in such a manner! Why, they'd be lucky if he didn't have them all hung from the yardarm!

When, after a few minutes more, no one appeared to check on him, let alone release him, Devlin began to roar. In his best authoritative bellow, he cursed, "Nate! You scurvy sea dog! Get your arse in here, or I'll have you flogged to within an inch of your worthless life. Do you hear me, you sneaking bilge rat?"

The cabin door opened, but to Devlin's shock, it was not Nate, or any other of his crew, who entered. It was

Eden who strolled in so calmly. Aboard his ship! No doubt dooming them all to a watery grave!

"Do cease that infernal yelling, Devlin," she instructed him blithely, "or we'll have to gag you, as Nate originally intended." She set the tray she carried on the desk opposite the bed and turned to face him, her hands on her hips as she looked him over with a cool, gloating smile. "My, I rather think I'm going to like having you at my mercy this way."

His eyes were nearly bulging from his head, his face blotched with fury, and she hoped he was not about to go into some sort of fit and die. His mouth worked soundlessly until he finally managed to get his lungs and tongue in working order once more. Sailors an ocean away should have leapt to attention as he raged, "Get off of my ship!"

Eden merely smiled down at him. "And do what, Captain? Swim back to Charles Town? We are several hours out at sea."

"I don't care how you manage it," he snapped. "I just want you gone! Immediately! Before you send us all to wrack and ruin!" He groaned and thrashed about, trying unsuccessfully to jerk loose of his restraints. "Hellfire! I'd rather have the devil himself aboard, than a woman! You know that!"

"Now, Devlin, don't fash yourself so. We've taken care of it. Think you that Nate and the crew would have me aboard if we had not?"

"I've no idea what Nate might do these days, for I'm beginning to think love has reduced his brains to a puddle of mush within his foolish head! Blast him, anyway! And blast you as well!" He glowered up at her.

Eden glared back. Then she turned back to the tray she'd brought in, caught up the cloth napkin, and wadded it into a ball. With a determined gleam in her eye, she walked slowly toward him, her intent obvious.

"Eden Winters, don't you dare! You'll live to regret it, if you do," he warned darkly.

She shook her head at him. "You should know by now what I will dare when I want," she told him. "As for regrets, we'll simply have to wait and see, won't we, Captain Kane?" As he opened his mouth to argue further, she shoved the cloth between his teeth, successfully muffling his curses.

"Now then," she cooed, stepping back to study her good work, "that's much better." She made to leave, halting at the doorway and smiling as he continued to yank futilely at his bindings and rail at her through the muzzle, his black eyes blazing at her. "I'll be back later, and if you are more prone to listening, I'll further explain matters to you. I'll also feed you the meal you would already be digesting, had you been more civil."

It was Nate who next entered the captain's quarters, regarding the bed, the taut-tugged ropes, and the lunging pile of ghost-inhabited clothes with a crooked grin. "Ah, lad! If only ye had listened sooner, ye could have saved yerself all this trouble. And us as well."

Devlin grumbled at him from behind the cloth.

"Save yer breath, Dev. I'm not here to listen to yer threats. I've only come to help ye attend to yer more private needs, since Eden can't be expected to do it. The lass has seen altogether too much o' yer bare arse already, if ye take my meanin'. Fact is, ye should be thankin' yer lucky stars we got ye out o' Charles Town when we did, for Janie was riled enough to nail yer hide to the stable door for buzzard bait."

Devlin's answer was a low, threatening growl.

After loosening the bonds securing Devlin's stocking-clad ankles to the footboard, Nate pulled a crockery chamber pot from beneath the bed. "Now, I'm gonna untie one o' yer hands so ye can unbutton yer breeches and tend to business, but don't ye go tryin' nothin' funny. We dressed ye so I can see what ye're up to, and if I see yer free hand anywhere near the other, ye'll be askin' for a lump on yer noggin—and the next time nature calls, ye'll be goin' in a nappy, jest like a newborn babe," he warned.

This was the first time Devlin had given a thought to his clothing, but now that Nate had mentioned it, he saw that he was, indeed, dressed in one of his visible outfits. There were even pieces of colored yarn tied about his fingers and wrists, the better to enable his captors to determine the exact movements of his hands and feet. Though he could not see it, he could also feel some sort of band about his brow, encircling his head, and could only assume they had reasoned a hat would have fallen off too easily.

From the looks of it, they appeared to have given a good deal of careful consideration to all aspects of his abduction, down to the smallest detail. It would now be his task to discover one detail they had missed, and to put it to his advantage when they were least expecting it—much as Eden had done with him.

Though he was tempted to toss the pot at Nate's head, Devlin thought better of it. Not because of his friend's warning, but more to lull the man into believing Devlin was beginning to accept the situation, becoming a more cooperative prisoner. Let them drop their guard, as he had done. It would serve them right, and him well, when he managed to turn the tables on them.

With that in mind, he tried to hide his temper when Eden returned to the cabin on Nate's departing heels.

"Are you ready to eat now?" she asked.

He nodded.

She bent over him and yanked the gag from between his teeth. Skin went with it, his mouth being so dry now, and Devlin's good intentions flew to the winds.

"Damn and blast, woman! Did you have to take half my flesh with it?"

"Still your usual charming self, I see," came her unrepentant rejoinder. She did, however, offer him a cool drink of water, which he was forced to accept from her helpful hand.

The food on the tray was now long congealed, but when he complained, she chided him. "If you had behaved yourself earlier, 'twould not be cold, so you have only yourself to blame. Now, open your mouth like a good boy."

He offered a sneer, but with his stomach rumbling, he did as she bade. After taking three large mouthfuls of toast laden with egg and ham, his teeth clamped down firmly on her fingers.

"Ouch! Let loose, you ogre!" she screeched, rapping him sharply on his aching head to effect her release. " 'Tis not fitting, or wise, to bite the hand that feeds you. Try that again, and I just might decide to let you starve until your manners improve."

"Then stop shoving that slop in so fast," he demanded fretfully, twisting about to rub his smarting head briskly against his pillow, in lieu of being able to do so with his hand. "Or have you a mind to choke me, Eden, since you give me no time to chew the food properly?"

"Now, there's a thought." She did take more care from that point on, however.

When she had finished and seated herself in a nearby chair with her sewing, he asked irritably, "How is it that you are not suffering any ill effects from your first sea voyage? I would have thought you would be headfirst in a slop jar for the next week."

She gave him a complacent grin. "Sorry to disappoint you, Devlin," she said, not sorry at all. "And how are you enduring the aftereffects of the sleeping potion?"

He scowled, remembering how he had guzzled the wine so eagerly, with nary a word of prompting from her lying lips. "You think you are clever, don't you, my sweet? But you were not clever enough to escape unscathed, were you? And what is next, Eden? A hue and cry for marriage?"

She laughed in his face. "Who says I want to marry the likes of you? Ah, yes! I can see it now. Years of you being tied to my side—not for any love of me, but simply because without me you cannot function as a normal person. Surely, sir, that is every girl's dream!"

He blinked in surprise. "My pardon for so offending you," he avowed testily. "So! If not marriage, what *do* you want?"

"I assumed that would be obvious, even to a thickhead such as you. I want you to apply for pardon."

"And you paid the price for such with your lovely body?" he said, arching a brow at her. "Duchess, has no one taught you to get the prize before paying the cost? 'Tis much more productive done that way round."

Eden was simmering. It showed in the heat of her gaze. "Had I made such a bargain with you yesterday, or the day before, would you have agreed?"

He grinned and shook his head. "Nay, but 'twould have been amusing to see how far you would have carried the game."

"Would it?" she asked, all too sweetly. Rising, she set her sewing aside. "Shall we see about that?"

He frowned at her, not at all certain what she meant. His brow furrowed further as she stepped to the door and threw the lock. Then she began to unbutton the front of her dress. His eyes widened. "What are you doing, wench?"

"Why, playing more 'games,' of course. And testing your theory. Were you not saying, in essence, that having once tasted them, my charms are less tempting to you? That they would gain me naught? Shall we see if I am still capable of 'amusing' you?"

Eden took her own sweet time with the fastenings until she had opened the front of her dress from chest to waist. Slowly, before Devlin's disbelieving eyes, she pulled loose the stomacher which filled in the deep vee of the gown's bodice. She tossed it onto the bed to land at his side.

Her fingers toyed with the sash about her waist, easing the fabric from the pretty bow it had formed. When the ribbon slid free, she held it out before her, sliding the lustrous satin through her fingers. Then, on inspiration, she bent forward to glide the slick length over Devlin's body—an act which would have been much more impressive if he'd been nude. Still, she noted with immense satisfaction that he swallowed hastily when she dragged it over his bare throat and caressed his lips with it.

"Eden, you are playing with fire," he warned thickly.

"Oh? And what are you going to do about it, my dashing pirate?" she taunted, reaching her arms around to unhook her skirts from their side loops. She eased the dress from her shoulders, ever so slowly exposing her ruffled petticoat fully to his view. With a delicate shrug of her shoulders, the cloth fell to her waist and caught there for just a moment, awaiting the sweet shimmy of her hips, which sent it floating to her feet.

Next came her petticoats, all four of them. Again Eden rid herself of them in the most tantalizing fashion, and with each enticing twitch of her hips, Devlin felt himself grow warmer, his manhood swelling uncomfortably within the confines of his tight breeches.

Her eyes shifted knowingly to his crotch, and she laughed softly. "Are you amused yet, Devlin?" she mocked. "Do you like what you see?" Bending to remove her slippers, she presented him with a tantalizing glimpse of her breasts over the gaping top of her chemise.

He groaned. His mouth watered with longing to take hold of the proffered fruit displayed so temptingly beyond his reach. "Enough, vixen," he ground out.

"Not nearly," she countered saucily.

There were eight tiny ribbons along the front of her chemise. Devlin counted each of them, watching in fascination as Eden's fingers lovingly untied them, dawdling over the process until he wanted to scream at her to hurry. With each that came undone, more of her sweet, pale flesh was exposed. Again, she lagged over the band at her waist.

A fine sheen of perspiration glistened at her throat and chest, the only thing that now seemed to hold the fabric over her breasts, shielding them from his avid gaze. It was the only hint that she might be nervous. Or was it simply too warm in the cabin, despite the wide window opened to the extreme aft of the ship, where prying eyes could not see in? It certainly felt stifling; sweat beaded upon his own brow and ran in rivulets into his damp hair.

Like the temptress she had suddenly become, Eden peeled the cloth from her breasts, her shoulders, her hips. As it pooled at her feet, she stood proudly before him, clad only in the sheerest of stockings and her lacy garters. As if she had all the time in the world, she pulled the pins from her hair, letting the silken mass tumble down her back and across her breasts, only barely veiling them within its waving strands.

Though not large, her breasts were beautifully formed, firm and round, the rosy crests dimpling prettily in the breeze from the window. Or perhaps it was the hot glow in Devlin's black eyes that made them spring to attention so eagerly. As if she'd read his thoughts, Eden's tongue crept out to lick her lips, moistening them as he wished to do to her breasts and those perky pink nipples. Her hands slid smoothly along her body, teasing him until his own curled into fists. Her palms cupped her breasts, thrusting them tauntingly before him.

"Do you want them, Devlin?" she purred. "Shall I give you a taste?" She bent over him, holding them just shy of his reach.

"Better yet, perhaps you'd like to feel them," she suggested with a smile that would have put a sea siren to shame. "Shall I undress you?"

Devlin could only groan as she tugged his shirt free of his breeches, pushing it up his chest and over his head. With his hands bound as they were, the garment caught at his wrists and hung there like a drooping flag of surrender. Next she unbuttoned his breeches. As she tugged them over his hips, to a point just above his knees, his turgid shaft sprang free, and Devlin gave a muted sigh that at least this part of him was to be released from its bindings. Perhaps if Eden were to see this wanton act to its conclusion, he would soon feel further relief.

But that was wishful thinking. Bent solely on tormenting him, Eden slid her body along his. Starting low on his thighs, she glided upward, dragging her breasts slowly over every inch of quivering male flesh she had just exposed. "Does that feel good, love?" she whispered.

"Aye, witch. You know it does," he admitted, straining the words through gritted teeth. She rewarded him with a shower of light, wet kisses.

Her silken hair spread over him, trailing softly in the wake of her hot mouth and burning breasts, like fingers of flame. Her legs, still encased in the sheer stockings, slithered over his, one knee coming to rest lightly atop his aching manhood, stroking its throbbing length as his flesh leapt and arched in helpless response.

Just when he was sure he was about to explode for

need of her, Eden drew back slightly. "Admit that you want me, Devlin," she commanded softly.

"I want you. Come over me."

"How much? What would you give to have me now?"

"For pity's sake, sweetling," he moaned. "Can't we discuss this afterward?"

"Nay. That is not what you told me before, when you were mocking me so well. You said not to relinquish the price before the prize."

"I'll not apply for pardon, Eden," he grated, his body screaming for hers, for that sweet, mindless relief only she could give it.

"Aye, you shall," she insisted, sliding from atop him. "Mayhap not just yet, but you will concede." She rose and stood looking down at him, her face flushed with her own unappeased desire. "You taught me that as well, Devlin. You made me want you until I granted you exactly what you sought. Now the shoe is on the other foot, and I intend to make it fit just as tightly. Think on it, love." Her glance slid to his engorged manhood. "Think long and hard."

Chapter 23

*I*t was the most delectable, intense torment
Devlin had ever experienced. He could not believe the
speed and ease with which Eden had discarded her previous prudery. Having once been initiated into the delights of the flesh, she now seemed to revel in her
newfound female prowess, flaunting her seductive powers with all the artfulness of an accomplished courtesan.
He could only conclude that such talent must be inborn
in some women, and once released, it was stunning to
behold. And extremely erotic.

The woman was also ruthless, taunting him day and
night. Everything she did, even the most innocent act,
seemed to further excite his desire for her. The scheming witch was out to break him, and apparently would
not cease trying until she got him to agree to her demands. Though the moment of his defeat had yet to arrive, Devlin was not at all sure how much longer he
could survive this sensual onslaught. She was fast turning him into a blithering slave to her charms.

Each night, Eden crawled into his bed, buck-naked,
to curl her soft, smooth body next to his. All night long,
he lay awake and painfully aroused—feeling her, smell-
ing her, yet unable to do a thing about it! Indeed, she

had him completely at her mercy, and Eden did not seem at all prone to sympathy over his sad plight. Rather, she seemed to enjoy it immensely, to devise even more innovative ways to torture him.

He came to live in anticipation of those moments when she would rise to stretch the weariness from her body, arching up on her toes, her arms reaching far over her head. The elegant turn of her throat enticed him nearly as much as the forward thrust of her breasts and hips. And the supple gyrations she employed at such times was enough to get a rise out of a corpse!

She made an art of the simple act of dressing and undressing, her movements easy and graceful, her hands lingering on all the places he wanted so desperately to touch: stroking her stockings over her long, shapely legs; her fingers sifting through her cinnamon hair; shimmying into her petticoats and letting them slither over her slender curves.

Even while sewing or eating, she was a tempting baggage. The tip of her tongue would creep out to catch between her teeth, or to lick a morsel of food from her lips or her fingers. Simply to tantalize him further, she would often apply similar measures toward him, lapping and sucking crumbs from his lips and chin, even from his bare chest, and he would almost lose his mind.

When she wasn't tormenting the daylights out of him, and sometimes while she was doing so, they talked. Once she had described to him in minute detail all the precautions she and Nate had taken to counter her presence aboard ship, Devlin relaxed a bit. Still, he didn't feel absolutely comfortable about having her here. It was like waiting for the other shoe to drop. Of course, comfort wasn't something he was frequently experiencing these days anyway. And they would simply have to wait to see how well the priest's blessing would work.

"Explain one thing to me, Eden," he requested one

day. "If you don't wish to wed me, then why have you gone to such lengths to try to convince me to apply for pardon? I don't understand it at all."

She gave him a long, contemplative look, as if deciding how best to word her reply. Then she said softly, "Because I want you to be safe. I don't want you needlessly risking your life, with every navy in the civilized world bent on your capture. It would kill me to learn that you'd met your end on the gallows, your body left there to rot as a warning to other corsairs."

"Sweetling, there are risks to everything in life. I wouldn't have to be pirating to slip on a deck and break my neck, or to choke on a chicken bone, or to die of unknown causes in my own bed."

"Aye, but those would be accidents, or effects of nature. As a brigand, you would be bringing about your own demise, don't you see? And for what? A cache of jewels? A handful of gold? A few years of grand adventure? Even Nate sees the wisdom of quitting while he can, with his head still atop his shoulders."

"Nate is becoming an old fuss-fidget. Besides, he has a good ten years on me, and I'm not so ready to settle into my rocking chair."

"Age hasn't a thing to do with it, Devlin," she argued. "Nor has wanting to marry or raise a family. The plain truth is right before you, but you refuse to see it. Your days of roaming the seas and stealing to your heart's content are numbered. 'Tis an occupation which is soon to be abolished altogether, by countries and kings and common folk all working hand-in-hand to see piracy stamped out, once and for all. I simply do not want to see you breathe your last along with it."

Devlin hated to admit it, but some of what she said held more than a grain of truth. Military vessels were becoming more numerous and their men more vigilant all the time, as well as more determined and skilled. Even the port authorities were less prone to accepting bribes, and stolen goods were harder to unload, bringing lower prices than in years gone by.

Perhaps, whether he wished it or not, the time had come, to consider his future more carefully, to decide what he might want to do with the rest of his life if sailing beneath his own flag, under his own rules, was no longer possible. But he wanted the choice to be his, made in his own way, in his own sweet time—for his own reasons.

Not that he didn't appreciate Eden's brand of persuasion. Truth be told, he was relishing most of it. Despite his constant discomfort, he was curious to see how long she would continue with it, and how far she would go to gain his agreement. And he was becoming more intrigued by her with each passing moment.

He simply wanted the decision to be his own.

Three days into their voyage, Devlin managed to badger Ethan, his cabin boy, into loosening his bonds. The lad had come in to clean the cabin, as was his assigned duty. Eden had gone for her usual mid-morning stroll on deck and was not there to witness the threats and curses Devlin heaped upon the poor boy's head. Fortunately, Ethan was too well-trained, and too loyal to his captain, to disobey for long.

"But I promised Mr. Hancock I wouldn't untie you," he protested, even as he bent to the task of setting Devlin free. "He and Miss Winters will know 'twas me, and I'll get my ears boxed for sure."

"Then we won't tell them, and they'll be none the wiser," Devlin replied, pulling his wrists free of the slackened restraints and flexing them. "You just leave the ropes looped loosely, and I'll slip in and out of them as need be. Just remember what I said. Nate will be in to see me each day and will surely tighten the knots again. You must come in after him and ease them once more. Forget, or disregard my orders, and 'twill be more than your ears you'll have to worry about."

A short while later, after having stretched his muscles and indulged in an excellent cigar, making sure the smoke drifted through the open window, Devlin slipped back into his ropes—just a heartbeat before Eden came through the door. His lips twitched with a desire to laugh; his eyes sparkled with deviltry.

Hers did too, for an altogether different reason. " 'Tis time you had a good washing, Devlin," she stated in a no-nonsense tone, placing a jug of steaming water on his desk.

"Sweetling, I really don't think now is the time," he told her, after first recovering from her bold announcement. Though the idea of having her bathe him was a novel one, rather like having one's fantasy come true, Devlin didn't want to test his endurance quite so fully as yet. With freedom a mere twist of his wrists away, he wasn't sure he could keep from ravishing her, and he didn't want to give the game away just now.

Eden had retrieved the washbowl, filled it with hot water, and was approaching him, washcloth in hand. "Now, you just lie back and enjoy this," she said.

He would try. He just hoped he could succeed.

Eden peeled his clothing from him. Again, his shirt caught at his wrists, and for the first time, Devlin considered this a boon. Perhaps it would help him to remember to keep his hands where they belonged, away from Eden. Somehow, with much tugging and pulling, she succeeded in dragging his breeches nearly to his ankles. Well, if the shirt was aiding him, the breeches were doing twice the trick. Even should the leg restraints slide over his feet, his trousers would hobble him admirably. For all intents and purposes, he might as well still be bound.

She started with his face, which should have been a safe enough place to begin. But this was to be no ordinary scrubbing. Devlin soon discovered that his lips were extremely sensitive, and she really didn't have to breathe into his wet ears that way, did she? Lord, he was so riddled with chill bumps that if anyone could see him now, they would take him for a plucked goose!

She swathed his chest with soap, creating a mass of frothy bubbles amid his chest hair. Then she spent an inordinate amount of time weaving intricate patterns through the lather with her fingertips, before tormenting him a second time with a rinsing. Though Devlin had never considered himself ticklish, when she washed his sides and his armpits, he almost leapt from the bed. Only by holding firmly to the loosened ropes did he keep from jerking free of them. Even the bend of his arm, his palms, his fingertips—when she finally got round to them—were amazingly attuned to her touch.

With his ankles and wrists bound to each other, she was able to nudge him onto his side. Whereupon, she proceeded to give his back equal attention. She'd scarcely begun when Devlin was groaning in appreciation, his eyes closed to savor the pleasure, hard-put to remember when he'd enjoyed anything more.

Suddenly his eyes popped wide. The woman was clutching his bum! By damn if she wasn't! And sneaking her slippery fingers between his legs to feel at other parts of him as well!

By the time she had washed and rinsed his legs, missing not one sensitive spot along the way, Devlin was ready to die of pure bliss. It seemed not even the soles of his feet or his toes were to be spared. Then, inevitably, her hands were caressing his upper thighs, his stomach. Finally, his pulsating manhood. It rose and fell in tandem to her touch, like a cobra entranced by a flute.

Teeth grated, Devlin forcefully reminded himself not to grab for her, not to roll her beneath him and plunge into her. There would be time enough later to pay her back for her playfulness. If he survived this interlude!

Sweet heaven! Now she was licking at him with her warm tongue, lapping at him like a kitten at a platter of cream! Any minute now, he was going to lose control, and surprise the devil out of her!

Then she was settling herself astride his hips, her skirts pulled up and out of the way, her lips caressing his chest. "Tell me how to do this, Devlin. Please!" she entreated, breathing unevenly.

He obliged eagerly. "Close your hand about me, pet, and guide me into yourself. Lower yourself upon me, as slowly and easily as you must, and as far as you can."

For a moment he thought she might stop, even at this final stage—and if she did, he would strangle her! But his fears were unfounded. In the next second, she was sliding down upon him, her hot, wet sheath wrapping itself tightly about him. It was so heavenly that he almost failed to hear her whisper, "Devlin! I'm so full with you! But I need to move. Oh, hurry! Tell me how!"

"Ride me, sweetling, as you would a horse. Up and down. Brace your hands on my chest, and ride me hard."

For someone who'd never spent much time astride a horse, Eden was more than adept at riding her man. Soon both of them were bucking and arching and colliding in perfect rhythm, writhing against one another in search of the ultimate ecstasy. Their cries blended, as together they found it at last, glorious waves of splendor washing over them, drowning them, hurtling them toward rapture's shores.

"Why?" he panted afterward, as her head rested over his thumping heart. "Why did you give me all of yourself now, when I've yet to bend to your wishes?"

She raised her head and smiled at him through the veil of her disheveled hair. "This time was for me, Devlin Kane. You might have gained your pleasure as well, but I know that this time was mine."

He answered with a wry grin. "Then I can only hope you want your own satisfaction again soon, vixen. Very soon indeed."

Another confrontation of no small import arose when Eden decided that Devlin's hair could use a trimming. At that announcement, his face clouded ominously. "Nay!" he exclaimed. "Try it, woman, and there are no bonds which can hold me."

He was so adamant that Eden backed away, scissors still in hand. "Devlin, why are you getting into such a snit over such a small matter? Heavens! I have cut it for you several times now since we've met, and I've yet to do it badly."

"Aye, but those times were ashore, not aboard ship."

"Pray, explain what difference that should make."

"It makes all the difference, as Nate or any of the crew will verify. To trim hair or pare nails aboard ship when the weather is fine is sure to bring a storm."

"Oh, of all the rot!" she huffed. "I swear, you sailors have more silly superstitions than anyone I've ever heard." In an aside, she added, "I cannot recall Mother ever telling me that Grandfather believed so foolishly."

"Your grandfather?" Devlin echoed. "What has he to do with anything? Did he also sail?"

Eden glanced at him in surprise, only now aware she'd spoken aloud. "Aye, Devlin, he did. To hear Mother speak of him, he was a wondrous man to know. Many times, I've wished he would have lived past my second year, for I scarcely remember him. My single recollection is of sitting on his lap and yanking at his beard, which I must have found immensely intriguing. He laughed heartily and patted my head."

She smiled at the memory, then asked softly, still caught up in her thoughts, "Do you think mayhap that is why I've not been prone to the usual malaise at sea? Might I have inherited his sea legs?"

Devlin shrugged. "That is beyond my reckoning, Eden. But you may consider yourself fortunate to be so blessed. However, we've had fine weather and smooth seas thus far. You might still experience a few ills should we encounter a storm. Therefore, regardless of your own thinking, t'would be wise to heed my warning and apply your shears solely to your sewing."

Eden was to discover that many more things were forbidden aboard ship. One of these was whistling, which also brought storms and was considered mocking the Devil. But since whistling interfered with, and was often mistaken for, the piercing tones of the bo'sun's pipe, used to signal various activities on deck, this superstition made some sense to her. Killing seabirds was also forbidden, and eagles, hawks, and falcons were often brought along as tokens of good fortune, which explained why Zeus, visible or not, was still revered among the crew. They'd even delayed sailing from Charles Town until the bird had been retrieved from Eden's home and installed once more aboard the *Gai Mer.*

She also discovered why sailors, pirates in particular, so often wore an earring, some men donning two or more. The tradition hailed back to a time when doing so was thought to improve eyesight, a definite benefit at sea, especially useful in spying other ships and avoiding treacherous shoals. Very vaguely, almost as if she wished it so, she recalled that her grandfather had sported a glint of gold in his ear. She would have to ask her mother to be certain, but it was not at all unlikely.

On a whim, more to test the theory than for purposes of adornment, Eden donned a pair of garnet ear bobs she'd packed into her valise. With their inner fire, garnets were considered objects of good luck, and Eden was curious enough by now to want to test them.

When she foolishly admitted as much to Devlin, he laughed uproariously. "Ho! Not so ready to poke fun at the rest of us now, are you, pet?" His dark gaze strayed to the slight bulge in her pocket where her little sack of codfish stones rested. "I know about the stones also, so you may as well admit that you're every bit as drawn to charms as the rest of us."

Her lips protruded in a fetching pout. "I am simply conducting an experiment, Devlin. To see if any of this has even a morsel of validity."

"Aye, sweetling," he agreed on a chuckle. "But if nip should come to tuck, I'd wager you'd swallow those stones to stay afloat rather than risk losing them."

Devlin was alone and unbound in his quarters, with only Zeus for company. With his keen hearing, the big bird had taken to alerting his master of approaching footsteps, well in time for Devlin to resume his supposed captivity. Suddenly the ship's bell rang out the alarm. From on deck, shouts arose. Without a thought of continuing his ruse, Devlin dashed to his sea chest and quickly retrieved his broadsword and pistols. On the run, he checked their load and shoved the guns into his belt.

Aside from Eden, no one seemed surprised at his abrupt appearance on deck, though a few hastily crossed themselves at the sight of their captain's bodiless clothes rushing toward the helm. "What goes?" Devlin queried, assuming immediate command.

Nate nodded toward the starboard horizon, handing Devlin the spyglass. "We've company, Dev. Two ships with sails full and gainin' on us."

Devlin peered through the lens, his brow furrowing. "They sport no colors," he mused. "Likely, brigands such as ourselves."

"Aye," Nate concurred. "But we ride high in the water, with no plunder fillin' our holds. Seein' this, they surely know we've nothing to steal. Why, then, are they so intent on catchin' us?"

Devlin's eyes narrowed. "A good question, old friend. What say we discover the answer? Give the order to swing about. We'll meet them straight on, and if 'tis a fight they're wanting, they'll have it shortly. Even with but two-thirds of our normal crew, we can still give 'em a challenge they won't soon forget."

Nate gave him a queer look. "I'm not gonna bother askin' how ye got yerself free so fast, but I am wonderin' if ye intend to greet the challenge dressed as ye are. To be sure, ye'd likely scare the bejesus out o' every last man, if that's yer purpose."

Devlin cursed in frustration. "Damn me, but I'd love to enter the fray as a normal man again! While this business of being a half-spirit has some merit, I find no sport, and little honor, in wielding my sword against an enemy who cannot see me." Finding no help for it but to change into his ghostly attire, he was intent on returning to his cabin when he nearly collided with Eden.

"Which one of your men untied you?" she demanded heatedly.

He grabbed her arm, propelling her alongside him. "I've no time for petty squabbles now, Eden. We've ships to meet, and likely a battle forthcoming."

He shoved her ahead of him into the cabin, again making his way to his chest. Locating his invisible clothes, he began to change into them. "I want you to remain here. Lock the door behind me and open it to no one until I send word that 'tis safe to do so." From his belt, he tossed her one of his pistols. "Arm yourself with this, and if anyone breaks through that door, shoot them. You do know how to fire a gun, I trust?"

She nodded, too caught up in watching him dress to notice much save the excited gleam in his dark eyes. "You are looking forward to this confrontation, aren't you?" she accused. "Fairly relishing it."

He flashed her a white-toothed grin. "Aye, Eden. I *do* enjoy my work—nearly as much as I have fancied these last few days at your tender mercies. When the battle is won, mayhap I can return the favor, sweetling. In the interim, 'twill give your agile mind something to dwell upon besides your fears."

"Devlin," she said hesitantly, "I overheard what you told Nate. Does it truly bother you so, to meet your enemy unseen?"

"Aye, Eden, it does. 'Tis unscrupulous to hold such unfair advantage over an opponent, and I detest it to the marrow of my bones. When I pit my wits and my sword against another, I want to come away knowing 'twas a fair fight I won."

She gave a miserable nod. "I think I understand what you are saying, and I suppose if I were a man I would feel much the same." On a defeated sigh, she rose to fetch a length of black cloth from her sewing material. "Change back into viewable clothing, Devlin. I think I have a solution to your problem."

He stopped in the midst of fastening his sash about his waist. His startled gaze met hers. "You do?"

"Aye." She held the cloth out to him. "Your hood, Sir Pirate," she declared somberly. "If we cut eyeholes in a square of this, as one might do with a mask, and drape it properly over your head so that your vision is unimpaired, it should serve the purpose. Of course, you might also want to secure it with a neckerchief, to keep it from slipping out of place, and mayhap wear your hat atop it as well."

Devlin stared at the cloth in consideration. "With gloves over my hands, and visible weapons and clothes, my body will be totally discernible," he marveled. "This is wonderful, Eden!"

She wasn't so certain. However, she kept that thought to herself and told him, "You do realize that this hood will be suitable only under circumstances such as this. 'Twould not be appropriate attire for a stroll down the streets of Charles Town, lest you send people screaming in fear, and ruin all the goodwill you have striven so hard to gain with the citizens there."

"Nor wise to wear for an audience with Governor Rogers?" he added with a querying look. "Is that why you have not suggested such a fine disguise until now?"

"Nay, Devlin. I simply hadn't thought of it before. I wish I hadn't thought of it now."

"Well, I am overjoyed that you have," he admitted. He quickly changed clothes again, and with her aid, donned the new hood. Viewing the result in his looking glass, he was well-pleased with the intimidating image reflected there.

He turned to her, his eyes aglow. "I'd love to kiss you just now, but 'twill have to wait until the battle is won and my mouth is free of this covering." His gloved hand came up to stroke her cheek. "Fear not, Eden. Lock the door after me, and stay safe. I shall return soon, and together we will celebrate the victory."

Chapter 24

*E*den perched nervously on the edge of the bed. She paced. She peered out the large window, but saw nothing save endless ocean, for her only view was behind the *Gai Mer*. With her ear to the locked door, she listened anxiously for the sounds of battle.

For what seemed an eternity, all was curiously silent. Then the cannons roared, and the crew cheered. A minute or so later, the frigate lurched slightly to one side, accompanied by the clanking and scraping of grappling hooks seeking their marks. Suddenly Eden wished again for that awful silence, for the air was rife with shouts and the distinctive clash of steel upon steel. Shots rang out, and with each sharp report, Eden flinched. Her imagination running wild, she clenched her hands together and prayed fervently, hoping God would hear her pleas and spare Devlin and Nate and the rest of the *Gai Mer*'s crew, though neither she nor they probably deserved His divine intervention.

On deck, Devlin was in his glory. Sword drawn, he fought at Nate's back, as was their customary arrangement, to protect each other from an unseen rear attack. All around them, their comrades did likewise. With relentless determination, and his usual nimble skill, he swiftly dispatched several brigands on their merry way to hell. All the while, even as he dueled with remarkable finesse, he was anxiously awaiting the arrival of his archrival, the captain of the lead attacking ship.

Even as changed in appearance as Swift was, after near-death on that deserted island, and the lengthy interval since they'd last parted, Devlin had immediately recognized him at the helm of the enemy ship. Half-prepared though he'd been, it had still come as a shock to see his old foe alive—to view that familiar flat-mashed nose, those same thick, sneering lips that had cursed and taunted him for so long, and those piercing, deep-set gray eyes that had never failed to make Devlin think of slimy creatures slithering from a grave. Evil oozed from this man, who had reveled in the most dastardly deeds known to mankind, who had gleefully dragged innocent men and boys into his rancid web of sin—capturing them and forcing them to his will by means of whips and chains, starvation and keelhauling, until they eventually bent to his bidding. Devlin knew his day would not be complete until he and his nemesis met face-to-face in a final, deadly confrontation.

At this very moment, Swift was edging toward Nate's blind side. Not that the quartermaster could have done much to prevent it, had he been aware of the approaching danger. He was tending off an opponent from his front, trusting Devlin to protect his back.

As he watched Swift's approach, Devlin's smile was diabolical. The sneaking bastard was in for a rude awakening, one Devlin was only too glad to provide! Quickly, he dispatched his own adversary, just in time to prevent Swift's sword from striking at Nate from behind. With righteous anger, Devlin met the man's thrust with his own. Their swords clashed in midair.

Devlin laughed aloud. "Come on, you spineless cur!" he roared. "If 'tis a fight with the Devil you seek, you've damned well found it!"

Swift's sunken eyes went wide with surprise at hearing Devlin's voice resounding from beneath the fearsome black hood before him. "Thought ye'd seen the last of me, didn't ye, lad?" he jeered, recovering quickly. "Ye always were a hasty pup, and too squeamish for yer own good. Now ye'll pay for that failing, and for those endless months I spent marooned on that little spit of worthless sand."

Swift slid his blade free, only to have his next lunge met more forcefully than the last. "Did ye know I feasted on Dobbs's flesh for a week?" he taunted further. "Sucked his skinny bones dry, I did. And I'll do the same with yers."

Though Swift's words revolted him, as they were intended to, Devlin kept his head, concentrating all his efforts and his anger into his sword arm. Assuming the offensive, he flashed his blade forward in a series of furious thrusts that left his aging opponent no more time or breath for talk. Though Swift somehow managed to parry a number of the masterful blows Devlin leveled at him, he could not keep the pace for long. Soon he sported several small wounds, courtesy of Devlin's superior skill. Then, inevitably, Devlin's steel found its mark, driving deep into Swift's right shoulder. The man dropped his sword, grabbed at his wound, and stumbled to his knees before Devlin's hooded gaze.

Suddenly the moment of Devlin's absolute triumph was upon him. At last he would collect his full revenge for his lost youth, his forfeited dreams, all the agony he had endured at his former captor's hands. He drew back his sword for the single, deadly thrust that would pierce Swift's heinous heart and send his black soul to everlasting perdition.

But at that exact moment, before he could deal Swift the final, fatal blow, Eden's frantic screams resounded over the clamor of the ongoing battle. Despite knowing he should never look away from an opponent until the contest was completed, well aware that he was breaking a primary rule of successful swordsmanship, Devlin jerked his gaze from his cowering prey and searched for Eden in the mad melee.

"There!" Nate shouted, waving his sword in the direction of the lower deck. She was being dragged before a burly seaman, a knife held to her throat. Two more grinning accomplices followed close behind, their flashing cutlasses successfully holding her would-be saviors at bay.

Devlin turned back, intending to quickly finish the task before him and rush immediately to Eden's aid. To his profound shock and dismay, he discovered that Swift had seen his chance to escape and managed, miraculously, to crawl away. He was now being aided over the rail by two of his crewmen.

"We'll meet again, Kane!" the man threatened. "I'll hound ye till yer dying day!"

Cursing softly, Devlin raised his sword in answer. "If you survive your wounds, Swift. May they putrefy and kill you slowly!"

At his back, newly engaged with yet another foe, Nate yelled, "Go, Dev! Save Eden! I can fend for meself! The lass can't!"

Devlin's feet could not carry him rapidly enough. Spying a line close by, the far end of which was attached to a spar of the mainmast near where Eden now struggled, Devlin hacked it loose. Taking only enough time to secure his sword at his side, he grabbed the line with both hands and launched himself from the quarterdeck. Feet first, he soared downward like an avenging angel, knocking several men aside as he went. The last of these were the two rogues guarding Eden's captor. They went sprawling, and were quickly set upon by their eager enemies.

Devlin landed with a thud little more than an arm's length from Eden and the fellow who held her. Never had he seen her eyes so wide with fear, her face so white. Yet, when he appeared so suddenly before her, a glimmer of faith was immediately born in her tearful face. That simple confidence that he would save her sent a lump to Devlin's throat. Even as she stood there, her life in peril, she believed in him completely.

In all his days, Devlin had never been as humbled by a mere look, or as frightened as he was at this moment. Her captor's blade was a hairsbreadth from her slender neck. One slip of the man's foot, one errant bump against his elbow, and Eden's life could end horribly.

In that instant, as he gazed into her trusting eyes, Devlin knew the truth he'd been denying for so long. He loved this woman, with all his heart and soul. He loved her quiet beauty, her dauntless spirit, the very essence of her being—and he would gladly give his life to spare hers, if need be. Hopefully, such sacrifice would not be required of either of them this day.

As Eden's captor watched, a taunting grin on his broad, flat face, Devlin whipped his hat from his head and sent it sailing. The man laughed, but his evil cackle caught on a horrified gasp as Devlin's hood followed suit, revealing no head beneath the black cloth. In that moment, while the man stood immobilized by fear, Devlin grabbed his forearm and pried it, and the threatening knife, away from Eden's throat. She stumbled free, her skirts tripping her as she tried to run. She tumbled to the deck, struggling to regain her legs beneath her.

No sooner had she fallen than Devlin was jostled from behind, two combatants crashing into him. One of Eden's flailing feet caught his, further eroding his precarious balance. Devlin staggered forward, his body thrown against that of Eden's attacker, their arms and the knife caught between them.

The man's agonized scream reverberated in Devlin's ears so loudly it might have been his own. When he found his footing and stepped back, he beheld his opponent stuck fast to the mast behind him, impaled on the very knife he'd held against Eden.

Behind Devlin, at his feet, Eden gagged. A hasty look around them assured him that the battle was won, that he could safely attend to Eden without imperiling the lives of his mates. With the ragged remnants of his crew, Swift was escaping in one sloop, the grappling lines severed and the ships drifting further apart with every surge of the sea. The second enemy ship, which had sustained the most damage in the opening exchange, was being left behind, forfeited to the victors.

Even now, Nate was capably directing the removal of dead bodies from the deck, ordering the confinement of several prisoners, and recruiting aid for the remarkably few members of the *Gai Mer*'s crew who had been wounded—none fatally, so it appeared. They had been extraordinarily fortunate, and would all live to fight again—perhaps to meet Swift at another time, another place, for an even more momentous conquest.

As gently as possible, Devlin hauled Eden to her feet and guided her toward the nearest rail, lending support while she relieved her stomach of its contents. When she had heaved her last, he gathered her trembling body into his arms and carried her back to his quarters. His cabin door hung crookedly on bent hinges, but he succeeded in shoving it shut again, affording them the privacy they required.

" 'Tis done with, love," he crooned as he bent over her. She was curled into a ball on the bed, her knees drawn up to her chest, sobbing as if she would never stop. His big hand stroked her hair. "There's naught to fear now, sweetling. You're safe."

"I . . . I know!" she said, hiccuping. "I . . . you saved me. I knew you would. I . . . just can't s-seem to stop sh-shaking."

Gathering her back into his arms, he held her, rocking her. Her hands were like ice, while her cheeks were flushed with vivid heat. "Oh, Devlin!" she wailed, throwing her arms about his waist and burying her face against his chest. "I've never seen such carnage! Until you appeared to rescue me, I've never been so scared! Not even when Tilton was choking me!"

"Tell me, Eden. Tell me all of it. Let it free, lest it grow in your mind and fester there."

"Those men! They beat the door down! I thought if I stayed in . . . I'd be safe . . . The door was barred . . . My shot missed." She was stammering and crying, her words all but incoherent, yet he heard within his heart what she was trying to tell him. "They grabbed me, and they were going to . . . but they had no time, and thought it better to take me to their ship. They wanted to . . . to . . ."

"I know, sweet. I know what they intended. Just assure me they did not harm you, for I'll never forgive myself if they did."

"Nay," she confirmed. Then she scrubbed at her lips with her fist, as if to negate her claim. "God! I can still feel the horror of those lips on mine! And their hands clutching at me . . . at my clothes!"

Devlin stiffened. "Eden, the truth now, on your honor. Did those men violate you? Did they do more than kiss you and grab at you?"

"Nay. I swear it. But I still feel so dirty, as if their slightest touch has defiled me."

"Then let me make you clean again," he said softly. "Let me take away the memory of their touch, and replace it with my own."

Slowly he peeled away her clothes, taking the utmost care not to upset her further. His hands stroked tenderly, his touch as light as the brush of an angel's wings. His lips whispered over her bared flesh in a lover's promise.

When at last she lay naked before him, her quivering

somewhat abated, he fetched soap and water, and began to bathe her. He applied the damp cloth gently, thoroughly, his intent not to excite but to soothe, to make her feel cleansed and treasured. On the side of one breast, he saw the violet shadow of a bruise arising, and for a moment he wished he could kill the man who had put it there. But the man was already dead, and could not be slain twice. Shoving such thoughts from his mind, he reminded himself that this was not the time for contemplating revenge. It was a time for cherishing the woman he loved.

Like a loving parent attempting to ease a child's pain, he placed a petal-soft kiss over that bruise, and others he discovered—on her arm, her throat, her fragile jaw. Her lips were slightly swollen, either from brutal advances or the scrubbing she'd administered, and he took extreme care not to abrade them further. No part of her, from head to toe, escaped his healing touch. Even her hair received his attentions as he relieved it of its pins and gently combed it through his fingers.

By this time, Eden's eyelids were beginning to droop, the adventures of the day taking their final toll. Yet, when he would have wrapped her in a thin blanket and left her to rest, she objected.

"Nay, Devlin." Throwing her arms about his neck, she refused to let him go so easily. "Please. Stay with me. Lie with me. Love me."

Though he'd never been particularly intuitive to a woman's emotional state, Devlin realized she needed this comfort. Despite her recent fright, she seemed to crave his reassurance, to know that she was still desirable to him. But this, too, he must achieve through a delicate wooing. This could be no rough-and-tumble mating, the seeking of fleshly pleasures before all else.

Easing himself down beside her, Devlin drew her into the haven of his arms. For long minutes, he did no more than caress her, murmuring sweetly to her between lingering kisses. He thought perhaps this might be enough for her for now, that if she were to relax sufficiently, she would soon drift into slumber.

But Eden had other intentions. It was she who thrust her tongue into his mouth, seeking to deepen their kisses. She who drew him more tightly into her embrace, who rubbed her slender limbs over his so enticingly. She who brought her breasts to his lips, a tantalizing offering. And she who shamelessly undressed him and took him in hand, stroking the silken length of him to rigid attention.

All of Devlin's best intentions took wing. His mouth, his hands, became more demanding than he'd meant for them to be. But Eden was just as eager, urging him on, meeting him move for move. Her fright at the hands of her assailants had long since burned to ashes in the flame of their mounting desire, and when he came over her, into her, she was ready for him, her body welcoming his.

As one, they climbed the golden stairs, each step taking them higher, further than they'd ever gone before. For a timeless, breathless moment, they stood poised on the brink of eternity, the world spinning dizzily around them. Then they plunged over the crest together, falling, crying out, clinging tightly as rapture claimed them, enshrouding them in the shining folds of its resplendent robes.

She slept peacefully afterward, her arms still about him. It was some time before Devlin had the heart to leave her, and only then because ship's business demanded his attention. There were crewmen awaiting his orders, the wounded to tend, prisoners to question, punishments to mete out—and, thankfully, Eden awaiting him when these gruesome tasks were done.

Eden's grand scheme had come to an end, and now she was at a loss as to what to do about it. With Devlin unbound and once more in command of the *Gai Mer,* circumstances were drastically altered. She cornered Nate and asked, "Are we still headed for New Providence? Or has Devlin redirected the ship in search of those pirates who attacked us?"

Before her future stepfather could answer, Devlin appeared behind her as silently as a big cat. With a low growl to match, and a taunting smile, he purred softly into her ear, "I'll have plenty of time later to catch up with Swift, my precious pet. At the moment, Nate is more determined to gain his pardon, so he can rush home and wed your mother."

Her relief was so evident that he had to laugh. "Still hoping to reform me before we get there, Eden? Ah, but you do have a problem with that now, don't you? No longer can you dangle such tempting rewards beneath my nose, like a carrot before a donkey, the ultimate prize for my agreement. You shall have to think of some other means to gain my consent, but having given all to the cause, what is left for you to offer? What more could I possibly desire that I've not already gleaned?"

Fortunately, Nate had wandered off, allotting them their privacy, for which Eden was profoundly grateful. With no audience to hear their words, she faced Devlin squarely, her chin tilted at an imperious angle, her eyes assessing him. "Have you ever had a mistress, Devlin?" she asked with feigned calm.

Devlin nearly swallowed his tongue. Of all the things he might have expected her to say, this was the last. "A mistress?" he echoed stupidly.

"You do know what I'm talking about, don't you?" she persisted with a too-sweet smile. "At various times, I believe they have been called paramours, pillow friends, companions, amorata, lovers. Of course, they all mean much the same thing." Again she posed her question. "Have you ever had one?"

"Nay." His eyes narrowed speculatively. "Why do you ask?"

"Would you like one?"

"Come to the point, Eden. Are you suggesting such an arrangement between us?"

"If you want. After all, we are more than slightly familiar with one another now, and there is no longer the matter of my virtue to consider. Also, we have fairly well determined that I am not a curse to your ship or your crew, so that is no longer an issue. I would be able to travel with you, wherever you go, should you decide to keep sailing."

His smile was sardonic. "In return for your continuing favors, I would be expected to apply for pardon, I assume?"

"Most assuredly."

"And what if I decline your gracious offer?"

"If, by the time we reach New Providence, you do not decide to plea for amnesty . . . how shall I put it? The cow will cease to give milk."

"Aptly phrased. However, you have neglected a major factor. What if I choose to keep the 'cow,' whether she wishes to stay or not? Given her sensual nature, I'm sure I can convince her to give milk again, and still not have to pay the price for it. In other words, my haughty duchess, I could simply keep you captive, and have my wicked way with you all I wish."

"You think so?" she challenged.

"I know so."

She gave a careless shrug. "Mayhap, but what would be the fun of it then, having to force me each and every time, when I have offered myself to you willingly, if only you agree to my terms?"

"And how long would you stay with me?"

"As long as you continue to desire me."

"That long, eh?" he mused, cocking a brow at her.

"You do realize that you could be in your dotage by then."

She awarded him a saucy grin. "And you could be cocking up your toes long before."

His countenance turned more reflective. "Why would you offer to spend an indeterminate amount of time with me as my mistress, yet claim not to want marriage? I fail to see your reasoning, Eden, for surely a wife has the better lot."

Her smile melted away. "Unfortunately, I cannot foresee marriage working well for us, even should you decide to settle down. As I said before, Devlin, as long as you remain disembodied, there would be too many obstacles to a normal life. Were I to marry, I would want children."

"You could very well be carrying my child even as we speak, or has that thought not crossed your mind?"

"How would that be possible?"

"Come now, sweetling," he scoffed. "With bedding comes begetting. Surely, by now, you realize how offspring are conceived."

Eden blushed. "But you are a ghost. A spirit. At least by half. Certainly, such a thing is not possible. Is it?"

"How in blazes should I know?" he retorted. "Becoming invisible as I have done is supposed to be equally inconceivable. However, I assume we'll discover the truth of the matter sooner or later, particularly if we continue to enjoy one another as passionately as we have of late."

"Oh, dear!" Eden murmured, her eyes wide. "That puts quite a different light on things, doesn't it?"

"If you are thinking of recanting on your delightful proposition, forget it," he advised her. "The offer shall stand as originally tendered. I'll let you know my decision upon docking in New Providence."

Chapter 25

*D*evlin examined the hole in the cabin wall where Eden's shot had ended, rather than hitting her attackers. It was just above the perch where his falcon so often roosted. "Damn me, Eden!" he exclaimed. "If Zeus had been tethered here when you fired, you might have blown his poor head off!"

She rolled her eyes and sighed dramatically. "Another opportunity lost! However, with a bit of practice, I suppose my aim would improve. It was, after all, the first time I've ever fired a gun."

He frowned. "When I handed the pistol to you, I asked if you knew how to fire it, and I distinctly recall an affirmative nod from you."

She returned his scowl. "I did manage to discharge it, Devlin," she reminded him tartly. "You didn't question my aim."

He sketched a mock bow toward her. "My fault entirely, Miss Winters. An error we shall soon remedy. You are quite right, my dear. If you have aspirations of keeping company with me, you should become more proficient with the weapon. We shall begin practice sessions immediately."

First he taught her how to check the load, how to

clean the pistol, how to load it herself and check the prime. Then he had her carry it on deck, where he set up targets for her. Standing behind her—the safest place to be now that she sported a loaded gun in her shaking hands—he showed her how to position her body correctly, how to steady the heavy weapon with both hands, and how to take aim.

"Do try not to destroy too much of my ship while you are about this, or cause undue damage to our newest prize, which presently rides to the aft." Swift's captured ship, the *Dame Anise,* was being manned by a portion of Devlin's crew, and would accompany the *Gai Mer* to New Providence. Later they would decide if the ship should be sold or kept, the total worth of the vessel and its cargo split amongst the crew. "Also, I would prefer no new wounds to any of my crew, if you don't mind, sweetling," he instructed wryly.

She tossed him a grin over her shoulder. "Have you considered what a chance you are taking, arming me with a weapon? Upon reaching New Providence, I could very well hold you at gunpoint until you sign the governor's proposal."

One blond brow rose in challenge. "You would shoot the man you love?" For a moment, she stared at him, nonplussed. "You're not going to deny your love for me, are you, Eden?"

Finding her voice, she asked, "Would you believe me if I did?"

He smiled. "Nay, darling. I would not."

Eden had but two days to sharpen her shooting skills before they reached the Bahamas. They sailed past the first large island and numerous smaller ones, wending a route between them toward New Providence Island, where the new governor now resided. The cays and islands were lushly tropical, with vivid flowers and bright-plumed birds, but for the most part they were un-inhabited.

The surrounding waters were a sparkling turquoise, much the same color as Eden's eyes, a fact Devlin was quick to point out to her. "The first moment I saw you, I fell in love with your eyes. They remind me of these sun-kissed seas, so very beautiful and full of mystery."

The largest of the islands they passed was dotted with huge stands of enormous pine trees. But the bright-pink birds lining the shore were what caught Eden's attention. "Oh, look!" she exclaimed, almost jumping in glee. "Why, I declare, I've never seen a rose-hued stork before!"

Devlin chuckled and shook his head. "Those aren't storks, sweetling. They're called flamingos. A different bird altogether."

"I don't care. I think they're marvelous!" She yanked at his arm. "Stop the ship, Devlin. I want one of those birds!"

At this he laughed harder. "Eden, you'll see more of them on New Providence. There is no need to drop anchor here. Besides, I imagine they're a bit tricky to bag, love."

"Right," Nate put in from a few feet away. "And if ye're gonna run amok tryin' to catch one, 'twon't be on that island. 'Tis said to be haunted by wee creatures nestin' in the pines."

Even more intrigued, Eden asked, "What sort of wee creatures?"

"They call 'em Chickcharnies, and they be like lep-rechauns."

"Oh, how exciting! I want to see one!"

The men shook their heads in tandem. "Nay. They're fey things, and fickle, too. One minute as good as little cherubs, the next as evil as demons," Devlin told her.

"And no tellin' which mood they'll be in if ye chance across 'em," Nate added. "Ye can go chasin' yer flamingos on New Providence, lass, but forget the Chickcharnies."

New Providence Island was much smaller than Eden had expected. Along its northeastern coast, another tiny island lay within shouting distance, helping to create a natural harbor between the two. This was where the *Gai Mer* and *Dame Anise* dropped anchor.

The town itself was something of a disappointment, after Eden's great anticipation. Actually, it was little more than a village, though a busy one. There were more ships at anchor, and more seamen rushing about, than Eden had ever seen at one time in Charles Town.

"The place hasn't had time to prosper as it should have done," Devlin explained when he saw her disillusionment. "Both the French and Spanish launched attacks just ten and five years past, and since then it's been more of a pirate haven than aught else. The Bahamas are within easy reach of the trade lanes, and a convenient place to rest and relax between raids."

"More'n likely the reason 'twas chosen for this meet," Nate added. "Where else would ye gather so many brigands in one place at the same time?"

"Aye," Devlin agreed solemnly, his dark gaze alert for anything amiss. "I imagine 'tis also the reason they set Woodes Rogers in charge, since he was one of us a few years ago, though he has always claimed that he was into legitimate privateering more than actual piracy. A dubious distinction, at best. I suppose he is to be our shining example, for the rest of us to trust and follow. We can only hope this is not all an elaborate trap."

No sooner had they rowed ashore than Devlin's mind was set at ease on that score. The offer was legitimate. Governor Rogers was on the island, and doing a brisk business in reform. As the three of them made their way to his offices, Nate and Devlin were stopped by a fellow buccaneer. "Ye gonna apply for the King's pardon?" he asked.

At Devlin's reply, Eden's knees went limp. "Aye," he answered with a wide grin, slanting a wink in her direction. "'Tis an offer I can't refuse."

Nate nearly danced in the street. "I knew ye'd see the right of it!" he proclaimed gladly, little knowing the full extent of Eden's persuasive measures. "Ye won't regret it, Dev."

" 'Twill be up to Eden to see that I don't," he said dryly, "since she's gone to such lengths to convince me. Also, agreeing to reform my ways does not mean I am willing to forego my revenge against Swift, you understand, for that is private business, and no concern of the King's, nor that of his men."

There was a long line at the governor's offices, and Eden feared Devlin would not have the patience to wait so long. Eventually, they faced a harried clerk, who was busily scribbling names into a ledger and setting up audiences with Rogers as quickly as possible.

"The soonest you can speak with him will be three days hence," the man advised them sourly. "Ten o'clock in the morn." He handed Devlin a paper. "List the name of your vessel, and those of your crewmen. Bring the list back with you at that time, and Governor Rogers will see all of you then."

"What are we supposed to do till then?" Nate demanded.

"That is entirely your problem," the clerk responded irritably. "But if you want amnesty, you'll appear promptly at the appointed hour."

Devlin flipped a gold coin in the air. It landed with a soft *thunk* on the fellow's ledger. "Would that help you find an earlier interview for us?"

"Nay, but four more of its kind might," came the reply.

Devlin produced the necessary coins.

"Tomorrow. Same time. That's the best I can do."

"Good enough."

They walked off, Nate grumbling. "And they call us thieves!"

While Nate returned to the ships to give the news to the crew, to post the watch and release the rest of the men from their usual duties, Eden and Devlin meandered through the streets. Eden's mood brightened considerably when they came upon the market square. Devlin's did likewise.

"What shall I buy you, wench?" He dragged her to a nearby stall, where woven hats and baskets were displayed. Eden gasped at the price of the simple straw hat he purchased for her, and laughed when he plopped it atop her head. "Can't have you getting that pretty nose burned," he quipped. "The sun is much hotter here than you are used to."

Eden saw huge displays of big, perfectly shaped conch shells. There were mounds of sea sponges, and she bought several of these to take home to friends and her mother. For Jane, as a wedding gift, she purchased delicate coral ear bobs and a matching necklace. Alongside were several similar items made of tortoiseshell.

"Is this where you got the hair combs you gave me?" she asked Devlin.

He nodded, his dark eyes twinkling. "Did you think they were stolen?" he teased.

"The thought crossed my mind a time or two," she admitted sheepishly. "I also wondered about the cargo you stored at the warehouse. You can't imagine my relief when I discovered 'twas mostly innocent trade goods to be bartered to local merchants."

"What did you think it was?"

"The skeletal remains of your victims, of course," she announced with a wry grin. "After all, you are a pirate of some repute, are you not?"

They dined on crayfish stew, a spicy native mixture

that set Eden's eyes to watering, and washed it down with banana-flavored rum drinks. For dessert, they treated themselves to flaky coconut tarts, still warm from the oven, and more banana rum.

By the time they encountered the stall offering parrots for sale, Eden was more than a little giddy. Poking her lips into a pout, she asked the proprietor, "Don't you have any of those darling flamingos? I had my heart set on one."

"Those birds are nice to look at," the man told her, "but you wouldn't want one for a pet. Now, if 'tis their bright feathers you want, I have a friend who hunts them. But you can't catch them and keep them penned up. They die right off."

Eden frowned. "I don't want feathers. I want a live bird. Devlin has his falcon, and I want a bird of my own."

The man grinned and winked at her. "Why, a falcon's nothing compared with a fine bird like this," he said, producing a big green-and-blue parrot. "Give this fellow enough of your time and attention, and he'll soon learn to talk. That's something a hawk will never do."

"Truly?" she asked in amazement. "He can be taught to speak?"

"Absolutely."

Eden gave a brisk nod. "I'll take him." Turning to Devlin, she ordered, "Pay the man, Devlin."

"Now wait just a blarsted minute, Eden," Devlin replied, in a huff. "After all the grumbling you've done about Zeus, you expect me to buy this ragtag parrot? I'd rather be shot than take this moth-eaten thing aboard the *Gai Mer.*"

"In that case, would you care to lend me your pistol?" she mumbled. Immediately, she changed tactics, gazing up at him with soft, pleading eyes. "Please, Devlin? Buy the damned bird."

He never knew whether it was that beseeching look

or her unexpected curse that turned the trick. Whichever, Eden got her pet.

"Well, as I live and breathe," Rogers said, leaning
back in his chair with a huge grin. "Look who we have
here. 'Devil' Kane in the flesh. I must admit, I doubted
you would come."

"I could walk out as easily as I entered," Devlin was
quick to reply.

"Don't you dare!" Eden hissed. "I swear I'll shoot
you with your own gun if you change your mind now."

Rogers's attention swung to her. "Ah, and who is this
fetching lady? The person responsible for your sudden
change of heart, mayhap?"

"I make my own decisions, Rogers, as well you
know," Devlin responded stiffly. He did, however, bend
to propriety enough to introduce the two. "This is Miss
Eden Winters, of the Carolinas. Eden, may I present the
slightly less than honorable Woodes Rogers."

Rogers laughed. "My pleasure, Miss Winters." His
brow furrowed thoughtfully. "Winters. That name
sounds familiar. Are you associated with the family that
owns the warehouse in Charles Town?"

Eden blinked in surprise. "Aye. 'Twas my late father's establishment, which my mother and I now hold.
In fact, we've just sailed from there, after concluding a
rather nasty bit of business with thieves who were attempting to destroy the company. Captain Kane and Mr.
Hancock were most helpful in routing the scoundrels
from our midst," she added in the men's defense.

"Is that so?"

Nate stepped forward. "The lass tells ye true. An'
I'm not just sayin' that b'cause her ma and I are
plannin' to wed, soon as we get our pardons and return
to Charles Town."

"Ah, so you are going to become a legitimate busi-
nessman, Mr. Hancock," Rogers said with an approving

nod. "That does relieve my mind, knowing that you will have decent employment to keep you on an honest keel. And what of you, Devlin? Have you similar plans?"

"Nothing so solidly decided," Devlin admitted. "I may continue to sail."

"With what?" Rogers asked congenially. He sat forward, elbows on his desk, hands together in a prayer-like pose, fingers tapping his long chin. "Your frigate may be required as forfeit, to ensure your compliance with the terms of your amnesty."

"What?" Devlin roared, taking a threatening step forward, forcing Eden along with him to remain in touch. "There was nothing of this mentioned to me!" Of course, Devlin himself had heretofore failed to disclose the news that he now commanded a second ship, a fact he intended to keep quiet, especially in light of this recent development, which Rogers seemed to find so amusing.

To his credit, Rogers didn't even flinch. "The matter is being left to my discretion," he explained calmly. "If you can convince me of your sincerity, you may still retain possession of your vessel. However," he added, waving a hand for silence when Devlin would have spoken, "you will have to register the ship under British dominion, and choose a new name and flag for her."

Devlin looked as if he had just received another jolt of lightning, and the thunder accompanying it. His handsome face was dark with suppressed anger. "You know as well as I that 'tis bad fortune to change the name of a ship. You're a fool even to ask it. 'Twill not gain you many entries on your precious roster, Rogers, should you place such stout restrictions on brigands yet leery of your offer. While I expected the request to sail under the Crown, and will even agree to relinquish my present flag, the *Gai Mer* must retain her present appellation." As would the *Dame Anise,* he thought, with Rogers none the wiser.

"Then, as much as I regret it, I am afraid I must reject your application for pardon," Rogers said. "If the rest of your crew still wish theirs, and agree not to sail under your command, theirs will be granted. As will Mr. Hancock's, if he forfeits his claim to the ship."

Eden was thinking frantically. She could not allow this to happen! Surely there was some way around this problem, if only she could conceive it quickly enough. "Wait!" she exclaimed. "There must be another solution which would satisfy everyone, if we just apply ourselves to finding it."

Devlin scowled. "I see none. The *Gai Mer* will remain as such."

" '*Gai Mer*' means what, in English?" Eden asked, unable to recall her smattering of self-taught French under such a stressful situation.

"It translates to 'Joyous Sea,' or 'Gay Sea,' if you prefer," Rogers supplied.

"Would that suffice? The name, after all, would mean the same," Eden suggested hopefully.

"Aye." Rogers nodded.

"Nay." This from Devlin. "To my mind, the letters painted on a ship's side must remain true, the same number and the same characters she was christened under."

"Blast you for a stubborn jackass!" Eden exploded. "Devlin Kane, you are the most obstinate man ever born! Is it not enough that 'Gay Sea' has the correct amount of letters? Must you demand a complete miracle, when half of one will do quite nicely?"

Another burst of laughter came from Rogers, the only person present who seemed to find anything remotely humorous in their predicament. "The lady knows you well, Kane," he claimed. "She might also have given us the key to this dilemma. If you insist on retaining the same characters, perhaps they can be rearranged in a different order to spell yet another name. Would that suit?"

Devlin thought for a moment, then gave a reluctant nod.

The next few minutes they spent trying to arrange the six letters into some sensible order. At last, Devlin achieved one. "Margie," he pronounced to one and all.

Eden frowned up at him, her eyes narrowed suspiciously. "Who is Margie?" she demanded. "The name came to you with wondrous ease, Devlin, leading me to believe you have known such a woman."

"Well, there was a tavern maid in Lisbon, who sported a similar name," he mused. "What was it she was called? Margo? Marlie? Nate, do you recall?"

"I might, if you could describe her looks to me," Nate offered.

"Never mind, Nate," Eden told him firmly. "We'll simply have to find something else. I refuse to sail on a ship named after one of Devlin's doxies."

"Now who is being stubborn?" Devlin accused irritably. "That being the case, 'tis up to you to find another name, or 'twill rest on your head if my pardon is denied for your jealousy."

"I am not jealous," she objected heatedly. Still, she applied herself to her given task, with the aid of pen and paper supplied by the governor, and soon offered an alternative. "Mirage," she announced with a satisfied smirk. "Now, I defy you to find fault with that, for 'tis of a nautical theme and also fitting to your present circumstances, Captain Kane," she added slyly.

"What circumstances?" Rogers questioned, not understanding Eden's reference to Devlin's ghostly demeanor, while the others present grasped her meaning immediately and chuckled.

Eden gave a feminine shrug. "Nothing much, really.

'Tis more a private jest than aught else, referring only
to the way Devlin seems to come and go on a whim."

"Will it do then, Devlin?" the governor asked.

"Aye. Is all else settled as well?" Again, he remained
silent about the ship he'd won from Swift. When the
proper time came, if ever it did, he would then register
the *Dame Anise* under the British flag using similar
methods of disguising her true identity.

"There is one additional matter to address," Rogers
stated authoritatively. "Since I am well aware of your
awesome reputation as a pirate, and the delight you
have taken in your brigandry to date, I fear I must at-
tach a condition to your pardon, and to Mr. Hancock's
as well. If, in the course of the following year, it should
come to my ears that either of you have resumed the
activities you are about to renounce, your amnesty will
be immediately revoked, and you will be considered an
enemy of the Crown, as if this meeting had never been.
On the other hand, if you remain lawfully employed
during this period, you will receive a commendation
from the King, and quite possibly a reward of some
kind for honoring his faith in you."

"I see," Devlin said, frowning. "Does this mean that
you are taking a personal interest in my cause, Rogers?
I little care for a warden on my tail."

"Then I suggest you keep a clean slate, Kane. Mayhap you should return to Charles Town with your lady
and your friend, and apply yourself to some enterpris-
ing endeavor there for a time."

"The better for you to account for my whereabouts
and my actions?" Devlin's brow rose sardonically.

Rogers merely smiled. "It would simplify the process
greatly," he concurred.

With a helpful nudge from Eden's elbow, and much
grumbling, Devlin complied. The proper papers were
signed, and the frigate duly registered under her new
name of *Mirage*. At the conclusion, Rogers presented

Devlin with a British flag, reminding him to display it alongside a new banner of more suitable representation than his current pirate pennant.

They were on their way out the door when Rogers suddenly said, "Miss Winters, I should like to extend my belated sympathies on the death of your grandfather. I met him just once, but was much impressed with the man. For a brigand, he was a good sort, and had a reputation of being inordinately fair in his dealings with his friends and crew."

Eden could have melted through the floor, especially when Devlin stopped short and speared her with a dark look. "Thank you, sir," she replied meekly, attempting to pull Devlin from the room before anything else could be revealed.

Devlin refused to be budged. "Excuse me, but I seem to have missed something," he stated quietly. Too quietly for Eden's peace of mind. Turning to Rogers, he said, "Eden has spoken of her grandfather being a sailing man, but she failed to mention that he was a corsair of some notoriety."

Rogers chuckled. "Does the name Black Jack Blake ring a bell in your mind, Devlin? He was a bit before your time, but quite renowned. He barely missed swinging on the gallows, retired from piracy soon after, saw his only daughter married to Eden's father, and settled in Charles Town, to spend his remaining years in leisure."

"How very enlightening," Devlin said with the smile of an alligator contemplating a tasty morsel. "Thank you for illuminating Eden's celebrated ancestry more clearly to me, Rogers. I bid you a good day."

Chapter 26

With every step back to the ship, and despite Nate's hovering presence, Devlin railed at her. "You deceitful little baggage! All the while you were berating me for my nefarious trade, you were deliberately concealing the fact that you are not so far removed from such dealings yourself. Why, I'll wager your father's business was built, at least in part, with funds from your grandfather's coffers!"

" 'Tis not exactly the sort of thing one shouts from the rooftops," Eden declared in her own defense. "Nor does it make me a brigand by association or relation, so do not try to tar me with the same brush. From what little I remember of him, I adored my grandfather; and from the things she has told me of him, my mother loved him as well. That does not mean we approve of his methods, or that we follow in his shadow, imitating them."

"Blood is said to be thicker than water, my sweet. And the apple does not often fall far from the tree."

"My, you are simply running over with proverbs this morn, all nicely suited to your purposes, of course."

"What I am is angry, Eden. Both you and your mother conspired to pull the wool over my eyes."

"We did not lie to you, Devlin."

"Nay, you merely neglected to tell the whole truth of the matter."

"What difference could it possibly make, whether my ancestors be pirates or preachers? Would it make me any more or less than I am? The only thing my grandfather's life has done is to teach me some very important lessons that I might not make the same mistakes he and my grandmother did."

"Such as?" Devlin prompted.

"He taught me the price one pays for greed. While my grandfather was about his pirating, my grandmother nearly worried herself into an early grave. He, too, almost met an untimely end, more times than any of us can count. He came very close to being hung for his crimes, only a corrupt official and a hefty bribe saving his neck, even as the gallows' rope was being fitted around it. Fortunately, he decided not to tempt fate further after that harrowing experience. However, 'twas too late to save my grandmother. Her poor heart gave out soon after.

"So you see, Devlin, I have learned how devastating this lawless life can be to all concerned. It robbed Grandmother of her youth and her health, Grandfather of his beloved wife, and Mother and me of their loving presence. I scarcely got to know either of them, except through the stories my mother related to me, that their memory should live on."

This explained much to Devlin, now that he considered it. Why Eden had been so worried about him, why she'd done everything in her power to convince him to cease pirating—even to the point of sacrificing her virtue and offering herself as his mistress. All to the cause of saving him from the same grief Black Jack Blake had met.

Only partially mollified, Devlin turned a scowl on his quartermaster. "Did you know of all this, Nate?"

"Aye," his friend admitted readily. "Janie told me when I asked for her hand. O' course, she swore me to silence, and I thought if she wanted ye to know, she'd tell ye herself. Or leave it to Eden."

"See there, Eden? Your mother told Nate. You might have been just as honest with me."

"There is a difference, Devlin. Mother and Nate are to be married."

"So should we," he answered gruffly.

Eden stopped and stared at him. "I beg your pardon?"

"You heard me well enough. I think we should marry."

"Why?"

"Why not?" he countered. "Damnation, woman! If I'm good enough to be your lover, then I'm good enough to be your husband."

Nate bit back a chuckle. "Ye two certainly are a pair! Usually, 'tis the woman wailing such nonsense, and here Devlin is, miffed to his ears, his male pride takin' a whipping, while Eden drags her heels in a grand show o' reluctance."

"You're only suggesting such folly because you know I'll refuse," Eden stated obstinately. "Should I agree, you'd most likely run for your life."

"Agree then, and find out if you're right," Devlin challenged.

She was tempted. Ever so tempted. But her better sense won out. "I still say the primary reason you want me is that I'm the only female available to you in your lamentable state. What if I should consent? Suppose we married, and in a few months you regained your body? What would you do then, Devlin? Regret your choice? Sail off one day and never return? Bemoan your hasty action and take solace in the arms of other women? When I wed, I want a faithful husband, one who loves and desires only me, always and forever."

His eyes were as soft as black velvet, his voice gruff with emotion as he bared his soul to her. "I do, Eden. I fear I'm well and truly beguiled by you. Never has any woman touched my heart as you have done. I want no other for wife—or lover. I never shall. Laughing, loving, or spitting mad, you are the most bewitching wench I've ever known, and my world would be empty without you to brighten it for me."

Eden gazed up at him, tears swimming in her eyes. "Oh, Devlin! You cannot know how long I've yearned to hear those words from your lips. But there are so many problems in our path. Though my heart tells me yes, my head warns against it."

"Listen to your heart, my darling," he implored her. "Together we can face the difficulties and overcome them."

Eden still wasn't sure. "How would we manage it?" she asked hesitantly. Glancing about at the throng of pirates crowding the streets, she added, "I doubt there's a minister to be found within leagues, or any duly sworn captain, for that matter."

"There is Rogers," Devlin reminded her. "Not only is he a legitimate captain, but governor as well. He has the authority."

"Aye, but he's so busy with the pardons. Would he have the time, or even be inclined toward the idea?"

"I've no doubt he'd find it vastly amusing," Devlin assured her. "The man has a twisted sense of humor. Believe me, he'll make the time, if only to have a part in seeing me relinquish my freedom."

"I always thought, if I were to be wed, that 'twould be in church, with my mother and my friends to share my joy," Eden said wistfully.

Then she looked up into Devlin's face and saw the hope and adoration shining there, the promise in his eyes. On a sigh, she shoved her regrets aside, and her worries with it. Devlin was right. They were meant for each other, and there wasn't anything they couldn't brave together. Somehow, some way, they would endure, and with enough faith and prayer, perhaps someday Devlin would regain his visibility. But to wait until then to marry him could cost her the one true love of her life.

"I yield, most gladly," she told him softly, her heart overflowing.

No sooner were the words free of her lips than Devlin grabbed her into his arms and whirled her around until both were dizzy with delight. Nate went into a jig, cheering with glee. All about them people stopped to stare. When at last Devlin set Eden on her feet again, it was only to grab her hand and rush off with her to gain another appointment with Rogers before his bride-to-be could revive all her previous objections.

Rogers's wide grin threatened to split his face. "I vow, Kane, you and your lady are providing me with more entertainment than I'd hoped to find on this assignment. I get to lend a hand in ushering you not only into a lawful life, but also into holy wedlock."

"When you are finished crowing and patting yourself on the back, mayhap we could get on with it," Devlin suggested impatiently.

Rogers gave a final chuckle and began shifting through the papers on his desk. Finally he found the book he sought. "Ah, here 'tis," he said, turning to a marked page. Glancing up, he told them, "You must forgive me, but yours is the first marriage ceremony I have had the privilege to perform under my new title as governor, and I would hate to omit anything important through my lack of practice. After all, we do want it completely correct and legal."

"What of the banns?" Eden asked, frowning as she suddenly recalled that point.

"Fortunately, not only do I have the power to marry

the two of you, I have also been granted the right to waive the banns, should I see fit," Rogers stated importantly.

He turned to his clerk, who was standing nearby. "Do we have all the proper papers and witnesses?"

The man nodded.

"Well then, let us begin. Miss Winters, Devlin, please stand before me and join hands."

Although he had to read the ritual verbatim, Rogers's resonant voice added just the right touch of solemn dignity and sincerity. As she listened to the words that would bind her to Devlin for a lifetime, and recited her vows, Eden's last-minute nervousness deserted her. There was a sense of rightness, of completion, about pledging herself to the handsome man at her side, as if two halves of a whole were finally being united.

Her gaze met Devlin's, searching for any doubts she might find lingering there—and found only love and adoration lighting his warm dark eyes. That, and a twinkling of amusement as she promised to honor and obey him, for richer or poorer, for better or worse.

Aside from his brief touch of humor, Devlin was as proud as he'd ever been as he took this wondrous woman for his wife. Indeed, for all the rush, she looked particularly beautiful this day. Her hair was a tumble of curls, artfully arranged in a shining cascade of fire-kissed waves and topped with a coronet of delicate blossoms. In her slender hands she carried the bouquet he'd given her just this morn, a glorious array of vivid tropical flowers he'd picked for her himself. But the glow on her face outshone the brilliant petals, bespeaking her happiness more eloquently than any words she might offer. She was a vision, the embodiment of all his hopes and dreams.

At the end of the rite, Devlin accepted a plain gold band from Nate and slipped it upon Eden's finger. It had the look of having been worn, the feel of having been prized by another woman before her. Even as she was wondering where he had gotten it, he said earnestly, "Jane entrusted this to Nate, with the wish 'twould soon be put to its proper use, almost as if she knew what was to come. Thus, 'tis with the very ring which your father bestowed upon your mother's hand, that I now wed my own lovely bride."

Tears welled in Eden's eyes as she accepted this shining symbol of her mother's blessing and Devlin's pledge. "I shall cherish it dearly, but not half as much your love, which I shall treasure endlessly and with all my heart."

After such a hurry-up, few-frills wedding, Eden was delightfully surprised when Devlin arranged for a short honeymoon. Prior to meeting Devlin, if Eden had been asked where she dreamed of going on her wedding trip, she might have said England, or Rome, or even Boston, simply for a change of scene from Charles Town. Never had she expected to spend her first night as a married woman in a tropical paradise, with an entire island all to herself and her new husband.

Almost before the ink was dry on their marriage document, Devlin whisked Eden back to the *Mirage*. With a minimal crew to man the ship, Devlin directed them through a maze of islands. By mid-afternoon, the newlywed couple had been willingly marooned on a tiny, remote isle.

"Return for us in three days, and not a minute sooner," Devlin instructed Nate, as he handed Eden and their supplies into the jolly boat. "Unless the entire world is at peril, do not dare to show your face until then, old friend."

At her first step upon the beach, Eden was enchanted. "Devlin, look!" she exclaimed in awe. "The sand! 'Tis pink!" Quickly, as if to explain this strange phenomenon, she glanced about, sure that the sun must be about to set and was painting the beach with its rosy hue. The sun, however, was still riding high in the sky, blazing its white heat earthward. "How can this be?"

Devlin laughed. "I ordered it so," he teased her. "Just for you."

For an instant, before she caught the twinkle in his eyes, she nearly believed him. Which made him laugh all the more. "Actually, duchess, while 'tis not a common occurrence, neither is it truly rare. I believe 'tis a result of the waves hitting the reefs and shore in a specific manner, differently from the way it does in other places. When it does so, it first deposits numerous shells, and then proceeds to crush them into sand; but under these special conditions, with these particular types of shells, the result is colored sand."

His explanation made sense, at least as much of it as she understood, but she was almost sorry she'd asked. No matter how it had happened, the effect was spectacular. As was the tiny isle itself. Palm trees swayed gently in the breeze. Flowers blossomed in profusion. Gaily colored birds dotted the trees, lending their voices to the soft, salty air.

" 'Tis paradise," she breathed, twirling slowly around, trying to take in everything at once, letting the essence of the place surround and swamp her senses. "A marvelous, hidden haven."

Sweeping her into his arms, Devlin grinned down into her rapt face. "A veritable Garden of Eden," he agreed with droll humor. He wagged his brows at her in his best imitation of a villain about to pounce upon a sweet young innocent. "The perfect place in which to sin, don't you think?"

She giggled joyously. "Silly man. We're married. If 'twas sinning you wanted, you should not have wed me, but kept me as your mistress."

He shook his head, serious now. "Nay, Eden, my love. Though you may have been a delightful mistress, 'tis not the role for you. You were made to be a wife—my wife."

"I'm glad, Devlin." She sighed. "Ever so glad."

"So am I." Then his previous mischievous mood returned. "However, marriage does not preclude sinning. Does the church not list lust as a sin? And greed? And gluttony? Madam Kane, before our time here is o'er, I intend to satisfy my immense hunger for you, to avail myself of your charms until I am too weak to stand, and to ravish you as no man ever has before or ever shall after. And you, my sweet, wanton bride, are going to love every moment of it. This I swear to you."

In the hours that followed, he made good his promise. He made love to her in ways Eden had never imagined possible. When they both lay limp, weary, and replete, they slept entwined in one another's arms.

Several hours later, Eden roused to find the sun low on the horizon, setting over the sea in a blaze of color. "Come," Devlin told her, pulling her onto wobbly legs. "While you have been napping, I have been seeing to our housing."

Eden gave him a look which clearly said he'd had too much sun atop his golden head. "What housing?" she asked, looking about the beach with a confused frown. "I see naught but trees and bushes and sand. Did you build a cottage of sand somewhere?"

"Nay, wench. If you will but follow me, I shall show you a much better cottage than one built of sand. 'Twill make a castle dim in comparison."

He led her away from the beach, forging a trail through the brush. At length, they came upon a little glade in the midst of which lay a tiny pond of fresh water. On the far side of the clearing, a pile of earth and rocks had formed a small grotto, and it was there that Devlin had set up their supplies and started a fire. Several rugs and pillows cushioned the dirt floor of the minuscule cave. Into the cracks of the stony walls he had wedged hooks, and from these hooks now hung a single hammock.

This last, Eden eyed askance. "Devlin, there is but one hammock," she said, wondering if he was already tiring of her now that his lust had been blunted.

"Aye." He nodded. "Why would we have need of two when we'll be using only the one?"

Eden caught at the word "we," her pulse racing away with itself. Still, she could not believe the two of them could sleep in that contraption, large as it was, without one of them tumbling out of it. "Devlin, 'tis not possible for both of us to sleep there, is it?"

He sent her a rakish wink. "'Tis possible to do much more than sleep in it, Eden. After we've eaten, 'twill be my pleasure to enlighten you."

Despite all they had shared mere hours before, Eden still felt her cheeks heat up at the look he gave her, the devilish glow in those black eyes which locked her gaze to his. Release came only when her stomach gave a loud growl, startling them both.

"Come, wench, feed me," he ordered playfully, leading her toward the fire and their small cache of foodstuffs. "Let us see if my new wife knows her way about the kitchen."

"Kitchen?" Eden chortled. "For a caveman and his woman, mayhap."

He waved a hand about them. "Behold, madam. Your cave. Your fire. Your hungry mate."

They dined on fish Devlin had purchased fresh from the market just prior to sailing, and on rice Eden found among their stores. They quenched their thirst on coconut milk. Then Devlin poured a dram of rum into the half shells, and they savored the liquor-flavored meat of the fruit one heady bite at a time.

Between sips and sweet kisses, Devlin admitted he had not chosen this island by chance. He and his crew had been here before. "Which is how I knew 'twas not inhabited, and of the existence of this hidden glade, and the supply of fresh water. Without it, this paradise would be little more than a pile of sand. Certainly no place to be stranded, even with a beautiful lady for company."

His fingers brushed her cheek and clung to her skin—not through any lingering effort on his behalf, but because they were sticky with rum and coconut. He stared in amusement. "Wife, we are in sad need of washing, lest we find ourselves permanently stuck to one another." He rose, helping her up after him. "Come, milady. Your private bath awaits."

He pulled her toward the pond, its calm surface illuminated by the flickering flames of their fire and the full moon now rising overhead. Stars winked in the velvet-black sky. Even in darkness, the night was beautiful, ripe with the intoxicating perfume of tropical flowers.

While Devlin divested himself of his breeches, the only clothing he'd seen fit to don since their lovemaking on the beach, Eden hesitated. She eyed the pool with trepidation. When Devlin turned to find her still wearing her dress over her otherwise nude body, he held out a hand to her. "What is wrong, love? Having trouble with your hooks? I'll be more than willing to help you with them."

She stood staring at the pond, as if she expected a monster to arise from its depths. "Devlin, what sort of creatures lurk in there?" she asked in a small voice. "It could be most unwise to disturb them."

"There are but a few harmless fish, Eden. Nothing dreadful, I assure you. This pool is fed by a spring and does not connect with the sea."

"Surely there are snakes and such," she persisted.

"Snakes in paradise?" he scoffed. "Not possible."

"There was a snake even in Eden."

"Nay. That was Satan in disguise. The only devil

here is the one before you, and you have him well tamed."

She grinned. "Do I? I think not. I rather hope not, for I find him extraordinarily appealing when he's being wicked."

"Then wicked I shall remain, simply to please you. Come now, Eden. Shed the dress and I'll teach you how to play mermaid and sea dragon." His lascivious look was exaggerated in the extreme.

Though she laughed, she shook her head. "You forget, Devlin. I cannot swim."

"Is that your worry? Fair maiden, I would never allow you to drown. Moreover, the pool is very shallow, little more than waist-deep."

Further assurances were necessary, as Devlin eased the dress from her and urged her gently into the water with him. Her trembling fingers gripped his like tentacles, her eyes huge with uncertainty, her teeth clamped over her lower lip as she inched cautiously into the water. Only her trust in him kept her moving, until both of them stood in the center of the pond, the water lapping just beneath Eden's breasts.

Once she realized that her feet were planted firmly on the sandy bottom, and the water nowhere near covered her head, Eden's tension began to ease. The water was soothing, the temperature sun-warmed to nearly that of a tepid bath. With Devlin's arms still securely about her, she relaxed into him, her bare flesh sliding sinuously against his.

She released a pent-up sigh. "This feels heavenly. Just don't let loose of me."

"Never," he promised, his breath tickling her ear. If anything, his hold tightened, only to loosen slightly as he began to stroke her silken curves, his touch smooth and sensual as he bathed her breasts and belly with warm, wet hands. In the cool night air, her dampened nipples dimpled instantly, calling up an echoing response deep within her belly. His hands wandered lower, beneath the dark surface of the pool, gliding over her hips and buttocks, slipping between her thighs to a place even warmer and wetter than the water surrounding them. Eden moaned, and tried to turn more fully into his arms.

"Not yet," he murmured. "We've all the time in the world. Enjoy the feel of the water caressing your body. Flow with it. Become one with it."

Eden would rather have become one with Devlin at that juncture, for his hands were performing marvelous magic upon her slick skin. Stroking. Arousing. In counterpoint to the soothing lap of the water. His sharp white teeth nipped playfully along her flesh, creating gooseflesh in their wake. His lips praised her with a thousand kisses. Slowly, surely, he built her passions to the very edge of desire as she quivered in his embrace.

Just as her emotions threatened to boil over, he lifted her, wound her silken legs about his waist, and swiftly impaled her on his swollen staff. Rapture burst upon them, within them, like a white-hot comet streaking through their trembling souls to meld them evermore.

Eden lay limp in his arms, her legs now dangling in the water, her eyelids drooping with slaked passion. To save her life, she could not call up an ounce of energy.

Or so she thought.

Just then, something brushed against her calf. Her eyes popped wide. "Devlin?" she whispered anxiously. "Did you just graze your leg against mine?" She hadn't thought he'd budged.

"Sweetling, I'm much too sated to move a muscle at this moment."

Again, something swept swiftly past her ankle. With a shriek of alarm that brought several birds flying from their roosts, Eden clamped her arms about Devlin's neck, dug her toes into his thighs, and began climbing up his long, wet frame. Before Devlin knew what hit him, his wife had scrambled up his chest and draped herself around his shoulders, her bare bottom poking skyward. Her fingers scraped his scalp, threatening to yank him bald, and her arms were wound about his face. She was shaking violently and whimpering like a child."

"It touched me! It tried to bite me!"

"*It* was probably no more than a tiny fish, which you most likely frightened into an early death with your screaming," he told her calmly, trying to pry her arms from his eyes and nose. "Climb down from there."

"No! It will eat me! Get me out of here!"

"I would if I could see where I was stepping," he said with a long-suffering sigh. As one of her clawing fingers poked into his eye, he yowled. "Ouch! Damn, woman! Don't blind me altogether!"

He lurched toward the shore and somehow managed to reach it without tumbling both of them beneath the water. Once there, he had to peel Eden from her perch atop his shoulders. Gently, he cradled her in his arms, torn between laughter, pity, and annoyance as he carried her toward the grotto. "In the morning, when you can see for yourself how small and innocent those fish are, you're going to feel like a silly twit."

In an effort to calm her, Devlin snuggled the two of them into the molding confines of the hammock. There, he held her and crooned to her in the gently swinging bed. By the time he'd deftly demonstrated that coupling could be achieved while swaddled in its net folds—and with exceptional results and remarkable maneuverability—Eden had long since forgotten her fright.

Chapter 27

*T*hey spent part of the next day, and the two that followed, exploring the tiny, sun-kissed island. They strolled the beach, collecting shells and scampering about in the surf. They lunched on bananas and coconuts. They reveled in the beauty surrounding them, treasuring this precious time alone, and each other.

Upon returning to their secluded glade that first morning, they found a flock of flamingos feeding in the pond. Still determined to catch one, no longer intimidated by the pool's depth or its finned inhabitants, Eden crept slowly into the water. When she turned back to locate Devlin, she found him lounging on the bank, a blade of grass stuck between his teeth, watching her in amusement.

"Come help me," she hissed, gesturing at him to join her.

He shook his head in mute refusal and waved her on, a wide grin splitting his face.

Muttering silently to herself about lazy husbands, Eden inched along, trying not to disturb the water with her furtive movements. All in all, she did better than Devlin expected, coming to within a body's length of the skittish birds before they became alarmed and took flight. Eden sprang after the nearest one. Her fingers grazed its bright plumage, plucking a single bright feather from its wing before the flamingo made good its escape.

Eden's leap landed her off-balance. Suddenly her feet slipped out from beneath her, and she fell with an awkward plop. Her posterior smacked the sandy bottom of the pond, bouncing her sideways. Thrashing about, she came up on her hands and knees, her head still under water. She opened her eyes, frantic to find the surface—and came face-to-face with Devlin.

In that instant, with his cheeks puffed with air, his hair floating about his head in a golden nimbus, and the added distortion of the water making his eyes seem to bulge, he looked like some strange sea bass. Eden burst out laughing. Devlin did likewise. They rose from the water in a foam of bubbles, both of them sputtering and cackling and clinging to one another.

When they'd at last gained some control again, Eden waved the dripping feather before Devlin's nose. "See?" she exclaimed triumphantly. "I almost caught him."

"That you did," he agreed on a chuckle, giving her a great hug. "Too bad you didn't have some salt to sprinkle upon his tail."

She smiled. "There is always tomorrow to try again. If not, I still have my feather as a memento."

The flamingos did not return the following day. Eden and Devlin had the pool to themselves. Between sensual bouts of passion, he taught her to float on her back, and even to take a few strokes. It was a start at least, and if they hadn't kept reverting to more amorous pursuits, she might have learned more. Eden was well satisfied with what she did learn, however—particularly those lessons conducted in Devlin's arms, with his body locked to hers and ecstasy a few short moments away.

On their final morning, they awoke to bright sunlight and a peculiar sense that they were no longer alone on the island. It was more an odd intuition than anything truly tangible, at least at the start. Then, above the slight rustling of palm leaves, they heard voices, carried to them on the ocean breeze. Another fact immediately came clear. All the chattering birds were now silent, further announcing invasion of their remote domain.

Eden turned wide eyes toward Devlin. "Nate?" she whispered doubtfully.

"I don't know, but I don't think so." Devlin slid from the hammock, lifting her free of it after him. "Get dressed. Quickly," he murmured into her ear. "And be very quiet about it."

"What about you?" she asked softly. For this short, private trip Devlin had not brought his invisible clothing along. At this moment, it was freshly laundered and hanging on a drying line in his cabin aboard the *Mirage*. The only undetectable items he'd kept with him were his sword and longknife.

"I'm at a better advantage as I am," he replied, glancing down at his nude body. "'Tis you they'll see, if they spot either of us. I think it wiser if you hide with our goods while I go investigate."

Hurriedly, he helped her gather their meager furnishings and their sacks of supplies and stash them in the bushes. He stationed her behind a big palm tree several paces from the path. "Don't make a sound, no matter what you hear or see. Stay out of sight and wait for me." He planted a swift kiss on her soft, trembling mouth, and hastened away as silently as the specter he half-seemed to be.

The voices were coming from the beach, near the spot where Devlin had pulled the longboat ashore and concealed it beneath a stand of palms. As he drew closer, he was relieved to note that his and Eden's footprints from the previous days' excursions had been wiped clean by the wind and tide. He hoped their unexpected intruders would never realize the island was already occupied.

Just beyond the edge of the trees, where the beach began, Devlin spied two men. No ordinary men these, but pirates. And not just any cutthroats. To his astonishment, there stood none other than Blackbeard himself, and one of his crew. At their feet was a huge sea chest, the weight of it making a sizable indentation in the sand.

So, Devlin thought to himself with a grin. *The sly fox is about to bury some of his famed treasure, right here before my very eyes! What a stroke of fortune!*

That thought was still forming in his mind when Blackbeard and his mate hefted the chest between them and lugged it to the base of a large palm tree. While Blackbeard and Devlin watched, the other fellow began to dig. A short time later, Blackbeard deemed the hole deep enough, and together they lifted the chest into it.

The second man then proceeded to shovel the sand back into place. He was bent forward to the task when Blackbeard raised his sword and speared him through the back. Without a sound, the crewman fell into the hole which was to become his grave as well as the hiding spot for Blackbeard's treasure.

Devlin winced. It went against his principles to kill a man when his back was turned. Even the worst scoundrel deserved a fighting chance to defend himself. Of course, not all pirates adhered to that rule. A dead man told no tales.

Blackbeard was known for jealously guarding his secret caches of stolen wealth. It was said not even his wife knew their whereabouts. That being so, Devlin could not understand why the crewman had foolishly accompanied Blackbeard to this island. Surely he'd suspected something of this sort would happen. The only answer was that greed had blinded the poor looby, hastening his own demise.

Blackbeard had now finished smoothing the shovel over the sand to remove any evidence that it had been disturbed. Within the hour, the sea breeze would complete the job. This spot on the beach would soon look no different from any other.

With his hands on his hips, Blackbeard threw back his head and let loose a chilling roar of laughter. "Rest in peace, Stimmons," he said, snickering nastily. "Guard my prize well, you stupid sea dog."

With a final glance around to be certain there was no one lurking about, Blackbeard strode back to the waiting dinghy and rowed off. It was Devlin's guess that the brigand had ventured at least three islands away from the area in which his ship lay anchored. In this maze of isles and cays, even the crewmen awaiting him there would never be able to guess where their murderous captain had stashed his treasure.

Only Blackbeard knew for certain. And Devlin.

A chuckle rose in Devlin's throat as he imagined Blackbeard's surprise when next he came to this island to retrieve his pilfered booty—and found only Stimmons's bleached bones. And perhaps a note of thanks from his relentless ghost-devil.

Devlin was very secretive when he returned to in form Eden that the men they'd heard talking had gone, and that it was safe for her to come out of hiding now. From the gleam in his eye, she knew he was excited about whatever he'd seen or heard, but as much as she wheedled, she could not get him to tell her about it. "Wait and see," he said.

Though their unexpected visitors were no longer a threat, Devlin thought it wise to remain in their bower until the *Mirage* returned for them, lest they chance upon more unwanted intruders. He admonished her to stay behind when he gathered their belongings and took them to the longboat.

Reluctant to leave their tropical hideaway now that their time here was nearly over, Eden willingly complied, spending the last few hours of her honeymoon savoring this special place which would linger in her mind and heart forever. When at last Devlin rowed them out to the ship, tears shimmered in her eyes as she bade a final farewell to their island paradise. She hardly noticed that their longboat seemed more encumbered than it had been on their arrival, their rugs and bags heaped high in the center of the small craft. Nor did it strike her odd when Devlin unloaded most of their cargo himself, carrying it straight to their cabin.

A short while later, he led her into their quarters and locked the door behind them. With a sweep of his hand, he gestured toward a large chest which stood in the center of the room, taking up a good deal of the floor space. "Prepare yourself, sweetling," he warned her cheerfully. "You are about to receive a wedding gift a queen would envy."

The lock had already been broken, and Devlin quickly flipped the lid open, watching Eden with gleeful expectation. She gazed in dumbfounded astonishment, her eyes huge and her jaw slack. She could not believe her eyes. Surely, at any moment she would awaken to find this was all a glorious dream. It couldn't be truly happening. This chest overflowing with gleaming coins and jewels simply could not be real!

"Oh, my!" she exclaimed breathlessly, her hands clasped to her chest. "Devlin, I've never seen such a sight in my life! Are those actual gems? Is all that gold and silver genuine?"

"Aye. Eden, my love, you are looking at a good portion of Blackbeard's secret cache. 'Twas he who came to the island this morn to bury it. And now 'tis yours."

Eden sank to her knees before the open coffer. "I

can't believe it," she murmured, thrusting her hands into the tangle of treasure. When she raised her cupped palms, they were dripping with strands of pearls, loose jewels, rings, and coins. Every gem she'd ever heard of, and some she did not recognize, sparkled and winked back at her in a dazzling display.

For the first time, she could understand what made men risk their lives in pursuit of such fabulous treasure. How good, decent men could be lured into becoming highwaymen and pirates. Why men would scale mountains, trek through steaming jungles, and burrow far beneath the earth's surface for such wealth.

It wasn't merely the adventure, or the challenge, or the danger. It was this—the dream of someday holding this much wealth in the palm of one's hands. Of jewel-imbedded chalices, of piles of gold, of priceless gems the size of hen's eggs. The search for elusive grandeur, evolving from simple greed into something much stronger—more of a quest, a relentless fever, that only a prize of this magnitude could hope to cure.

"Devlin, is this really ours?" she asked softly, shock still strong upon her. "God's teeth! There must be more wealth here than in all of England."

"I doubt that, though it is impressive, isn't it? I'd love to be there when Teach discovers it's missing. He'll be fit to be tied."

"What shall we do with it all?" she said wonderingly.

"Whatever we please, my sweet. We could build a grand house anywhere you want—or two or three if you desire. We could start a business of our own, perhaps in shipping. That would please Rogers no end, I imagine. You and I could travel wherever we wish, and you could see the world as you've always longed to do. The possibilities are limitless."

"Oh, Devlin! That would be wonderful! But we must keep some back and invest it for the future. And I do hope you won't mind sharing a bit of it with those of your crew who applied for amnesty, for they will need some means of beginning anew, now that they'll no longer be pirating for a livelihood."

He nodded. "I intend to see that they have a decent start on their new lives, whether they choose to remain in my employ or not. We've been through many a good and bad time together, and I would not see them turned out with naught in their pockets."

Digging into the mound of treasure, Devlin extracted a diamond tiara, which he promptly placed upon Eden's head. "I've called you duchess, and now you truly look like one," he proclaimed. His admiring smile turned teasing as he held out his hand to assist her from her knees into his arms. "You know, I've always wondered what it would be like to make love with a royal wench."

"My blood is not blue,' she reminded him, shivering delightedly as his fingers deftly released the fastenings along the back of her dress.

"For that I am profoundly grateful," he assured her, his lips nibbling along the curve of her slender neck. "Methinks I would much rather bed my own hot-blooded pretender than a real duchess anyway. But do indulge my secret fantasy a bit, won't you, sweetling?"

She played her part to perfection. She remained perfectly still as he bound her nude body to the bed with cool ropes of silver and bejeweled chains of gold. "Am I to be your prisoner, as well as your imagined duchess?" she asked, breathlessly excited by this new game.

He cocked a taunting brow at her. "Why not? I was yours, and turnabout is fair play. Now you shall see what torment you put me through, for I intend to apply the same measures to you."

He proceeded to drench her flushed skin with necklaces and bracelets of glittering gems—sapphires, emeralds, rubies, and diamonds. Eden gave a small shriek as he plopped one dazzling topaz, not yet mounted in a proper setting, into her navel.

He stood back to admire his work, nodding his approval as he divested himself of his own clothes. "You look like a sultan's favorite dancing girl," he told her, his voice rough with desire. "A pasha's love slave."

"Nay," she denied, her eyes outshining the jewels. "Not a pasha's, but a pirate's."

His smile was particularly wicked as he reached once more into the treasure chest and pulled forth a long strand of pearls. "'Tis said that pearls acquire an added sheen when warmed by a woman's flesh. Shall we test that theory now, my sweet?"

With tantalizing slowness, he drew the smooth gems over her lips, her throat, then wove them around her aching breasts and across her crested nipples. She sucked in a sharp breath as he trailed them lightly over her quivering stomach, snaked a path down her trembling thighs, and slowly up again. His long fingers caught the beads into a shorter length, holding them taut on their string as he delved between the hot folds of feminine flesh so sweetly bared by her outspread legs. The pearls, now so silken and round and warm, stroked her intimately. One following the other, adroitly applied by Devlin's hand, they kneaded smoothly, repeatedly, at that tiny, throbbing nubbin of desire, until Eden was arching helplessly beneath their sensual caress.

"Please," she begged, her voice quaking on the brink of splendor. "Devlin, please!"

With a low laugh that rang with pure male satisfaction, he brought her to her peak. While she was yet in the throes of ecstasy he came swiftly over her, fusing his body to hers, thrusting her immediately into another wondrous spasm. Her moist depths sucked hungrily at him, like a pulsating satin glove; squeezing, pulling, greedily milking his seed from him as he blissfully accompanied her on a mad journey to rapture's realms.

"What a passionate princess you are, my love," he avowed softly, his damp brow resting in the delicate curve of her shoulder. His lips kissed her there, tasting the dew of her spent ardor.

She answered with a low laugh. "First a duchess, now a princess. Honestly, Devlin, you do exaggerate so extravagantly. What shall I be next—a queen mayhap?"

"Aye." He sighed contentedly. "Forever my sassy duchess and the queen of my heart."

They were on their way home with pardons in hand, sailing swiftly toward Charles Town and all that was so achingly familiar to her. Yet, in a strange way, Eden's life in the Carolina colony now seemed but a distant dream, something that had happened a century ago that had to do with someone else entirely. So much had occurred since they'd left, and she had changed so dramatically in so short a time. If not for her mother, Eden wasn't at all sure she would want to return to that sedate, restrictive life.

To her surprise, she found herself suddenly sympathetic to Devlin's way of thinking. Here, on the sea, with the breeze tugging at her hair, the sun and spindrift softly kissing her flesh, Eden experienced a sense of freedom she'd never known. As far as the eye could see, there was nothing but rolling, sparkling waves. At night the stars appeared close enough to touch, the moon majestic and mysterious. Each morning the sunrise was glorious to behold, and each sunset seemed more magnificent than the last, as if the sky were being painted with promise by God's own hand.

"I wish we could stay here, in the middle of the ocean," she told Devlin one evening, as they watched the moon rise in a cloudless indigo sky. "Sailing endlessly." Cradled before him, his arms bound securely about her waist, she turned her face up to his with a winsome look. "Could we do that, do you suppose? Just the two of us?"

"Wishful dreaming, my pet," he answered with a regretful crook of his lips. "How would we live?"

"We have the treasure. Surely that is enough to see

us through several lifetimes, without the need to pirate and bring Rogers down upon our necks."

"Aye," he agreed. "But a frigate of this size requires a crew, so we would not be entirely alone. Also, we would still need to put ashore for supplies, and for the men to indulge their baser needs."

Eden rolled her eyes. "How delicately phrased," she teased.

He ignored her and continued with his list of reasons why her wish could not come true. "No doubt, soon you would miss your mother, and drive me to distraction with your whining."

"I do not whine," she countered with a haughty sniff.

He chuckled. "I fear you could learn to do so with astounding ease, especially if you should find yourself with child and want Jane at hand."

Eden sighed, acknowledging the wisdom of his words. "I suppose a ship would not be the most suitable place to raise a child," she conceded. "And I do want to bear your children." She frowned, a disturbing thought having just occurred to her. "You *do* want children, don't you, Devlin?"

He hugged her close, his lips grazing her upturned cheek. "Aye, Eden, I do. I want a long, lanky red-haired daughter with sea-sparkled eyes, an abundance of freckles, and a sassy mouth—the spit and image of her mother."

Eden's elbow connected sharply with his ribs. "Want what you will, but I intend to have a strapping son with sun-blond locks and midnight eyes, and the supreme arrogance of his father."

"Do you now?" he purred into her ear, his black eyes dancing. "Well then, Madam Kane, we'd best see what we can do to speed things along." He swept her into his arms, and his long strides carried them swiftly toward their cabin. "Let it never be said that I did not do my utmost to fulfill your dearest desires."

Chapter 28

*T*hey sailed into Charles Town harbor with the early-morning tide, almost a full month after leaving it. To Eden's eye, nothing much had changed during their absence. No major fires or Spanish attacks had destroyed the town, no unexpected floods or plagues barred their departure from the *Mirage*.

No sooner had they walked through Eden's front door than Jane came dashing down the staircase in her night robe. She skidded to a halt, the expression on her face a mixture of hope and anxiety.

With a huge grin, Nate hurried forward to envelope Jane in a crushing embrace, twirling her around. "We got the pardon, Janie girl!" he proclaimed. "Set the date and send for the preacher!"

A joyous smile wreathed Jane's features, only to melt quickly away. Easing back from him, she gazed up at him with tearful eyes. "Nathan, my love, when you hear what I have to tell you, you might want to rethink our plans. Though I sincerely hope you won't be too terribly upset."

Nate frowned, as did Devlin and Eden. When Jane hesitated, chewing her lip in the same nervous manner Eden often employed, Nate said somberly, "Spit it out,

Janie. Whate'er 'tis, we'll solve it together. What's wrong?"

On a sob, Jane declared, "'Tis not something so easily resolved, and certainly nothing we planned. Nate, I'm going to have a child. Our child."

All three listeners stood there stunned. Nate looked as if he'd been poleaxed. Jane's face was as pale as parchment. "A . . . a babe?" Nate squeaked out, the picture of astonishment. "I'm gonna be a father?"

Jane nodded, her hands clenched together so tightly that her fingers appeared blue. "I . . . I know it comes as a shock. It certainly did to me. I just need to know how you feel about it."

Nate gave a sharp shake of his head, like a man trying to rid himself of the lingering remnants of a nightmare. "Janie," he croaked. Then a smile to rival the sun lit his wrinkled features. "I'll be damned. I'm gonna be a papa!" He swept her back into his arms and peppered her face with kisses. "Woman, ye couldn't have greeted me with grander news if ye'd just told me I was crowned King of England! How? When?"

At last Jane joined him in his laughter, relief making her giddy. "You know very well how, you randy old goat!" she replied with a silly grin. "As to when, I assume you want to know how soon the child will arrive. According to my calculations, along about next April And I can't tell you how glad I am that you are thrilled about it. I wasn't sure you'd take to the notion."

"How could I not?" he replied. "Oh, Janie, we're gonna be a real family. You an' me an' the babe, an' Eden an' Devlin too." He set her on her feet, but kept his arm firmly about her. "We've got news as well, though not as startlin' as yers. Hold on to yer nightshirt and say hello to yer son-in-law, Janie. Eden and Devlin got themselves married in New Providence."

At this, Jane positively glowed. Tearing herself loose from Nate's hold, she darted forward to gather her daughter to her breast. "Eden, I'm so happy for you both. I was hoping, praying that things would work out between you, even with all the complications still before you."

Her pleased gaze found Devlin, and she reached out a hand to him. "Am I correct in guessing that my daughter finally succeeded in her relentless attempts to convince you to apply for amnesty?"

Devlin grinned and squeezed her slim fingers. "Aye. She worked her wiles on me until I could do no less. And I'll wager we'll be starting a family of our own not far behind you and Nate. Congratulations, Mother Winters."

Jane chuckled. " 'Jane' will suit, Devlin. No sense in assuming formality at this late date."

Eden had yet to say a word. When Jane turned back to her, the younger woman's eyes were still slightly dazed. "Oh, dear!" Jane said softly. "It seems we've well and truly shocked you." Gently she led her daughter toward the nearest chair. "Come, Eden. You look as if you are about to swoon, and I am the one who is supposed to be prone to such behavior just now."

Eden allowed herself to be seated while the other three gathered around with looks of concern. At length she remembered to breathe, the air whooshing out of her lungs in a tremendous gush. "Oh, my! Who would have believed this?" she said weakly. She turned a quizzical gaze on her mother. "Mama, are you certain? How can this be? I'm . . . you're . . ."

Jane's eyes narrowed in tender warning. "If you dare mention my advanced age, I swear I'll take a switch to your backside, Eden Winters. I am only just forty. Not near ready to be fitted for a shroud, and not yet past my childbearing years, as nature has seen fit to prove. While I'll admit it was not to be anticipated, neither is it totally phenomenal."

Eden gave a confused nod. "But is it safe for you to

carry a babe now? You haven't been well for so very long."

"Sweetheart, don't fret. I am as healthy as a horse," Jane assured her, and the men as well. "My inability to walk was more in my head than in my body. Strange as it may seem to you, I am looking forward to having this child. I've always regretted not being able to supply you with sibling playmates, and while this little one will not grow up alongside you, it could do so with your children, if you are likewise favored."

Eden answered with a wan smile. "I'm glad for you, Mama. Truly. 'Tis just such a surprising development."

"I know." Jane laughed. "Think how I felt when first I suspected. And with all of you gone, I had no one in whom to confide. Lord knows, everyone is going to be horrified when they learn of it. Tongues will be wagging throughout Charles Town, most especially when the baby arrives prior to the usual term. Mayhap my considerable age will prove a benefit after all, if only to excuse the early birth."

Nate's eyes popped wide again. "Merciful heavens, Janie! Ye must get hold of that preacher for an immediate weddin', I won't have my son born on the wrong side o' the blanket, or with folks whisperin' about him."

"Isn't that just like a man," Jane declared, shaking her head. "Tell him he's going to be a father, and he's all set to order jackboots and breeches."

"Devlin wants a daughter," Eden said, her eyes catching her husband's. She rose from her chair to give her mother a belated kiss. "I can scarcely believe that I will soon have a baby brother or sister, after all these years. 'Tis truly mir ... mir ... aculous." Her words drifted off tremulously, but it wasn't merely due to her roiling emotions. Suddenly, as she clung to Jane's smaller frame, dizziness threatened to overcome her.

Dark clouds swirled around her, her vision narrowing to a spiraling tunnel.

"Devlin?" she called out fearfully, reaching for him.

Feeling her daughter starting to sway, Jane promptly shoved Eden into Devlin's ready arms. "Set her down and press her head betwixt her knees," she instructed brusquely.

Devlin did as Jane suggested. The irreverent thought crossed his mind that he'd rather have Eden's head between *his* legs, but he didn't imagine Jane would find that amusing at the moment. Actually, neither did he when he caught his first glimpse of Eden's milk-white face.

"Breathe deeply, pet," he told her. "Nice deep breaths. Come on, Eden, I've got you. Cease fighting it. If you relax, 'twill soon pass."

Slowly Eden's world began to right itself again, but no sooner did it stop spinning than she clamped a hand over her mouth and attempted to bolt from her chair. Realizing the problem, Jane grabbed a nearby vase, hastily dumped its bouquet of flowers onto the floor, and thrust the vessel under Eden's nose.

"Blessed saints!" she said chuckling dryly. " 'Twould seem all our prayers are to be answered at once. Unless I miss my guess, I'd say we've two breeding women in the same house, and two untried fathers-to-be. What merry mayhem this heralds!"

Despite the limitations imposed on him by his invisibility, Devlin strove to conduct as much business as possible without requiring Eden's presence. His bride was often indisposed these days with recurring bouts of nausea and light-headedness, as was her mother. Jane had been correct in assuming that Eden was breeding, and as near as they could figure, the child was due sometime in June, with only a few weeks separating the birth of Nate and Jane's babe from Devlin and Eden's.

Taking all this into consideration, Devlin concluded that it would be best to delay any search for Swift until after the arrival of the babies. Finding the fellow might prove a lengthy venture, and Devlin did not want to be separated from his wife just now. Nor did he wish to miss the momentous occasion of his first child's birth, merely to mete out revenge on his old enemy. Besides, until the proper time came to go after Swift, there was plenty to keep him busy right here in Charles Town.

In exchange for Devlin's help at the warehouse, Nate reciprocated by aiding Devlin in the purchase of property along the wharf. With the two ships as a start, Devlin now had his sights set on developing a small shipping firm, in partnership with Nate, and employing many of their former shipmates. Putting his carpentry skills to work, Devlin was also renovating the *Dame Anise*, which Swift had allowed to fall into sad disrepair. Once the ship had been restored to his satisfaction, Devlin would rename her. By rearranging the letters, the *Dame Anise* would become the *Sea Maiden*, and be legally registered as such. For now, Devlin initiated new business with the *Mirage* as his only merchant ship. It was a beginning, the dawn of a new dream.

Months earlier, when Jane and Eden had needed his support so badly, Devlin had bought into the warehouse; and upon his marriage to Jane, Nate owned part of the company as well. The two businesses went hand-in-glove, one complementing the other under the dual supervision of the two friends. Goods stored at the warehouse were often contracted to be transported by the new shipping company, which was titled Kanecock Shipping, a combination of the owners' surnames. Likewise, goods arriving on the company ships would be regularly consigned to Winters Warehouse. Thus, both businesses benefitted, earning a handsome profit at both ends.

Aside from this, Devlin's improvements to the *Dame Anise* so impressed other ship owners that he was soon besieged with requests for similar repairs to other vessels. Eden found this latest development vastly amusing. "For a man who once claimed that piracy was the easiest road to riches, you are fast disproving your own words. You now have three profitable means of income, and if things keep on as they are, you'll own half of Charles Town in short order."

Devlin laughed, but admitted to further aspirations. "I've considered building a rooming house, mostly for use by the men working for us. They are currently letting rooms all over town, wherever they can find space, and some are living in deplorable conditions. There simply aren't enough accommodations available. They need a decent place to lay their heads at night, and edible food, at considerably less cost than they are being charged now, or they'll be back at brigandry before you can shake a stick. Even if they don't resort to their former trade, they won't be worth their wages if they are ill-fed and weary from lack of a proper bed."

"Ah, I see yet another enterprise in the offing," Eden predicted with an impish look. "You shall have to form your own building company. Then, if the price of lumber is too high for your liking, you'll start a timber business and a lumber mill, and God knows when I'll ever see your face again, let alone any other part of your anatomy. Despite my complaints of late, mayhap 'twas a good thing you got me with child when you did, for you'll soon be much too busy and fatigued to attend to such a vigorous activity as bedding your wife."

She pulled a mockingly mournful face, throwing a forearm over her brow. "Woe is me, the wedded widow of an ambitious man!"

Devlin laughed at her antics, playfully tossing her to the mattress and smothering her with kisses. "You sassy, lusty wench!" he growled, nipping at her nose. "If ever I fail to satisfy your needs, you have permission to box my ears. Until then, kindly stifle your imagined grievances and apply yourself to salving the wounds you have inflicted upon me with your rapier-sharp tongue."

"What wounds?" she countered, giggling. "I see no obvious evidence of any."

He cocked a brow at her in comic dismay, his gaze traveling downward to his upstanding manhood. "But, sweetling, note how painfully swollen I am, and 'tis all your doing."

They spent a pleasant interlude relieving his lamentable state.

At the start, like many an expectant father Devlin was reluctant to continue their amorous ventures, afraid some harm might come to Eden or the babe nestled in her womb. Nate had similar notions, and it was left to Jane, the only one with previous experience in these matters, to educate them. Though she managed this feat in ladylike fashion, she was necessarily forthright. Witnessing two burly pirates of dangerous repute stammering and stuttering and blushing like schoolboys caused her untold amusement.

While their husbands were about the business of earning a living, the two women settled down to serious sewing. Both would soon need clothing more suited to their expanding figures. They also had scores of diapers and wee ruffled gowns to create, baby blankets and lace-edged bonnets to crochet, and booties to knit. Eden's old cradle was brought down from the attic and dusted, the old mattress thrown out and a new one made for it, in anticipation of Jane's delivery. Rather than purchase another cradle for his and Eden's child, Devlin had promised to craft a new one himself, and Eden was eager to see the finished product, certain it would be the finest ever built.

Since their return from New Providence, and following Jane and Nate's hasty wedding, the two couples had resided beneath the same roof. For the most part, this was convenient, the four of them getting on very companionably. There were times, however, when privacy was at a premium, and every time the bedsprings creaked loudly in the still of the night, whether they be hers or those in the room across the hall, Eden cringed with mortification. There was also the matter of continuing to conceal Devlin's invisibility from Dora, no mean feat these days, with Eden plagued by nausea and dashing off in search of a slop jar at any given moment.

Devlin decided it was time to consider acquiring a home of their own. The problem was the lack of suitable housing currently available. Nearly every standing dwelling already had a family residing within its walls, and the few that didn't weren't fit for habitation. The obvious solution was to build a house, which, to be done correctly, would take many months.

Devlin applied himself to the task immediately, drawing up the plans himself and sending for the necessary materials, many of which had to be transported from elsewhere in the colonies and from as far away as England. Though he intended to do most of the carpentry work himself, and to oversee that which he could not fit into his busy schedule, much of the labor fell beyond his expertise.

He wanted the place built of stone, to withstand the seasonal storms and lessen the chance of damage from fire. That, and the fireplaces, required the skills of a mason. The twisted ironwork he desired as enhancement for the veranda and porch had to be specially contracted with a master forger. Extra laborers would be needed to install the flooring, the interior structure, and the roof. There was a well and a root cellar to be dug, windows to place, doors to be made, not to mention furniture to fill the dozen rooms he was including in the plans. Altogether, this house was the largest endeavor he ever hoped to undertake, and Devlin shook his head in wonder that he'd ever thought life ashore would be dull.

Chapter 29

*T*hey hadn't been back from New Providence a month when pirate ships once more appeared in the harbor. With the memory of Blackbeard's attack still fresh in their minds, the irate townspeople immediately sent up a hue and cry. They were tired of constantly being harassed by these lawless cutthroats, and were bound and determined to have no more of it.

With the ink hardly dry on their pardons, and a portion of their sympathies still leaning toward their fellow brigands, Nate and Devlin were satisfied to sit back and let others handle the problem. They recognized the lead ship as that of Stede Bonnet, a comrade with whom they'd worked in the past on a few ventures. Though notorious for his success as a sea robber, he was not noted for being particularly bloodthirsty or vengeful. For the most part, he and his crew preyed on trade vessels, rarely bothering common citizens, and Devlin expected no different now from the man whom many called a "gentleman pirate."

For the first couple of hours things were peaceful enough, and it looked as if the buccaneers meant to do no more than replenish their supplies and go on about their business elsewhere. Then all hell broke loose.

From their prime position near the mouth of the harbor, the pirates began to waylay all incoming and outgoing ships. Cannon shot flew hot and heavy, the smoke so thick that ships began colliding with one another in the harbor.

The brigands boarded several merchant vessels, carrying the bloody fight to the decks. In the ensuing fray, men on both sides were wounded, though fatalities remained remarkably few considering the extent of the conflict. In the end, the pirates confiscated two of the most seaworthy trade ships and ordered the defeated sailors into dinghies, that they might safely reach shore. The remaining ships were plundered of all worthwhile cargo before more shot was leveled their way in an effort to scuttle them sufficiently to make it impossible for them to give chase.

From the warehouse dock, Devlin and Nate watched the battle unfold, casually making wagers on who would win the day, pirates or merchants. Neither felt inclined to join a fight which was not theirs, and possibly forfeit their pardons.

Then the volley of cannon fire began to rake those ships anchored closer in, and those tied up at the docks. Whether the shots were going wild, or deliberately aimed toward damaging every ship in the harbor, mattered not. Most particularly when one of the frigates last hit was the *Dame Anise*.

Want it or not, the battle had now been brought to Devlin and Nate's doorstep, and the two friends were furious. No one, but no one, got away with scuttling their property! Especially not Stede Bonnet, whom they had considered a decent rogue and a jolly mate. The *Dame Anise* might not be the best vessel afloat, but they had plans to renovate her into a fine little cargo ship. She and the *Mirage* were to be the foundation of their joint venture into the shipping business, and they certainly didn't need anyone delaying their progress before they'd gotten a decent start of it.

"Hellfire!" Devlin let loose with an enraged curse. He gave a final glower at the departing pirates, then turned to Nate. "Despite all our good intentions, it seems you and I can't stay out of the fray. Ready the *Mirage*. We're going after those blackguards."

"Cap'n, the *Mirage* is on a run to Boston, and not due back for a fortnight," Nate reminded him. "We're as land-bound as beached whales."

"Damnation!" Devlin raked his fingers through his hair. "Now's a hell of a time to be stranded ashore, one ship gone and the other damaged!" He heaved an exasperated sigh. "There's no help for it, I suppose, but I swear as soon as the *Mirage* makes port, we're after that sorry lot. Bonnet will not get away with this!"

It soon became apparent that others of the townspeople were of the same mind. Disgruntled and longing to fight back, merchants were quickly gathering under the command of Colonel William Rhett. They set about outfitting two sloops and assembling enough sailors to chase after the fleeing pirates.

The *Mirage* returned the day before Rhett's expedition was due to set sail. All through the night, Devlin and his men worked to unload the incoming cargo and take on sufficient supplies to last throughout their search for Bonnet.

The colonel was pleased that Devlin and his crew would be joining them on their mission. "We appreciate your help in this matter," he told Devlin. Regardless of Eden's presence at her husband's side, the man felt compelled to add, "To be truthful, I wasn't convinced you were serious about reforming your ways. For all our sakes, I'm glad you are. It's good to have a man of your caliber on our side."

Devlin didn't bother to explain that it had taken a broadside to his own ship to muster him to action.

What Rhett didn't know wouldn't hurt him, but playing defending heroes certainly put Devlin and his crew in a better light in the eyes of any citizens who still harbored similar doubts.

Though she understood why she could not accompany the men, Eden could not help being disappointed at getting left behind. While she knew Devlin was more than capable of protecting himself, she also knew she would worry herself ragged until he returned safely. She did not even have the consolation of knowing that Devlin would be invisible to his enemy, for he intended to make use of his hooded disguise once more, and thoroughly relished the opportunity to employ it. For this short venture, it would suit admirably indeed as he temporarily assumed a role echoing that of his former pirate image, though presently in defense of justice. "Devil" Kane lived on—lawfully reborn.

Before he left her, however, Eden intended to give him a time to remember, something to remind him what awaited him on his return. When he came dragging into the house in the wee hours of the morning he was to sail, after working so hard to ready the *Mirage* for the voyage, Eden was awake and waiting for him. He was so weary that he could scarcely stay afoot long enough to wash and haul his tired body onto the bed.

Once he was there, Eden urged him onto his stomach. "You just relax, darling," she whispered. "I've a cure for all those sore muscles."

He was half-asleep as she poured warm oil over his back. Naked herself, she straddled his hips, massaging the soothing liquid into his skin, leaning into her task until he groaned in grateful relief at the magic her slick hands were performing.

As she applied like measures to his buttocks and thighs, he gave a muted laugh. "Sweetling, I might be bone-tired, but I'm not dead. Don't start anything you aren't prepared to finish."

"Oh, I'm not done by half yet," she told him in sultry promise.

A few minutes later, she rolled him onto his back and devoted herself to allaying the tension from his neck, his aching arms and shoulders, and his broad, furred chest. "Sweet heaven, that feels marvelous!" He sighed. "I just might employ your skillful services more often."

She gave a low laugh, her fingers wandering downward, the massage quickly becoming temptation. "I am a woman of many talents, sir. Shall I demonstrate further?"

"Please do," he murmured encouragingly, his dark eyes slitting open to gleam at her.

Soon they were both as slippery as wet seals, their bodies gliding smoothly together as Eden lowered herself upon his rigid staff. Weariness became but a memory, their easy, lingering lovemaking assuming the ethereal softness of a sweet, sensual dream. As one, they drifted from ecstasy into slumber, their bodies still entwined.

At last they sailed, with high hopes and great determination. Since Stede Bonnet was known to cruise the Carolina coastline, Devlin hoped they would soon encounter him and quickly conclude this business. First they headed south, thoroughly investigating every island, cove, inlet, and river mouth. There was no sign of Bonnet or the two ships he'd captured. Halfway through the first week, they turned north again, disappointed but undaunted. They made a brief stop in Charles Town to ensure that Bonnet had not put in another appearance there, then continued north the following morning.

For five days they searched the coast. At dawn of the sixth day, their efforts were finally rewarded. They spotted Bonnet's flagship and the two trading vessels lying at anchor at the mouth of the Cape Fear River. From the look of it, he'd stopped there to refit his small fleet, and to repair damages incurred in the fight in Charles Town Harbor.

Rhett was in the lead sloop. Motioning for the others to follow, he headed his ship toward the mouth of the river. The second sloop followed close at hand, prepared to help block Bonnet's passage to the sea.

At the helm of the *Mirage,* which was trailing the other two sloops, Devlin tried to signal the others to wait, to beware of the shallows and sandbars that lay ahead. But in the excitement of the moment, his warning went unheeded. Rhett's sloop ran aground near the left bank. The captain of the other sloop, unfamiliar with the river's tricky current, found his vessel swept into the shallows at the right edge of the river, where it, too, stuck fast. It was left to Devlin to skillfully guide the *Mirage* between the two, the only one of them to successfully negotiate the shoals.

Meanwhile, Bonnet had become aware of the encroaching danger and was weighing anchor. While exchanging rapid fire with the *Mirage,* he attempted to pilot his own ship, the *Revenge,* through the small passage left to him. His efforts failed when the *Revenge* also ran afoul of a sandbar, trapped midway between Rhett's sloop and the *Mirage,* his two remaining prize ships blocked in the river behind him, with no route of escape.

They still had some mobility, however, as did the *Mirage.* While the two Charles Town sloops were busy with the dual tasks of defending themselves and trying to free themselves from the shoals, Devlin took charge of returning fire from the pirate prize ships. Thus occupied, he and his crew could not readily board the *Revenge,* as they had hoped to do at the start.

To everyone's disbelief, the battle raged on in this

manner for five interminable hours. Cannons roared, muskets blazed, taunts were exchanged all the while. Red-hot gun barrels belched out thick smoke, and the air hung so heavy with it that the acrid odor lent its taste to the tongue.

It was not until Devlin's men had subdued the barrage from the enemy sister ships that the fight began to wane and boarding became possible. The battle then turned to fierce swordplay and hand-to-hand combat as Devlin divided his crew, sending half onto each enemy prize ship. Into the thick of the fray he flew, his sword flashing, leading his men to a quick victory.

Casting a look about, Devlin realized that the incoming tide was rapidly raising the water level in the river's mouth. Any minute now, Rhett's two sloops would break free of their groundings. But so would Bonnet's flagship, which alone faced the ocean and stood a good chance of making a fast escape once it slid free of the sandbar.

With little time to spare, Devlin signaled Nate to secure the captured ships, then hastily divested himself of his hood and clothing. Now unseen, his invisible knife clasped between his teeth, he dived into the water and swam to the *Revenge*. Dripping water after him, he hauled himself aboard just as the sleek little sloop floated free of its moorings.

Bonnet stood on the quarterdeck, bellowing orders to his crew and wearing the wolfish grin of a man who has just found himself locked in a roomful of love-hungry nymphs. "By damn! We're off and running with the wind now!" he shouted gleefully.

"Not quite, old friend," Devlin corrected on a low growl, slanting his knife blade toward Bonnet's windpipe.

Stede's eyes rolled to the side in a futile attempt to see his foe.

"Give it up, Stede. Call your men away from their

stations into the center of the deck, where they may all be readily accounted for, and issue the command for a calm, orderly surrender. Or would you rather die here and now, your blood staining your boots?"

At about this same time, Colonel Rhett's ship broke loose of its own sandbar, and headed directly toward the *Revenge,* with the obvious intention of boarding her. To the colonel's vast astonishment, after all the fierce combat that had gone before, the *Revenge* suddenly hoisted a flag of truce. Incredibly, Bonnet did not even attempt to fight further, but lay down his weapon and surrendered with remarkably good grace, his men rapidly following suit. The battle was won, the brigands captured.

Devlin swam back to his ship undetected, donned his pirate's uniform and hood, and once again confronted his former friend, who was now ensconced in Colonel Rhett's makeshift brig. "How very wise of you to surrender when you did, Stede," he commented wryly.

Bonnet eyed him warily. "That voice. I know that voice, yet I cannot place it. Remove your mask and reveal yourself."

"Nay. I cannot show my face as yet, but you do know me well. We've shared a few adventures, you and I, and hoisted a few tankards along the way. Did you not recognize the *Gai Mer,* though she now flies a new flag and bears a new name?"

"Devlin?" Stede questioned, peering more closely in an attempt to see the man beyond the enveloping mask. "Devlin Kane?"

"One and the same, Stede."

"Damn your eyes! Why didn't you say so? And why are you now aligned with those who would hang me? We're mates, Dev."

"We were, until you shot holes through the hull of my newest ship back in Charles Town Harbor."

"I'll pay for the damage if you'll but help me escape."

"I cannot, Stede. Woodes Rogers would not take kindly to that, you see, after I have so recently sworn my fealty to the Crown."

Bonnet sighed. "Got your amnesty, did you? I considered it as well. Now I wish I had made the voyage to New Providence, rather than chance my luck too far."

"Aye. If not for Nate and my new bride, I might be in the same spot, right alongside you, a little late and a great deal sorry."

Sometime later, during the search of Bonnet's ship, a young woman was found locked in Stede's quarters. The poor lass was in a pitiful way, half-crazed with fright and pathetically grateful to her rescuers. Some weeks past, Bonnet had captured her and spirited her away with him on the *Revenge,* keeping her hostage to his private pleasures. Shamed and despoiled, she was nonetheless anxious to be returned to her loving family, who no doubt thought her dead by now.

Upon seeing this unfortunate woman, and learning all she had suffered at Bonnet's hands, Devlin's sympathy for Stede immediately vanished. Thinking of Eden, and how he would feel if she had been Stede's victim, Devlin could only hope the girl's relatives would receive her back into their keeping with open arms and all the compassion she deserved.

Nate was of a similar mind, though his thoughts went further. "Dev, if ye hadn't acted so quickly and stopped Stede from sailin', the poor lass might yet be with him. Though the colonel and his men be claimin' they saved her, 'twas really yer doin'. I'm right proud o' ye this day, and Eden will be too, when she hears."

Devlin scowled at him, ridiculously embarrassed by Nate's lavish praise. "I'm no bloody hero, Nate, and well you know it."

"Aye, ye are, Dev," Nate argued. "Like it or not. By heavens, lad, if ye're not careful, ye'll turn into a bloomin' saint!"

Chapter 30

*T*he *Mirage* sailed into Charles Town Harbor just behind Colonel Rhett's small fleet, and immediately the crew found themselves acclaimed as champions along with the rest of the returning party, though Rhett received the lion's share of the credit for leading the successful expedition. Eden became exceedingly miffed when she learned they could not reveal the most vital part her husband had played in executing Bonnet's capture. But Devlin was content to note that the townsfolk openly appreciated the aid he and his men had delivered, and that they now seemed proud to claim him as one of their own.

Stede Bonnet and his crew were promptly jailed, awaiting their coming trial. While most of Stede's pirates were held under heavy guard at the watch house, he and his quartermaster, David Herriot, were lodged separately at the home of the town constable.

When Devlin questioned Colonel Rhett about this unusual arrangement, the old man told him, "It appears that some of our town officials still consider Bonnet a gentleman pirate, despite his recent actions, though I myself fail to see their reasoning. It has to do with the fact that the fellow was born and raised to be a gentleman, that he is well educated, especially compared to most of the riffraff pirating the seas, and that before he turned to brigandry, he owned a plantation in Barbados."

Devlin gave a derisive snort. "Bonnet came by his plantation through marriage, not merit. Furthermore, he soon abandoned his labors and his wife for a more adventurous life. He claims his wife was a shrew and drove him to seek some measure of peace from her harridan's tongue by taking to the sea. For my money, he simply wanted more gain for less sweat."

Rhett nodded in agreement. "There are some who do not concur with you, however. Between the two of us, those who do not and are even now begging leniency on Bonnet's behalf, are those who have previously done business with the man, or others like him, and despair of having their names linked with his in court. It would not surprise me if Major Bonnet managed to escape some dark night with the help of those who most fear what his testimony before the judge might do to their own characters."

As had happened once before, following Devlin's rescue of Blackbeard's beleaguered prisoners, he now experienced the same curious result. After being touched by Eden and becoming visible, he found he could remain visible for some time after she broke contact. This time the mystifying tendency was stronger and lasted longer. Rather than being normal for mere minutes, he could now walk about freely for upward to two hours or more. And, when he felt himself beginning to fade, if he concentrated his thoughts and energies against it, he could sometimes prevent himself from disappearing so soon. When he did fade altogether, he could instantly be restored to view simply by brushing Eden's hand, or her sleeve, and remain discernible for another couple of hours.

This development was extremely encouraging, leading all of them to hope for his complete recovery in the near future, Eden most of all. Though her pregnancy seemed to be progressing nicely, she was often plagued by worries that her child would be afflicted with its father's invisibility. Try as she might, she could not relieve her mind of that dreadful prospect, though Devlin assured her she was being foolish.

"Darling, the child will be perfectly normal, with all its fingers and toes."

"Aye, but will they be perceivable? Worse yet, will the poor mite appear and disappear in the blink of an eye, come and gone like an errant breeze?"

"Better that than with its mother's outrageous imagination," he told her. "Sweet heaven, Eden! You are driving yourself daft, and I'll wager a hundred pounds that you are fretting yourself into fits for naught. Expectant mothers are supposed to remain calm and think tranquil thoughts, not dredge up every horrible consequence likely to occur, and more that are pure drivel."

" 'Tis more than drivel," she argued. "You have merely to look at yourself to see that the impossible can happen."

"I still say you are being a silly twit. But I suppose that is to be expected. Your mother did warn me that breeding women are often prone to emotional disturbances, but I mistook her to mean tears and angry outbursts, not fanciful nonsense and outright derangement."

Eden glared at him. "I'll remind you of that when our child arrives only half visible, O Wise One. Then we'll see who is being irrational."

Autumn was fully upon them before they quite knew where the time had gone, and though Charles Town was not yet completely free of the threat of tropical storms, the torrid temperatures fell to a more pleasant level. This was a great relief to them all, but especially to

Eden and Jane, who were miserable enough in their delicate conditions without the added heat and humidity.
Eden clung to her mother's prediction that the dizziness
and nausea would cease within another few weeks. Unfortunately, by then her figure would have begun to ex-
pand, and her trim waistline would be but a fond
memory.

For the time being, however, it was marvelous to
have a fuller bosom, which she hoped to keep after the
baby was born. Her added dimensions in that area had
Devlin deliriously fascinated, quite like a boy with a
new toy, and he could scarcely look at the straining
bodices of her gowns without salivating. The poor man
walked around in a state of constant arousal, and their
lovemaking was showing no signs of diminishing in
frequency or quality. Though Eden wouldn't have believed it possible, it was more passionate with every
passing day.

There was yet another love affair blossoming in the
household these days, though Devlin could scarcely
credit it. Zeus appeared to be beak-over-tail-feathers in
love with Eden's parrot! It was lunacy and didn't make
a bit of sense, but there was no way to convince Zeus
that a falcon could not become enamored of a parrot.

"This is the craziest thing I've ever seen," Devlin
marveled, half-despairing that his precious falcon had
lost his senses over such a gaudy female bird. "Zeus
and Rum Pot?"

Eden had named her feathered friend while still
under the misconception that Rum Pot was a male, but
the appellation was fitting since the parrot had an inordinate liking for rum, and would pilfer a drink from
anyone's cup whenever possible. Perhaps more curious
than Rum Pot's preference of drink, or the odd attraction betwixt the birds, was the fact that the parrot appeared capable of viewing the invisible hawk, while no
one else, save Devlin, could do so.

Eden thought the feathered courtship was hilariously funny, particularly as Rum Pot was playing coy, making Zeus work for every scrap of her attention and often mocking him terribly. "Devlin, calm yourself," she told him. "If Zeus is like most men, he'll soon tire of the chase. Besides, Rum Pot is not giving him much encouragement."

"You think not?" he disputed. "Then why is she making eyes at him at this very moment?"

The parrot was preening herself, but since Eden could not see Zeus, she hadn't been aware that Rum Pot was putting on this fetching act for the falcon's benefit. She had to rely on Devlin's word that Zeus was presently transfixed with Rum Pot's come-hither display.

Eden shook her head in befuddlement, then gave a fatalistic shrug. "Oh, well, I suppose 'twill work itself out somehow. After all, look at the two of us. Who would ever have thought we would make such a perfect pair?"

"There is a difference, my sweet. According to several sources, the Bible for one, like consorteth with like, and birds of a feather flock together. These two are definitely not birds of a feather, and what they are aiming toward goes against all the laws of nature."

Eden laughed. "So speaks my husband, the expert, who even now cannot explain the bolt of lightning from out of the blue which rendered him invisible. That, too, was supposed to be impossible, love. This world is ever full of surprises, is it not?"

"That, and sassy women," Devlin agreed, getting in the last word.

At the end of October, just a few days before Stede Bonnet's trial was to begin, the pirate captain and his quartermaster managed to escape in the middle of the night, much as Colonel Rhett had predicted. Though it couldn't be proved, it was believed that the guards had been bribed to turn a blind eye to their prisoners' flight. It was curious that Bonnet did not take the *Revenge,* or any other adequate ship anchored in the harbor. Devlin attributed this to the fact that two lone men could hardly sail a ship of that size without the aid of a crew. He suspected Bonnet and Herriot would return as soon as they could gather enough mates to reclaim their sloop.

Governor Johnson was furious. Immediately, he offered a reward of seven hundred pounds for their capture, dead or alive, and appointed Colonel Rhett to head the search. As luck would have it, however, a fierce squall was brewing, forcing the search party to postpone their departure until after it had passed.

The weather worsened steadily, and it soon looked as if they were due for a full-fledged tempest, if not an actual hurricane. Cursing the fact that he hadn't been able to gauge the extent of the gale early enough to transfer the *Mirage* to sea, and the *Dame Anise* away from the dock, Devlin headed to the harbor to secure the two ships as well as he could against any damage they might sustain. Then he and Nate hurried home to latch the shutters tightly over the windows, move porch furniture indoors, and generally make the house and grounds as snug as they could.

For three long days, the wind howled, beating rain upon the house in gusts that rattled the shutters. Thunder roared like an enraged bear until Dora was loath to venture into the kitchen by herself, afraid she would be struck by lightning even through the tightly shielded windows. By dawn of the fourth day, when the gale finally began to ease, everyone was irritable from lack of proper sleep and from being restricted to the house for so long.

Finally, by mid-morning, the storm had abated sufficiently for the men to go forth and assess the loss. The house and stable were unharmed, but Eden's henhouse seemed to have taken the brunt of the damage. The roof had blown half off, and a good number of ducks and chickens had flown the coop. Several lay dead, littering the rear lawn.

Next, the men went down to the docks to evaluate how well their ships had weathered the tempest. To Devlin's vast relief, the *Mirage,* lying at anchor in the center of the harbor, had escaped unscathed. The *Dame Anise* had not fared so well, however. Necessarily tied up at the wharf, she'd taken quite a beating, and it would take much time and effort to restore her to seaworthy condition. It was hardly a consolation that they'd scarcely gotten a good start at refurbishing the crippled vessel, for now it would take twice as long to get her ready to sail.

"I swear this frigate has become a millstone about my neck," Devlin bemoaned. "She is my personal albatross. Mayhap 'twould be better to sell her to the first buyer with coin in his pocket and be done with it."

"And do what? Buy another?" Nate asked. He shook his head. "Nay, Dev. She's a good little ship, only wantin' someone to see to her care. Don't throw good money after bad by purchasin' someone else's raft o' problems."

They returned to the house to find Eden weeping copiously. Sure that something dreadful had happened, Devlin rushed to her side. "Darling, what's wrong? Is it the babe? The demise of your chickens? I'll buy you more, you know."

Seating himself next to her on the divan, Devlin pulled her to him and kissed her sweetly on the lips. Almost instantly, he recoiled, his expression one of horror. "Damnation, Eden!" he exclaimed. "What on God's glorious earth have you been eating?" He swiped hastily at his mouth, as if to remove the awful taste.

"Raw radishes," she answered, as Jane erupted into peals of merriment.

"Radishes?" Devlin echoed stupidly. Then he sighed. He should have expected as much. "That, I suppose, is the reason for your weeping. Lord knows, the small bit I sampled from your lips was strong enough to put hair on your chest, let alone a tear in your eye."

Eden nodded, turning her swimming turquoise gaze to his. "They're very hot," she admitted, her voice still husky. "Mother cautioned me to eat them with buttered bread, but I was too eager for them to wait that long. Of a sudden, I simply had to have radishes, or die wanting them."

Devlin looked perplexed, and Jane took pity on him. "Cravings, Devlin," she explained. "Most expectant mothers experience them at some time during their term. For myself, I've had the strongest yearning for calf's liver, though I normally don't care for it."

He shook his head, as if still not able to comprehend this strange female phenomenon. "Liver I can understand to a point, but radishes? Sweet heaven! 'Tis a blarsted wonder she hasn't set her stomach aflame, and the babe with it! At the least, she'll have a bad case of indigestion to accompany her stomach upsets."

"Nay, Devlin," Eden informed him, "the nausea seems to have disappeared entirely and quite abruptly. Now 'tis only this curious longing for radishes that plagues me."

"Well, I can only hope this leaves as well. And soon. I don't mean to offend you, pet, but you have the breath of a dratted dragon. I expect to see smoke and flames erupt from your mouth at any moment. Certainly, it does not promote intimacy."

While Eden glared at him, as if to say she would be enduring none of this if he hadn't gotten her with child in the first place, Jane commented with a wise chuckle, "Fear not, young lovers. This, too, shall pass."

"Until it does, I strongly suspect neither of us will get much rest at night for Eden's complaints of a burning stomach," Devlin predicted. "Why is it no one thinks to advise fathers-to-be of all these problems before they occur?"

"Most likely because 'tis so much fun surprising you with them," Eden told him with a smirk. "And because, if we have to suffer, you might as well share some of it right along with us."

Just when it seemed that the seas had finally calmed enough to sail after Stede Bonnet, two new pirate ships appeared at the mouth of Charles Town harbor. Rumors flew that the brigands intended to sack the town. Some wondered if Stede Bonnet was among them, intent on regaining his own ship and a bit of revenge in the bargain.

While the two pirate vessels sat patiently at anchor, as if daring the first foolish merchant ship to cross their path, the town fathers quickly put a plan of attack into action. Four ships, the *Mirage* included, were hurriedly outfitted for battle and disguised as common traders, their cannon hidden beneath loosely constructed packing crates. When all was ready, they sailed as a group toward the mouth of the harbor, Devlin once more covered with the black hood that was fast becoming his trademark.

He wondered why he'd allowed Colonel Rhett to recruit him so effortlessly. Was it simply because he had so little opportunity now to play the rogue, that he missed the excitement of battle on the seas? Or was it his love for Eden that sent him rushing out on this rescue mission, to save her precious town from sacking and make her proud? He rather suspected it was the latter, and that somewhere along the route Eden had not only stolen his heart, but gone a long way toward reforming him as well—despite himself.

Their ruse of disguising the ships worked. Mistaking the vessels for unarmed merchantmen, the pirates opened fire ... and were immediately met with an answering barrage. One sloop was hit broadside beneath the waterline and instantly began to take on water. She was easily boarded, her crew subdued and arrested in short order.

At this turn of events, the second pirate ship took flight, heading toward the open sea where the brigands hoped to outrun any pursuers. It was only then, through his viewing glass, that Devlin got a good look at the captain on the bridge of the fleeing sloop. It was none other than the nefarious Captain Swift!

Devlin immediately issued orders to give chase. For three hours, the *Mirage* stalked the enemy ship, forcing its crew to alter their course numerous times, until finally the brigands turned to face the challenge being offered them. There was hardly time for a brief exchange of advance volleys, with little damage incurred to either ship, before they drew alongside each other. Even as the grappling hooks found their marks, Devlin took the conflict onto the decks of Swift's sloop, Nate and several mates close behind him.

Swift was awaiting him on the poop deck. No sooner had Devlin and his quartermaster landed before him than they were quickly surrounded by half a dozen of Swift's men, all with weapons drawn and leveled at the two friends.

"We meet again, Kane," Swift said in greeting, a sneer twisting his lips. "As I told ye we would."

"What's this, Swift?" Devlin replied, casting a curious glance about him. "Is your shoulder wound yet so bad that you cannot fight me yourself, but now need others to do the deed for you? I am flattered indeed, that you deem me so formidable that it would take so many men to accomplish the task."

Over the noise of the battle being waged around them, Swift gave a harsh, derisive bark of laughter. "Don't exalt yer sword skills to such heights, my man."

His brow rose as he added, "Or should I say, my *phantom?* Which is why I am takin' such drastic precautions now, though I'm not certain I truly believe such drivel as I've heard."

Momentarily taken aback, Devlin was still formulating the question in his mind when who should step into his view but Dudley Finster! "Ah, now the light begins to dawn," Devlin drawled, eyeing the scrawny accountant with distaste.

Evidently feeling safe with so many men guarding Devlin, Finster swaggered forward, the sun glinting off the lenses of his new spectacles. He stopped before Devlin and smirked up at him, his long pointed nose and protruding teeth giving him the look of the weasel he was. "Thought you'd seen the last of me, didn't you?" he taunted. "'Twas my good fortune to encounter Captain Swift a few weeks back. The good man redeemed me from that lecherous old fart you sold me to."

"Of course, I would never have ransomed such a mewlin' runt had he not possessed such interestin' information about ye, Devlin," Swift put in. "However, we acquired a pair of eyeglasses for the fellow, and he's since been earnin' his keep by tabulatin' my treasure. So my coin was well spent."

Devlin gave a contemptuous snort. "I'd take care letting the man so near my purse, were I you," he warned. "He's puny, but exceedingly greedy for his size."

Swift chuckled. "Aye, but he'll soon have his sticky fingers out of my wealth. Once ye are properly dealt with, he intends to return to Charles Town and court yer lady, Devlin."

"My wife," Devlin corrected, leveling a superior look at Finster. "Eden and I are wed, as are Nate and Jane. So you see, Finster, your schemes are all for naught."

"Not so," Dudley countered cunningly. "With both of

you dead, your widows will once again need someone to look after them—and their business interests."

"Ye'll not find 'em such an easy mark this time round," Nate predicted.

"Enough of this bickerin'," Swift announced. Waving his sword in a broad arc, he indicated the ongoing fray between their crews. "Tell yer men to throw down their weapons and surrender, Kane."

"Nay," Devlin replied. "I'll not forfeit their lives with my own. They'll fight or not, as they choose."

Again Swift gave a gruff laugh. "Still such an arrogant pup! And so absurdly noble! So be it, then. But before we send the two o' ye to yer watery graves, let's have a look beneath that black hood, shall we? I've yet to be convinced of Finster's wild tales of specter pirates, but I do wonder what ye're hidin' behind that cloth. And while we're about it, let's see if ghosts can bleed like mortal men."

As his men stood ready to strike Devlin and Nate down at their slightest move toward their own defense, Swift's cutlass swung up toward Devlin's face, the tip of his blade barely snagging the fabric.

At the same time, the sky above them was suddenly rent with the hair-raising shriek of an enraged falcon. There came a mighty swoosh of displaced air as the bird swooped downward with a frantic flapping of huge wings and the savage rake of razor-sharp talons. All accompanied by the terrified screams of the big hawk's victims as they raised their arms to fend off this invisible winged avenger.

Taking full advantage of the unexpected aid, from such an unanticipated source, Nate and Devlin wasted no time in disabling a number of their guards. Nearly as surprising as Zeus's attack, two of Swift's cohorts now turned their weapons on their own mates, charging at their fellow brigands with astounding fervor, if little actual skill.

As soon as Zeus ceased clawing at Swift's head and flew off as mysteriously as he'd come, the enemy captain quickly recovered his wits. While Devlin was yet occupied in another clash of swords, Swift came at him, leveling a broad swipe at Devlin's head. Had the weapon met its mark, it would have severed Devlin's head from his shoulders. A fortuitous lunge to administer a final blow at his current opponent was all that saved Devlin's neck.

Instead, Swift's cutlass slashed through Devlin's plumed hat and continued its hissing arc to find another, less fortunate target—the stunned accountant who'd lost his eyeglasses during Zeus's attack and had not yet managed to find his way clear of the fray. The fatal blow caught the little man across the forehead, and with nary a cry from his bloodless lips, Finster pitched forward, dead before he hit the planking.

Free now to engage Swift, Devlin met his rival eagerly. For long minutes they battled, steel ringing loudly upon steel as their swords clashed again and again. From the start, Devlin assumed the offensive, steadily backing his adversary across the deck before his relentless advance. Finally came the moment when Swift's spine met the rail edging the top deck. He had no more space to retreat.

"'Tis your choice, Swift. Either surrender to me now, and I'll return you to Charles Town for hanging, or you can die here, on the blade of my sword."

In a desperate effort to avoid either fate, Swift made a clever attempt to launch himself over the barrier behind him. With little room to maneuver, and needing sufficient leverage to clear the rail, he lunged hastily forward. It proved a mortal mistake, as he sorely misjudged his ability to deflect Devlin's weapon at the crucial moment. The point of Devlin's sword wavered, flexed back again and speared full into Swift's chest.

On a pained gasp, Swift leaned sharply away, and tumbled backward to the deck below.

Devlin peered down at his archenemy. The man had landed heavily and now lay unmoving, his neck bent at an impossible angle. A small pool of blood darkened his chest, just over his lifeless heart.

Though Swift's death did not cheer Devlin nearly as much as he'd anticipated, relief flooded through him. With a final look at the sinister man who had brought him so much grief, and would torment him no longer, Devlin turned away. He had more important tasks to attend to. Men to command and a ship to secure—a life to live.

Little else was left to be done save for deciphering the curious business of the two opposing corsairs who had rallied to the defense of the *Mirage*. Come to discover, the pair had been impressed into Swift's service much in the same manner as Devlin himself. Neither had chosen piracy for his career, one being an able gunsmith and the other a competent tailor, and both were grateful to be rescued. They begged transport back to Charles Town, where they hoped to be allowed to ply their true trades.

So it seemed that once again, Devlin had had a hand in rescuing innocent victims from a vile brigand's clutches. To his mind, it was fast becoming an annoying practice. Blarst it, this time it had even cost him his favorite hat!

Chapter 31

*A*s soon as their surviving prisoners were bound and thrown into the hold for safekeeping, Devlin put a portion of his crew in charge of sailing the captured ship back into port. Then Devlin and the *Mirage*'s remaining forces set out in search of Bonnet—who, unless the situation had altered in the past few hours, was still eluding the law.

Since their pursuit had taken them south of Charles Town, they cruised the coastline on their return route home, thoroughly investigating every likely area along the way. They had reached the mouth of Charles Town Harbor, and were about to enter it, when they chanced to spot Colonel Rhett's vessel to the north of them, traversing the seaward shore of Sullivan's Island. Suddenly Rhett's ship changed course, heading toward the far end of the island.

Curious as to what the colonel had spotted, Devlin headed the *Mirage* on the same tack. They pulled alongside the sloop just as Rhett and his men were clambering into their jolly boats. Cupping his hands about his mouth, Devlin called out loudly, "Ahoy, Colonel! What goes?"

Rhett turned quickly, almost tumbling himself into

the water in his excitement. He pointed toward the island, where a battered, abandoned skiff had been washed up on the rocks, and bellowed back one word. "Bonnet!"

It was all that was necessary to rouse Devlin and Nate to action. Into their dinghy they flew, rowing to shore mere seconds behind Rhett and his band.

The group split into sets of two and three men, and quickly spread out to search the small island. Devlin and Nate stayed together, heading into the dense, damp underbrush, employing their cutlasses as machetes to clear their path. They were making so much noise that there was no way Bonnet and his quartermaster could fail to hear them coming. Though they communicated by hand signals, the rattle and crackle of brush and branches announced their approach as loudly as a cannon report.

They had passed a point perhaps a quarter of the way across the narrow isle when the back of Devlin's neck began to tingle alarmingly. Without stopping to question his actions, he swiveled about, drawing his loaded pistol from his belt at the same time. From the corner of his eye, he caught a brief flash of movement in the nearby brush. He barely managed to shove the unsuspecting Nate aside in time to level his weapon and shoot. In that same instant, his enemy fired as well, and it was only thanks to poor marksmanship that Devlin did not receive a ball in his chest. Rather, the missile tore through the left sleeve of his shirt, leaving behind a thin, bloody groove the length of his forearm.

His opponent was far less fortunate, for Devlin's aim proved true. The man gave one hoarse shout of disbelief and pain, followed by the sounds of mad scurrying through the bushes. Weapons drawn, Devlin and Nate dashed forward, keeping carefully under cover now. Arriving at the place where Devlin had spotted the gunman, they found Herriot lying dead at the base of a tree, shot through the head.

Leaving him there, the two friends took off after Bonnet, following the trail of broken branches and fresh footprints. It was a testimony to Bonnet's desperation that they chased him for a full ten minutes before running him to ground.

Immediately upon realizing that he'd been caught, Bonnet threw down his weapon and raised his hands above his head in surrender. Only then did he finally recognize his captors, and his flushed face turned hopeful. "Let me go," he implored breathlessly. "For old times' sake. I swear I'll give up pirating. I'll go back to my plantation, and my wife, if she'll have me, and petition for special amnesty. I give you my pledge as a fellow Brethren."

"We're no longer members of the same league," Devlin reminded him callously. "Nor would I wish to align myself with the man you have become, Stede, a man who would hold an innocent woman against her will and ravage her repeatedly and without mercy. The old Devlin Kane might not have cared, but the new one does. Therefore, 'twill do you little good to plead for pity from me."

"Nor from me," Nate concurred. "If 'twere left to me to decide, I would shoot you where you stand, and let the buzzards feast on your rotten innards. However, that'd be cheatin' the good citizens of Charles Town out o' yer hangin', and they're lookin' forward to the grand event. So, what say we get marchin', and give them folks somethin' to cheer about?"

It was only after the two friends returned to the *Mirage* that Devlin became aware that he had lost his disguising hood somewhere amidst the dense tangle of underbrush on Sullivan's Island. He'd gone to his cabin to examine the wound to his arm. As he stood at the washstand, he glanced upward—and caught his reflection in the wall-mounted mirror. For a moment, he thought nothing of this, as he had now become accustomed to being discernible for hours at a stretch. But then the truth dawned upon him. He had not been in contact with Eden since early morning. It was now sunset, and he was still visible!

Though his hood was gone, probably lost hours before, Nate and Bonnet and Rhett's men had seen him clearly. Devlin had no doubt he would have known immediately if any of them had viewed him as some freakish phantom! His breath caught in his throat, hope rising within his chest. Could this possibly mean what he desperately wished it did? Could he finally, at long last, be fully revived? Had Swift's death somehow triggered his ultimate restoration? Or had something entirely different effected a cure?

When Devlin reached home, cautiously elated, Eden was ecstatic. It was she who came up with the true test of the matter, and as much as it pained him, Devlin agreed. "In order to be certain, we must avoid touching each other for a few days," she told him.

"Drat it all, Eden, do you know what you're asking of me? After all these months, 'tis second nature to me to be in almost constant contact with you. I don't honestly know if I can stop myself from doing so."

"Well, you simply must, so we can know for sure whether or not you are really cured. Mayhap 'twould be best if you were to live on the ship, or move a cot into the warehouse office for a short time. That way, neither of us will accidentally ruin the experiment."

Devlin groaned. "As often as I have prayed for this advent, the cure now seems worse than the ailment."

"Not the cure," she corrected solemnly. "The proof of it."

She took another crunchy bite of radish on buttered bread, and Devlin caught a whiff of the pungent aroma from across the bedroom. As his eyes began to water, he waved a hand to disperse the fumes. "You win, duchess. We'll give it a three-day trial. If I become invisible before then, home I come. If not, you have that space of time in which to stuff yourself with radishes, to your burning heart's content. If God is kind, your odd obsession with the obnoxious root will be adequately satisfied by then, and I will no longer hesitate to share the same air as my lovely, fire-breathing bride."

For the next three days, Devlin avoided the house. With the *Mirage* on another shipping run, he slept in the warehouse office, as Eden had suggested, and took to carrying a small mirror with him so that he could readily check the state of his visibility. Afraid of doing anything which might send his body back into revolt, he minced about as if he were walking on eggshells.

He was irritable as all hell at being forced into "exile from Eden." Once he had thought of it in those exact terms, he found a small dose of dour humor in his current situation, and developed a good deal of sympathy for Adam and Eve into the bargain. He might have told them that true temptation came not in the form of an apple. For him, temptation was a tall, sweetly curved lady with sparkling turquoise eyes, a lilting laugh, and a tart demeanor. One who had quickly become a habit he didn't want to break, an addiction he adored.

It was one thing to be away from her on business, to be separated by miles of sea. It was quite another to know that she was mere minutes removed from his touch, warm and waiting and eager, yet completely forbidden to him, all by their own design. It was a unique torture.

Eden was equally miserable. She tried to keep busy to counter it. But in the wee hours of the night, when their bed seemed to have grown to twice its actual size, she missed Devlin terribly. Now, at long last, she was experiencing but a meager measure of what her mother had felt after her husband had died. Eden couldn't imagine how dreadful it must be to know that one's husband was forever gone, never to return again. At least she could anticipate having Devlin back in her arms in no more than three days, and if it took all that time, it would mean he was well and truly restored to his normal self. For this she would endure almost anything. She'd even give up radishes!

Like Devlin, she could scarcely bear having him so close at hand, yet so completely inaccessible. At every turn, she found herself tempted to rush over to the warehouse and see how he was faring. Alone in their room, she paced for hours. She curled up on the bed and snuggled her face into his pillow, breathing in the lingering scent of him. She dreamed of him at night, and fantasized about him all day, until she was certain she'd go mad.

By the appointed hour of his return, Eden was as edgy as a rusted razor. When Devlin finally walked through the door, she raced for his arms. "I hope you are cured, my love," she told him as she threw herself into his welcoming embrace, "because I never want to be separated from you like this again. I have even decided that if you choose sailing as your trade, I and our child will voyage with you."

Laughing, he hugged her to him. "Oh, you will, will you? Don't I get anything to say about it?"

"Nay. 'Tis decided. Now, tell me that all is well."

"Aye, sweetling. At least for now. Hopefully, for always."

As he at last set her on her feet, she pulled him toward the bottom of the hall stairs, the twinkle in her eyes telling him she was scheming some sort of delightful mischief. "Come," she urged, tugging at his hand. "We simply must celebrate this grand and glorious event."

"Upstairs?" he questioned, mocking her with a raised brow.

She nodded.

"Mayhap in our bedroom?"

"Aye, dunce. Now do hurry, will you?"

"My, what a lusty wench you are, to have missed my loving so much," he teased, deliberately dragging his steps.

"You don't know the half of it," she claimed boldly. "Now, unless you want me to undress you where you stand, and have my wicked way with you right here on the stairs, kindly move your bloomin' bum a bit faster."

He was sorely tempted to call her bluff, but resisted—just barely. "Aye, aye, duchess!" he replied with a smart salute. The two of them ran hand-in-hand up the stairs and scarcely shut the bedroom door behind them before they began tearing at each other's clothes.

He needed a bath, and he needed her, and it seemed his bride was well prepared to give him both—at the same time! She'd shielded a large section of the bedroom floor with an oilcloth tarp, over which she'd spread several blankets. In the center stood the copper tub, half-filled with bathwater.

"Mama would have fits if we flooded the floor and brought down the dining-room ceiling," she explained with a giddy grin.

In her eagerness to jerk his shirt over his head, she nearly strangled him. Then she tried to remove his breeches before his boots, and he almost broke a leg in his efforts to untangle himself. Likewise, he ripped the sleeve of her gown in his haste to undress her, and completely forgot to peel her stockings off before tumbling her into the tub.

The protective covering for the floor proved prudent, for by the time their raging passions had finally been slaked, there was more water outside the tub than in it.

"Good God, how I missed you!" Devlin growled into her wet ear.

"I'm glad," she murmured, lazily lathering soap into swirls on his chest. "As much as I suffered, I was hoping you were, too."

He chuckled and squeezed her close. "Ah, Eden! Our biggest problems are behind us now, duchess. After six long months, I am completely normal at last. The businesses are coming along well. We'll soon have a new house and a new child. And Swift and Finster will bedevil us no more."

She raised her head to smile at him and licked a drop of water from his chin. "You can *bedevil* me as often as you wish, my love."

His black eyes glittered with ardent promise. "I intend to, my sweet. Very often indeed."

Though Eden and Devlin had spent the better part of the night reveling in their reunion, they were rudely awakened at first light by a loud chorus of the most cacophonous squawking Eden had ever hoped to hear. It wasn't hard to guess that the ear-piercing noise was coming from the parlor, where Zeus and Rum Pot had been tethered to their perches. Devlin grabbed for his britches, while Eden yanked on her night rail. In tandem, they rushed down the stairs.

Eden skidded to a halt just inside the room, her eyes wide in disbelief. "Gadzooks, Devlin!" she swore breathlessly. "I always supposed Zeus was big, but I had no idea how large until now!"

"You can see him?"

"I most certainly can," Eden replied, glowering. "And I must say, he is looking extremely proud of himself. I also fancy I know the reason why." She pointed a finger at Rum Pot, who was weaving to and fro on her perch, looking dazed and ruffled. A scattering of bright plumes littered the floor.

Devlin gave a muffled laugh. "I'll be switched! That snooty bird of yours has finally gotten her comeuppance!"

Eden jabbed him sharply in the ribs. "That heathen pile of feathers you call a hawk has finally gotten his claws into my parrot!"

"More than his claws, from the look of it," Devlin countered with a chuckle. "Lord only knows what sort of odd chicks will hatch, should their curious union produce eggs."

"One might ask the same of our offspring," Eden reminded him sourly.

Not at all put off by her surly mood, and freshly inspired by Zeus's success with Rum Pot, Devlin carted Eden back to bed for another lusty romp in the sheets. By the time they came up for air, Eden had long since gotten over her pique at the hawk. If the two birds were destined for each other, who was she to gainsay their union?

For now, it was Devlin's turn to question matters. "I wonder what has caused Zeus to reappear now," he mused. "Do you suppose the effects of the Saint Elmo's fire merely wore off gradually, rendering the two of us whole again?"

"Possibly," she allowed. "Then again, when you regained your visibility, Nate suggested it might have been the good deeds you had performed, for after each incident your visibility returned a bit, until you were completely cured."

She recounted the three separate times. "After you saved those unfortunate prisoners from Blackbeard's clutches, when you rescued that young woman Stede Bonnet had held prisoner, and after you helped to free the two men Swift held in bondage. All admirably selfless acts."

"True, I did improve after each, but what of Zeus?" Devlin asked.

"He performed his own heroic feat when he swooped down on Swift and his men, providing a much-needed distraction, which no doubt saved both your life and Nate's. A deed for which I will be eternally grateful."

"Then you agree with Nate, that these acts of valor redeemed our bodies?"

"Not entirely." Eden's smile grew wide as she gazed at him with adoring eyes. "Nate has his theory, but I have one of my own. I believe love cured both of you—that only when you had fully surrendered your hearts and received a matching measure of devotion and passion in return did all fall right with your world again. I also suspect that is why I could view you when no one else could, and why Rum Pot could apparently see Zeus. We were your God-chosen mates, you see, specially selected to love and aid you. Some might claim it magical or mystical. I say 'tis the power of love."

Devlin simply declared it wondrous, and prayed that the splendor of it would shine brightly all through their lives, and beyond.

Epilogue

Eden and Devlin stood on the veranda of
their hilltop home and looked out over the magnificent
view of the harbor spread out below them. At the sound
of childish laughter, they each turned, smiling, to watch
two toddlers, one blond and one dark-haired, chasing
clumsily after a butterfly in the lawn. The youngsters
were healthy, happy, and as mischievous as puppies.
They were also the light of their parents' lives.

Nathan Rogers Hancock, named after his father and
the man who had granted Nate his pardon, had arrived
two and a half years ago in April, just as Jane had predicted. A month later, James Devlin Kane had made his
grand appearance, and Eden had cried grateful tears
when Devlin had suggested having Jamie carry on her
beloved father's name.

The children were constant companions, and it was
odd to think of them as uncle and nephew to each other,
for they were more like twin brothers, with the excep-
tion of their looks. Eden had wanted a son with Devlin's sun-kissed locks, and she'd gotten her wish.
However, as if to please both parents, the Fates had
seen fit to endow their child with Eden's turquoise
gaze. At the moment of his birth, Eden would not have

cared if Jamie had been born with twelve toes, so thankful was she that he had arrived beautifully visible to one and all.

For three years now, Devlin had also remained discernible, as had Zeus. The queer romance between the falcon and the parrot had yet to bear offspring, but the birds were still enamored of each other, so that eventuality yet remained. After all, stranger things had happened, as Eden and Devlin well knew.

Eden stooped low to catch her small son as he came tumbling up the porch steps and launched himself at her skirts. Laughing, she picked him up and settled him atop her right hip. "Whoa there, little lad! You're going to pitch yourself onto your head, trying to run so fast on those chubby legs of yours."

Devlin awarded her a mock glare. "Jamie's legs are perfect," he claimed. "Just right for a growing boy."

"If you say so," Eden answered, trying unsuccessfully to stifle a snicker at Devlin's proud paternal attitude. "Still and all, 'twill not be long before he is too heavy for me to lift."

"Aye, he's growing fast and tall, this one."

"Well, I hope the next one remains petite and darling," Eden told him with a sly gleam in her eyes.

"The next one?" Devlin echoed suspiciously, bending to scoop little Nathan into his arms as the child came dashing at him. "Eden, are you trying to tell me you're breeding again?"

She nodded. "I'm surprised you haven't noticed. But then, you've been so wrapped up in your adorable son that you scarcely take any notice of me these days," she teased.

"If that be the case, how is it that you are with child?" he countered.

She shrugged playfully. "It must have happened when I laundered your breeches, I suppose."

"Nay, minx," he said, laughing and tweaking her

nose, then Jamie's and Nathan's in turn. "We both know full well how it happened. Most likely, 'twas the night you performed that ridiculous harem dance for me."

She grinned in remembrance. "As I recall, you didn't think it was so ludicrous at the time. Nonetheless, I do imagine you are correct in assuming that our daughter was conceived that night."

He cocked a blond brow at her, his son immediately imitating the familiar gesture. "What makes you so sure this one will be a lass?"

"The lemons."

"Lemons?"

"Aye, Devlin. Surely you've noticed that I have developed a passion for lemons. I thought you'd be grateful 'tis not radishes this time round."

"I am, duchess. Believe me. Anything is an improvement over those noxious roots."

"Then you're pleased with my news?"

He pulled her to him, both children crushed happily between them. "More than pleased, Eden. Thrilled. Elated. Overjoyed at the prospect of a daughter—and the blessed absence of radishes!"